TWILIGHT'S LAST GLEAMING

DANE RONNOW

TWILIGHT'S LAST GLEAMING

A NOVEL

MOHAVE PUBLISHING

Copyright © 2018 by Mohave Publishing, LLC

Mohave Publishing, LLC
P.O. Box 6912
Kingman, AZ 86402

Printed in the United States of America

First Printing 2018

ISBN 978-0-9979857-1-9
ebook ISBN 978-0-9979857-2-6

www.mohavepublishing.com

*For Dianne, who doesn't care much
for the genre, but loves me just the same.*

ACKNOWLEDGMENTS

Special thanks to John C. Ronnow,
Eagle Scout and U.S. Army combat veteran,
5th Special Forces Group (Green Beret), Vietnam,
for suggestions in story development
and giving rise to the characters
Chris Tanner and Miles Ackerman.

Also, thanks to Bob Kaelin
and Robyn Ronnow Kaelin
for proofreading and encouragement.
Robyn was standing on a beach in Honolulu
the night of July 8, 1962, but never knew
what the flash in the sky was until I
asked her to read the manuscript.

Principal Characters

UNITED STATES GOVERNMENT

Edmund Wheeler: President of the United States

Jan Hutchens: Vice President of the United States

William Denton: National Security Advisor

Elaine Richardson: Secretary of State

Patrick Wilkinson: Secretary of Defense

Margaret Beck: Secretary of Homeland Security

Douglas Chambers: Secretary of the Interior

Roger Townsend: Secretary of Energy

Bob Larson: White House Chief of Staff

Spencer Cochran: Speaker of the House of Representatives

General Thomas Macfarland: Chairman, Joint Chiefs of Staff

Admiral Fletcher Powell: Director of National Intelligence

Admiral Carroll O'Sullivan: Director, Defense Intelligence Agency

Matthew Donovan: Director, National Security Agency

Michael Attwood: Director, DEFSMAC branch,
   National Security Agency

Naomi Hendricks: Senior intelligence analyst, DEFSMAC branch,
   National Security Agency

Scott Winter: Intelligence analyst, DEFSMAC branch,
   National Security Agency

Paul Lundgren: Intelligence analyst, DEFSMAC branch,
   National Security Agency

General Wilson Tuckett: Commander, North American
   Aerospace Defense Command

Lieutenant-General James McNaughton: Deputy commander,
   North American Aerospace Defense Command

OTHER CHARACTERS

Neil and Nancy Hayes: Residents of northwest Arizona

Christopher McAvoy: Captain, Delta Airlines flight 322

Nathan Hayes: First Officer, Delta Airlines flight 322

Chris Tanner: Resident of Big Spring, Texas; former Green Beret,
   5th Special Forces Group, Vietnam

Miles Ackerman: Resident of Big Spring, Texas; former Green Beret, 5th Special Forces Group, Vietnam

Henry and Arvella Gardner: Residents of Clay City, Iowa

Audrey and Evie Lane: Residents of Springfield, Missouri

Avery Stokes: Resident of Ash Grove, Missouri

Hal Decker: Deputy sheriff, Greene County, Missouri

Kyle and Julie Ward: Residents of Lewiston, Idaho

Everett King: Investment banker, San Francisco, California

Jordan Stanley: Investment banker, San Francisco, California

Burke Abbott: Investment banker, San Francisco, California

Silas and Muriel Davenport: Residents of Winslow, Arizona

Harlan Hicks: Resident of Winslow, Arizona

Jack Davis: Senior engineer, Palo Verde Nuclear Generating Station

Carl Ferguson: Resident of northwest Arizona

TWILIGHT'S LAST GLEAMING

INTRODUCTION

July 8, 1962
10:40 p.m. Hawaii-Aleutian Daylight Time
Johnston Island, North Pacific Ocean

At the north end of Johnston Island—a barren patch of land two miles long and a half-mile wide—a PGM-17 Thor intermediate-range ballistic missile stands on Launch Emplacement One, gleaming white in the floodlights. Weighing fifty-four tons, standing sixty-five feet in height, and capable of lifting 2,200 pounds, the United States Air Force rocket is America's primary launch vehicle for nuclear weapons.

Here on Johnston Island, part of an atoll 890 miles from the nearest populated land mass, the PGM-17 is used to launch nuclear warheads in various high-altitude tests. It is the height of the Cold War between the United States and the Soviet Union, and nuclear weapons development is the focus of national defense.

Tonight's launch, named Starfish Prime, will gather data on the effects of a nuclear explosion in the vacuum of space. Sitting atop the rocket is a 1.44 megaton hydrogen bomb that will be detonated at an altitude of 250 miles.

At 10:41 the launch pad is cleared. Personnel are moved to the blockhouse, a cramped concrete bunker packed with equipment and observers, less than a half-mile away. Instruments are checked, recorders are started, lights flicker and gauges spring to life.

At 10:46:28 the ground shakes as the rocket fuel ignites, and the missile rises slowly off the concrete pad with an ear-splitting roar, then accelerates into the night sky. Sixty seconds later, observers emerge from the blockhouse to watch the rocket, now a distant spot of light in the darkness, disappear altogether.

At 10:57:30 the rocket reaches an altitude of 660 miles. The reentry vehicle containing the warhead separates from the missile and begins its descent back toward the surface.

At 11:00:09 the warhead explodes 248 miles above the North Pacific Ocean.

Eight hundred ninety miles away on the island of Oahu, the mood is festive as a number of hotels in Honolulu are playing host to 'rainbow bomb' parties, named for the vibrant colors that fill the sky after detonation of the nuclear bomb at high-altitude. Roof tops and verandas are crowded with guests hoping to catch a glimpse of the phenomenon.

At nine seconds past eleven local time, a brilliant flash lights up the night sky. A split-second later, street lights are blown out and residential burglar alarms are set off across the city. Electrical power is out in some areas and a telephone microwave link between Kauai and the other Hawaiian Islands is dead.

In a matter of seconds, the sky is filled by a deep red glow, broken by bright, white, finger-like filaments that slowly align with the earth's magnetic field lines. Over the next seven minutes the red glow turns purple, then phosphorescent green, and is visible from the Midway Islands to New Zealand.

On Johnston Island, personnel in the block house watch as needles are pegged on instruments used to measure electrical phenomena resulting from the detonation. Electrons scattered by the explosion and traveling near the speed of light have created a powerful electromagnetic pulse, or EMP, that impacts electrical equipment and radio frequency waves. Apart from the disturbances in the Hawaiian Island chain, military aircraft 500 miles away lose radio communications.

Within days of the test, satellites begin to fail from radiation collecting in a belt around the earth. The first to fall victim is TRAAC, a U.S. Navy satellite launched to measure radiation from atmospheric nuclear tests. Then NAVSAT, a satellite used by the Navy to provide accurate location data to Polaris ballistic missile submarines.

In the weeks following, nine more satellites fall victim to the radiation, and within six months nearly half of all satellites in Earth orbit at the time of the Starfish Prime test have failed. Among these is Telstar I, America's first telecommunications satellite.

Meanwhile, the Soviets also are testing the effects of high-altitude nuclear explosions. On October 22, 1962, a 300-kiloton warhead is detonated at an altitude of 180 miles over Kazakhstan. The EMP fuses 350 miles of overhead telephone lines and sends a surge of electrical current through 650 miles of underground cable, starting a fire that destroys the Karaganda power plant.

It was obvious at the moment of the nuclear blast in the Starfish Prime test when instrument needles jumped off the scales on the equipment in the Johnston Island blockhouse, that the effects of EMP were much stronger than scientists anticipated. But it wasn't until much later, long after data was evaluated and reports were filed, that scientists and engineers began to look at EMP in a completely different light—not as a consequence of a nuclear detonation, but as a primary effect to be exploited.

In the early 1960s the arms race between the United States and the Soviet Union was running full tilt. Both sides were stockpiling thousands of warheads in preparation for a possible nuclear conflict, and there appeared to be no end in sight. By the 1970s it was understood that a country could have a nuclear arsenal of thousands of weapons, and if it came to war, use those weapons to destroy the adversary by launching hundreds of weapons via missiles, bombers and submarines. With the understanding of EMP, though, it became clear that by using just a few nuclear weapons optimized to create the strongest EMP field possible, a country could destroy the enemy's electrical infrastructure, eliminating the adversary's ability to wage war. This became significant as the use of electronics grew.

By the turn of the century, sophisticated computer systems were running practically every aspect of modern society—banking and finance, delivery of food and fuel, municipal power and water, communication, medical services and police and fire protection, as well as national defense networks and military operations. Worldwide communication through computers and cell phones had become commonplace, and servers across the globe became storage points for personal and corporate records, as well as hundreds of trillions of dollars of investments—the wealth of the planet.

On the one hand it was the most efficient method of delivering product and services imaginable. On the other, it was modern society's Achilles' heel. Every segment of infrastructure relied on another. If one failed, they all would fail ultimately. And the entire system depended on one thing alone—an uninterrupted supply of electricity. And destroying the ability to move electricity was exactly what EMP did. That, and rendering electronic equipment useless.

A nuclear electromagnetic pulse consists of three components: E1, E2 and E3. E1 is an extremely fast and very intense electromagnetic field that induces high voltage in electrical conductors. Lasting less than one-millionth of a second after the explosion, E1 destroys computers, servers, cell phones and other electronic devices.

E2 is similar to lightning. It is an intermediate pulse lasting from one microsecond to one second after the explosion. In theory, electrical systems could be protected against E2 by the use of surge protectors. But because the E1 field has already destroyed electronics, including circuits used by surge protectors, E2 is unimpeded in further damaging electrical equipment.

E3 is a comparatively slow pulse, beginning several seconds after the burst and lasting hundreds of seconds, caused by the rapid expansion of the nuclear blast pushing the earth's magnetic field out of its way. Similar in effect to a geomagnetic storm caused by a solar flare or a coronal mass ejection from the sun, the E3 component induces current into long electrical conductors such as high-power transmission lines and destroys electrical transformers, stopping the flow of electricity.

The area of damage depends on the strength of the nuclear device and its altitude at the time of detonation. Positioned 200 miles above the central United States, a nuclear bomb has a line of sight to both east and west coasts, as well as north into Canada and south into Central America. When detonated, that bomb will destroy electronic equipment and electrical transmission capability in most of North America.

From 1960 until the late '70s, the nature of EMP and its destructive capabilities was relatively unknown outside the realm of nuclear weapons technology. But it was simply a matter of time until rogue nation-states with nuclear ambitions would have the knowledge and technology to develop an EMP weapon.

In the mid-1990s North Korea began work on a nuclear weapon. On October 9, 2006 the first bomb was tested. Based on data obtained, it was declared a failure by nuclear experts. A subsequent test on May 25, 2009 reinforced the belief that North Korea was unable to produce a working nuclear weapon.

It was several years before experts began looking at the tests from a different perspective. What if the North Koreans were not interested in pure explosive power as with conventional nuclear weapons? What if they were developing a bomb strictly for use as an EMP weapon? With the resources available to North Korea they would never be able to build a stockpile of weaponry that would upset the balance of nuclear power in the world. With a single nuclear EMP weapon, though, they could destroy a nation's infrastructure, leading to that country's collapse. All they would need is a missile that could boost the weapon into low-Earth orbit—a capability demonstrated in 2012 when North Korea launched a satellite into space.

By the early 2000s, novelists and movie makers were immersed in the concept of EMP. Books were written describing the collapse of civilization. Movies and television series were created around similar plot lines, and while much of it was sensationalized, there was an element of truth to it. And that truth was terrifying to contemplate. Experts understood this and began working to educate those in a position to protect our national infrastructure. By 2001, Congress had established the EMP Commission under the National Defense Authorization Act and appointed a panel of independent experts to explore the effects of a high-altitude EMP on the United States.

In 2004 the commission reported their findings to Congress, describing in House testimony the catastrophic effects of a high-altitude nuclear explosion over the central United States. Banking and finance, delivery of water, food and fuel, communications, police and fire response, as well as internet connectivity, would collapse immediately. Services that continued would do so only as long as fuel for emergency generators was available.

Even more dreadful to contemplate, the commission estimated that two-thirds of the population that had not died in the chaos and lawlessness following the initial grid collapse would be dead by the end of the first winter due to starvation.

Congress presented these findings to the Department of Homeland Security, prepared to budget expenditures necessary to secure vital aspects of national security. But there was no budget request. In fact, there was no response from DHS other than to say that as a nation we were totally unprepared for an EMP attack. Another panel of experts was commissioned. More findings were presented to Congress. And still there was no plan to deal with the growing threat of EMP.

Then, in 2011, a novel titled *One Second After* by William Forstchen climbed *The New York Times* best-seller list. It was the story of one man's struggle in a post-EMP world. In the Afterward, Forstchen quoted a letter from U.S. Navy Captain Bill Sanders, who called *One Second After* not so much a novel as a warning.

According to Sanders, "Our technologically oriented society and its heavy dependence on advanced electronic systems could be brought to its knees with cascading failures of our critical infrastructure. Our vulnerability increases daily as our use and dependence on electronics continues to accelerate."

At this writing, nothing significant has been done to protect the national power grid. The North American Aerospace Defense Command—NORAD—has begun moving critical communications equipment back into Cheyenne Mountain in Colorado Springs, a Cold War relic abandoned in 2006 when NORAD moved most of its operations to nearby Peterson Air Force base. In an article in *The Wall Street Journal*, Henry F. Cooper and Peter Pry write, "Why the return? Because the enormous bunker in the hollowed-out mountain, built to survive a Cold War-era nuclear attack, can also resist an electromagnetic pulse, or EMP."

The article states that despite the potential threat, there is no effort underway in Washington to protect civilian electronic infrastructure, even though a prolonged nationwide blackout could result in chaos and death on an unimaginable scale.

Excerpts from *The Report of the Commission to Assess the Threat to the U.S. From Electromagnetic Pulse Attack*

Committee on Armed Services
House of Representatives
108th Congress, Second Session
July 22, 2004

[Testimony from transcript, pages 69 and 70, Roscoe Bartlett, congressman from Maryland, and Dr. Lowell L. Wood, member of the commission.]

Mr. Bartlett: [. . .] Dr. Wood, your characterization of this is a large continental time machine that would move us back a century in technology, and my question then was, "But, Dr. Wood, the technology of a century ago could not support our present population and distribution," and your unemotional response, "Yes, I know. The population will shrink until it could be supported by the technology."

When I look at the technology of a century ago and where we are today, Dr. Wood, I would imagine that that shrink might be a good two-thirds of our present population?

Dr. Wood: The population of this continent late in the 19th century, sir, was almost a factor of 10 smaller than it is at the present time. We went from where we had 70 percent of the population on the farms feeding 30 percent of the people in the villages and cities, to where 3 percent of the population on the farms at the present time feeds the other 97 percent of the country.

So just looking at it from an agricultural and food supply standpoint, if we were no longer able to fuel our agricultural machine in this country, the food production of the country would simply stop because we do not have the horses and mules that were used to tow the agricultural gear around in the 1880s and 1890s.

So the situation would be exceedingly adverse if both electricity and the fuel that electricity moves around the country, the diesel fuel and so forth, if that went away and stayed away for a substantial interval of time, we would miss the harvest, and we would starve the following winter. [. . .]

[Portion of the closing statement by Curt Weldon, congressman from Pennsylvania, page 75.]

Mr. Weldon: [. . .] It is just unfortunate it has taken us five years to get to this point when we first started raising this issue with our leadership—this is not a political statement—all the leadership in both the military and non-military, pooh-poohed the idea of this ever happening.

It is real, it is significant, and we are unprotected. [. . .]
[Full transcript at http://commdocs.house.gov/committees/security/has204000.000/has204000_0.HTM]

Between 2008 and 2014, three more hearings were held, all addressing threats to the national grid—two from cyberattacks, one from EMP—all emphasizing the catastrophic outcome of a collapse. As of this writing, Mr. Weldon's statement before Congress in 2004, more than fourteen years ago, still holds true: The threat is real, it is significant, and we are unprotected.

PROLOGUE

WASHINGTON, January 31, 9:35 a.m. EST (AP) - In a stunning development today, Russian president Victor Burkov announced his country is severing economic ties with Europe, the United States and Canada, and is expelling their diplomats and giving foreign businesses—which include auto makers Ford, General Motors and Volkswagen—60 days to shutter their plants and leave the country.

The announcement came at 5:00 p.m. Moscow time, just as the opening bell rang at the New York Stock Exchange. Trading was suspended 12 minutes later as the Dow Jones Industrials plummeted 10 percent, the biggest single-day decline in market history. The Nasdaq and S&P 500 suffered similar losses.

The move comes on the heels of Tuesday's Wall Street mayhem following China's sale of $1.2 trillion in U.S. Treasury bonds, a move that threatens to destroy U.S. debt markets. The wholesale bond dump sent the dollar into free fall and gold skyrocketing.

While tensions between Russia and the west have been rising for more than four years—a result of economic sanctions that have decimated Russia's economy—the trigger for Moscow's action this morning is widely believed to be the passage of a bill in Congress authorizing the U.S. Treasury to seize Russian assets in U.S. banks, coupled with the European Central Bank's declaration that it would no longer recognize transactions with Sberbank—Russia's largest bank, serving more than half the population of Russia and one million businesses—and with VTB, Russia's second largest bank.

Amid these alarming economic developments, Russia is moving warships into the Gulf of Oman. Military analysts see this as an immediate threat to Saudi Arabia, who, along with Turkey, is fighting alongside Syrian rebels in their civil war against Syrian president Sayid al-Sharaa. Russia and Iran are providing weapons and troops to Sharaa's forces.

Western leaders have called for an emergency meeting to discuss Russia's actions and possible responses.

Part I

The Unraveling

1

Friday, February 7
5:40 p.m. Eastern Standard Time
The White House
Washington, D.C.

President Edmund Wheeler stood behind his desk in the Oval Office, looking out the window at the snow-covered South Lawn of the White House, deep in thought. Three years into his first term, he was desperate to regain a sense of equilibrium as financial markets, central banks and currencies spiraled out of control. His immediate concern was for the economy, now teetering on the brink of collapse following China's wholesale dump of more than a trillion dollars in U.S. Treasuries. The move—widely regarded as economic suicide—demonstrated to Wheeler a no-holds-barred response to his decision to restrict Chinese investments in the U.S. Now, as the trade war between the U.S. and China threatened to disrupt global supply chains, Chinese warships were converging in the South China Sea, confronting U.S. Navy missile cruisers.

Across the Atlantic, the European Union was on the brink of disintegration, unable to regain its footing after Great Britain's exit, then slammed by the forced resignation of Germany's chancellor. Terror attacks in more than a dozen of Europe's largest cities were occurring with alarming frequency and violence against Muslims had reached epidemic proportions.

In the Middle East, Syria's civil war, now in its seventh year, had reduced the country's three largest cities to ruins and displaced more than eight million refugees. With Russia backing Syrian president Sayid al-Sharaa, and the U.S. supplying arms to rebel forces, it was anyone's guess as to how long it would be before the U.S. and Russia were engaged with each other in direct conflict.

Of deeper concern to Wheeler was the deteriorating state of affairs with North Korea's leader Lee Yong-hwa. Following a large-scale joint military exercise with U.S. and South Korean troops in April, Lee's threats of striking the U.S. were punctuated by the test firing of a ballistic missile capable of reaching the west coast of the United States. That test failed, but it sent a clear message that North Korea was further along in missile development than previously thought, and experts recognized it was a simple matter of time before a successful test was accomplished.

Over the next four months, tensions between the U.S. and North Korea escalated rapidly, marked by eight more missile tests—each one demonstrating a rising level of capability—and another nuclear test. In September, the secretary of Defense and chairman of the Joint Chiefs outlined a list of military options, including a preemptive strike. Three days later, President Wheeler ordered a third U.S. Navy strike group to the waters off the Korean peninsula.

Then, in a move that would have far-reaching political and economic implications, China announced a landmark trade agreement with Russia and unloaded its holdings in U.S. debt—over a trillion dollars in ten-year Treasury bonds—crushing the U.S. debt market.

Wheeler's prospects were, in a word, grim. Now, standing in the Oval Office, his mind went back to the Republican national convention three and a half years earlier. News of a scandal involving the party's leading candidate had broken. Damage control kicked in immediately, but to no avail. Going into the convention, the assessment was that the candidate had no chance of winning the primary. Worse, the consensus held that none of the remaining candidates stood a chance of winning the general election.

With the debacle threatening to upend the party, the Republican National Committee finally came to an agreement—draft the party's most influential governor, Edmund Wheeler. Trouble was, Wheeler wasn't interested in being president. He made that clear a year earlier when they asked him to run, and his feelings hadn't changed.

When push finally came to shove, Wheeler told the party bosses he didn't feel competent to lead the nation in a time of such global upheaval. In his words, "This country needs a wartime president, not a governor." Not surprisingly, the committee's only concern was taking the White House, along with House and Senate seats. Wheeler countered with the idea that what was best for the party may not be best for the country, a notion bordering on heresy as far as the committee was concerned, and they rejected it. With the stipulation that he could pick his running mate, Wheeler finally relented, and on the third ballot he won the Republican nomination. Then, in November, against all odds, he won the general election.

It was a victory Wheeler never expected. As he prepared to occupy the White House, and with concern for his ability looming in his mind, he thought back to a piece of advice his father had given him decades earlier. The senior Wheeler—a successful businessman and respected leader in the oil exploration industry—told his son the best leaders surround themselves with smart people, then listen to them. Those leaders make the critical decisions, but they are decisions shaped by experts.

That advice was foremost in his mind when he filled defense-related cabinet and security posts with retired military, and gave his field commanders broad discretionary power in executing military action as they deemed necessary.

"The days of basing the defense of our nation on tentative posturing are over," he stated in a press conference. "We have the best military leaders in the world, and we are going to let them do their jobs. If they say we should go in, we're going in. If they say we need to bomb, we'll bomb. And the first clue the enemy will have concerning our intentions will be when a missile drops through the roof of the building they're hiding in."

Democrats screamed bloody murder, some suggesting that Wheeler's cabinet and intelligence picks were the basic ingredients for a military coup. But the thinking among political analysts was that the country should get used to a president who was singularly focused on getting America off its knees and back into the role of leader of the free world, and a superpower to be reckoned with.

By his fourth month in office, the discussion around the tables of the Sunday talk shows was that Edmund Wheeler—a man who never wanted the White House—would be one of the greatest presidents to hold the office, or one who would crash and burn on a scale never before seen. Nobody with an opinion that carried any weight thought otherwise. Now, just over three years into his first term, misgivings and self-doubt were taking a toll on the president.

Wheeler shook his head as his thoughts returned to the present. He turned away from the window and reached into a desk drawer for a bottle of antacids. He shook four tablets into his hand and popped them in his mouth, chewing slowly, eyes closed. A moment later his phone rang. It was William Denton, the National Security Advisor, calling from the White House Situation Room.

"Sir," Denton said, "the Israelis have launched a massive air strike against Iran's nuclear facilities."

Wheeler leaned forward, his brow furrowed. "When?" he asked.

"It's underway. The chairman of the Joint Chiefs and director of National Intelligence are here. I've called the secretary of State. She'll be arriving shortly." Denton paused. "Russian fighter aircraft from Khmeimim—the Russian airbase in northwest Syria for operations against the rebels—are flying southeast through Iraqi airspace."

"Do we know what they're doing?"

"No, sir. But if they get involved, we'll want to have the secretary of Defense here as well."

"Make the call. I'll be down in five minutes."

"Thank you, sir."

Wheeler hung up the phone, then sat in his chair, attempting to gather his thoughts. A momentary dizziness gave way to nausea, and for a few seconds he thought he might throw up. He closed his eyes until the feeling passed, then drew a deep breath and stood. "Let's find out what the smart people think," he said aloud.

He left the Oval Office and walked down the hall to the elevator, then descended to the White House basement. A minute later he walked into the Situation Room. Seated at the conference table were Denton, Admiral Fletcher Powell, director of National Intelligence, and General Thomas Macfarland, chairman of the Joint Chiefs of Staff. They stood when he entered.

"Mr. President," they spoke in unison.

"Gentlemen," Wheeler replied, slipping his jacket off. He draped it over the back of the chair at the end of the table, then walked to the far end of the room where a large flat-panel wall screen displayed a tactical map of the Middle East. Centered on Saudi Arabia, the Persian Gulf and Iran, the map was crisscrossed with lines indicating flight vectors and icons depicting aircraft in flight. Wheeler studied the map for a moment, then turned to Denton. "Fill me in."

"IAF fighters have been in Iranian airspace for just under an hour," Denton said. "A number of targets have been destroyed, beginning with the offensive missile sites at Tabriz and Imam to eliminate the possibility of a retaliatory strike against Israel. Following that, they hit Iran's primary underground enrichment facilities—Natanz and Fordo."

"Weren't those supposed to be impenetrable?"

"We thought so, with twelve feet of steel-reinforced concrete underneath forty feet of earth. It takes thirty thousand pounds explosive force to punch through that kind of bunker and destroy it."

"The biggest thing the Israelis have," General Macfarland said, "is the BLU-113. Conventional military wisdom says it's not enough to penetrate those bunkers. But that wisdom is based on just one drop—fly in, release your bombs, and fly out."

Wheeler nodded. "And the Israelis aren't conventional."

"No, sir. They sent twelve F-15s to Natanz, thirteen to Fordo, each one carrying a pair of 113s. The jets came in thirty seconds apart and pounded the bunkers with successive hits."

"Drilling down."

"All the way to the bottom. The last bombs exploded inside the bunkers, creating enormous blast pressure."

"And this destroyed the facilities?"

"Completely, Mr. President. Satellites show craters at Natanz and Fordo that are at least five hundred yards wide and nearly two hundred feet deep."

Wheeler stared at the general for a moment. "Twelve F-15s attacking at thirty-second intervals . . . that's at least six minutes."

"Yes, sir."

"Seems like a long time to be on enemy radar when you're flying an attack. What are the Iranians doing while this is going on?"

Admiral Powell stepped in. "That's where it gets interesting. The Saudis provided E3 Sentry aircraft—same thing as our AWACS—to conduct concentrated electronic interference."

"Meaning?"

"Jamming radar, scrambling radio communications, disrupting homing signals." He paused, raising his eyebrows. "They downloaded a software virus—most likely an Israeli design—into the defensive missile control system of every site they planned on bombing. It appears to have been one hundred percent effective."

"Leaving the Israeli jets free to roam the countryside, destroying whatever they want with little risk of being shot down."

"That's what it boils down to, sir."

"So there have been no Israeli losses."

"That's correct."

"How many other aircraft besides the twenty-five F-15s?"

"Fifty F-16s. Seventy-five fighters total."

Wheeler shook his head. "Unbelievable."

"Yes, sir."

"Any Saudi losses?"

"None so far."

"Are they flying anything other than the E3s?"

"Yes. Along with providing electronic cover, they're refueling the Israeli jets. They've got six aerial tankers in the air over the Saudi-Kuwaiti border. The Israelis topped off their tanks after the flight from their bases in Israel—a nine hundred-mile trip—and they'll need refueling when they return from Iran."

Wheeler turned and looked at the map on the screen, nodding slowly. "They pulled it off," he said quietly.

Along with support for a strong military and a foreign policy aimed at strategic alliances, a major plank in Wheeler's campaign platform had been unwavering support for Israel. Some political analysts suggested it contributed heavily to his victory in the election. And during the process of appointments to key positions, he asked potential nominees point-blank, "What are your feelings toward Israel?" No one who vacillated on that issue would be an integral part of the Wheeler administration.

Denton, Macfarland, and Powell, as well as the secretaries of Defense and State, had expressed not just strong support for the state of Israel, but a desire to deepen ties and solidify the view globally that the U.S. and Israel were committed partners in the war against aggression in the Middle East. Further, Wheeler reached out to Saudi Arabia and Jordan, promising to defend those countries against terrorist expansion in the region in exchange for their military support of U.S. operations. Later, when ISIS began attacks along shipping lanes in the Strait of Hormuz, the United Arab Emirates turned to Wheeler for help and he responded.

As a tightly-knit coalition emerged, the relationship between Russia and Iran deepened in support of Syrian president Sayid al-Sharaa. With the U.S. firmly behind the rebels, and Russia threatening Saudi Arabia and Turkey, many believed the war in Syria would completely envelop the Middle East and pull the U.S. into direct conflict with its old Cold War adversary.

In the end, Russia's relationship with Iran was very much like America's with Israel and Saudi Arabia. Now, with Israeli jets bombing Iran's nuclear infrastructure, and Saudi Arabia facilitating that attack, Russian warships in the Gulf and fighters flying south over Iraq brought home a menacing reality. Wheeler would go to great lengths to avoid a battle with Russia tonight. But he would not turn away from his allies.

His thoughts returned to the Situation Room as the door opened and Secretary of State Elaine Richardson and Secretary of Defense Patrick Wilkinson walked in.

"Mr. President." They greeted him and shook hands.

"Thank you for coming on such short notice," Wheeler said. "Please have a seat." The two sat opposite General Macfarland and Admiral Powell, and looked at the map on the wall screen. Wheeler took his seat at the head of the table. "Mr. Denton," he said, "please continue your briefing."

Denton recapped what the others had covered so far, then moved ahead, describing the destruction of the Iranian centrifuges used to enrich uranium, the yellowcake facility at Isfahan, and the military base at Parchin, which also served as a bomb manufacturing plant. "Presently, of the seventy-five fighters launched by the Israelis, around fifty are on their way back. They will refuel a second time before returning to their bases in Israel. The remaining fighters appear to be en route to a second yellowcake production facility at Ardakan and the heavy-water reactor at Arak.

"As near as we can tell, Arak is their northernmost target in Iran. The bulk of the remaining fighters are headed that way, most likely to provide fighter support for the attacking aircraft. The longer these jets stay in Iranian airspace, the greater the possibility of Iranian air defenses recovering from the radar jamming and frequency blocking imposed by the Saudi E3s. Still, remarkably, there have been no losses of Israeli fighters or Saudi support aircraft."

"There are Russian fighter aircraft over Iraq," General Macfarland said. "The fact that they are flying this time of night and are in Iraqi airspace is reason for concern. There is considerable tension between Russia and Saudi Arabia over their alliances in Syria. Throw in the fact that the Saudis have made this attack possible, and there's a lot of room for things to go sideways. At the same time, Russian warships stationed in the Gulf of Oman have moved into the Strait of Hormuz, four hundred fifty miles southeast of our strike groups. That also is cause for concern. If Russian fighters get involved in a conflict, those warships could try to tip the balance."

"Mr. President," Secretary Richardson said, "you've got a framework alliance with Saudi Arabia and you've expanded your promise to stand with Israel." She looked around the table. "I think all of us here agree with you on that. Under the circumstances, though, we need to think about how far we will go to protect the Saudi and Israeli air forces if Russian fighters attack them."

"We have an alliance with Israel," Wheeler replied, "and nothing the Russians do will change that. And we have an agreement with the Saudis. While there is no formal document yet, the lack of ink on paper doesn't change our commitment to them."

"The Russians aren't going to touch the Israelis," Admiral Powell said. "If they go after anyone, it'll be the Saudis."

"And the Saudis won't leave their own tankers defenseless," Defense Secretary Wilkinson said. "They'll scramble fighters."

"Regardless of what the Saudis do," Richardson said, "I believe the president would be wise to prepare for conflict with Russia tonight." She turned to Wheeler. "They are testing you, sir. You were elected due in part to your support of Israel and agreements with Saudi Arabia and Jordan. I believe the Russians are looking for an opportunity to see exactly where you stand now."

Admiral Powell stood, looking at the map. "I think we're about to find out," he said, pointing. "Aircraft just popped up south of where those Saudi tankers are flying. If they're not F-18s from one of the Navy strike groups, they're Russian fighters flying up from their aircraft carrier in the Strait."

The words were barely out of his mouth when a voice came over the intercom. It was from the Watch Floor—the multi-tiered information center for the Situation Room, manned by three duty officers, a communications director, and an intelligence analyst. "Russian fighters flying up from the Strait are over the Persian Gulf," a duty officer said. "Four SU-33s on a heading of three-two-zero, eighty miles west-northwest of the fleet."

Denton stood and crossed the room to the display. "Project their flight vector, airman." A single line appeared on the display, running from a point fifty-five miles off the coast of Saudi Arabia, northwest through Khafji, eight miles southwest of the Saudi-Kuwaiti border. Three Saudi refueling tankers were in the sky over that point. "What's their ETA at Khafji airspace, airman?"

"Three minutes."

"Those Russian fighters flying south over Iraq are a ruse," Macfarland said. "We're sitting here wondering what they're up to all the while these other guys are barreling up through the Strait."

"Flying below radar all the way," Powell said. "They went right past our strike group."

Wilkinson nodded. "If they shoot down those tankers, the Israelis won't have the gas to make it home."

"Give us tighter scale on the map," Denton said. The view zoomed to an area centered on the Persian Gulf. The tankers were approximately twenty miles apart, circling 25,000 feet above the desert south of the Kuwaiti border.

"Saudi fighters are scrambling out of Abdulaziz," the duty officer said. "Eight F-15s heading northwest to Khafji airspace." He paused, then spoke again. "The southernmost E3 is turning and heading to Khafji airspace." Another pause. "Carrier Strike Group Eight is launching aircraft. They're on a northwest vector to Khafji airspace. ETA, just over three minutes."

"Airman," Wilkinson said, "project Strike Group Eight." A number of dots appeared in the Persian Gulf one hundred miles southeast of Khafji. Wilkinson turned to the president. "Strike Group Eight is one of two operational formations in the Gulf. The associated carrier is the USS *Harry S. Truman*. There's a second strike group stationed thirty-five miles east of the *Truman*—Strike Group Two— with the USS *George H. W. Bush*. It's likely the *Truman* is launching fighters to monitor the situation in Khafji airspace, but also to be close to the action if things go south."

"And what are the chances of things going south?" Wheeler asked. "Your best estimate, General."

"As it stands right now, not much of a chance. Having our fighters up there with the tankers is going to give the Russian fighters pause. They may harass the Saudis, but they won't engage."

"Firing on anybody would be suicide for the Russians," Powell said. "They're outnumbered at least fifteen to one. If fighters from the *Bush* get involved, it's thirty to one."

"Russian fighters are four miles from location," the duty officer spoke. "They're pinging the tankers."

"Pinging the tankers?" Wheeler said.

"Using radar to lock on to a target," Wilkinson said.

"Those tankers are Airbus A300s," Macfarland said, "same airframe as a commercial passenger jet. They can't evade like a fighter can. They have countermeasures, but those usually aren't successful if the aircraft can't maneuver quickly."

"Missiles have been launched," the duty officer said.

"So much for harassing them," Wheeler said.

Powell shook his head. "What are they thinking?"

Everyone in the room was standing now, watching the wall display in silence. Ten seconds later the duty officer spoke again. "First missiles have missed their target."

"The E3 is jamming the homing frequencies," Macfarland said. "But when they get close enough for guns, it's over. The E3s can't stop that. Those tankers will be sitting ducks."

"Two more missiles launched," the duty officer said. "Saudi fighters are on location and are pinging targets." He paused. "Missiles launched from Saudi fighters." Another pause. "Four more Saudi fighters departing Abdulaziz. Six more Russian fighters moving up through the Strait."

"It's about to get busy up there," Powell said.

Wheeler looked at the floor, shaking his head for a moment, then glanced at Powell. "Call me a pessimist, but I have a feeling we're about two minutes away from shooting at the Russians."

Ten seconds later, the duty office spoke again, this time with emotion. "Two Russian SU-33s have been hit by Saudi missiles and are going down. Saudi aircraft firing missiles again. Hold on . . . an anti-ship missile has just been launched from a Russian cruiser in the Strait. It's headed for Strike Group Eight."

"Now we've got trouble," Wilkinson said.

Wheeler stared at Wilkinson for a moment, then spoke. "Can the strike group defend itself against that missile?"

"The carriers have Sea Sparrow missiles, as well as the Phalanx. Those are gatling guns—"

"Yes or no, General."

"Yes, if they're not swarmed by anti-ship missiles."

"Let's hope it stays at just one." Wheeler turned to Denton. "Bill, get the commander of Strike Group Eight on the horn. Then get a call through to President Burkov."

With the exception of Denton and Wheeler, the remaining people in the room were riveted to the wall map. Wheeler pulled Secretary Wilkinson aside. "What are the chances the strike group takes a hit?" he asked.

"One missile," Wilkinson replied, "no chance. Multiple incoming?" He shrugged. "They come in low and extremely fast. One could get through."

"What's our state of readiness?"

"DEFCON 4."

"I have the commander on the line," Denton said.

"Put it on speaker," Wheeler replied.

"This is Captain Ethan Holloway, commander of the USS *Truman*. Talk fast. We're busy here."

"Captain Holloway, this is the president. You are not to return fire on the Russian warship that fired the missile unless you are hit. Do you understand?"

"Yes, sir."

"I am trying to contact the Russian president to persuade him to stand down on this attack. Meanwhile, defend yourself against incoming missiles, but do not fire at Russian ships."

"Yes, sir."

"Good luck, Captain."

"Thank you, sir." The line went dead.

"Impact from Russian anti-ship missile in ninety seconds," the duty officer said. "It's targeting the *Truman*. Two more Russian fighters have been hit. Both are going down." He paused. "Four more anti-ship missiles have been launched from the Russian cruiser."

Secretary Richardson turned to General Wilkinson, her eyes wide. "They want war," she said.

"It looks that way," Wilkinson replied.

"Can we get Burkov on the line?" Wheeler asked impatiently.

"The Russians are not answering our call," Denton replied.

"How long to missile impact?"

"Airman," Denton said. "How long before the first missile reaches the *Truman*?"

"Sixty seconds," the duty officer replied. "Missiles two through five, two minutes." A pause. "Four more anti-ship missiles launched from the Russian cruiser."

"To hell with this," Wheeler said. "Bill, get Captain Holloway."

Five seconds later, Holloway's voice came over the intercom. "Yes, Mr. President."

"Captain Holloway, return fire at the Russian vessels." He paused. "Give them both barrels."

"We have one hundred sixty barrels on eight ships, sir."

"Rain fire on them, Captain."

"With pleasure, sir."

"Captain Holloway," Powell said.

"Yes."

"Admiral Powell here."

"Yes, sir."

"Good hunting."

"Thank you, sir."

Wheeler turned to Secretary Wilkinson. "Patrick, bring us to DEFCON 3." Wilkinson nodded and reached for a phone.

"The *Truman* has stopped the first anti-ship missile," the duty officer said. "Four more anti-ship missiles have been launched."

"Twelve inbound," Wheeler said.

The president returned to his seat at the head of the table. The others took their seats one by one, staring at the map on the wall screen. Nobody spoke. The silence was finally broken by the duty officer. "The *Truman* has been hit by a Russian anti-ship missile. Her cruisers are returning fire."

Denton turned to the president. "Should we keep trying Burkov?" Before Wheeler could answer, the duty officer's voice came over the intercom again.

"Forty anti-ship missiles have been launched at the Russian fleet, along with thirty-six F-18s from the *Truman* and twenty-four from the *Bush*."

Wheeler looked at Denton. "The Navy is going to have a conversation with him now."

2

Monday, February 10
12:05 p.m. Eastern Standard Time
National Security Agency
Fort Meade, Maryland

Within the complex and largely undisclosed framework of the National Security Agency is a Department of Defense project known as the Defense Special Missile and Aerospace Center. Jointly administered by the NSA, the Defense Intelligence Agency, and the National Geospatial-Intelligence Agency, DEFSMAC is the focal point of U.S. missile and space intelligence, providing alerts, assessment, and analysis of foreign missiles and satellites to national agencies and command authorities.

Within DEFSMAC's operational structure is a subbranch tasked with analyzing satellites and space-based hardware with a focus on rogue nations that possess or are actively working toward possessing nuclear weapons. Working closely with the North American Aerospace Defense Command (NORAD), Space Defense

Operations Center (SPADOC), and the United States Northern Command (USNORTHCOM)—military commands located at the Cheyenne Mountain Operations Center in Colorado Springs—it is staffed by senior intelligence analyst Naomi Hendricks, and mathematicians Scott Winter and Paul Lundgren.

Operationally, this unit is a branch of DEFSMAC. But among NSA administration and staff, and the military commands at CMOC, it is referred to as Rampart.

For the past ninety minutes, Hendricks, Winter and Lundgren had been analyzing a satellite launched that morning from the Semnan Space Center in Iran. The first thirty minutes were spent combing through data received from Space Surveillance Network. The rocket lifted off at 17:30:10 Iran Standard Time—14:00:10 UTC—with the satellite reaching orbit seven minutes, fifty-eight seconds later. It was travelling 17,261 miles per hour at an altitude of 201 miles, completing one orbit every ninety-one minutes.

From this information and other parameters, Winter—a specialist in orbital mechanics—modeled the satellite's track over a Mercator projection of the earth and displayed it on the main wall screen. On either side of this were smaller screens displaying data on this satellite, as well as previous launches of Iranian satellites.

Hendricks knew without looking at the old data that today's launch was a carbon copy of everything the Iranians had put up over the last nine years—altitude, inclination, orbital period. But in the back of her mind was the intelligence gathered on Iran over the last eighteen months concerning their relationship with North Korea, and specifically whether or not the North Koreans were sharing nuclear weapons technology with the Kashani regime.

She returned to her desk and sat, feet up, a half-dozen pages of handwritten notes on her lap, then reached for the Department of Defense report she browsed earlier that morning detailing the Israeli attack against Iran. She read for a minute, then looked up at the orbital track, an idea taking shape in her mind that was troubling. She was never comfortable with the launch of an Iranian satellite, but now she was worried.

"Did you guys read the official take on Israel tearing up Iran?" she asked.

"Yeah," Lundgren replied, shooting a foam basketball across the room. It sailed over Hendricks' head and into a makeshift hoop attached to the opposite wall. "That's five in a row," he said to Winter. "You owe me lunch." He turned to Hendricks. "Couldn't happen to a nicer bunch of terrorists."

"Have they said anything?" she asked.

"Iran?"

"Yes."

"Like what?"

"Death to Israel. Death to America." She shrugged. "Death to whoever is ticking them off at the moment."

"Nope."

"Doesn't that strike you as odd?"

"Depends on your definition of odd," Winter said.

Hendricks leaned forward and typed on her keyboard. A moment later she read aloud, "Differing markedly from the usual, ordinary, or accepted; peculiar; not regular, expected, or planned."

Lundgren chuckled. "You asked for that one, buddy."

"Walked right into it," Winter said. He shot and missed. "That's Naomi's fault." He turned to Hendricks. "Odd. You mean like—"

Hendricks held up a hand. "Scott. This isn't like the Iranians. Especially after this." She waved the report.

"She's right," Lundgren said. "After that attack, they'd be running their mouths a mile a minute. And warming up the missiles."

"The Russians too. Four of their ships are lying at the bottom of the Strait of Hormuz. Why aren't they threatening us?" She crossed the room to the wall display and stood, arms folded. Her eyes traced the orbits, but her mind was on the report. The more she thought about it, the more concerned she became. Lundgren watched her for a moment, then sank a hook shot from across the room.

"Lunch, times two." He smiled at Winter, then walked over and stood next to Hendricks. "What's on your mind, boss lady?"

Winter picked up the basketball and dropped it on his desk. "She thinks it's a weapon."

"You know me," Hendricks said. "The way I see it, the minute they can put one up there, they will."

"Sure," Winter replied. "You can plan on it. But they didn't do it with a Safir. The most that rocket will lift is a couple hundred pounds. A weapon—and I assume you're thinking nuclear—is going to run a ton, maybe more."

"Are you sure they launched it with a Safir?"

"It's all they've got."

She nodded, then turned back to the orbital track, focusing on the sixth orbit. At 6:03 p.m. Eastern Time, the satellite would pass over Nogales, Arizona heading northeast, exiting the U.S. over Marquette, Michigan six minutes later. Hendricks thought for a moment, then crossed the room and glanced at her desk calendar. "When was the Iranian Revolution?" she asked.

"Demonstrations against the Shah started in 1977," Lundgren said. "It went on a year and a half. Ended in '79."

"When did Khomeini take power?"

Lundgren stared at Hendricks, thinking. "The tenth of February." He paused and glanced at Winter. "Forty-one years ago today."

Hendricks sighed. "I've got a bad feeling about this one, guys."

Iran was a source of deep concern for Hendricks. Their negotiation tactics—dialogue cluttered by obfuscation and evasion, punctuated by long periods of silence—were, in Hendricks' mind, thinly veiled attempts to slow the progress of inspections while work toward a nuclear weapon continued under wraps.

When the White House announced in 2013 that an accord with Iran was on the table, U.S. intelligence agencies quietly parted company with those who thought an agreement would force Iran to abandon its nuclear program. They weren't outwardly vocal in their suspicion of Iran—at least to the point of inhibiting progress in the negotiations—but took a wait-and-see position, seeking to protect U.S. interests without burning bridges.

Six months after signing the accord in July 2015, Iran shipped the bulk of its low-enriched uranium to Russia, fulfilling a key provision of the nuclear deal. And while proponents of the accord celebrated this as a significant slowdown in the breakout time to a weapon, a majority of analysts—Hendricks among them—saw the loss of uranium as little more than a hiccup for Iran. The breakout time was set back a mere six months. And the nuclear reactor at Arak, which was to be shut down completely by the end of the year, was still operational well into 2016. And it was producing plutonium, an easier path to a nuclear weapon than uranium.

The most unsettling aspect in Hendricks' mind was Iran's long-standing partnership with North Korea, beginning with the North's first successful test of an atomic bomb. Following that, the two countries collaborated on all things nuclear, from construction of centrifuges and the plutonium reactor at Arak, to development of missiles. And while sanctions cut off the shipment of missiles from North Korea to Iran, they didn't eliminate the flow of information from Pyongyang—specifically, the technology needed to miniaturize a warhead for use on an intercontinental ballistic missile. And it was this exchange that Hendricks considered most dangerous. This is what kept her up at night.

She turned from the orbital track and faced Winter and Lundgren. "None of this strikes you guys as out of the ordinary," she said.

"I consider anything Iran launches into space out of the ordinary," Winter replied. "But a threat?" He shook his head. "No."

"You guys remember the cargo that was shipped from Pyongyang to Tehran two years ago? They moved it by truck to that weapons development facility."

"Parchin," Winter said.

Hendricks nodded. "That cargo is the key to all of this."

"You think it was a weapon?"

"Yes."

"Satellites didn't pick up any radiation signature on the cargo when it shipped from Pyongyang," Lundgren said.

"I know. I think it was the components to build the bomb, not the bomb itself. They ship the hardware, then it sits at Parchin while the Iranians are putting together enough plutonium to make it work. Once they have that, the North Koreans come back and assemble everything. Two months ago, a crate was shipped from Parchin to the launch facility at Semnan. If that crate was the same one that was shipped from Pyongyang, I think it was the bomb fully assembled and ready for launch. The North Koreans are at the launch site when it shows up." She paused, thinking. "And the Russians are there—"

"Wait," Winter said. "You think the Russians are involved?"

"It's a hunch."

"Based on what?"

"Eighteen months of intelligence."

"The same intelligence we've looked at a dozen different ways."

Hendricks sat on her desk. "When I look at what we have on North Korea and Iran, but particularly the time frame when bomb technicians were traveling back and forth, then this—" she held up the DoD report, "—Israel taking out Iran's nuclear facilities, and Russia's bright idea to go after a U.S. Navy aircraft carrier . . . I get the feeling it's all connected."

Winter glanced at Lundgren, then back at Hendricks. "I get the feeling their satellite is just a satellite—communications, weather, mapping, maybe surveillance." Hendricks nodded but didn't reply, instead, focusing on the wall screen with the orbital track. "You're serious about it being a bomb," he continued.

"Do I look serious?"

"This is what she does," Lundgren said. "She doesn't shoot hoops. She doesn't do math. She just looks for trouble."

Winter nodded. "Well, she's good at it."

"Come on, guys," Hendricks said. "You know how it works around here—we do whatever we want. You play basketball. I look for threats to national security."

"Are you asking which is more important?" Lundgren said.

Hendricks smiled, then crossed the room to the wall display and pointed to the ground track's sixth orbit. "See this? That's the satellite crossing the central U.S." She turned and faced them. "If this is what I think it is and we don't do something about it, a little over five hours from now the United States is going dark. No electricity. And it won't be coming back any time soon."

Winter stared at her. "You think it's an EMP weapon."

"I do." She walked back to her desk and sat. "I'm going to think out loud for a while. Feel free to chime in with any ideas you have." She reached for a folder. "Or you can shoot hoops."

Winter looked at Lundgren, then sat on Hendricks' desk. Lundgren pulled up a chair. "Deal us in," he said.

"This is a recap," Hendricks began, "so bear with me. December thirtieth, 2015, Iranians with a background in weapons development travel to Pyongyang. One week later, North Korea conducts its fourth nuclear weapons test. Three weeks after that, North Korean bomb techs travel to Tehran. While they're there, the mysterious cargo is shipped from Pyongyang. It shows up at Chabahar, Iran's southernmost seaport. They move it to the weapons development facility at Parchin.

"Over the next two weeks, the North Koreans are camped at the weapons complex—doing what, we don't know, because they're in an underground facility and our satellites can't detect anything. March eighth, they pack up and go home.

"Over the next six months the North Koreans and Iranians travel back and forth eight times. On three separate occasions when the North Koreans are in Iran, they travel to Semnan. But every time they're in the country, they're at Parchin. As far as we know, the crate doesn't move from the middle of March to the end of August.

"September second, Iranian bomb techs travel to Pyongyang. On the ninth, North Korea detonates it's fifth nuclear weapon." She set her notes on the desk. "You see a trend here?"

"Bomb geeks gone wild?" Lundgren said.

"Not exactly what I was thinking, but close enough. So how long would it take Iran to enrich enough plutonium for a warhead in the twenty-kiloton range?"

"With what they had before the Stuxnet virus?" Winter said. "A year, to a year and a half."

"All right. We know that Stuxnet shut down their production from June 2009 through late 2012, and talk of an accord was good reason for them to cool their jets through July 2015."

"Add the threat of sanctions," Lundgren said, "and they're idle through June 2016."

"Now fast forward to late September," Hendricks continued. "The North Koreans show up in Iran, head to Parchin and work under wraps until November fifteenth. Then a crate is moved to Semnan and the Russians show up."

Winter nodded. "The time frame fits."

"Bottom line, guys, I think the satellite they launched this morning is a nuclear weapon."

"It's plausible," Winter nodded. "Up to the point of trying to get it off the ground." Hendricks sighed, then leaned back in her chair and closed her eyes. "Naomi," Winter continued, "we're all on the same page as far as Iran being a threat. And dropping a bomb on us the first chance they get? Nobody in this line of work thinks otherwise." He paused. "But not today."

"There's absolutely no way it's a weapon?"

"It's the rocket. It can't lift the weight. And the Safir is the only thing they have." He glanced at Lundgren, then back at Hendricks. "For the sake of discussion, let's say they could lift it into orbit. If I let my mind run—which is your strong suit, not mine—I can imagine North Korea and Iran collaborating to attack the U.S. But I don't see Russia in the mix. Yes, they were at the launch site when the North Koreans were there, but doing what?"

"That's what I'm trying to work out." She turned to the wall display, looking at the orbital track, but running things through her mind, desperately trying to make a connection, all the while fighting a rising sense of frustration. Hendricks relied on Winter and Lundgren to keep her in check. She was the right brain of Rampart— the imagination—letting her mind run with ideas regardless of how wild they seemed. Winter and Lundgren were the left side—logical, mathematicians focused on probability. The three of them worked together like a finely-tuned machine, a system of checks and balances. But there were times when Hendricks felt like she was dragging a car without wheels across a parking lot.

She stood and faced them. "You guys need to step out of your wheelhouse on this one," she said. "Your playbook isn't going to explain it. The pieces that make up this picture are different than what we're used to seeing."

"Like Russia deciding out of the wild blue to wipe out the United States," Winter said.

"That's just it. This isn't out of the wild blue. It started six years ago. Russia seizes Crimea. We hit them with sanctions. Then they muscle Ukraine. In the eighteen months following that, they're pounded with more sanctions—against their banks, corporations, pretty much everyone who has any influence. The EU slaps them with travel bans. We push Turkey to block their pipeline. We hit their energy and defense sectors. By the first quarter 2015—"

"Naomi." Winter held up his hand. "I get it. We crushed them economically. But they didn't launch this satellite."

"Listen, Scott. Russia got fed up, plain and simple. They'd had enough. Iran hatched a plan with North Korea to take us out, and Russia was ready to be a part of it. The attack on the *Truman* that triggered the destruction of their ships was to justify their role in this." She paused. "It was a sacrifice to set the stage."

Winter stared at Hendricks. "You asked if I can say there's absolutely no way that's a weapon," he said. "I can't. What I can say—and I'm saying it because part of my job is to keep things in the realm of probability—is this is a stretch, even for you."

"Come on, Scott."

"You get out there, Naomi. I'm not saying that's bad. Some of our best work has come from you climbing out on a limb and dangling in the breeze. You're fearless."

"But."

"This is past that. It's beyond belief."

"You don't like the idea of a nuclear bomb in orbit."

"I'm quirky."

"What would we be talking about if that satellite had been launched this morning from Pyongyang?" she said. Winter stared at her in silence, then looked at Lundgren.

"She's right," Lundgren said. "We're not ready for Iran to have a nuclear weapon. A year from now? Maybe. Naomi looks at this and asks, 'What if North Korea gave them a bomb three months ago?'"

Winter nodded, thinking. "Okay. Set aside North Korea and Iran for a minute. And Russia, assuming they're involved. China comes to mind. They're not going to sit still for an attack like this, and I don't care what they've got going with Russia." He paused. "China is the world's number two economy for one reason—the world's number one economy. There is no way they're going to upset that apple cart. Yes, they mess with us every chance they get—cyberattacks, stealing secrets, that's what they do. But if our ship sinks, so does China's. They go back to the 1970s—a centrally-planned, closed economy that's going nowhere."

"I don't think China knows about this," Hendricks said.

Winter looked at her, then shook his head. "It's still a stretch, Naomi. Truthfully, more of a leap. A really long leap."

Hendricks started to speak, but Lundgren stopped her. "Let me hit replay," he said, "but from a different angle."

"Dazzle me," Winter said.

"Last Friday, Israel sends everything they've got against Iran. They tear the place apart. They take out defensive missile sites, which, of course, makes sense since they're flying an attack. But they destroy air bases too. And Iran's two offensive missile sites. Technically, it's an act of war. But—and this is a big but—Israel has the support of the U.S. One of the constants in the Middle East is the fact that Iran won't attack Israel no matter how badly they want to, for fear of U.S. retaliation. And our commander-in-chief is very fond of Israel.

"Russia, who is watching from the Strait of Hormuz, decides to test Wheeler's resolve. They start with a response to the attack by the Israelis and Saudis. Then, in a brain-gone-haywire moment, they attack the U.S. Navy. It's suicide, but there it is nonetheless."

"The sacrifice," Winter said.

"From Naomi's point of view, yes."

"Go on."

"When the smoke clears, Iran and Russia know for a fact that Israel, Saudi Arabia and President Wheeler are serious as a heart attack. Now throw in North Korea. The one thing they have in common with Iran—apart from being certifiably insane—is they hate the U.S. in a wildly deranged way. And the big difference between them and Russia is that Russia would never start a war with us, mutually assured destruction being what it is. Iran and North Korea would because they don't think from one minute to the next."

Hendricks pointed a finger. "And Russia knows they would."

"Exactly," Lundgren said. "The question then becomes, if the U.S. could be taken out before it could launch missiles—and I mean in a heartbeat—"

"Electromagnetic pulse," Hendricks nodded.

"—would Russia care that the U.S. as a global economic force is gone? No. China cares, but it's too late. They become strategic partners with Russia and move on."

"Russia becomes the sole provider of natural gas to Europe and the Middle East," Hendricks said. "Iran becomes the leader in oil. And what does China need more than U.S. consumers?"

"Oil," Winter replied.

"Exactly. China becomes the world's economic superpower. Russia and Iran dominate the Middle East." Hendricks paused. "Goodbye, Israel."

Winter looked at Lundgren, then back at Hendricks. "Goodbye, America," he said quietly.

"It makes sense," Lundgren said, "in an every-man-for-himself kind of way."

Winter stared at the floor for a moment, shaking his head. "This is so far out there, I feel like I need a telescope to see it."

"I know, Scott," Hendricks replied. "Believe me, I know." She paused. "I need you to find something wrong with it."

"I'm trying." He looked at Hendricks, then past her, his mind pouring over the last twenty minutes of discussion. He walked slowly across the room, absorbed in thought, glancing up at the orbital track. He turned back to Hendricks. "Would Russia be involved in something like this," he said, "knowing we could still hit them with sub-launched weapons after our grid has collapsed?"

"Orders from NORAD."

"Yes. CMOC is bullet-proof. Even after the lights go out, anyone inside that mountain can still contact the subs."

"I know. I think Russia believes their role in this won't be discovered. They're backstage actors."

Winter held up his hands. "I can't find anything wrong with it. Other than lifting a heavy weapon into orbit." He paused. "I hate to keep bringing it up, Naomi, but they didn't do this with the Safir."

Hendricks sat down and closed her eyes, rubbing her temples with her fingertips, wondering now if she was hung up on this theory because it validated her worst fears about Iran. She had the utmost respect for Winter's opinion, for his ability to look at arguments logically, free of emotion. Lundgren too. At the same time, she couldn't ignore her feeling about this satellite, a feeling so strong she felt it was screaming at her.

Then it hit her, and she practically jumped out of her chair. "I don't believe it—it's been staring me in the face all along. CMOC would have a heat signature on the launch, wouldn't they?"

"Sure," Winter replied.

Hendricks pointed at him. "The rocket was Russian. That's why they were at the launch site."

Winter stared at her for a moment. "That would change everything. Paul, check SSN. I'll check CMOC."

Hendricks turned back to the orbital track. She was anxious to close this loose end, but fully aware that with each step toward a resolution, they moved closer to a terrifying reality. If that was a weapon orbiting Earth, things were going to change dramatically. If it was an EMP weapon, it could all be over in an instant.

"Bingo," Winter said a minute later, looking up from his computer. "Heat signature was from a Russian Zenit."

Lundgren stood. "That has a fifteen-ton lift capacity."

Winter nodded. "It could launch a multi-megaton warhead with about twelve tons to spare."

"Why would they use that?" Hendricks asked.

"No clue," Lundgren replied. "They could have lifted a five-megaton warhead with an Angara—smaller rocket, less fuel and a lot easier to set up and launch."

"The question I have," Winter said, "is why didn't we get this tidbit with the orbital data two hours ago?"

Hendricks turned to her desk and dialed the direct line to the Cheyenne Mountain complex, then hit speaker. It rang twice.

"Colonel Keating here."

"Naomi Hendricks at Rampart. Have you got a minute?"

"Yes."

"We just queried the CMOC database on the Iranian satellite launched today. The heat signature is from a Russian Zenit."

There was a pause on the other end of the line. "Ms. Hendricks, can I put you on hold for a minute?"

"Yes."

Forty-five seconds later, the gravelly voice of General Wilson Tuckett, commander of NORAD, came on the line. "This is General Tuckett, Ms. Hendricks. It pains me to admit it, but this heat signature was lost in the shuffle. It should have been flagged hours ago."

"Are you concerned about it?"

"I'm trying to think of a good reason to use that rocket to lift a satellite. More than that, though, I'm wondering why Russia would give the Iranians a heavy-lift launch vehicle regardless of what they were putting up there."

"Sir, we're looking at intelligence gathered over the last eighteen months on Iran and North Korea. With this heat signature, we believe the satellite launched this morning could be a weapon."

"Russian?"

"North Korean. We think they helped Iran build a bomb. The Zenit would be more than capable of lifting it into orbit."

"What's your bottom line?"

"We think it's an electromagnetic pulse weapon."

"Jesus," Tuckett whispered.

It wasn't until that moment that Hendricks was hit with the enormity of the situation. As an analyst, she was all about the details, working through a theory as if it were a massive jigsaw puzzle, focusing on the colors and contour, the fit of the pieces. Lundgren and Winter—mathematicians—were the same. Together they hammered out concepts that were mind-numbing in complexity, sometimes never pushing back until everything had fallen into place.

General Tuckett was a big-picture person. He saw the end game immediately. Hendricks sat down and drew a slow breath. "Sir, the satellite crosses the U.S. between 6:03 and 6:09 Eastern Time tonight, tracking over the central U.S. at around 6:05. We see that as a possible point of detonation."

"Have you told your directors?"

"We're still working it out. I wanted your take on the Zenit."

"Make the call, Ms. Hendricks. Get it in front of them ASAP. If you're right about this, every minute counts."

"Yes, sir."

"We'll look at it on our end, see if our people have any ideas." He paused. "I hope you're wrong about this, Ms. Hendricks."

"So do I, General."

"Tell Attwood to get with us if he has any questions."

"I will, sir. Thank you." Hendricks ended the call, then turned to Winter. "Your thoughts."

"As wild as it is to contemplate," he replied, "it's actionable."

"We've got to be rock-solid on this, guys." She pointed at her phone. "I'm going to call Attwood. He's going to want credible. If he gets it, this could end up in front of the president. Now rewind the last thirty minutes. More than being plausible, is it credible?"

"The intel's good," Winter said. "The reasoning is sound. The Russian booster is the tipping point."

"Can you think of any reason to use a rocket that big to put a satellite in orbit?"

"No. But I agree with Tuckett. The question is why would Russia give Iran a heavy-lift vehicle for any reason, satellite or otherwise?" He paused. "If this is what we think it is, it would have been in the works at least six months ago. That rocket was sitting on the launch pad at the Semnan Space Center ready to boost a warhead long before Israel bombed Iran's nuclear facilities and the Navy sunk those Russian warships in the Gulf."

"I know." She turned to Lundgren. "What do you think?"

"It's solid," Lundgren replied. "But we're analysts, not politicians. You've got to keep that in mind when you're talking to Attwood. Donovan too."

"You think there may be some resistance."

"Naomi, this is huge."

"He's right," Winter said. "Jump to the end—Donovan signs on and sits down with the president. Now put yourself in Wheeler's shoes. This isn't like closing a train station or a stadium based on a terrorist threat. This is the immediate shutdown of every nuclear power plant in the country. Grounding all air traffic. And that's just for starters."

Lundgren nodded. "Logistically, it's Mount Everest."

Hendricks picked up the phone and dialed the director of DEFSMAC. He answered on the first ring.

"Michael Attwood."

"Naomi Hendricks in Rampart, sir. We have a threat."

"I'll be there in three minutes."

"Thank you."

She hung up the phone and turned to face the wall displays. "Let's get visuals up there. Dump the old satellite data. Scott, calculate the line-of-sight distance of an electromagnetic pulse from two hundred miles above . . . Kansas?"

"That's the geographic center of the U.S.," Winter said. "If I wanted to maximize the effect of an EMP, I'd set it off over Nebraska. Maybe even South Dakota. In northern latitudes, the earth's magnetic field is stronger. It's going to push the pulse toward the equator. By the time it hits the ground, it will be centered at least two hundred miles south of where the weapon was in orbit."

"Make it South Dakota," Hendricks replied. "Paul, put together three maps of North America—physical, political and population density. Take Scott's data and overlay all three maps with a red circle showing the affected area."

"Weapon yield?" Lundgren asked.

"Twenty kilotons, high gamma output."

Ninety seconds later the displays flickered, and three maps appeared. Hendricks stood in front of the screen displaying the population density map. The red circle extended from approximately three hundred miles off the coast of California, east to Nova Scotia, and from the Northwest Territories in Canada, south to El Salvador.

"My God," she whispered, "that's all of North America."

"Ninety-seven percent of the population," Lundgren replied.

"With no electricity. No lights. No heat."

"No food or water," Winter said.

Hendricks nodded. Her worst fears of an attack by Iran were now being realized, step by step. She knew the outcome, and there was nothing she could do to steer events leading up to it, or slow them down. All she could do was watch them unfold.

"Welcome to my nightmare," she said quietly.

3

9:45 p.m. Iran Standard Time
Tehran, Iran

Anatoly Markovic and Stepan Ivanov sat in the back seat of a Mercedes sedan as it sped up the Lashkari Expressway, heading to the 1st Tactical Air Base at Mehrabad International Airport. The two had been present at the launch of an Iranian satellite four hours earlier—Markovic as a major general in the Strategic Rocket Forces of the Russian Federation, Ivanov as a member of the Federation's Ministry of Science and developer of the satellite's guidance software. Now they were returning to Tehran where they would board a military jet and fly back to Moscow.

A dozen times over the past six months Markovic had considered his role in the satellite's mission, experiencing feelings of apprehension, then distress, and as the launch date neared, trepidation. He could see no outcome other than the ultimate economic demise of Russia, and quite possibly nuclear war with the United States. He was aware of the military installation in a mountain in Colorado from which the launch of nuclear missiles could be ordered, even after the collapse of the nation's electrical grid. He was aware too of the possibility, however remote, that the U.S. could destroy the weapon before it detonated in space. That was his singular focus as he stared out the window of the sedan.

Markovic's military career began in the KGB—the primary security agency in the Union of Soviet Socialist Republics. He would not have had any qualms back then about a mission such as this, and certainly would never have questioned the motives behind it. He was rising in the ranks and developing a deep hatred for the United States of America, an implacable enemy of the Soviet Union.

Under the leadership of General Secretary Mikhail Gorbachev, his views began to change. During a meeting in New York between Gorbachev and President Ronald Reagan, Markovic—the head of Gorbachev's security detail—got a firsthand glimpse not only of America as a bastion of capitalism, but of the culture as well. Driving down the streets of New York City in a presidential motorcade, he stared out the window at the myriad small shops and large businesses, the theatre marquees and thousands of people in brightly colored clothes, some even singing and dancing on the sidewalks.

But of all his experiences in the city, the most profound was with a street vendor selling hot dogs. The car carrying Gorbachev and Reagan pulled to the curb, and the two men got out and bought a hot dog. Markovic did the same. The man selling them appeared overjoyed as he prepared them for these world leaders and members of their entourage, laughing as he told them jokes, talking excitedly about his city and waving his arms in a way Markovic later learned was the normal manner of speaking among New Yorkers.

That trip left an indelible impression on Markovic, and he reflected on it frequently in the years following. During conversations with Gorbachev—a man for whom he held deep respect—he was surprised to learn that the General Secretary's political views were moderating, and with Gorbachev's move toward political transparency and a hybrid communist-capitalist economy, Markovic's own political views were moderating as well.

With collapse of the Soviet Union in December 1991 and the dissolution of the KGB, Markovic found himself in the upper echelon of the SVR, Russia's newly-formed Foreign Intelligence Service, and in a completely different frame of mind politically. Gone was the hostility and mistrust toward nations seeking to build relationships with Russia, and with a newfound freedom that didn't exist in the KGB, he sought to build ties that would stabilize Russia's role in the world. This he would do covertly.

Now, as the sedan slid to a stop in an airport hangar, he knew what he must do. He and Ivanov boarded the military jet and sat in the rear. As Ivanov opened his briefcase, Markovic asked to see the orbital data. Ivanov pulled a folder from the briefcase and handed it to him, then watched as he thumbed through the pages. A minute later Markovic stopped, pulled a phone from his pocket, then took a picture of a page.

"What are you doing?" Ivanov asked.

Markovic considered the young man's question as he typed a recipient and phone number. Would it help if he described what life was like in the Soviet Union? Perhaps Ivanov would understand if he knew President Burkov was steering Russia back to those days of economic and cultural repression.

He turned and looked at Ivanov. "I'm trying to save our way of life, Stepan. I'm trying to keep the United States and Russia from destroying each other." Then he hit send.

4

1:20 p.m. Eastern Standard Time
National Security Agency
Fort Meade, Maryland

Hendricks leaned back in her chair, trying to relax. Even with her eyes closed she could still see the image of the orbital track as if it were burned into her retinas. She looked up at the population density map, and suddenly her mind was flooded with thoughts of her mother and father, of everything they taught her about being prepared for disasters. Of everyone she knew, her parents would be among the few who would survive an EMP attack—a life without electricity and everything that depended on it.

Her mind went back to a summer she spent with her family after college, but before NSA. One week was spent hunting, fishing and camping—what her dad called 'roughing it.' She loved every minute of it. She loved the outdoors, but also just being with her mom and dad and brother, helping set up camp, pitching a tent, gathering firewood and cooking over a fire.

She still remembered the first time she helped her father start a fire with flint and steel. She was eight years old. "I could use matches," he told her, "but this is way cooler. This is pioneer science." He held a short piece of a broken iron file in one hand. In the other, a piece of flint and a small swatch of charred cotton fabric. He struck the edge of the rock several times with the file, each time sending a spark flying onto the cloth. Finally, one took hold, and a tiny circle of orange began glowing in the middle of the black fabric. "That's an ember," he said. "Blow on it gently." She did, and it glowed brighter, spreading as it slowly consumed the cloth.

"Now let's turn that into a camp fire." He picked up a handful of tinder—a strip of juniper bark he had twisted and crumpled until it was a loose ball of shredded fiber—and carefully tucked the char cloth inside, the ember still glowing. He gently squeezed the wad of tinder around the cloth, then held it close to her face.

"See it glowing down in there?" he asked. She nodded. "Blow on it again, very gently." She did, and it grew, glowing brighter. He pushed the tinder closer around the ember. "Again," he said. She continued blowing until a wisp of smoke wafted up through the tinder. "Again," he said, "a little more breath this time."

Each time she blew, the ember grew brighter and the smoke heavier, until at last the tinder burst into flame. Startled, she leaned back, then looked up at her dad, eyes filled with excitement.

"Cool!" she exclaimed.

"You are a fire goddess, little missy," he smiled, placing the burning tinder on the ground. "Now we make it bigger." He handed her a pair of gloves, then picked up a handful of small twigs he'd gathered before they started the fire. "Starting with these," he said, "take one at a time and carefully lay it on top of the tinder."

"The fire's getting bigger, Daddy," she said, adding the sticks.

"That's right, sweetheart, so we move back a little and add bigger sticks. These are called kindling."

A minute later the fire was crackling and popping. She stood next to her father, marveling at this—her first fire.

"Mom!" she called. "I made a fire!"

"Oh, my goodness!" her mother said, emerging from the tent. "Look at you, sweetheart!" She joined them and watched the flames, smiling down at her.

"Can we cook on it, Mom?"

"Absolutely."

She remembered that meal as if it were yesterday—a Dutch oven stew with cornbread, and apple cobbler for dessert—and while it may have been because she helped start the fire, or the fact that it was campfire cooking rather than something prepared in the convenience of a kitchen, it stuck in her mind as being one of the tastiest meals she'd ever eaten.

Over the years, her parents taught her how to expect the unexpected and prepare for it, from building a makeshift shelter with nothing but tree limbs and leaves, to foraging for food, to advanced first aid techniques. She learned how to trap small game with a snare, how to fish with a few feet of monofilament line and a hook, using bait she found under rocks at the edge of the water—her father called them 'rock rollers.' She learned how to read topographical maps and find her way with a compass, how to determine her latitude by the angle of the stars.

Suddenly she was overcome by an intense yearning for those days of life in the outdoors with her parents, of learning all she could about preparedness, survival—in her father's words, Scouting 301. Her knowledge was extensive. But right now she was overwhelmed by the feeling that it wasn't going to be enough.

Her thoughts returned to the problem at hand when the door to the office swung open and Michael Attwood entered. "What's happening?" he asked. He glanced at the maps with red circles. "A population density map? That can't be good."

Hendricks crossed the room and pointed to the orbital track on the main display. "This is the ground track of a satellite that made orbit a few hours ago, launched from Iran. The booster used to lift it was a Russian Zenit. It can carry fifteen tons into orbit."

"That's a lot of rocket for a satellite, isn't it?"

"It is. We've been analyzing relevant data for the last two hours. We now think the satellite is an electromagnetic pulse weapon."

"Detonated in orbit."

"Yes."

He stared at her for a moment, then turned back to the orbital track. "Present position?" he asked, pointing to the blue circle.

"Yes, sir. West-southwest of New Zealand, on its third orbit."

"And the track in red?"

"First orbital ascension over the U.S."

"And this is when you think it will detonate."

"Yes."

"Why not here," he pointed to another track, "when it's descending? It still crosses the central U.S."

"This is just a hunch—trying to think like they would—but setting it off after it's dark on the east coast would maximize confusion in the largest cities."

"It would," he said. "But whether or not they think like you is another matter." He turned back to the display. "When is this ascending pass?"

"Crossing the U.S. from 6:03 to 6:09 Eastern."

Attwood nodded, then turned to the population density map. "The red circle is the affected area."

"Yes, sir."

"Population?"

"Six hundred million," Lundgren said.

Attwood closed his eyes for a moment, then turned to Hendricks. "All right. Give me the lowdown."

Hendricks nodded. "First, we just got off the phone with NORAD. I wanted their take on the Russian booster."

"Who did you talk to?"

"General Tuckett. He's concerned."

"If Tuckett's concerned, I'm concerned."

Hendricks spent the next ten minutes going over the data, starting with the North Korean scientists traveling to Iran eighteen months earlier, then working forward, ending with Israel's attack in Iran and the destruction of Russian navy vessels. "The recent U.S. sanctions against Lee Yong-hwa directly, as opposed to sanctioning the regime, resulted in him threatening nuclear war. He's done that before, of course, but this time the North is very close to Iran. Things could turn. Lee doesn't have a rocket that will lift a weapon this heavy into space. But Iran does, courtesy of Russia. Based on everything we know right now—the intelligence, the heat signature of the launch vehicle, NORAD's thinking and, frankly, a hunch, our analysis points to a credible threat."

Attwood nodded. "If this is what you think it is, and we can't stop it, it's game over."

"I understand, sir. That doesn't change our conclusion."

"I know. I'm trying to wrap my head around your conclusion."

"Sir, we threaten to shut off the lights in Russia, Iran and North Korea. Tell them right now that's what will happen if this weapon is detonated over U.S. soil. Worst-case scenario, they ignore us, and we lose the grid. We've still got subs out there. NORAD's still functioning. They send word to target those three countries with high-altitude air bursts, just like they're doing to us." She paused. "If we go dark, they go dark."

"That's an idea we can keep in reserve," Attwood replied. "If it comes to that and they respond, it would be a happy ending to a short horror story. But they haven't been talking to us lately."

"There's another approach," Lundgren said.

"I'm listening."

"Open this up to S32."

"Tailored Access Operations?"

"Yes, sir. That division is home to the best hackers in the world—Access Technologies Ops. They could infiltrate every network in Iran, Russia and North Korea, and wipe them out."

"You're suggesting an all-out cyberattack?"

"Yes, sir. We plant viruses in every computer network we can find over the next few hours. We systematically cripple banking and finance, government, military and civilian systems. We destroy their infrastructure from the inside."

"That's another one we'll keep in reserve. What's your level of confidence on this?"

Winter and Lundgren glanced at each other. "Eighty-five percent," Winter replied. Attwood nodded, thinking.

"Sir," Hendricks said, "for ten years we've recognized the inevitability of Iran getting their hands on a nuclear weapon. We just didn't know when. That uncertainty diminished with North Korea's involvement over the last year. Now we look at it from the standpoint of triggers—escalation in tension, a spike in conflict."

"Are you talking about the attack in the Persian Gulf?"

"That, but also events leading up to it—Russia's aggressive behavior toward NATO over the last six months, their economic treaties with China, then severing ties with the west a week ago."

"So today," Attwood said, "right now."

"Eighty-five percent," Winter replied. "The Russian booster changes everything."

"That's it. Eighty-five percent."

"We deal in probability," Hendricks said, "not certainty. Eighty-five percent is our way of saying, 'Plan on it.'"

A moment later, Hendricks' cell phone chimed. Then Winter's computer. Then Lundgren's, followed by five other workstations.

Hendricks tapped the screen on her phone. "A secure message from MI6." She looked at Attwood. "London."

"MI6? How often do they contact you?"

"Never."

Winter and Lundgren moved to their work stations. "It's not text," Winter said. "It's an image." Ten seconds later, a single page appeared on a screen to the left of the orbital track. "It looks like a satellite guidance program—tabular data." He walked to the wall display and studied the image. "Look at the last line."

"Plus zero nine, zero five, thirty-seven," Hendricks read aloud. "Four three, dot three nine three zero seven, minus nine seven, dot one three four two five."

"A time and coordinates," Winter said. "Paul, place a marker on the orbital track at launch plus nine hours, five minutes, thirty-seven seconds." A moment later a small red circle appeared in the U.S., upper Midwest. "What's the location?"

"Nineteen point five miles southwest of Sioux Falls, South Dakota," Lundgren replied. "Parker Township."

"Put another marker at those coordinates—forty-three point three nine three zero seven latitude, minus ninety-seven point one three four two five longitude."

"Same place. Sioux Falls, Parker Township."

Hendricks closed her eyes, her heart sinking. For the first time in her career at NSA she was praying she was wrong, that somehow, by some kind of miracle, all this data—the launch of the satellite, the intelligence on North Korea, Iran and Russia, the discovery of the rocket's heat signature and now the message from MI6—would be nothing to worry about, that it would be exactly what Winter suggested earlier, a communications satellite or a weather platform.

Then Lundgren spoke. "The message originated in Tehran."

Attwood pulled out his cell phone and dialed the director of NSA. "Matthew, Michael Attwood. We need you in Rampart. It's urgent." Slipping the phone back into his pocket, he turned to Hendricks. "How many of your people are at lunch?"

"Three."

"Support staff?"

"Yes."

"Are they essential to any of this?"

"No."

"Send them home when they get back. You three stay." He turned to leave. "I'll be back in ten minutes. If the director gets here before I do, give him a magazine."

"Sir?"

"Do not brief him until I return."

"Yes, sir."

Attwood stopped at the door. "Nobody comes in here except me or Matthew Donovan. Nobody leaves." He paused. "I hope you understand the need to keep this quiet for now. No calls to anybody. Not friends. Not family."

5

10:15 a.m. Mountain Standard Time
Northwest Arizona

Neil and Nancy Hayes stood on the deck of their mountain home, watching the clouds in the east give way to bright blue sky and sunshine. A foot of new snow had fallen overnight, and the air was cold and still, the silence broken only by the sound of mule deer making their way through the trees.

"It never gets old," Neil said. As if on cue, a whisper of breeze blew through the ponderosa pines and the snowflakes on the boughs swirled into the air like glitter on the sunlight.

"It's beautiful," Nancy smiled. "It's like a postcard."

He put his arm around her, pulling her close. "It's like a little piece of heaven, isn't it?"

Neil and Nancy had moved to the mountains from the city five years ago. The adjustment had been minor—Neil had grown up hunting and fishing, so he was no stranger to life in the outdoors, and Nancy, although living in cities most of her youth, was a country girl at heart. A simple drive up the mountains when it was possible was a getaway for her; the idea of living in them, a dream.

The rural property was perfect for gardening and small livestock, and before long they were wrapped up in a serious push toward self-sufficiency. Neil wasn't fond of the term 'prepper,' but that was pretty much where he and Nancy were today. They raised chickens, rabbits and ducks, preserved food and started a pantry, all with an eye on becoming more self-reliant.

It was a pleasing lifestyle. It wasn't easy, but it was worthwhile. The days were quiet, even serene, when sitting on the deck with the sound of a gentle breeze blowing through the forest was relaxing. And nights were spectacular when the sky was clear, stars spread like a carpet across the inky blackness.

"Ever miss the city?" Nancy asked, leaning on the railing.

"Like a rash," Neil replied.

She laughed, then gazed down at the road in front of their home. "I think this is the most snow I've seen since we've been up here."

"It's hard to tell with the drifting, but I'm guessing there's close to thirty inches on the road down there."

"Are you're still thinking of driving to Las Vegas?"

"I am."

"With all that snow?"

Neil looked down at his pickup parked in front of the house. At the rear of the truck the snow was up past the bumper. In front it had drifted over the top of the hood. "I'll have to dig it out," he said. "But four-wheel drive will get me to the highway. I'll use chains if I have to." He paused, reading the look on her face. "I need to get the last of the solar equipment."

She sighed. "I worry about you in that old truck."

"Old truck?"

"Well, let's see. A 1972 Dodge . . . my math is a little rusty . . . ten times forever, carry the one. Yes. Old truck."

"Do me a favor and keep your voice down. I don't want the 'old truck' to hear you talking like this."

She laughed. "What is it with guys and their pickups? Anyway, I'm freezing." She turned to the door. "I'll cook bacon and eggs if you'll make waffles."

"I'll make waffles if you come to Vegas with me," he said, following her inside.

"Nope." She walked into the kitchen and opened the refrigerator. "I'm staying here where it's warm and cozy. I've got a fireplace, a good book and hot chocolate, maybe a bit of Kahlúa." She set bacon and eggs on the counter. "I'm set."

"It'll be a road trip."

"Don't. I'm staying here. And I'll be praying your truck doesn't fall apart on the highway."

Neil laughed. "I love you," he said, taking her in his arms.

"I love you too, cowboy." She kissed him. "You know I'm just giving you a hard time about your truck."

"I don't mind. I think it's funny."

Nancy laid strips of bacon in the pan while Neil mixed waffle batter. "You watch the news this morning?" he asked.

"Yes. And I find myself wondering if we have enough put away if the world blows up."

"You mean food?"

"Food . . . toilet paper."

"These days, I get the feeling that no matter how much we put away, it's not going to be enough."

"What do you mean?"

"You remember when we started this self-sufficiency thing?"

"I do."

"And we were looking at it not just from the standpoint of basic disaster preparedness—the power goes out for a month, or we get ten feet of snow—but from an end-of-the-world perspective. A solar flare takes out the grid, or some other catastrophe. There's no food or water. All we've got is all there is."

"Sure."

"And I'm reading those survival blogs online that are talking about the deep-forest compound with razor wire, booby traps and snipers' nests, everybody running around in camo with AR-15s."

"You were pretty wrapped up in it."

Neil smiled, spooning batter onto the waffle iron. "That's putting it nicely. Fact is, I went overboard. Anyway, I'm reading articles written by these guys who think the only way to survive a full-blown collapse is to hunker down, watching the world through a riflescope and protecting your stash, which, in their book, is a fifty-year supply of everything from guns and gasoline to beans and Band-Aids."

"A bunker mentality."

"Exactly." He shook his head. "It quit clicking with me."

"I remember your thinking changed. You quit talking about prepping all the time."

"It wasn't prepping in general. Having enough food, water, stuff like that, for several weeks—and I think that's a minimum—makes sense. But I think when a person starts living for that eventuality, an end-of-the-world event, they lose touch with what's really important. I get the idea of survival, but when people close the door on everyone else, ignoring their plight . . ." He paused, lifting the waffle from the iron and pouring more batter.

"I have this picture in my mind of everything falling apart. Chaos from one end to the other. People shooting at anything that moves. Cars on fire. A few days after it begins there's a knock on the door. And circumstances being what they are, I'm careful. I've got a loaded gun. But when I open the door, there's a young couple—husband and wife—and two little kids standing there. They look like they've been dragged behind a truck. They're tired. They're beat. They're starving. And the look in their eyes tells me we're their last hope." He shook his head. "I wonder how many preppers in that situation—the world is coming apart, and they're locked and loaded behind steel doors in darkened rooms—would turn them away."

"How many would even answer the door?" Nancy asked. She lifted the strips of bacon out and placed them on a paper towel, then cracked eggs in the pan. "I guess that's what you meant by never having enough put away. You take care of the less fortunate, people who can no longer take care of themselves. Share what you have. Help them get back on their feet."

Neil pulled the second waffle from the iron. "It's not giving away what we have. It's helping people, then finding out what they can do. Can they tend a garden? Sew clothes? Build things? Maybe someone who knocks on your door is a doctor or nurse. Someone else comes, then two or three others. You're building a community."

Nancy set the plate of bacon and eggs on the table. Neil followed with waffles, then they sat and said grace. Nancy poured coffee and they started eating. "I get the need for security," Neil continued. "God gave us brains with the idea that we use them, and if everything falls apart, there are going to be bad people out there. But when good people close themselves off, hiding out, hoarding what they've got and forsaking everybody else . . ." He shook his head. "If we don't play our cards right when society hits the wall, we'll never get it back. We treat each other with compassion and respect or it's over. There's nothing left."

"It's funny," Nancy said, "I used to think if everything fell apart, we were going to end up in a bomb shelter or something, with a lot of food, and nobody but each other." She patted his hand. "I love you dearly, but I don't know if I could handle that."

"*Blast From the Past*," he nodded.

She laughed. "What was the wife's name?"

"Helen. Swilling vodka martinis to cope."

"And screaming."

Forty-five minutes later, Neil returned from shoveling snow away from his truck, and stood by the front door in a parka and snow boots. "I should be home by four or five."

"Carl Ferguson called while you were outside," Nancy said. "He's got the new antenna ready on the radio repeater. He wants you to give him a call from White Hills, see how the reception is."

"Will do."

"And could you go by Costco or Sam's Club and pick up some cases of canned food?"

"Anything in particular?"

"Chili, stew, albacore. Fruit and vegetables. Juice." She paused. "As much as you have room for."

Neil studied her for a moment. He knew the look. "You think something's going to blow up."

She shrugged. "I have a feeling. It won't go away."

He nodded. "Anything else?"

"Nathan's flying today."

"Where?"

"JFK to LAX."

"I'll wave at him when he passes over Las Vegas." He smiled and hugged her. "Love you."

"You too. Be careful."

"Always." He hugged her again, then walked out the door and made his way through the snow to his truck.

6

The mood in Rampart was tense as Hendricks, Winter and Lundgren, DEFSMAC Director Michael Attwood and NSA Director Matthew Donovan assessed the situation. Fifteen minutes after sending the message to the NSA, Leland Brookhurst, Deputy Chief of MI6—Britain's Secret Intelligence Service—was on a secure phone call with Donovan. He began by confirming he relayed the message from Tehran.

"There's not much I can tell you about this," he said. "The message was sent to our people at Hostile Intelligence Services by a high-ranking Russian military official in the SVR. He is one of a handful of people working for unfriendly governments, with whom we maintain a back channel."

"You consider him an ally," Donovan said.

"In a manner of speaking."

"But the information is reliable."

"Yes."

"Was there anything more to the message than what you forwarded to us?"

"No."

"You haven't contacted him?"

"Our communication with him is one-way. He sends information to us. For us to respond would establish a relationship that would compromise his position with the government of Russia." Brookhurst paused. "He is not a double agent, Mr. Donovan. His allegiance is to Russia, not Britain."

Donovan considered that for a moment. "Do you know what he was doing in Iran?" he asked.

"We're not certain. A rocket was launched this morning from Semnan Province. We assume it carried a satellite. Our intelligence indicates Russia was involved."

"To what extent?"

"They provided the launch vehicle."

"Do your people know what the satellite's mission is?"

"No."

"An educated guess?"

"I would need to know what is located in that part of South Dakota that would interest Iran or Russia. Perhaps something sensitive in terms of national security."

"Nothing we're aware of."

Brookhurst paused. "If anyone would know, it would be NSA."

"We have a theory it may be an electromagnetic pulse weapon," Donovan said.

Five seconds passed before Brookhurst replied. "If that theory is correct, it would be most unfortunate for the United States."

"Indeed."

"I don't envy your task of sorting through it."

"Yes, well, if you come up with anything new, any ideas—"

"Educated guesses?" Brookhurst said.

"Anything," Donovan replied. "Please contact us directly."

"Of course." Brookhurst paused. "Good luck."

"Thank you." Donovan ended the call, then turned to the others in the room. "So, we have the Russians giving Iran a launch vehicle capable of lifting something heavy into space. We have an SVR agent sending data that contains coordinates and a time—which happen to align on the satellite's ground track at Sioux Falls—to MI6 in London. And we have your analysis," he nodded at Hendricks, "tying North Korea to Iran, and giving Iran and Russia motive to act against the United States." He paused. "It's a lot of dot connecting. At the same time, NORAD is concerned. We don't take that lightly. I spoke with General Tuckett. He considers this satellite a potential threat with high confidence."

"Are you going to tell the president?" Hendricks asked.

"Of course. But it will be difficult to convince him."

"With respect, sir, would it be easier if it were an attack on the White House or the Capitol building?"

Donovan smiled. "Your point is taken, Ms. Hendricks. It tells me you know full well the depth and magnitude of this. Understand that I know it too. If it is an EMP, this country is on the verge of losing the electric grid, and with it, the national infrastructure." He paused. "NORAD is not enthusiastic about the ability to target and destroy the satellite."

His last sentence hung in the air a full ten seconds before anyone spoke. "Matthew," Attwood said, "we've got what we need. We should get with the president. He's the one who's going to have to make the tough decisions."

"Make the call," Donovan replied. He turned to Hendricks. "I need this in a report. Quickly. Be concise." He glanced at his watch. "Send it to my phone. I'll print it at the White House."

"Yes, sir."

He crossed the room to the door, then turned back. "I'm in your corner on this, Ms. Hendricks." He nodded at Winter and Lundgren. "All three of you. It's compelling work. I'm not convinced beyond a shadow of doubt, but persuading me is not the problem. Persuading the president is."

"Thank you, sir," Hendricks said. Donovan nodded, then left the room. Hendricks turned to Attwood. "I keep thinking about the rocket used to lift the satellite into orbit. It doesn't make any sense. They could have accomplished this with an Angara booster." She paused. "There's more to this than we realize."

"Keep digging," Attwood replied. "See what else you can find." He turned to the door, then stopped and glanced at the orbital track. The satellite was over the North Pacific Ocean, heading toward British Columbia, four hours from detonation. He turned back to Hendricks, Winter and Lundgren. "If there's anything you need to take care of," he said, "tie up loose ends, whatever, stay close to your phones." He walked to the door. "Be here at five o'clock sharp." Then he left.

"Tie up loose ends?" Lundgren said. "Like what, closing escrow on a bomb shelter?"

"This is right out of *The Twilight Zone*," Winter added.

"You guys know what this means," Hendricks said. "A complete grid collapse."

"Urban warfare," Lundgren replied. "People will kill you for a bottle of water." He paused. "It could just as well be an asteroid impact. This will take a little longer, but everybody dies."

Hendricks was not a mother, but there was a maternal instinct kicking in that she couldn't ignore. Despite being close to her in age—early thirties—Winter and Lundgren were in many respects like ten-year-old kids running around with capes and lightsabers—headstrong, precocious, and a little nutty.

More to the point, over the six years they had worked together, she had seen moments of pain and sorrow that underscored a part of them that was alone and scared. This was one of those, and she felt an overpowering urge to hug them and tell them everything would be all right. Trouble was, she knew their lifestyles. For them, everything would not be all right.

"Not everybody dies," Hendricks said. "Are you guys willing to leave Maryland to survive?" They stared at her, not understanding. "Apart from this job, is there anything keeping you here?"

"Where are you going with this?" Lundgren asked.

"She's bugging out," Winter said.

"Exactly," she replied. "I have a plan, and it doesn't include dying of starvation or being killed by crazy people. My question is, do you guys want to come with me?"

"That's out there, Naomi," Lundgren said.

"Out there, Paul? How about the end of modern civilization as we know it? Does that sound out there? You're good at math—what are your chances of being alive a month from now with no food or water, no medical services and no law enforcement?" Winter and Lundgren stared at her in silence. "If you guys want to stack the deck in your favor," she continued, "go home and pack."

"How do you pack for a grid collapse?" Lundgren asked.

"Clothes meant for hard work, outdoors, hiking, that kind of stuff. It's February, so cold-weather gear. Jeans, cargo pants, hiking boots or work boots, coats, gloves—"

"I don't have boots," Winter interrupted.

"Who doesn't have boots?"

He held up his hands. "I'm not like you, Naomi. I don't camp, I don't hike. I ride a bike."

Hendricks nodded. She'd be picking up clothes for them while she was out. She jotted down their sizes—shoes, waist, inseam—then stuffed the paper in her pocket. "Any important papers, birth certificates, stuff like that, bring them. Your laptops and spare batteries. Chargers. Flashlights and batteries. If you've got backpacks, use them to carry what you're bringing."

"Laptops?" Winter asked. "With no electricity? No internet?"

"I've got a folding solar array. It's portable. We can charge the batteries in a lot of these devices. Even without internet, a laptop is nice to have." She paused. "This is important, guys. If the grid collapses and we leave, we might not be coming back here. Ever. If there's anything that's important to you and doesn't take a lot of space—photos, mementos, anything special—bring it. Money is not going to be worth anything before long, but for the first week or so, it will still buy stuff. Empty your bank accounts unless they won't let you. If that's the case, get as much as you can."

They stared at her in silence, overwhelmed. Hendricks stepped directly in front of them. "You guys have been great to work with. You're brilliant, funny . . ." She paused. "I can't let you guys stay here knowing you won't make it. I just can't."

"What if the satellite isn't an EMP weapon?" Lundgren asked. "What if nothing happens?"

"Then this is a fire drill. But the bigger question is what happens if it is an EMP weapon, and NORAD—or whoever—can't shoot it down?" She looked at her watch. "Be back here in two hours. Meet me in the parking lot off Dennis and Emory, southeast corner."

Winter and Lundgren nodded, then left. Hendricks sat behind her computer and began putting together a report, pulling pieces from her files. Twenty minutes later, she emailed the document to Donovan, then stood, looking at the orbital track. "If only we could be wrong," she said. Then she walked out the door.

7

2:45 p.m. Eastern Standard Time
The White House
Washington, D.C.

"I'd be less concerned if the Russians were threatening us with a nuclear strike," President Wheeler said, pacing the floor in the Oval Office. "It's not knowing what they're up to that's maddening. We sank four of their ships. Why aren't they yelling at us?"

Wheeler's chief of staff, Bob Larson, sat across the room. "What if we release a statement," he said, "something to the effect that the White House believes the attack against the U.S. Navy was not President Burkov's doing, but a navy commander gone rogue, serving the interests of a splinter faction of the Russian government?"

"You mean let Russia off the hook."

"It might get them talking."

Wheeler shook his head. "What's the mood out there?"

"It's split, as you might expect. Most of the Republicans in the House and Senate say the Russians fired first."

"And the Democrats?"

"They think you've lost it. They're afraid of all-out war."

Wheeler pulled a bottle of antacids from a drawer in his desk, shook four of them into his hand and popped them in his mouth. "What is it about this job that people will do anything to get it? I've been here three years; it feels like thirty."

"It's a bad time, Mr. President. There's enormous pressure."

"It's overwhelming, Bob. Everything is falling apart."

Larson shook his head, not knowing exactly what to say. He knew the president wasn't sleeping well and that he was going through a half-bottle of antacids every day. He knew also that Wheeler was drinking rather heavily at night. "Is the White House doctor giving you anything to relax?"

"Yes," Wheeler replied. "I take a sedative at night. He doesn't have anything I can take during the day that won't leave me groggy." He drew a slow, deep breath, then exhaled loudly, turning from the window to face Larson.

"Do you think it was a mistake to sink those ships in the Gulf?"

"Don't do this to yourself, Mr. President."

"Do you think it was a mistake!"

Larson paused. "They fired first, Mr. President," he said quietly. "They attacked a U.S. Navy warship."

A moment later the phone rang. Wheeler flinched, then walked to his desk, picked up the phone set and yanked it from the wall socket, then threw it across the room.

"Nobody's home," he said.

8

Naomi Hendricks pulled her truck into the Sam's Club gas station on Russett Green East, off Laurel Fort Meade Road. She parked at the pump, then unloaded ten 5-gallon gas containers, uncapped each of them and started filling them with gas.

This was her last stop before returning to work. She had driven home first to swap her car for the truck—a 1979 Ford F250 four-wheel drive. It could haul a lot of weight and cross rough terrain. She put together her camping gear—two tents, sleeping bags, tarps, Coleman stove and lantern, axes, bow saw and flashlights. In a large duffel bag, she packed Marine combat fatigues, denim jeans, canvas cargo pants, thermal underwear, heavy wool socks and an assortment of T-shirts, mostly gray and black. In a smaller duffel she packed eight-inch desert boots, insulated pac boots, three pairs of athletic shoes and an assortment of gloves. In a second small duffel she packed winter coats and hats.

She lifted her Jansport backpack out of the closet. It was already packed with her 'bug-out' supplies—two sets of clothes, tarp, bottled water, two jars of peanut butter and a dozen granola bars, compass, fire starter kit, first aid kit, sewing kit, duct tape, a fixed-blade knife and lightweight ax, and 500 feet of paracord.

From the garage she retrieved a dozen flat-folded cardboard boxes. She estimated this was going to be all she had room for in the back of the truck while allowing space for food and water, extra gas, and anything Lundgren and Winter might bring. The first four boxes would hold the sleeping bags, tents, lanterns and flashlights, as well as the rest of the camping and outdoor gear she had accumulated over the last few years, everything from small cook stoves and cookware, to knives, whetstones and fire strikers.

Other supplies were not so much things she would need on a road trip that would be formidable as they were items that would be in short supply after a grid collapse. Fifty tubes of lip balm, Ziplock bags of bar lotion and a dozen small containers of skin balm, both made by her mother. Band Aids, gauze pads, ointments and surgical tape. One hundred twenty broadheads—sixty for deer, sixty for elk—for hunting arrows. Disposable lighters, pencils and erasers, pocket flashlights and folding knives. The list was long and varied.

As she moved through her home assessing what would go and what would stay, she was in a different frame of mind than if she were moving from one place to another. Streamlining was essential—if it wasn't necessary or couldn't be used to make something necessary, it stayed. There was only so much room in the truck.

An exception to this was a small box of photographs. She wasn't one to have dozens of framed pictures on the walls of her home, but she did have an abundance of pictures of family and friends, of various outings and adventures she'd been a part of. These she would pull out and pour over occasionally, cherishing the memories they evoked, mostly laughing, sometimes crying.

The box of photos went into a larger box along with a dozen or so books—Hawke's *Green Beret Survival Manual*, Wiseman's *SAS Survival Handbook*, Forgey's *Wilderness Medicine* and Auerbach's *Medicine for the Outdoors*, along with a copy of *Emergency Care and Treatment of the Sick and Injured*—the standard textbook for EMT training courses, given to her by her father. These books were indispensable when it came to surviving under adverse conditions.

She moved to an upper shelf where the novels resided. These she pondered for a minute. Her first impulse was to pass them by—they weren't important. Then she was struck by something her father told her, the idea that if the world as we know it ever came to an end, it might be nice to have some literature to remember what life was like before everything fell apart. She pulled *The Collected Poems of Robert Frost*, Thoreau's *Life in the Woods* and Hemingway's *The Old Man and the Sea* from the shelf.

She was getting ready to close the box when another book caught her eye—*The Essential Calvin and Hobbes*, a collection of the popular comic strip by Bill Watterson. She opened it and thumbed through the pages, smiling, remembering Sunday mornings with the newspaper. *Calvin and Hobbes* was a staple, and if she had only a few minutes to spend with the paper, the comic strip was what she turned to first. It was, as the title of the book implied, essential.

Next she moved to the kitchen where she packed canned food and the contents of her spice rack, three twist-type can openers and a dozen basic cooking utensils. From the pantry came the sugar—unrefined and brown—salt, pepper, molasses, two containers of old-fashioned Quaker Oats and four boxes of Cream of Wheat.

From the bottom cupboard she retrieved her cast iron cookware—a large Dutch oven, three skillets, two griddles and a wedge pan for making cornbread. She thought back to a trip she took with a friend who told her she packed lighter than any woman she knew. She replied, "I left my cast iron home."

This set of cookware weighed sixty pounds. She never took it when she went backpacking, for obvious reasons, but she always had at least a skillet when she was camping out of her truck. Her father had given the set to her when she was getting ready to move away from home, telling her, "Good cast iron is an heirloom. It never gets old, it never wears out. It's ideal for cooking over a fire, and in a pinch, it'll stop a bullet." She smiled, thinking back. Her response to that last part was, "I hope whoever I might be cooking for would be pleased with the meal."

She lugged the box to the living room and set it by the others, then looked around. Her words to Lundgren and Winter echoed in her mind, "You won't be coming back." She was leaving most of her belongings, but she wasn't troubled by it. She could live with what she carried in her truck, and be content with that.

The last things she packed were her firearms—a .30-06 hunting rifle with scope, a 12-gauge pump shotgun and a 9-millimeter semi-automatic pistol—and a dozen boxes of ammunition for each.

Everything fit in the back of the truck with a fair amount of room to spare. She packed along both sides of the truck bed, putting the heaviest boxes and bags ahead of the rear axle for better weight distribution, leaving a two-foot space down the middle for gas containers and whatever Winter and Lundgren might bring.

She went back into the house and changed into military camouflage pants, lace-up boots, a black T-shirt emblazoned with Blind Faith in hot-pink lettering, and a hooded, wool-lined denim jacket. Back in the living room, she stood in the middle of the floor and took one last look around, then walked out.

From the garage she retrieved her tool box and a second spare tire for the truck. With the one slung under the rear of the truck, this would give her two for the trip. She loaded the second one in the back with the tools, along with a box containing spare radiator hoses and clamps, accessory belts, a set of spark plugs, two gallons of coolant and five quarts of motor oil. She inspected the load, then closed the tailgate and locked the camper shell.

It was a short drive from her home to the Walmart Supercenter off the Baltimore-Washington Parkway. She purchased the gas containers and clothing for Lundgren and Winter—cargo pants, heavy socks, insulated coats with hoods, leather work gloves, and two large duffel bags. She considered buying hiking boots there, then decided against it. For about the same price, she could get military boots at the Fort Meade PX located just ten minutes from NSA.

She also purchased one hundred feet of quarter-inch cotton rope, a twelve-volt fuel pump and wiring that would run it from the truck's cigarette lighter, and fifteen feet of rubber fuel line. As a backup to the electric fuel pump, she bought a small hand pump.

From Walmart, she drove across the parking lot to the Sam's Club where she bought four cases of canned food—albacore, stew, chili and chicken noodle soup—two large jars of peanut butter and a quart of honey, four loaves of bread, five boxes of granola bars and three kinds of crackers, a large bag of apples, a large bag of oranges, three bunches of bananas and drinking water in twelve 2-gallon jugs, and two cases of bottles.

With minor adjustments to the load already in the truck, she managed to fit everything with easy access to the gas containers. She tied everything in place with rope to prevent the load from shifting, then boosted the second spare tire onto the steel roof rack above the camper shell and lashed it securely in place.

From the Walmart, she drove across the parking lot to her branch bank where she withdrew five thousand dollars with only a minimum of fuss. When Hendricks caught the teller sizing up her appearance, she smiled. "We're taking an expedition of sorts. Several weeks in the wilderness. Maybe longer."

"An adventure," the teller said.

"That I can promise," Hendricks replied.

Five minutes later, she was zipping up a bank bag filled with fives, tens and twenties. "Thank you very much," she said.

"Have a wonderful time," the teller replied. "We look forward to your safe return."

From the bank, she drove to the Sam's Club gas station, filled the containers with gas and topped off the truck, then drove to the PX where she purchased insulated boots.

Exactly ninety minutes after she left NSA, she returned. Pulling into the southeast parking lot, she saw Lundgren and Winter standing next to their cars. She pulled into a parking place next to them and climbed out of the truck. Winter smiled, taking in the camo, boots and jacket, then sizing up the F250 outfitted with brush guard, electric winch and four front-facing flood lights. "Just when I think I've seen it all," he said, "Lara Croft parks next to me."

"Lara Croft?" Hendricks replied. "Seriously?"

"That's definitely a new look, Naomi," Lundgren said.

"I'm guessing you guys packed Hawaiian shirts." She smiled and walked to the rear of the truck, then lowered the tailgate.

"Is that gas?" Winter asked, pointing at the containers.

"Yes," Hendricks replied. "Fifty gallons in the jugs. And the truck holds fifty in twin tanks."

"That should get us across town," Lundgren said.

"I'm hoping it will get us through Oklahoma."

"Then what?"

"We drain gas from cars abandoned on the road. I've got an electric fuel pump and hose. If we have to, we punch a hole in the tank and drain gas into a pan, then funnel it into the jugs.

She pulled three 15-quart polypropylene storage containers from the back. "I need your electronics—laptops, cells, whatever you've got that you want to protect from EMP."

Lundgren and Winter went to their cars and unloaded their gear, then carried it to the back of the truck. They unzipped backpacks and pulled out laptops and spare batteries, iPhones, MP3 players. "I hope it's okay to bring this," Lundgren said, producing an X-Box. Winter pulled one out of his pack and held it up.

"Me too," he smiled.

"Sure," Hendricks replied. "You can teach me how to play." She pulled two wide rolls of heavy-duty aluminum foil from the back, along with a roll of 6-mil painters plastic, aluminum tape and scissors, and set everything on the tailgate next to the containers. "Observe," she said. She cut a large square of plastic and wrapped it around a laptop computer, then folded the ends over and taped them. "Just like wrapping a present." Then she wrapped it in two layers of foil, folding it over on the ends and sealing it with tape. "Plastic first, to insulate the item from any static charge. Then two layers of foil to shield it against the electrical field generated by the EMP. And every seam is sealed with metal tape—absolutely no gaps in the foil. It has to be completely enclosed."

Winter examined the package. "A Faraday cage."

"Without the copper mesh and grounding, but it works."

Winter and Lundgren nodded, then started wrapping their gear. Hendricks pulled two more rolls of foil from the back of the truck and set them on the tailgate, then opened the passenger door and lay on the floor underneath the dash. Unscrewing the antenna and power connections to the radio in the dash and the ham radio in a tray fastened underneath, she pulled both units out and carried them to the back. Winter and Lundgren were finishing up and stacking neatly wrapped items on the tailgate.

"Perfect," she said, inspecting each one closely. She placed the items inside a storage container, carefully arranging them to fit without tearing the foil. She placed the lid on top, fastened it, and wrapped it in several layers of foil, then taped the edges flat. After they had filled and wrapped two of these containers, she placed each one in a cardboard box, then wrapped the box in foil and taped it.

"That's all there is to it," she said, sealing the last box. She reached in the back and pulled out several shopping bags and set them on the tailgate. "Boots, cargo pants, parkas, gloves—pretty much everything you guys will need to stay warm roughing it over the next week or so. Add it to whatever you brought from home. Here's a duffel bag for each of you to carry everything."

Winter and Lundgren looked at the pants, held up the parkas and picked up the boots. They looked at each other, then at Hendricks.

"I don't know what to say, Naomi," Winter said. He paused, and she hugged him. "Thank you," he said.

"You're welcome, Scott."

She turned and hugged Lundgren. He was tearing up when she pulled away. "Thanks, Mom."

"You're welcome. You guys are helping me just by coming along. I'm glad we're doing this together."

"Where are we going?" Lundgren asked.

"Arizona, where the air is clean, and the sky is blue." She nodded. "My parents live there."

"They'll have room for us?" Winter asked.

Hendricks smiled. "Like Mom and Dad say, 'There's always room for friends.'"

9

3:15 p.m. Eastern Standard Time
White House Situation Room
Washington, D.C.

"You've all been briefed on what's happening," President Wheeler said. "We've got some hard decisions to make, and little time to do that. We're not certain this is a weapon, so we're going to have to make difficult judgment calls."

Wheeler looked around the conference table. Present were four statutory members of the National Security Council—the vice president, secretaries of State, Defense and Energy—as well as the chairman of the Joint Chiefs of Staff, the director of National Intelligence and the directors of the Defense Intelligence Agency and the National Security Agency. Also attending were the National Security Advisor, the secretary of Homeland Security and the White House chief of staff. The commander of NORAD was teleconferencing in.

"I want this discussion to focus on three aspects," Wheeler said. "First, whether or not this is in fact an EMP weapon directed at the

United States. Second, if we proceed on the assumption it is, a realistic look at our ability to destroy it in space. Third—and again, assuming it's a weapon—who we notify and what we tell them."

"I'm not clear on what we think this is," Secretary of State Elaine Richardson said. "The NSA report is heavy on jargon. This satellite launched by Iran and now orbiting the earth . . . we believe this could be a nuclear bomb?"

Wheeler turned to Matthew Donovan, director of NSA. "This is your baby, Mr. Donovan. I'll let you fill in the blanks."

"Our people think Iran intends to cripple our electrical grid with an electromagnetic pulse," Donovan said. "It's referred to as EMP. It's a by-product of a nuclear detonation, in this case from a weapon in low-Earth orbit. When that bomb goes off, a burst of electromagnetic radiation traveling at the speed of light hits us and shuts down everything in its path."

"What do you mean by everything?"

"Anything with an electronic circuit. Computers, servers, cell phones, cars made in the last thirty years. There's a second component to EMP that travels through power transmission lines and overloads electrical transformers, blowing them out. That stops the flow of electricity from power plants to cities."

"Is this thing targeting a specific area? Are we talking about a city? A state? How many people will be affected?"

"North America, Madam Secretary. Approximately six hundred million people without power."

Secretary Richardson stared at Donovan for a moment, then looked around the table. Nobody spoke. She turned back to Donovan. "For how long?"

"Some areas could be without electricity for six months to a year. Maybe longer. It depends on how long it takes to repair or replace electrical equipment—transformers, substations. Even then, some aspects of everyday life will never be the same."

"And the services that require electricity—"

"It's all gone. That's what I meant when I said everything. There's no banking or finance. No stock market. Stores are closed. No food, no fuel, no municipal water supply. Nothing from a faucet. No radio communication. And when the fuel for generators runs out—two or three weeks at most—we reach the end of functioning medical services, police and fire protection."

Once again, Secretary Richardson looked around the table. She appeared lost. "Now that we've scared the hell out of everyone," Defense Intelligence Director Carroll O'Sullivan said, "maybe we can evaluate this situation and decide if there's actually anything we need to worry about."

Wheeler waved his hand. "You're up, Admiral."

"I've read the NSA report," O'Sullivan said, brandishing a folder. "I think it's fair to say their analysts are reaching."

"You don't think this is a threat," Wheeler said.

"No, sir."

"Please expand."

"All of the background intelligence regarding North Korea and Iran is old data. Our people have been all over this stuff for more than two years. Yes, North Korea and Iran have collaborated. That's no secret. And yes, North Korean physicists have traveled to Iran, and Iranian physicists have traveled to North Korea. But that's where the drama ends. There's no evidence they built a bomb." He held up his hands. "There's nothing there."

Admiral Fletcher Powell, director of National Intelligence, spoke. "Is it possible, Admiral O'Sullivan, that NSA's intelligence gathering led them into areas not charted by your people?"

"It's possible, but not likely. We share information."

"Is it possible that analysts within NSA's DEFSMAC division have arrived at conclusions based on shared information that, while not in agreement with your analysts, is rational?"

"Your point, Admiral Powell?"

"A contradiction in analyses between agencies is not unusual. I believe this is a theory that demands scrutiny."

"You think it's a weapon?"

"That's what we're here to discuss."

"And I'm saying I don't think it is."

"I understand. I'm leaning the opposite direction."

"Frankly, I find the idea absurd," Richardson said. She looked at the president. "To think Iran would launch an attack against the United States—even after Israel's attack on their nuclear facilities on Friday—is so far-fetched as to be inconceivable." She paused. "We have an accord with them."

Donovan leaned forward. "As long as we're being frank, Madam Secretary, I find that accord nothing more than political theater. It was designed by the previous administration as a demonstration of control over the Iranians. It slows progress in their nuclear program, but doesn't arrest it. In the end, the only thing it accomplished was to make the U.S. look like fools in the minds of the Iranian hierarchy, and in that respect it was a masterpiece."

"It's still an accord, Mr. Donovan, signed by seven countries. It's a binding agreement."

National Security Advisor William Denton responded. "With respect, Secretary Richardson, we went into the accord knowing it would do little more than hobble the Iranians. They're unpredictable at best, and to think they will ever adhere without reservation to an agreement limiting their nuclear program, let alone eliminating it, is fantasy. It's just not possible with them."

"I disagree, Mr. Denton. I've sat across the table from them and I am satisfied they will honor this accord if we give them a chance."

"Give them a chance?" Donovan scoffed. "Is there anybody in this room besides the secretary of State who thinks the Iranians would not bomb the U.S. the moment they have the capability?"

"Not a chance," O'Sullivan replied. "They're not alone on the world stage. They have to exercise restraint."

"And that's the divide between us, Admiral. I don't think the Kashani regime gives a damn what the world thinks."

"Would it be safe to say your analysts reflect your attitude?"

"It would be safe to say my analysts have no illusions about Iran's intentions. Or North Korea's."

President Wheeler leaned in and spoke quietly. "I guess it would be safe to say you gentlemen are on opposite sides of the fence." He paused, then pointed at O'Sullivan. "Continue."

"In the interest of time," O'Sullivan said, "I'll just say Defense Intelligence believes the premise is highly improbable. As a footnote, I must say this—" he held up the report, "—is some of the most convoluted reasoning I've ever read."

General Wilson Tuckett, commander of NORAD spoke. "It's a credible theory. And as far as the report being convoluted, nobody at Cheyenne Mountain has a problem understanding exactly what the analysts at Rampart are saying." He paused. "Mr. President, I think it would be a good idea to shift the focus of this discussion and address how we bring down the satellite if and when we decide that's the best course of action."

"If you don't mind, General," Wheeler replied, "we can get to the hows and ifs after we decide it's necessary."

"Depending on how long that part of the discussion plays, we may not have time to do anything if we decide it is a weapon."

"General Tuckett's right, Mr. President," Chairman of the Joint Chiefs Thomas Macfarland said. "Assuming we decide to destroy this satellite—"

"Attempt to destroy it," Tuckett said.

"Yes," Macfarland continued, "attempt to destroy it. If we decide to do that, it will take time to get the ball rolling."

"What are we talking about?" Wheeler asked.

"Ground-based interceptors—missiles originally deployed to defend the U.S. against a strike by nuclear ICBMs. They carry a kill vehicle that's designed to collide with a missile in the midcourse phase of its flight, or with the warhead in the terminal phase, destroying the target with kinetic energy. Testing of the interceptor has been limited, though, with mixed results. And that's against ICBMs. We've never attempted to shoot down a satellite in orbit with a ground-based interceptor."

"No guarantees," Wheeler said.

"No, sir."

Wheeler drummed his fingers on the table, looking from the video display to the military men seated around the table—General Macfarland, General Wilkinson, Admiral Powell and Admiral O'Sullivan. After a minute of silence, Secretary Richardson spoke.

"Mr. President, before we launch missiles to shoot down an Iranian satellite, we should carefully consider the impact that would have on future dealings with them."

Wheeler looked at Richardson. He started to speak, but was interrupted by Secretary of Energy Roger Townsend.

"Mr. President," Townsend said, "we're going to have to deal with the ninety-eight nuclear reactors in the country. It's not possible to reach cold shut-down in a matter of hours."

"Secretary Townsend," Denton said, "let's not—"

"Hold on, Bill," Wheeler said, holding up his hand. He turned to Townsend. "What exactly do you mean by cold shut-down?"

"It's not a problem to stop the fission process," Townsend said. "But the fuel rods in the reactor containments and the depleted rods in storage pools will have to be cooled for years."

"Years?"

"Yes, for uranium. A decade for plutonium."

Wheeler stared at Townsend for a moment, then at Denton. "Mr. Townsend," Denton said, "with respect for your position and your concern, it doesn't matter if we talk about that now, or a week from now. If we lose the grid, plants will be running on generators and there will be a risk of meltdown. There's nothing we can do about that. The simple fact is there are things we can deal with now, and things we can't. We need to focus this discussion. At the moment we're all over the board, and that's slowing us down." He turned to Wheeler. "Mr. President, have the Joint Chiefs get missile deployment in play. When they're ready, they hold for your order."

Wheeler nodded, thinking. Then Admiral O'Sullivan spoke. "I think we can save ourselves a lot of time and energy—not to mention resources—if we go back to square one and ask ourselves if this is really a threat."

"Admiral," Matthew Donovan said, "you're aware of the message containing land coordinates and a time which line up with the satellite's ground track."

"I am," O'Sullivan replied.

"And this doesn't worry you?"

"No."

General Macfarland leaned forward. "I'm struck by the fact that North Korean scientists—nuclear physicists—were in Iran at the same time cargo shipped from Pyongyang shows up at Iran's bomb development facility. According to the report, that cargo was moved from the facility to Iran's launch complex at Semnan."

"I don't believe the cargo trucked to the launch complex was the same cargo that arrived earlier from Pyongyang," O'Sullivan said.

"But the North Koreans were at Semnan when the cargo arrived. It's difficult to ignore the connection."

"What about the use of a Russian rocket to put the satellite in orbit?" Donovan asked.

"That was mildly interesting," O'Sullivan replied, "but nothing I'm worried about. It could be a simple matter of a satellite that was heavier than Iran's Safir rocket could lift."

"I keep going back to the nuclear accord," Secretary Richardson said. "Why would Iran risk everything they've invested?"

"To take us out of the picture," Donovan said, "for a number of reasons, including the complete destruction of Israel."

"I understand the scenario, Mr. Donovan, but the idea they're actually doing that—"

"As this spells out?" Donovan held up the report. He looked around the table. "I'm not sure how many of us are proceeding on the assumption that Iran talks tough, but would never actually follow through with an attack against us, or that Russia would never be part of something like this." He paused. "Rejecting this theory because it doesn't fit our notions of how foreign policy ought to work is a serious mistake."

Richardson shook her head. "I don't think the Iranian satellite is a weapon."

"Madam Secretary, the people that put this together aren't politicians. They don't consider how their analysis will impact policy, treaties or nuclear accords. All they do is look at data, sift facts—"

"Form an opinion," O'Sullivan interjected.

"Which is what we ask them to do. And they're good at it."

"You've got your analysts. I've got mine."

"Gentlemen," Wheeler said, "this isn't a contest."

"Mr. President," Donovan began.

Wheeler held up his hand, then turned to the secretary of Defense. "General Wilkinson, I'm interested in your thoughts on this theory."

"Frankly, Mr. President," Wilkinson began, "I'd like to know how Defense Intelligence can dismiss the coordinates and time in the message. I find those extremely compelling. The fact that MI6 would forward it to NSA tells me they thought it was important."

"I agree," Donovan said. He looked at O'Sullivan. "In the intelligence community, with an eye on national security, it doesn't bother you—or strike you as odd in the least—that Iran, with Russia's assistance, has placed an object in space that appears to pinpoint Sioux Falls, South Dakota?"

"You can ask the same question six different ways, Mr. Donovan," O'Sullivan replied. "The answer is still no. We went through NSA's report with a fine-toothed comb. We found a few points interesting, as I mentioned a minute ago, but nothing to indicate a threat to national security." He paused. "You're flogging a dead horse, Matt."

Wilkinson leaned forward and looked at O'Sullivan. "I also find it disturbing that Defense Intelligence casually dismisses Iran's use of a Russian launch vehicle."

"It wasn't a casual dismissal, General," O'Sullivan replied, "We considered it, but concluded it wasn't a threat."

"Mr. President," General Tuckett said, "NORAD is alarmed over the use of the Russian booster to lift that satellite. The fact that Russia would provide it, regardless of what Iran was putting in orbit, is a serious matter."

"Does it come as a surprise considering the relationship between Russia and Iran?" O'Sullivan asked.

"Arming Iran to fight the Sunnis is one thing, Admiral," Tuckett replied. "Giving them a launch vehicle capable of putting a nuclear payload in orbit is another matter entirely. Moreover, you seem to have no problem with the idea that Russia would give them a heavy-lift rocket, but you dismiss the notion that North Korea might have given them a bomb."

"Sorry, General Tuckett. I'm not convinced."

"Nor am I," Wheeler said. "It's a theory based on hunches, mathematical probability and what-ifs. Sweep all that away and you've got an Iranian satellite in orbit, which is what they've done four times in the past." He paused. "With no grid collapse, I might add."

Donovan studied the president for a moment, thinking about Winter and Lundgren and their ability to boil down difficult concepts with mathematics and probability theory. On the one hand it seemed almost absurd. On the other, their track record was impeccable—they were the best in the business. And when it came to bringing everything to bear—intelligence and hard facts as well as the hunches, mathematical probability and what-ifs—Hendricks was in a class by herself. Donovan had been skeptical when he left Rampart a little over an hour ago. But after discussing it with the director of DEFSMAC, then sitting here hammering it out with these people, he understood that a very large part of systematic analysis was a matter of reading between the lines.

"Mr. President," he said, "I understand your frustration with the way analysts approach a problem like this. But frankly, a lot of what we pay attention to in the intelligence world, particularly when there is little human intelligence to rely on, are—as you put it—hunches, mathematical probability and what-ifs." He paused. "It has served us well for decades."

"I'm sure it has, Mr. Donovan," Wheeler replied.

Donovan stared at the president. "Pearl Harbor."

"Oh, for crying out loud," Wheeler muttered.

"Roosevelt's intelligence people gave him actionable information, Mr. President, based on hunches, mathematical probability and what-ifs." Donovan paused, looking around the table, then back at Wheeler. "He didn't act on it."

Wheeler stared at Donovan, agitated, but said nothing. It was then that Donovan realized he was trying to plead a case with respect for Wheeler's position, but it was slipping through his fingers precisely because he couldn't bring himself to lock horns with the president of the United States.

At that moment, General Tuckett jumped in with exactly what Donovan was looking for. "Most of what we know about what's up there," Tuckett said, "we know because of Rampart. They are some of the brightest minds in the business. NORAD, SPADOC and

NORTHCOM work hand in hand with them analyzing every scrap of metal in space. But even if we set aside their hunches, we're left with the Russian rocket." He paused. "There is simply no reason for them to use the Zenit to launch a satellite—communications, ground mapping, weather, it doesn't matter—and the fact they did is a big, red flag. Further, to ignore a message sent by Russian intelligence that specifies coordinates that are optimum for disabling our country's power grid with an EMP, and a time—both of which line up with the ground track . . . I can't conceive of how this is not setting off alarm bells with you people."

"General Tuckett," the president began.

"With respect, Mr. President, I'm already neck-deep in this and I'm going to finish. NORAD is in the business of detecting threats in space and protecting the American people from them. That's all we do. I respect the Defense Intelligence Agency, but they are dead wrong on this. If we do nothing because this whole idea seems too far-fetched, a little over two hours from now, this country—actually, the bulk of the North American continent—is going to be thrown back into the nineteenth century. And it will begin with the deaths of around two million people when every passenger jet over the continent falls out of the sky."

Ten seconds of silence passed as Tuckett's last sentence sunk in. Wheeler looked at the others in the room as if learning a simple truth for the first time. "Are you suggesting we ground all air traffic, General?" he asked.

"Yes, sir. And I'm asking you to give the order to prepare a missile strike on the satellite."

Secretary Richardson shook her head. "Iran will have something to say about that."

"I doubt that, Madam Secretary. Less than seventy-two hours ago, Iran's nuclear ambitions were bombed into oblivion and they haven't said a damned thing about it. If you think they're suddenly going to get gabby because we blow their weapon out of the sky, you're seriously mistaken."

"And if it's not a weapon? What then?"

"We'll do what we always do when they get their panties in a bunch—give them a truckload of cash." He paused. "Has anybody tried to contact them?"

"We have," Wheeler replied. "They're not talking to us."

"Have we tried Burkov?"

"The Russians aren't talking either, General. We're in the dark."

"Does that tell us anything?"

Wheeler stared at the video display for a moment, then held up his hands. "I don't know what it tells us."

Wheeler's chief of staff Bob Larson spoke up. "Mr. President, I've read some of the House testimony on the impact of EMP. Some of it is striking, but other aspects are debatable."

"For instance?" Matthew Donovan asked.

"Some experts say cars will quit running. Others say that's not true. We don't know that planes will fall out of the sky. This has never happened before. We can't be certain what it will be like."

"I've read the testimony too," Donovan said. "And the most chilling aspect of it is the conclusion that eighty percent of the remaining population—those who aren't killed in the violence immediately following a grid collapse, or who don't die from disease and sickness—will be dead from starvation within a year." He paused. "I don't know about you folks, but I would hate to have that hanging around my neck when somebody is trying to figure out how and where to bury two hundred eighty million bodies." In the silence that followed, Vice President Jan Hutchens turned and stared at Donovan, eyes wide, her face ashen. Wheeler sighed, shaking his head, his aggravation now obvious to everyone in the room.

"There is disagreement with that idea," Larson said. "And frankly, Mr. Donovan, fearmongering isn't helping your case."

"Fearmongering, Bob?" Donovan leaned forward in his chair. "How in God's name—"

"This discussion is losing its focus," Admiral O'Sullivan interrupted, standing up. "I suggest we decide if this is a weapon or not based on the information we have. If it is, we go full bore—ground air traffic, notify federal agencies of an impending attack, and, dare I say, address continuity of government. And we fire everything we've got at the satellite." He paused. "If we decide it's not, we adjourn this meeting and get back to work."

"Like any other Monday," Donovan said.

O'Sullivan glared at Donovan. "Matthew—"

"That's enough, gentlemen." Wheeler made no effort to hide his impatience as he looked around the table. "Does anybody have anything else to add to this discussion?" he asked.

Vice President Hutchens spoke quietly. "I have to say, I'm somewhat baffled. I admit not knowing about this electromagnetic pulse as well as many of you. But from what I understand, the stakes are too high to simply say the NSA is mistaken, to ignore them and NORAD." She looked at the others, then back at the president. "If we ground air traffic, notify federal and state agencies, and try to shoot the satellite down, and we are wrong about it, we look incompetent. But if NSA is right and we do nothing, we're guilty of criminal negligence on a scale none of us have ever seen or can even imagine. We will have allowed the worst disaster in modern times without so much as a word to the public." She paused, shaking her head. "I don't know how we could live with that."

Wheeler looked at the vice president in silence, measuring her words against the certainty of Admiral O'Sullivan. He was torn now. He looked down at the table in front of him, attempting to focus his thinking and control his emotions. He was becoming desperate for answers, and at the same time angry because there were none.

Then Donovan spoke. "I agree with the vice president," he said.

"As do I," General Tuckett said. "We're wasting valuable time. We need to bring that satellite down, and make immediate preparations for what we do if we can't."

Wheeler stiffened, staring at Donovan for a moment, then at the video screen. He drew a slow breath, then exhaled, looking at the others one by one. When he came to Margaret Beck, secretary of Homeland Security, he spoke. "Secretary Beck, weigh in."

She looked directly at the president. "I'm trying to imagine the logistics. If we act on the NSA's intelligence, we will be forced to mobilize every aspect of our national preparedness plan, from FEMA on a nationwide basis, to the military. I'm assuming we would implement martial law, deploy troops in the streets, contact state governors, coordinate with local law enforcement." She paused. "The disaster relief alone is unimaginable. We're talking about food, water and medicine for three hundred fifty million people. And grounding commercial air traffic will take hours. Think back to 9/11 and the images of passenger jets parked on the sides of runways while others are still trying to land.

"On the other hand, there is no agreement—even among our intelligence agencies—that this is a valid threat. If we put the machine in motion to prepare for this and nothing happens, it will have a serious impact on the federal government's credibility. Confidence will drop dramatically."

Donovan stared at Beck, his mouth open. He pointed a finger, about to speak, when Wheeler held up his hand to stop him. "Secretary Beck, are you saying we should not act on this?"

"Yes, Mr. President. I say we do nothing."

"Secretary Townsend?"

"Shutting down the nation's reactors will be a massive undertaking, Mr. President. It will take years to cool the fuel rods. The plants have generators, but not years of fuel to run them. And the backup batteries will run out in a matter of a week or two."

"I understand. Do you think the satellite is a weapon?"

Townsend paused, looking around the table. "No."

Donovan pointed at Townsend. "Do you believe it's not a weapon because we can't manage cold shut-down if it is?"

"Matthew," Wheeler said, holding up his hand. The two men stared at each other for a moment, then Wheeler turned to the chairman of the Joint Chiefs. "General Macfarland."

"I find it odd that our intelligence agencies can be so far apart on this," Macfarland said. "It's as if they're talking about two completely different theories. Given the circumstances—and consequences—I have to agree with Ms. Hutchens' assessment."

Wheeler looked down for a moment, then back at Macfarland. His thin smile did little to hide his displeasure. "Do you think it's a weapon?" he said slowly, quietly.

"Yes, Mr. President. And General Tuckett makes a valid argument for trying to bring the satellite down immediately. If we do nothing else, we need to begin that process."

Wheeler turned away. "Admiral O'Sullivan?"

"I don't believe we have actionable intelligence."

"Do nothing?"

"Yes, sir, in the absence of further information."

"General Wilkinson?"

"I agree with the vice president, sir. Too much at stake. Furthermore, I think as commander-in-chief you should give serious thought to issuing an ultimatum to the Russians, Iranians and North Koreans."

Wheeler's eyes narrowed. "An ultimatum?"

"We tell them in no uncertain terms that if a weapon in space is detonated over U.S. soil, we will retaliate immediately with sub-launched nuclear weapons."

Donovan leaned forward. "That's what Rampart's senior analyst suggested. Her words were, 'If we go dark, they go dark.'"

"If we go dark, they go dark," Wheeler repeated slowly. He looked at each person sitting at the table, his emotions flaring. "Easy to say if you're an analyst in a cubicle at NSA. But a little more complicated if you're president of the United States—" he glared at Donovan, eyes flashing, his voice rising, "—threatening a nuclear attack against Russia, who could wipe us off the face of the earth if they wanted!"

In the uncomfortable silence following his outburst, Wheeler stood and stared at Donovan, fuming. Jan Hutchens looked down at her hands folded in her lap. General Wilkinson exchanged glances with General Macfarland.

Ten seconds later, Bob Larson spoke. "Mr. President, perhaps we should—"

"Bob," Wheeler interrupted.

"Yes, Mr. President."

"Shut up."

Wheeler looked down at the telephone on the table in front of him. His mind went back to throwing the phone across the room in the Oval Office and he winced at the thought. "We're finished here," he said quietly. He turned to walk out of the room just as Matthew Donovan's cell phone rang.

"Donovan," he answered. He listened for a few seconds, then spoke. "I'm going to call you back on a phone in the Situation Room." He disconnected, then dialed a number on the phone in front of him. "Mr. President, you'll want to take this call. It's from Rampart's senior intelligence analyst, Naomi Hendricks." He put the phone on speaker. It rang once.

"Hendricks."

"Ms. Hendricks," Donovan said, "the president is here. Please tell him what you told me."

"We received another message from MI6 in London," Hendricks began. "It's from the same source in Tehran, the Russian SVR agent."

Wheeler glanced at Donovan, then O'Sullivan. "It's the technical specifications for the satellite carrying the warhead," Hendricks continued. "It's Russian."

"How do you know that?" O'Sullivan asked.

"From thirty-two pages of Russian-language blueprints for a space vehicle built by Voschyat, a design group that grew out of the early Soviet space program." She paused. "This thing is the size of a minivan, which would explain the use of a heavy-lift launch vehicle. I'm going to put Paul Lundgren on. He's a mathematician and can explain this better than I."

A moment later, Lundgren spoke. "The satellite has a rocket engine capable of changing the satellite's orbit, Mr. President. And not in subtle ways, but a rapid increase in altitude of hundreds of miles. It has a liquid-fuel propellant tank large enough to allow extensive engine burns. And it has radar, coupled with a guidance computer. That means it can evade an incoming missile.

"What concerns our team at Rampart, though—at least from the standpoint of trying to target this with ballistic missile interceptors—is that the satellite uses stealth technology." He paused. "It has the radar cross section of a golf ball. Your interceptors won't lock on to it in time to hit it."

"General Tuckett here, Mr. Lundgren. The interceptor's radar can see an object two inches in diameter twelve miles away."

"Yes, sir, but traveling eighteen thousand miles per hour, the interceptor has just two seconds to react before it's past the satellite. Eighteen thousand divided by sixty twice is five miles per second." He paused. "Multiply that by two."

"The missile's computer sends course corrections to directional thrusters in milliseconds," Tuckett replied.

"Yes. But consider the time required for reaction. Having received the course corrections, those thrusters have to move the interceptor. And it weighs forty tons. By the time its trajectory has been

changed, it would be past the target. Probably miles past the target."
He paused. "It's the physics, sir. Mass and momentum, coupled with
inertia—the resistance to change in the state of motion."

"Bottom line, Mr. Lundgren," Wheeler said, "the satellite can't
be destroyed with missile interceptors?"

"That's correct, sir."

Wheeler leaned back in his chair and looked at the ceiling. "Have
we got anything in space that can take this thing out?" he asked.

"No," General Tuckett said.

"No super-secret anti-satellite weapon?"

"No, sir."

"Do you mean nothing we can talk about in front of people who
might not have clearance?"

"I mean we have nothing, classified or otherwise." Tuckett
paused. "The military has chased this for the last thirty years. We
still kick it around. But as of right now, we have nothing up there
that can destroy this satellite."

Wheeler looked at the table in front of him, shaking his head, ex-
asperated. Then Scott Winter spoke. "Mr. President, there's another
problem. We've been looking at what else is up there and the potential for damage to our space-based assets. The International Space
Station is going to be approximately three hundred miles from this
warhead when it detonates. It's in a different orbit, but it will be in
the warhead's line of sight, subjected to the same electromagnetic
pulse that's going to hit Earth."

"Who's speaking?"

"Scott Winter."

"You're saying they'll lose their electronics."

"All functions of the spacecraft, sir. The astronauts won't be able
to return to Earth."

Wheeler stared at the phone. "Ms. Hendricks, is there any doubt
in your mind this is a weapon directed at the United States?"

"None, sir. This last message from MI6 spells it out."

Wheeler stared at the phone, then looked around the table. "Is there anyone here who still disagrees with Rampart's theory?" He looked at O'Sullivan.

O'Sullivan glanced at the others, then back at Wheeler. "No, Mr. President." The others nodded in agreement.

Wheeler turned to his chief of staff. "Bob, contact NASA. Tell them they have—" he glanced at his watch, "—ninety minutes to get those people off the space station and on their way home."

"Yes, Mr. President."

Wheeler looked at the video display. "General Tuckett, I'm guessing NORAD would be the quickest avenue to getting commercial air traffic grounded."

"Yes, sir," Tuckett replied.

"Take care of it, please." Wheeler turned to his secretary of Energy. "Roger, begin the process of shutting down our nuclear power plants."

"You realize, sir—"

Wheeler held up a hand. "Yes. I know. We'll deal with it." He turned to the chairman of the Joint Chiefs. "General Macfarland, contact our military bases and have them batten down the hatches, do whatever they can to protect as much of their equipment as possible from EMP."

"Yes, sir."

Wheeler went on to order the appropriation of food and water from large grocery distribution centers, as well as fuel from refineries. He directed Homeland Security to get FEMA rolling, and State to contact the heads of government in Canada, Mexico and Central America. "Tell them what's coming." He turned to the secretary of Defense. "General Wilkinson."

"Yes, sir."

"If we go dark, they go dark."

"I'll put together a plan."

"Mr. President," General Tuckett said, "we shouldn't proceed on the assumption that Russia is going to sit back and simply watch as this unfolds."

"I agree," General Wilkinson said. "They'll go to full-alert status, most likely sending up bombers and preparing ICBMs for launch."

"What have we got that will survive the EMP?" Wheeler asked. "Anything we can counter with?"

"The submarines," Tuckett replied.

The room fell silent for a moment, everyone there thinking the same thing—nuclear war with Russia. Wheeler drew a breath and exhaled slowly. "Put together a plan, General."

"Yes, sir."

"Mr. President," Matthew Donovan said, "NSA is preparing a cyberattack on North Korea, Iran and Russia to cripple them from the inside—government, banking, security. There is a possibility we can disrupt Russia's ability to launch ICBMs."

"Go on."

"The NSA's Tailored Access teams can penetrate almost anything regardless of firewalls—internet connections, cable, fiber optics, satellite networks. The problem is poking around Russia's offensive nuclear weapons systems."

"They'll know we're trying to get in."

"Yes. And an attempt could push them to launch. But we may be able to kill their ability to see what we're up to by bringing down other systems before we go after launch capability."

"Look at every contingency. But wait for the EMP."

"Yes, sir."

Wheeler paused. "Your people did well, Matt."

"They're still on the line, if you'd like to tell them personally."

Wheeler nodded. "Of course." He leaned toward the phone, still on speaker. "You folks at Rampart still listening?"

"Yes, Mr. President," Hendricks answered.

"We never would have seen this coming . . ." he turned to Donovan, "without you folks following a hunch."

"Hunches are what we do, Mr. President."

"Thank you."

"Mr. President, there's something else you need to know."

"I'm listening."

"You have generators and fuel at the White House, but it's likely they're connected to the building mains through an electronic interface that monitors line voltage and handles automatic startup. The interface will be destroyed when the EMP hits, and the surge may damage the generator itself. You won't have backup power. The generators have to be completely disconnected prior to the EMP."

Wheeler turned to his chief of staff. "Bob, get with engineering. Explain the problem."

"Right away, sir."

"That would also be the case for any facility," Hendricks said. "City fire departments, police stations and hospitals across the country. If they have generators coupled to the mains through an interface, they must be disconnected before the pulse hits."

"Bob?"

"I'll send an emergency notification," Larson replied. "To federal, state, county and municipal entities. Saturation level."

"Thank you, Bob."

"You're welcome, sir."

Wheeler put his hand on Larson's shoulder. "I'm sorry I was short with you, Bob."

"No problem, Mr. President," Larson replied. "We're good."

Wheeler turned to the others. "I apologize for letting my emotions get the best of me. I hope you'll forgive me."

"I can't speak for anybody else," Admiral Powell said, "but a little yelling now and then can be a good thing. Gets the blood flowing."

"That it does," William Denton said. He stood and faced the others. "Let's sum up, people. We're a little over an hour away from losing power. We've got a ground stop going into effect for air traffic. We're shutting down nuclear reactors and arranging for fuel to keep them cool. We're waking up FEMA and blanketing the country with an emergency notification to disconnect generators prior to five fifty-five Eastern Time. For a lot of people that will be a general announcement that civilization as we know it is about to come to a screeching halt." He turned to Wheeler and raised his eyebrows.

"I'm going to address the nation," Wheeler said.

Denton nodded, then turned to the others in the room. "Let's be clear, folks. At five minutes to six, you'll want to be someplace safe. And keep this in mind—after this thing hits, you might have a car that runs, but you won't have a phone. That means you'll probably be walking wherever you go, and the only people you'll be talking to will be standing next to you." He paused. "Questions?" Nobody spoke. Denton turned to Wheeler. "Anything else, Mr. President?"

"The days and weeks ahead are going to be extremely difficult for all of us," Wheeler said. "Meetings like this one, with cabinet, intelligence and military, are going to be practically impossible to hold in view of limitations on travel and communications. That said, ideas, advice, any input for responding to what will undoubtedly be the worst disaster in the history of this nation, will be at a premium. Take care of your families first. Then, if at all possible, be available—and I mean here—to help. If you don't have a car that runs, we'll find you a ride." He paused and looked around the room. "We need your best thinking. In order to get that, we need you here."

"Does the White House have room for guests?" Vice President Hutchens asked.

Wheeler smiled. "Yes, we do. Anybody that wants to make this their home are welcome to do so." He paused, clasping his hands. "Everybody please be safe. We'll see you when we see you."

10

Hendricks, Winter and Lundgren were returning from the parking lot after arranging gear in the back of the truck.

"I'm not one to brag," Winter said.

Hendricks laughed. "Yes, you are."

"She's right," Lundgren agreed. "You brag—not in an I'm-the-smartest-guy-in-the-room kind of way, but more of a sit-back-and-let-everyone-realize-how-stupid-they-are kind of way."

"Really?" Winter said. "Seriously?"

"Yeah," Hendricks replied. "Really."

"Seriously," Lundgren added.

They walked another twenty feet in silence before Hendricks spoke. "You were about to say?"

Winter nodded. "We're good at what we do. I think back over the last few years, the work we've done, the way we've been able to pull things together . . . the work on this satellite was some of the best." He paused. "And I wish we'd missed it by a mile."

"That would be a gift, Scott," Hendricks replied.

They entered the building, went through security, then crossed the lobby to the elevators. Inside, Winter had just pushed the button when they heard someone call, "Hold the elevator, please." Lundgren held the door open and five seconds later Matthew Donovan and Michael Attwood stepped in.

"Thank you," Donovan said, facing the analysts.

"Any time, sir," Hendricks replied.

"Casual Monday?" he asked, nodding at her attire.

"Something like that."

"This may surprise you, but Blind Faith was one of my favorite bands in 1969. I was a senior in high school."

Hendricks smiled. "My father liked them too."

"It was some of Clapton's best work."

"Dad has it on vinyl." She paused. "Some of my fondest memories are of hanging out with him, listening to his albums at concert volume on his stereo . . . drinking beer and going deaf."

Lundgren laughed. Then Winter. Then Donovan, Attwood and Hendricks, and for a few seconds the tension of a nuclear weapon in space, and what they could or couldn't do about it, was gone. It was a moment each of them would remember for a long time afterward. Then it slipped away. The elevator door opened, and they filed out, brass and staff, then walked down the hall to DEFSMAC.

Inside the office, Donovan turned to the others. "That meeting was over five seconds before you called, Ms. Hendricks, with no resolution. Your timing couldn't have been better. So, we're on track—for what, I'm not sure. This is uncharted territory."

"What about the cyberattack?" Lundgren asked.

"We're going to proceed with the plan. Access Technologies will add to it, then fire it up once the grid goes down." Donovan turned to Winter. "You mentioned an assessment of spaced-based assets. I'm assuming we're going to lose NSA satellites."

"Some," Winter replied. "The initial burst will take out anything that's in the weapon's line of sight. Other satellites will fail over time from radiation left behind."

"We'll work with what we have. Let's get sat phones down here. I want to be able to communicate."

"Whatever else we think we might need post-collapse—computers, servers, routers, switches—should be moved to shielded areas and sealed off before the pulse hits. No open doors."

Donovan turned to Attwood. "Let's get teams working on this—moving equipment and establishing a satellite connection we can run all available networks through for outgoing access." He paused. "I guess it's time to let department heads in on what's happening. Give them the low down and tell them to plan for a full evacuation to the parking lot at five forty-five. I don't want anyone getting stuck in the building because some stairwell door lock won't open."

"I'll take care of it," Attwood replied.

Donovan turned to Lundgren and Winter. "Finalize the plan for a cyberattack through satellites," he said. "The people upstairs can add to it, then launch it."

"Anything goes?" Lundgren asked.

Donovan nodded. "Nothing's illegal on this one."

11

1:00 p.m. Pacific Standard Time
Las Vegas, Nevada

Neil Hayes was rearranging cases of food in the back of his pickup when Alex Eisley, proprietor of Solar Solutions, crossed the parking lot to the truck.

"You got room for a generator in there?" Eisley asked.

"What have you got?" Hayes replied.

"Seventeen point five kilowatts. Gasoline, sixteen-gallon tank. Runs like new. We refurbished it."

"How much?"

"A thousand."

Hayes looked at the solar equipment sitting on the tailgate. With these last few parts, he was looking at an even twelve thousand dollars for the entire system. Still, a good generator would add the backup he wanted. And the price was right.

"I can do that," he nodded.

"Great. My guys will help load it."

Back in the office, Hayes gave Eisley his credit card for payment, then leaned on the counter, looking up at the television on the wall. The Fox News talking heads were discussing the sinking of Russian warships in the Gulf.

"Crazy stuff, eh?" Eisley said. He handed Hayes a receipt.

"We live in crazy times," Hayes replied. He signed the receipt then slid it back to Eisley. "These days, nothing surprises me."

"You prep don't you, Neil?"

"A little."

"Yeah, the smart guy says 'a little' and has an underground bunker with a pantry the size of a grocery store."

Neil smiled. "No bunker."

"What worries you? I mean right now—today."

"North Korea. They've got the bombs. We just don't know if they have the rockets to launch them."

"What if they did?"

"They'd shut off the lights."

"Good call on that generator, eh?" Eisley stapled the receipt to the invoice and handed it to Hayes. "Let's load it up."

The generator was portable with pneumatic tires, but at 450 pounds, it took four men—two on each side—to lift it into the back of the truck. They rolled it to the front of the bed, then secured it with ratchet straps.

"Lowe's has a sale on five-gallon Eagle gas cans," Eisley said. "Twenty-five bucks."

"They're the gold standard. They last forever."

"You going back on the 215?"

"Yeah."

"There's a store on Pecos."

"Thanks, Alex." The two men shook hands, then Hayes closed up the back of the pickup.

"Drive easy, old friend," Eisley said.

"I'm going home—a horse headed back to the barn."

"Just keep the shiny side up."

"That I can do."

Hayes pulled out onto Sahara and drove east, then took I-15 to the 215. He purchased gas cans in Henderson, then stopped at a convenience store to fill them, top off the truck and pick up road food—Fritos, beef jerky, M&Ms and a soft drink—easy to eat behind the wheel without making a mess.

Back on the road, he took Highway 93 out through Boulder City, past Lake Mead, and was crossing the bridge into Arizona by three o'clock Mountain Time. Halfway across the span, he looked to his left, then his right, disappointed and a little irritated—as he was every time he made this trip—that the view of the river on the south side and the lake to the north, were completely blocked by a four-foot-high concrete wall.

His mind went back to a night in 1972—his truck was new—when he stopped on the dam, walked over to the short retaining wall and sat on top with his legs hanging over the side, looking down the 700-foot drop into the darkness where the lower Colorado River emanated from the bowels of Hoover Dam. It was back when the highway went across the dam—there was no bridge—and at 2:00 a.m. you could park your car in the middle and get out because there was nobody around to tell you not to. There were no security check points, no bomb-sniffing dogs, no terrorist threats.

That night, though, there was a Bureau of Reclamation police officer who pulled up in his car. He watched Hayes for a minute, then got out and walked over to him. "You okay, buddy?" he asked.

"Yeah," Hayes replied. "Just sitting here wondering how the fishing would be down there."

The cop thought about that for a few seconds. "Been drinking?"

Hayes nodded. "A few beers."

"You okay to drive?"

"Sure."

The cop studied him for a few seconds, then turned back to his car. "Don't fall off the wall," he said. "It's a long way down."

Hayes smiled. "Good advice." He waved as the cop pulled away.

Now, forty-seven years later, the dam was closed to traffic, and the bridge, despite being a marvel of modern engineering, was a road without a view. On the bright side, Hayes' truck, which was older than his adult children, was still a source of simple pleasure. He reached into the glove box and pulled out a CD—*The Eagles Greatest Hits*—and slipped it into the player, then rolled down the windows and turned up the volume. "This," he said, selecting track one, "is what driving is all about."

And the canyon echoed with the strains of "Take It Easy" as he crossed the state line into Arizona, leaving the bridge and its concrete walls behind.

12

Matthew Donovan looked at the orbital track on the wall display. The satellite was over the Solomon Islands on its sixth orbit, forty-five minutes from detonation above South Dakota. In twenty minutes, he and everybody else in the building would move to the parking lot. Then they would wait.

Lundgren and Winter mapped out a plan for a cyberattack against Iran, Russia and North Korea. It would be handled by cyber security teams in Tailored Access Operations, triggered when the grid collapsed. Hendricks was going over last-minute logistics, while elsewhere in the building, staff engineers were disconnecting generators and moving critical hardware to shielded areas.

Donovan crossed the room to Hendricks' work station and sat on the corner of her desk. "I've never wanted our analysts to be wrong more than I do right now," he said.

"I've been getting that a lot today," Hendricks replied.

"I keep thinking of six hundred million people without electricity, and before long, food, water, medical services, police protection." He paused. "It's mind-boggling."

"I know. I keep thinking of the phrase 'impending doom.' I have this awful feeling, bordering on panic. I feel like I'm going to scream. Or cry. I don't know which."

"We're all nervous. Uncertain." He looked at the orbital track again, then back at Hendricks. "The phrase in my mind right now is 'human frailty.' I think of the millions of people who are going to be hit broadside in less than an hour by something they won't see coming. And most of them are completely unprepared for it."

Hendricks nodded. "A few hours ago, this was just a theory. We put it together like we always do, fitting bits and pieces, stepping back, working out the rough spots as we go, not giving much thought to the impact. Now . . ."

A moment later, Donovan's cell phone rang. He looked at the display. It was Jan Hutchens. "Madam Vice President," he answered.

"Mr. Donovan, are you near a television?"

"Yes."

"Turn on CNN."

Donovan turned to Hendricks. "Can you turn on CNN, please?"

Hendricks pressed the remote and a wall screen lit up.

"—unconfirmed sources reporting an attack against the nation's power grid is imminent," the anchor spoke.

Donovan nodded. "The cat's out of the bag."

"I thought the president would be addressing the nation by now," Hutchens said.

Donovan checked his watch. "There's still time."

"We have reports that states are mobilizing their National Guard units," the anchor continued, "and that FEMA is preparing to respond to a widespread power outage. Additional reports indicate nuclear power plants in the U.S. and Canada are being shut down." The anchor paused, putting a finger to her ear, listening to her producer. Five seconds later she spoke again. "We take you now to the White House Oval Office."

"Here we go," Donovan said.

President Wheeler appeared on screen, sitting behind his desk. "My fellow Americans, I come to you this evening with news of an impending crisis that will affect each and every one of us, not just in the United States, but in Canada, Mexico and Central America as well. We have received reliable information from our intelligence agencies that an attack against our power grid is imminent."

He paused, glancing at the next few lines on the teleprompter. Wheeler had written the address himself, hammering it out even as his communications director was working with television networks and cable outlets to break into regular programming. He wanted to name the countries responsible and assure the American people that this attack—this act of war—would not go unpunished. It was his intention to tell the public that on his order, the secretary of Defense and the commander of NORAD would unleash a nuclear attack against Russia, North Korea and Iran, sending them into darkness—a life without electricity—as they were about to do to the United States. But in that moment he knew that to announce his intentions would be to risk a strike by Russia before U.S. missiles could be launched against them.

"At this time, we do not know who is behind this attack on our electric grid," he said.

Donovan nodded, watching the television. "Smart."

"I have been in contact with the Canadian prime minister," Wheeler continued, "and the president of Mexico. And while they are pursuing responses to protect their national interests, as your president I am taking the following steps to protect ours.

"First, I have instructed the director of FEMA to prepare a nationwide response to those in need of food and water, shelter, and medical assistance. The inventory held in distribution centers owned and operated by grocery store chains will be appropriated by the federal government for the purpose of providing necessities on a common basis. Likewise, fuel supplies throughout the country will be used to move food and water wherever required.

"Second, I have instructed the governors in each state to activate their National Guard units. They will be used to help with the distribution of food, water and medical supplies, and to supplement law enforcement in maintaining the peace. They will be acting as law enforcement personnel with the authority of any other peace officer, under the jurisdiction of municipal police departments, county sheriff's departments and state police." He paused. "Crimes against people and property will be dealt with swiftly and surely. I cannot emphasize this too strongly—lawlessness will not be tolerated.

"Municipalities will be tasked with consolidating information as it becomes available and passing it along through communications centers set up in town and cities. I have been told that amateur radio services, more popularly known as ham radio, may be our only means of communication between individuals and government entities. Amateur radio has always been the frontline of communications following disasters, and we will be relying heavily on the resources of ham radio operators to keep agencies in touch with each other, and with people seeking accurate information.

"There is no easy way to say this, but under these circumstances I must be absolutely candid. The United States—all of North America—is going to be without electricity for a considerable time to come. Damage to the electric grid will be extensive, affecting every region in the country. Repairs will be made, but some areas will be without power for months. Perhaps longer. We will get through this, but it is imperative that as compassionate citizens of this great nation, as friends and neighbors who care for each other, we work through this as responsible people with mutual trust and respect, helping, not hindering, recognizing that each person, no matter what their station, is of value to every other person. After all is said and done, we're in this together."

The president stood and walked from behind his desk to the middle of the floor. He looked down for a moment, reflecting, then back at the camera. "There was a time not all that long ago when our grandparents and great-grandparents toiled by the sweat of their brows and strength of their backs, preparing their fields, planting crops, harvesting food and taking it to market. These were honest, hardworking people feeding a nation. They led simple lives. They tilled the land, growing what they needed to eat, working sunup to sundown, warming their homes with a fireplace and lighting them at night with candles and lanterns. They built this nation with a pioneering spirit, sharing the fruit of their labor with those in need, and comforting the afflicted. Neighbors mattered. Churches were filled.

"In the days and weeks ahead and beyond, we will be tested as never before, challenged in ways most of us can't imagine. But America is a country of good and decent people, strong, resilient, and as our grandparents and great-grandparents built a nation through strength of mind and peace of heart, so too will we rebuild with that same strength of mind and peace of heart. I pray that each and every one of us may face our new reality with an enduring spirit of hope and determination, of love and compassion. May God be with each of us. May He hold us close. And may He encourage us as we move ahead."

13

3:30 p.m. Mountain Standard Time
Northwest Arizona

Delta Airlines flight 322 was fifty-five minutes from touch-down at LAX when they received a radio notification from Los Angeles Air Route Traffic Control Center. "All flights under Los Angeles Center's control, contact your flight operations immediately. Repeat, all flights contact your operations centers."

Captain Christopher McAvoy turned to his first officer, Nathan Hayes. "This is a first."

Hayes nodded, switching the radio channel to the Selective Calling Radio System—SELCAL—and called Delta Airlines Operations in Atlanta, Georgia. "Dispatch, three-two-two."

"Standby, three-two-two."

"They're busy," McAvoy said.

"I imagine they would be," Hayes replied. "What have we got, a few hundred jets in the air right now?"

"At least."

Forty-five seconds later, ops called back. "Three-two-two, be advised FAA is ordering an immediate ground stop nationwide. Repeat, full ground stop. Find a runway ASAP."

Hayes turned to McAvoy. "Find a runway?"

McAvoy glanced at Hayes, then keyed his mic. "Dispatch, how much time do we have?"

"Eighteen minutes, three-two-two." Ops paused. "Word from intelligence agencies is that a high-altitude EMP detonation is believed to be imminent—6:05 Eastern."

McAvoy and Hayes stared at each other for a few seconds. They both knew what an EMP would do to the electronics that controlled every aspect of aircraft operation, and that at 4:05 local time, their plane would drop out of the sky uncontrollably if it wasn't already on the ground somewhere.

"Las Vegas?" Hayes suggested.

McAvoy switched back to ARTCC. "Center, Delta three-two-two, can you estimate our time to LAS?"

"Three-two-two, fourteen minutes to tower hand-off, plus three to pattern entry, plus four to final, plus three to outer marker."

McAvoy turned to Hayes. "We can't make it."

"See that highway at our three o'clock, running north and south?" Hayes said, looking out his side window.

"Yes."

"That's 93. It runs from Boulder City all the way to Phoenix."

"You know it?"

"Like the back of my hand. I grew up here."

"How's your navigation?"

"I'm on it." Hayes pulled an aeronautical chart from his flight bag along with a pencil, a protractor and a calculator. After forty-five seconds of rough calculations, he glanced at the instruments. "Bad news is we're going to put the passengers on the ceiling."

"And the good news?"

"We can make wheels down from thirty-six thousand feet in eight minutes." He glanced at his watch. "That will leave us another eight minutes for rollout, stopping—wherever that will be—and engine shutdown."

"Tell me about the highway," McAvoy said.

"It's divided, two lanes each direction with a wide median—dirt and brush. There's a thirty-five-mile stretch that's straight, beginning about ten miles behind us—off our four o'clock—to twenty-five miles off our two o'clock. But there are high-tension power lines crossing the highway in several places, and at least a dozen entry points from rural communities. It would be impossible to block off the highway and keep it traffic-free, and that's assuming we could get the highway patrol or sheriff's department out there in time. The nearest city is behind us—twenty miles southeast.

"Forty miles farther up, there's another straight stretch that's about four miles long and flat as a table top—no hills, no power lines and no entry points. We'll have more time to set up for landing and still make it down with rollout to engines off before we lose everything. And the highway up there will be easier to block. There's a gas station that stays fairly busy. It's usually got at least a dozen cars and several tractor-trailer rigs parked."

"You're thinking of having them block the road."

"It's all we've got, Mac. I can get dispatch to make the call." He paused. "We can take a chance and just bring it down, but there's traffic on that highway—there always is. It's not an expressway, but there will be cars and a lot of semis. Worst case, we hit a car. It won't destroy the plane. But if we hit a tractor-trailer rig, it's over for everybody—passengers and crew."

"Make the call," McAvoy replied, "but give me the numbers first so I can advise Los Angeles Center, then get in position."

"You're going to bank right to a heading of three sixty and start your descent. Heading for final is three thirty—the direction the highway runs. There's no downwind leg or base, just straight in. We're at thirty-six thousand feet, roughly forty miles from touchdown. At five hundred forty knots, we have to lose altitude at a rate of seventy-two hundred feet per minute—four times as fast as we normally would."

"Angle of descent?"

"Nine point seven."

McAvoy sized up the highway as it came into view off the nose of the jet, then glanced at Hayes. "I don't think I've ever told you this, but you're a damned good copilot."

Hayes chuckled. "I hope you still feel that way twenty minutes from now."

"I'll let you know if I change my mind," McAvoy smiled. "Now let's get to work."

McAvoy contacted Los Angeles ARTCC and advised them of the new flight plan. Hayes called Delta Operations, requesting they Google White Hills Chevron in Arizona for a phone number, then call them and ask for help blocking the highway.

McAvoy finished with ARTCC and switched to the cabin PA system. "Ladies and gentlemen, we have been instructed by Air Traffic Control in Los Angeles to land as soon as possible. We can't make it to McCarran in Las Vegas, so we're putting down on a highway. We're going to make a rapid descent that may leave some of you feeling a little dizzy. We apologize in advance. When we get ready to touch down, I'm going to ask everybody to brace for impact. There's no cause for alarm, but we want to stay on the safe side. Flight attendants, prepare for emergency landing."

McAvoy switched off, then eased back on the throttles and pushed the nose of the aircraft down. He studied the terrain ahead, the ground cover and obstructions. Then he looked at the highway. He shook his head and glanced at Hayes. "I'm assuming you know this because you're a smart guy," he said. "But just as a friendly reminder, that highway was designed for cars and trucks. The heaviest thing that rolls down that road is a semi—around forty tons. We're pushing two hundred."

"You're worried we'll punch through the asphalt on touchdown and tear off the landing gear," Hayes replied.

"It crossed my mind."

"Do you garden, Mac?"

"A little."

"Not a lot of people around here do. Very little farming . . . because there isn't a square foot of ground in northwest Arizona that isn't as hard as steel-reinforced concrete. The highway will hold up." He paused. "I just don't know if it's wide enough."

14

5:40 p.m. Eastern Standard Time
Presidential Emergency Operations Center
White House
Washington, D.C.

President Wheeler, Defense secretary Patrick Wilkinson and Chairman of the Joints Chiefs Thomas Macfarland were in the Presidential Emergency Operations Center, a secure shelter and communications center located beneath the East Wing of the White House, hammering out a new command authority protocol. With a grid collapse, the ability of the President to communicate directly with military commands would be lost. The new protocol was simple—communication with commands, whether in the U.S. or other parts of the world, would be handled by the North American Aerospace Defense Command in Colorado Springs.

President Wheeler studied the maps on the wall displays for a minute, then picked up the phone and connected to NORAD.

"Tuckett here."

"General," Wheeler said, "we're proceeding on the assumption Russia will go to full-alert status, correct?"

"They've begun, Mr. President. Ten minutes ago. We're seeing activity at missile silos and bomber bases."

"You've got a plan in place?"

"Yes, sir." Tuckett went over the details of a strike involving the detonation of a single warhead at high altitude over St. Petersburg, Russia, saturating cities with an electromagnetic pulse. "We're waiting on word from NSA on the cyberattack."

"And if it looks like the Russians are going to launch before the NSA can implement their attack?"

"That's a possibility, Mr. President. A first strike by Russia would trigger a proportionate-response scenario with our ICBMs." He paused. "A nuclear exchange."

Wheeler looked at the map on the center display projecting the globe in Mercator projection. He had seen the Defense Department's scenarios—dozens of lines originating in Russia and curving up over the Pole, then back down to targets in the continental U.S. And, likewise, dozens of lines from the U.S. targeting Russia. He looked at Wilkinson and Macfarland. "Either one of you care to put yourself in Burkov's shoes? A best estimate on what he's thinking?"

"A couple of things, sir," Wilkinson said. "First, it's a safe bet he's working with the idea that we know everything concerning Russia's involvement with Iran and North Korea. It's how he thinks. He's planning for the worst. Second, if Russia detects a hack underway, a cyberattack on any aspect of their infrastructure—and it doesn't matter if it's their financial networks or their military—Burkov won't spend a lot of time working through it."

"He'll assume it's us."

"Yes."

"I agree," Tuckett said.

Macfarland nodded. "So do I.

"Worst case," Wheeler said.

"If Burkov believes we're going to act on what we know," Macfarland said, "he'll launch missiles."

"That's where my money would be," Tuckett said.

"General Tuckett," Wheeler said, "how long after you send orders to the submarines before they're ready to launch missiles?"

"Twenty minutes, give or take. The orders have to be authenticated. Once that's done, Weapons Control takes twelve minutes."

Wheeler nodded, then glanced at Macfarland and Wilkinson. "We wait." He looked at his watch. It was 5:45. "General Tuckett, you're going to be at the helm once the lights go out."

"I understand, sir."

"I couldn't ask for a better man."

"Thank you, sir."

"Godspeed, General."

"Godspeed, Mr. President."

15

3:45 p.m. Mountain Standard Time
Northwest Arizona

Neil Hayes was headed south on Highway 93, coming up on the White Hills Chevron when his cell phone rang. He glanced at the screen. It was Nancy.

"Hey," he answered.

"Neil, the president just addressed the nation from the Oval Office. There's going to be a nuclear explosion in space. It's going to shut down everything in North America."

He hit the brakes and signaled a turn into the station. "Do they know when?"

"Twenty minutes from now."

"Do you know when Nathan's flight left New York?"

"One o'clock Eastern time."

"He's still in the air." Neil pulled to a stop in the parking lot, then glanced at his watch and did a rough calculation. He stepped out of the truck and looked up, scanning the sky in a slow 360. He knew there were two high-altitude air routes that crossed over this part of Arizona—one roughly twenty-five miles north of him, the other forty miles south. He could see nothing to the north, but south of him he saw a single contrail turning off the route. Then he saw the jet descending.

"Neil?"

"I'm at the Chevron on ninety-three. There's a jet south of me that looks like it's going to try for the highway. It might be Nathan. On a five-hour flight, three forty-five Mountain time would put him in the neighborhood. But whether or not it's him, that jet is going to need help getting down. I've got to go. Call Carl. Make sure he knows what's happening. Then foil-wrap everything you can—laptops, radios—you remember what I showed you?"

"Yes. Be careful, Neil."

"You too." He pocketed the phone and headed for the front door of the store. Inside, a man behind the counter was calling out to customers. "Listen up, everybody," he said. "There's a commercial airliner that has to land on the highway."

"Who told you that?" Neil said, crossing the floor.

"Delta Airlines is on the phone."

Neil heaved a visible sigh of relief and closed his eyes for a moment. Then he looked at the man. "I need to talk to them."

"Hang on—"

"I know how to get that plane down safely, but I need to get word to the pilots."

"Back here." Neil followed him into an office in back and picked up the phone. "Who am I speaking to?" he asked.

"Delta Airlines Flight Operations, Atlanta."

"I can help your plane land, but I need you to contact them and have them tune to one forty-six point four forty megahertz VHF." There was silence on the other end of the line. "That's a ham radio frequency. Can you do it?"

"Yes. One forty-six, four forty."

"What's their flight number?"

"Three twenty-two."

"Thank you. Please do it now." Neil hung up the phone and walked out to the front of the store. "Who's driving those semis parked out front?" he called out.

"Right here." Two men raised their hands.

"You guys want to be heroes?"

They glanced at each other and smiled. "Hell, yes."

"Follow me."

Outside, Neil pointed to the north side of the parking lot entrance. "I need one of you to pull your truck across the highway over there. Block the southbound lanes completely, then lay road flares just like you would for an accident."

"I'm on it," one of the drivers said. He ran to his truck.

"You know this highway?" Neil asked the other driver.

"Yeah."

"About three miles south of here, the road curves left, then back to the right. Then there's a straight stretch about four miles long. Drive to the end of that—right before it starts to curve again—then cross over and block the northbound lanes."

"You got it. Block the road and lay flares."

"Exactly. And you're going to have to push it hard. That jet will be coming down any minute." The driver turned and ran to his truck. Five seconds after he climbed in, he was pulling out of the parking lot, twin exhaust stacks belching black smoke as the semi accelerated down the highway.

Neil drove his pickup fifty feet down the road, then stopped and got out, clipping a handheld transceiver to his belt. He walked to the back of the truck and grabbed a tape measure out of the tool box, then walked to the edge of the asphalt and measured the distance to the other side. He pulled the radio from his belt, checked the frequency, and looked up at the jet, now roughly eight miles away and coming down fast.

"Delta three-two-two," he called, "this is K7AZK."

In the cockpit of the Delta airliner, Nathan Hayes stared at the radio. "I don't believe it," he said.

"What's up?" McAvoy asked.

Nathan shook his head. "That's my dad's call sign." He keyed the mic. "Neil Hayes?"

Standing on the highway, Neil laughed out loud, then keyed the mic. "I'm at the Chevron station, Nathan."

"That's . . ." Nathan shook his head. "That's incredible."

"You're telling me. Now let's see if we can get you down without bending your jet. We've got two semis blocking the highway—one at the Chevron blocking the southbound lanes, the other is headed south to block the northbound lanes. He'll be there any minute."

"Is one side better than the other?"

"The southbound lanes. They resurfaced those a month ago."

"So, we've got four miles of straight. Any idea how wide it is?"

"I measured it—forty feet, edge to edge."

"It'll be close. Our main gear is thirty-six to the outboard tires."

"Not much room for error. But there are no guardrails. No road signs or billboards. No obstructions in the median. There's a power line that runs parallel to the highway, but it's a hundred yards west of the southbound lanes. You'll have plenty of wing clearance."

"The southern truck is turning across the highway right now," McAvoy said. "It's blocking the northbound lanes."

"He's your marker for touchdown. How far out are you?"

"Six miles."

"Winds are two-ten at five."

"Two-ten at five." McAvoy replied.

"We're going to button things up here, Dad," Nathan said. "Stay by the radio."

"You've got it. See you guys in a few minutes. K7AZK clear."

Nathan switched to Delta's Operations Center frequency. "Dispatch, three-two-two, we're setting up for a highway landing. Plenty of straight, good width, perfect visibility."

"Safe landing, three-two-two."

Then he called Los Angeles ARTCC. "Center, Delta three-two-two, we are three minutes from highway landing."

"Three-two-two, I've got two more behind you. Can you advise on the highway?"

"Four miles long, straight and flat. Forty feet wide, no signs, guardrails or poles. Traffic is blocked."

"Thanks, three-two-two. They have eyes on you. Give them room on rollout." The controller paused. "Safe landing."

"Thank you, Center. Delta three-two-two." He switched to the cabin PA. "Ladies and gentlemen, we're on final descent. Place any loose items on the floor and fasten your seat belts. Flight attendants, please take your seats."

McAvoy turned to Nathan. "I'm going to have my hands full bringing the plane down without a glide slope indicator. Can you handle the rudder?"

"No problem," Nathan replied.

"You're going to lose sight of the highway center line when we flare for touchdown. Can you keep us lined up?"

Nathan turned and stared through the windscreen at the highway below. The runway they left six hours ago was two hundred feet wide, giving the 767 a one hundred sixty-foot margin of error. Forty-five seconds from now he would have exactly four feet to play with. All it would take is a five-knot gust of wind against the vertical stabilizer and they could miss the highway completely.

"Piece of cake," Nathan replied.

McAvoy nodded. "All right then." He glanced out the window, then back at Nathan. "You ready?"

"Let's do this." Nathan tightened his shoulder harness, then focused on the instruments. "Two-one-zero knots indicated airspeed. Altimeter, two thousand feet. Rate of descent, eighteen hundred feet per minute, thirty feet per second."

"Speed brakes," McAvoy said. He pulled the throttle quadrant back slightly.

"Speed brakes extended," Nathan replied. Twenty seconds later he called out, "One-seventy KIAS, altimeter fifteen hundred. Rate of descent, twenty-five feet per second."

"Retract speed brakes. Flaps two, gear down."

"Speed brakes retracted. Flaps two, gear down and green."

Standing on the highway, Neil watched through binoculars as the 767 descended for a landing. He had seen a lot of things in his life that he would consider remarkable, but never a commercial airliner landing on a desert highway.

One thousand feet from their point of touchdown and two hundred fifty feet up, McAvoy called for full flaps. "Full flaps," Nathan confirmed. "Rate of descent eighteen feet per second." He looked out the side window before McAvoy flared, looking for a point of reference that would allow him to judge where the highway was when the nose came up. The fence line paralleling the highway was straight and true. He nodded. "Begin flare."

The jet drifted to the right as the nose lifted. Watching the fence line, Nathan pushed the left rudder pedal slightly. The plane pivoted, and he pushed the right pedal to straighten it out. "I can see the plane's shadow," he said. "We're sixty feet up, still centered." McAvoy pulled the yoke back a little more, then eased off, adjusting the approach angle. "One forty-five KIAS," Nathan called out, keeping his feet steady on the rudder pedals. "Thirty feet up. Rate of descent, ten feet per second." He keyed the mic. "Ladies and gentlemen, brace for impact." He glanced at the plane's shadow again. "We're good, Mac. Bring it home."

"Ten seconds," McAvoy replied, holding the yoke steady.

The jet sailed in over the semi parked on the other side of the median, its starboard wing clearing the trailer by just fifteen feet. Nathan saw the driver standing on the highway, waving, then he focused on the parking lane stripe and the plane's shadow. "We're there," he said. The main gear touched down on the road gently and a faint vibration ran through the airframe as the tires rolled along the rumble strips. Both pilots held their breath, praying the asphalt would support the weight of the airliner. It rolled another two hundred yards on the main gear, the cockpit dropping slowly until the nose gear finally touched down. McAvoy and Hayes breathed a sigh of relief as the jet rolled out smoothly, in perfect alignment with the highway, leaving a trail of dust in its wake.

McAvoy reversed engine thrust and applied brakes. The jet decelerated rapidly as the engines roared, bouncing slightly as it rolled across a concrete bridge that spanned a wash. Nathan watched out the side window as the starboard wing clipped the thin, whip-like branches from the taller mesquite bushes in the center median, then he glanced at the airspeed indicator.

"Forty knots," he said.

"Retract flaps," McAvoy replied.

"Flaps retracted." They rolled another quarter-mile in silence, then Nathan turned to McAvoy. "Nicely done, Mac."

"You too, Nathan," McAvoy nodded.

Neil's voice came over the radio. "Delta three-two-two, follow taxiway Foxtrot to terminal one. Observe ground crew batons."

McAvoy laughed. "Taxi Foxtrot to terminal, don't hit the ground crew, Delta three-two-two."

Neil smiled. "See you guys in a minute." He pulled out his cell phone and called Nancy. "Nathan's flight is on the ground."

"Thank God," she sighed. "What happened?"

"They landed on the highway."

"They landed an airliner on the highway?"

"It was unbelievable, Nancy. You should have seen it."

"I'm pretty sure the anxiety would have killed me."

Neil laughed. "Anyway, they're down. They're safe."

"Is Nathan coming home with you?"

"I don't know. There are two more jets coming in, which means there will be a lot of people in Whites Hills that need food and shelter. It's going to take some time to get things squared away here. It might be tomorrow before we get back. Did you reach Carl?"

"I did."

"After the lights go out, unpack one of the transceivers. Tune it to one forty-seven, two forty. That's Carl's repeater. When it's back up and running, use that frequency to call me if I'm not back." He glanced at his watch. "Do we know when this is supposed to hit? When the power is shutting down?"

"When they said twenty minutes, it was just a minute before I called you. That would make it about five after four."

"All right. Don't leave the house unless you absolutely have to."

"I won't." She paused. "Have you heard anything from Naomi?"

"I haven't. But I'm guessing she's smack in the middle of this. If it's a weapon in space, NSA is all over it."

"That does nothing to put my mind at ease. I assume we're talking about a grid collapse."

"We are."

"And our daughter is two thousand miles away."

"Yes. And she's one of the smartest people we know. She's capable. She knows how to think."

"Do you think she'll come home?"

"I know she'll come home." Neil waited for a response, but was met with silence. "Nancy . . . she'll make it."

"I love you, Neil. Be careful."

"You too, sweetheart."

Neil had no sooner ended the call when his phone chimed with an incoming text. It was from Naomi. It read, 'Wrapping up things in Fort Meade. Heading to AZ tonight. Bringing two friends. Will monitor ham freqs. Is Nathan flying? Love you.'

Neil smiled. "Just when I was thinking you were going to leave me in the dark," he said aloud. "Figuratively, of course." He tapped a reply. 'Nathan's OK. Landed on hwy 93. Beware bad guys on the road. Stay armed and watch your six. Love, Dad.'

He forwarded Naomi's text to Nancy along with his reply, then slipped the phone into his pocket and breathed a sigh of relief, knowing his family was accounted for. Naomi had a long trek ahead of her—a lot of nighttime driving in winter weather. But her biggest problem following a grid collapse would be people on the highway stopping vehicles and taking whatever they could. He wondered who the two friends were, what kind of help they would be when the chips were down and lives were on the line.

He drew a deep breath, then exhaled slowly. "She's smart," he said quietly. "She knows the score." But despite knowing this and his assurances to his wife, Neil knew he would fret over his daughter until she was safe at home.

He looked down the highway. The Delta jet was rolling slowly along the road toward him. Behind it, the second plane was touching down. The third plane was still in the air a half-mile out.

"Bring it in, guys," he said. "You've got just seconds."

16

6:03 p.m. Eastern Standard Time
National Security Agency
Fort Meade, Maryland

Night had fallen as one hundred forty people stood in the parking lot of the NSA building, milling about among the parked cars, waiting, wondering. These were directors, supervisors and remaining staff who had not been sent home an hour earlier. Equipment had been moved, generators had been disconnected, and plans were set, at least to the extent they could be based on very limited knowledge of what was about to happen.

Hendricks, Lundgren and Winter stood alone, facing northwest. The sky was clear and dark, and the light generated by the nuclear detonation almost thirteen hundred miles away from them—two hundred miles above South Dakota—would be visible twenty degrees above the horizon.

They talked for a minute, then Hendricks walked alone toward the west side of the parking lot, gazing out across the Patuxent

Freeway and the Baltimore-Washington Parkway to the communities of Russett, Carriage Hill and North Laurel. She looked up at the night sky and imagined the nuclear bomb racing through space, just seconds away from exploding. That reality took hold and for a moment she trembled, her knees wobbling. She looked out over the suburbs to the west and thought of all the people, many of them rushing home from work to prepare for a power outage, breaking out flashlights and candles, others racing for stores and gas stations to grab whatever they could—essential supplies—food and water, gasoline, flashlights and batteries.

Suddenly, thoughts she'd been pushing out of her mind the last two hours in order to concentrate flooded back in. This time she let them stay, dwelling on them as if to pay homage to ways of life that moments from now would be changed forever. She thought of those families—parents and children—retrieving flashlights from closets and lighting candles, pulling out a board game to pass the time. How long would it be before the outage was no longer an adventure for the kids? And how long before strangers with bad intentions came knocking on their doors? She thought of the tens of millions of people young and old, obsessed with the technology of smartphones and the internet. Seconds from now they would lose their lifeline. How many would move ahead? And how many would fold, unable to talk, think or feel without their connection?

Denton's words leapt to mind and she felt sudden compassion for these people—people for whom she had felt annoyance and a lack of patience. They would be just like everybody else—the families, the friends, blue collar, white collar, retired, the elderly and the children. When the lights went out, they all would be human. They all would be frail. And they all would be vulnerable.

She groaned, a lump rising in her throat, then closed her eyes, trying to maintain but struggling with emotions that were running wild. A moment later she opened her eyes and through the blur of tears saw a brief but intensely bright flash in the distance, lighting up the night sky. Then it was gone.

Hendricks stood motionless, looking at the suburbs to the west, then those south of her. The lights were still on. She looked north toward Baltimore and saw the glow from the city. She laughed, then called out to Winter and Lundgren. "Nothing happened!" She turned back toward Carriage Hill and North Laurel, wiping the tears from her cheeks. "Nothing happened," she repeated quietly.

Then she saw cars rolling to a stop on the Parkway—dozens of them. She stared, listening to horns honking as the few cars still running threaded their way around those that were stalled. She heard Lundgren shouting something she couldn't make out as he ran toward her. A few seconds later he reached her, out of breath.

"The E3 hasn't hit yet," he said.

"What?"

"The E3—the latent pulse. It hasn't hit yet." He leaned over, hands on his knees, catching his breath. "But it's coming."

Hendricks stared at him, and just as she opened her mouth to speak, the lights went out, plunging the area into total darkness, from Bowie, to Annapolis, north to Baltimore and beyond. She turned in a slow circle, straining her eyes to see a street lamp, a traffic signal, a lighted billboard—anything other than the few remaining headlights on roadways. There was nothing but the fading sliver of twilight gleaming on the western horizon.

"No," she whispered. She turned back and stared into the darkness for a few seconds, then sat on the ground and cried.

PART II

THE COLLAPSE

17

Monday, February 10
6:07 p.m. Eastern Standard Time

I t couldn't be seen or felt. It was silent, traveling at near the speed
of light, a massive pulse of electromagnetic energy that blanket-
ed an area more than three thousand miles in diameter, frying every
integrated circuit in its path. Electronics were destroyed a millisec-
ond after the bomb detonated in orbit. But it was another two minutes before large power transformers were hit and the flow of electricity across North America stopped. Inner cities came to a standstill
as passenger cars, taxicabs and buses stalled, blocking streets and
intersections. Stores, restaurants and office buildings emptied, and
subway and train stations shut down, leaving millions of commuters
in the dark, stranded, unable to reach their homes.

But the real nightmare was unfolding in the skies over North
America as passenger jets that were unable to land before the bomb
detonated fell from the sky, their pilots unable to control a single
aspect of flight—pitch, roll, yaw or engine thrust.

More than eighty percent of the commercial flights in the air at the time of the FAA's ground stop landed with no significant loss of life—a miracle in view of the time frame—as pilots worked heroically to bring their planes down before the EMP hit. Most landed safely at airports. But hundreds of jets came down on highways and in open fields. Those would remain where they were for months before being moved, monuments to the quick thinking of pilots, the lightning-fast reaction of the FAA, and—according to anyone who witnessed an airliner drop out of the sky and touch down on a paved highway, in a plowed wheat field or an open prairie, and stay in one piece—the hand of God.

But more than a thousand aircraft crashed with catastrophic loss of life. Roughly half of these flights were over ocean water. In these cases, pilots descended prior to the loss of power to an altitude that would make ditching in the ocean a hopeful alternative to an uncontrolled fall from thirty-five thousand feet. None were successful.

The 240,750 lives lost in air crashes were the first tragedy of the blackout. It would not be the last.

Candles, oil lamps and makeshift attempts to warm dwellings by burning wood indoors resulted in accidental fires that swept through entire neighborhoods. With no response by firefighters and no water to battle the blazes, fires burned out of control until all combustible fuel in their path was consumed, taking the lives of tens of thousands of home and apartment dwellers.

But the steepest loss of life would be to starvation, beginning a week following the grid collapse and continuing for months. Within seventy-two hours the United States found itself not in the nineteenth century—a time when most families lived on farms producing the nation's food supply—but in the Neolithic Revolution of 10,000 BC, before mankind underwent the transition from hunting and gathering to settled agriculture. At the time of the blackout, fewer than one in three Americans knew how to grow a vegetable—a single tomato or cucumber, let alone a garden capable of sustaining a family. Fewer than one in ten Americans knew how to fish. And fewer than one in fifty knew how to hunt. The sad but simple truth was that when it came to acquiring food, the average American knew little more than how to shop for groceries. And a surprising number knew only how to order their meals from a menu.

Food appropriated from grocery distribution centers following the collapse ran out within twelve hours, and with no fuel to operate agricultural machinery, and only a tiny fraction of the population having the knowledge to plant, cultivate and harvest crops without modern machinery and computerized production, the nation's food supply ground to a halt.

The prevailing argument among those who had any interest in arguing was the same as it always was when disaster strikes—where is the federal government? Why aren't they taking care of its citizens? The answer to those questions, at least in the minds of the relative few in modern society who subscribed to the notion of being prepared for disasters, was simple—it wasn't the federal government's responsibility to feed the nation, to clothe it, or to provide shelter, medicine or other basic necessities.

Despite the efforts of FEMA and the wildly optimistic estimates of what the agency could do following the detonation of an EMP weapon over the United States, the reality was that FEMA was equipped to handle less than one percent of the nation's most pressing needs. And that was under optimum circumstances concerning staff, resources and communications.

Within two hours of the blackout, the failure of satellites supporting FEMA's Broadband Global Area Network resulted in a complete loss of communications with field teams. Further complicating communications was the loss of radio transmission capability due to the intense ionization of the atmosphere following the nuclear detonation. VHF and UHF radio communication was possible, but only in line-of-sight distances along the ground, limiting communications to a few miles.

Twelve hours after the blackout, FEMA's National Response Coordination Center had lost generator power. Two hours later, the generators powering the Federal Regional Center bunkers shut down. And by the end of the first full day, the Department of Homeland Security's Critical Infrastructure Warning Information Network had collapsed, severing ties with FEMA and other federal agencies, as well as with state Emergency Operations Centers.

It was a staggering failure. And it was not unforeseen. For more than a decade Congress had known of the consequences of an EMP. FEMA had run a risk assessment of a grid collapse resulting from a solar storm, and the outcome was identical. Either scenario left America hanging by its fingertips. And while every analysis by experts pointed to a catastrophic loss of life, nothing was done. Hearings were held, reports were submitted, and articles were published, all as if to say, "We're looking at it." Eventually, the notion of a nationwide power outage caused by a high-altitude nuclear detonation was dismissed, and while some continued to sound the alarm, an overwhelming majority of politicians and military leaders were in agreement—it could never happen.

At 6:07 p.m. Eastern Time on February 10 that thinking changed, and with it, the future of America.

18

Deep within the granite interior of Cheyenne Mountain, NORAD was buttoned up for the first time since September 11, 2001, running on power supplied by six diesel generators. Communication with locations elsewhere in the U.S. was spotty, but with ballistic missile submarines operating in the North Atlantic and Indian Oceans, and strike groups in the Sea of Japan and the Persian Gulf, communications were functioning through the High Frequency Global Communications System.

Prior to the EMP, authority to issue launch orders was transferred to NORAD from the National Military Command Center at the Pentagon, and the Alternate National Military Command Center at the Raven Rock Mountain Complex in Blue Ridge, Pennsylvania. Details of strikes to be made were vetted by the president, the Joint Chiefs of Staff and the secretary of Defense. The decision to detonate a single high-altitude nuclear warhead over Nizhny Novgorod—245 miles east of Moscow—saturating Russia's twelve largest cities with an electromagnetic pulse, was made at 5:10 p.m. Eastern Time, following the meeting in the White House Situation Room. The ICBM carrying the nuclear warhead would be launched immediately following the National Security Agency's cyberattack against military, financial and security networks in Russia.

But at 6:25 p.m. Eastern—4:25 Mountain Time—an alert from U.S. Strategic Command at Offutt Air Force Base in Nebraska was sent to NORAD. General Wilson Tuckett was in the command center when an airman handed him the printout. Tuckett scanned the message, then read it aloud.

"Russian SS-18s are being fueled at Dombarovsky, Kartaly, Uzhur and Aleysk launch sites. Strategic missile strike against U.S. believed to be imminent." He handed the message to his second-in-command, Lieutenant General James McNaughton. "Prepare launch orders for the *West Virginia*," Tuckett said. "High-altitude barrage—eight Tridents, one hundred miles above ground level in a spread from St. Petersburg to the Kamchatka peninsula."

"That's going to leave a radiation belt that will take down a lot of satellites in low-Earth orbits," McNaughton replied.

"I know. We discussed it."

"Just going on record."

Tuckett nodded. "You know the odds of those Minuteman interceptors in Alaska taking out a Russian ICBM?"

"Not good."

"Better to lose a few tons of space hardware than an American city." Tuckett paused. "If those SS-18s make it out of their silos, we'll be in serious trouble."

Five hundred twenty-five nautical miles southwest of Iceland, midway between the southern tip of Greenland and Ireland, the

USS *West Virginia* slipped through the ocean depths, undetectable by surface ships or satellites. Its orders were to remain at depth until half past the hour, at which time it would come shallow and listen for orders to launch. An Ohio-class ballistic missile submarine, the *West Virginia* carried twenty-four Trident D5 ICBMs, each one with a platform of eight 400-kiloton nuclear warheads.

Captain Owen Clark stood behind the ship control panel between the Helm and the Diving Officer of the Watch. He glanced at the wall clock, then turned to the diving officer. "Make your depth two hundred feet."

"Make my depth two hundred feet, aye, sir," the diving officer replied. He pulled back on the control wheel as the Chief of the Watch commenced blowing water out of the sub's ballast tanks.

Clark leaned into the climb, then turned to the Chief of the Boat. "Extend the VLF antenna buoy."

"Extend the VLF antenna buoy, aye, sir," COB replied.

Three minutes later the ship leveled off. "Depth is two hundred feet, sir," the diving officer reported. "Zero bubble."

Clark pulled the mic from the overhead clasp. "Sonar, Conn, report surface contacts."

"Negative surface contacts," the sonar officer replied.

Clark turned to the diving officer. "Hover."

"Hover, aye, sir."

All hands in the control center remained silent as they awaited incoming radio transmissions. If none were received by 00:35, they would return to depth and remain stealthy until the top of the hour, at which time they would come shallow and listen again.

At precisely 00:30 the communications officer broke the silence. "Conn, Radio, Emergency Action Message coming in on VLF. We're decoding now." Eight minutes later the communications officer appeared on the control deck, a sheet of paper in hand. "Valid EAM, sir." He handed it to the captain.

Clark scanned the message, then turned to his executive officer and nodded. "Authenticate."

Both men crossed the control deck to the safe and opened it, the XO spinning the combination lock on the outer door, the captain working the tumbler on the inner door. Inside were two sealed authenticator cards and two missile launch keys on lanyards. Clark handed one card to the XO, the other to the communications officer. Both men snapped the cards open.

"Bravo Delta Delta Kilo Charlie Zulu Tango," the XO read.

The communications officer followed. "Bravo Delta Delta Kilo Charlie Zulu Tango."

"Bravo Delta Delta Kilo Charlie Zulu Tango," the captain read from the EAM.

"The message is authentic, sir," the XO said.

The communications officer nodded. "I concur, captain."

Clark retrieved the launch keys from the safe and handed one to the XO. The other he hung around his neck. Both men moved back to the control panel. Clark set the emergency action message on the map console behind the Helm, then pulled the overhead mic and addressed the ship's crew.

"We have an authenticated order for strategic missile launch. Weapons, Conn, spin up tubes one through four and twenty-one through twenty-four. This is the captain speaking."

Clark handed the mic to the XO. "We have an authenticated order for strategic missile launch. Spin up tubes one through four and twenty-one through twenty-four. This is the XO."

"Spin up tubes one through four and twenty-one through twenty-four, aye, sir," WEPS replied. In the weapons control room, WEPS and his second-in-command opened a twin-tumbler safe and removed the launch trigger. WEPS plugged it into the console, then reached above it and set the wall clock.

"Conn, Weapons, time to missile launch, twelve minutes."

Clark acknowledged the message. "Time to missile launch, twelve minutes." He replaced the mic, then looked at the Chief of the Boat.

"Pandora's Box," COB said.

Clark nodded. "Let's hope it's open-and-shut."

President Edmund Wheeler sat behind his desk in the Oval Office. He arranged papers in front of him, then looked at the camera set up across the room. Ten seconds later the White House communications director nodded at him.

"This video address is being sent by satellite to our allies across the globe," Wheeler began. "The United States has suffered an EMP attack launched by Iran, North Korea and Russia. We have lost our power grid, and with it the bulk of our national infrastructure, leaving the citizens of this great nation without basic necessities—food, water, sanitation, functioning medical facilities and police and fire protection. We are doing everything in our power to mitigate this disaster, but with our nation's agricultural production at a standstill, and without fuel for delivery of what little food remains available, we face a famine that threatens to decimate our population.

"For decades we have stood with our allies around the world, strengthening your economies with financial aid, your armies with military assistance. We have helped you recover from natural disasters with humanitarian relief. Now we reach out to you with a plea for assistance, asking that you help us as we have helped you."

Five thousand miles away, Russian president Victor Burkov laughed heartily as he watched the address from the Kremlin. He turned to his Chairman of the Government and the Minister of Foreign Affairs and raised a glass. "To the fall of the United States of America," he said. The three men toasted and drank.

"I have a message for President Burkov," Wheeler continued. "Over the last several years we have responded to your unlawful expansion—your takeover of Crimea and invasion of Ukraine—with sanctions against your businesses and banks. When you began cyberattacks against us, our response was increased pressure, all of this with the hope that you would respond as a reasonable man who wished for the same things we all want for our citizens—a strong economy and a healthy, productive lifestyle for our people.

"Now, not only have you aligned yourself with terrorist regimes, you have willingly taken part in their war against the United States." Wheeler paused. "President Burkov, you have shut off our lights, but you have not shut down our military forces around the world."

In the North Atlantic, the USS *West Virginia* rose to a launch depth of one hundred thirty feet. Launch tubes were pressurized, missile hatches opened, and eight Trident ICBMs left their tubes, boosted to the surface by compressed nitrogen. Breaking free of the water, the engines ignited and the missiles roared into the sky.

Captain Clark turned to the Diving Officer. "Make your depth one thousand feet."

"Make my depth one thousand, aye, sir."

Ballast tanks were flooded as the Diving Officer pushed the control wheel forward, and the *West Virginia* slipped back into the depths of the North Atlantic.

Six minutes later, air raid sirens sounded in Moscow. "What is this?" Burkov asked. He crossed the room to the window and looked out across Ivanovskaya Square. A flash of light from above turned nighttime into day. Then it was gone, and within seconds the Russian Federation was pitched into darkness.

"And to the North Korean dictator Lee Yong-hwa," President Wheeler continued, "my message is simple and straightforward. Over the years, world leaders watched as you gambled with the future of your people who looked to you for security, for a better life. You toyed with nuclear weapons and missiles as a child who plays with a gun, unaware of the consequences, the depth and magnitude of his actions. We abided your irrational behavior, hoping for a shred of reason, a glimmer of the understanding that you were steering your country, your people, to destruction." Wheeler paused. "Now you will reap what was sewn."

Sixty-seven hundred miles away in the Sea of Japan, three strike groups led by the USS *Ronald Reagan*, the USS *Nimitz* and the USS *Theodore Roosevelt* launched a fusillade of cruise missiles against North Korea, destroying artillery units targeting Seoul, South Korea, then military installations farther north. Power stations and oil refineries were targeted next, followed by seaports and the Yongbyon Nuclear Scientific Research Center. Finally, the residential compound north of Pyongyang, home of Lee Yong-hwa, was leveled.

The attack against Iran targeted all remaining military installations not destroyed by the Israelis. Launched from strike groups led by the USS *George H. W. Bush*, cruise missiles took out power stations, including hydroelectric dams and the Darkhovin and Bushehr nuclear power plants. Oil refineries and pipelines were destroyed, then strongholds of the Iranian Revolutionary Guard Corps and the Kashani regime, including the presidential palace.

The attacks lasted just eighteen minutes, leaving Iran's electrical infrastructure completely destroyed along with its military presence. Its government was in tatters. North Korea suffered identical losses and outcome of military and government. Both countries were without power and running water. Both were without functioning government. Both were ripe for overthrow by their citizens.

"The era of détente is over," Wheeler said. "To those who wish to harm the United States or its allies, know that we will come at you with the full force and fury of the greatest military machine in the world. We will not negotiate. We will not pick up the phone. We will reduce you to rubble and be done with it." He pushed back from his desk, then stood. "You've been warned."

19

6:15 p.m. Central Standard Time
Chicago, Illinois

Chaos was rampant in the Englewood neighborhood of Chicago as mobs, unrestrained by police, moved through city streets, breaking windows, trashing parked cars and setting fires, destroying the area block by block. West Marquette Road was a war zone as hundreds of people looted food and liquor stores, then set them ablaze and moved on, like a screaming, psychotic thrashing machine mowing down everything in its path.

Forty-five minutes earlier, police and National Guard troops had moved into Englewood and Fuller Park in large numbers, but were overwhelmed by rioters numbering close to a thousand, all of them armed and none of them backing down. Following an exchange of gunfire, police and troops pulled out and moved to Forest Glen, North Park and Bridgeport—areas of the city where their presence would accomplish something other than a body count, leaving high-crime areas to fend for themselves, and ultimately to burn.

It was during the pullout that a primer-gray van sped south on Harvard Avenue from West 64th Street, clipping stalled cars as it swerved to miss pedestrians running down the middle of the street. The driver, a girl in her late teens, was frantic to get out of Englewood. In the back of the van, her boyfriend lay bleeding from a gunshot wound to the abdomen.

Less than a minute earlier, the pair had fled St. Bernard Hospital's emergency room when a nurse called security. The boyfriend, still upright but bleeding profusely, grabbed his girlfriend by the arm and retreated to the van. They flew out of the parking lot with the girl behind the wheel and a dozen people chasing them, screaming obscenities and throwing rocks and bottles.

"Don't stop for anything," the boyfriend said. "No matter what happens, don't stop the van." He leaned out of the front passenger seat, fell to the floor, then crawled into the back.

Three blocks later she made a hard right on West Marquette, then jumped on the brakes. Fifty yards in front of her, a large group of rioters blocking the street turned to face the van. "Don't stop!" the boyfriend yelled. The girl stepped on the gas pedal, accelerating toward the mob. She was thirty feet away when a bottle with a burning wick hit the windshield and burst into flames across the front of the vehicle. The girl closed her eyes and screamed, then stomped the gas pedal to the floor. Seconds later, the van blew through the mob, sending bodies flying through the air like bowling pins, then disappeared into the night.

The 480 Crosstown between the Missouri River and downtown Omaha was a nightmare following a massive pileup involving more than a hundred vehicles. The EMP hit at rush hour, and in the space of a second or two, the area went from being bathed in a blinding white light, to complete darkness—this, on a freeway packed with cars traveling seventy-five miles per hour.

Ed and Valerie Bennett were driving in from Council Bluffs to spend an evening at Omaha's Festival of Lights when the sky lit up brighter than noonday. "What in the world?" Valerie said.

Ed looked up just as the light disappeared, then glanced at the dashboard where a dozen indicator lights blinked on and off, then back at the road ahead, now completely dark.

"We're in trouble," he said. "We've got to get off the road." The words had barely left his mouth when he was hit from behind, the impact shattering his rear window and knocking his car into another. Both cars spun, sliding across the emergency lane into the concrete barrier, then bounced back into the right-hand lane where he was hit broadside on the driver's door. The collisions seemed to go on forever. Then they stopped, and an eerie silence fell over the darkened highway. "Are you all right?" Ed asked Valerie.

"I think so," she replied. "Are you?"

"Yes." The shattered windshield was draped across the dashboard and hanging over Valerie's lap. Ed reached across her and fumbled with the glove compartment latch for a moment, then pulled out a flashlight. He turned it on and looked at his wife. Her face was dotted with tiny cuts. "Close your eyes," he said, pulling a handkerchief from his pocket. He gently brushed glass from her eyelids and cheeks, then from her hair. "Okay."

She opened her eyes. "I thought that would never end."

"I know," he nodded. He squeezed her arm. "Stay in the car." He forced the driver's door open, then stepped out, broken glass crunching under his shoes. Shining the light down the freeway he saw wrecked cars to the end of the flashlight's beam. He stepped forward, tripping over a twisted bumper lying on the road and falling against the side of a car in front of his. He turned to the driver's door and looked inside. A woman was slumped over the steering wheel.

"Are you all right?" he asked. There was no response. He gently leaned her back in the seat and shined the flashlight on her. Blood was spurting from a gash in her neck. He shook his handkerchief, then folded it and applied pressure to the wound, slowing the blood flow, but not stopping it.

"Valerie!" he called out. "I need your help!"

She struggled with her door for a moment, then stepped out of the car. Ed shined the light on the road in front of her. "Be careful," he said. "There's glass and debris all over."

She climbed over the hood of their car and stood next to him. "Is she all right?"

"She's unconscious and bleeding badly. Hold this handkerchief against her neck. You'll have to press hard."

Valerie took a deep breath, then leaned in the car and held the handkerchief against the wound. Ed took off his jacket, then tore a sleeve from his shirt. He wadded it up, then leaned in. "I've got it," he said. "Call 911."

She pulled her phone from her pocket and tapped the screen. "My phone doesn't work."

"Get mine. It's in my jacket."

She picked up the jacket off the road and reached in the pocket. A moment later she said, "Yours isn't working either."

Ed looked down the road and shouted. "We need help here!" He could hear people moving, but couldn't see anybody. He shined the light on the woman's neck. It was still bleeding. He pressed as hard as he could. "Can somebody help us!" he yelled. He leaned in again. "I can't stop the bleeding."

Valerie stepped to the front of the car. "We need help!" she screamed. "Please! Somebody help us!"

In Fort Smith, Arkansas, Les Dunlap sat in his darkened kitchen with a shotgun on his lap and a box of shells on the table, listening to the sound of gunfire. It had been going on for thirty minutes, intermittent and from random directions, but moving closer. He stood and crossed the living room to check the dead bolt on the front door, then returned to the kitchen and sat again, waiting.

He was working in his garage when the lights went out. He pulled a flashlight from a drawer in the workbench, turned it on, then walked to the end of the driveway and looked down the street. It was dark from one end to the other. His two grandchildren met him at the front door to tell him the TV was off.

"I guess dinner will be a little late," his wife said.

"We'll find something to eat," he replied. He set the flashlight on the counter by the sink, resting it on its base so the light reflected off the ceiling, illuminating the kitchen, then turned on the faucet to wash his hands. The water came out in a trickle, then stopped. He lifted the receiver from the wall phone and listened for a dial tone. It was silent. From the hall closet he picked up another flashlight, then walked into the den and switched on the portable radio. Nothing. He replaced the batteries and tried it again. Still nothing. He returned to the living room.

"I'm going for a walk," he said. "I'll be a few minutes."

"Can we go?" the kids asked.

"Not this time. You stay and keep grandma company. I'll be right back." He pulled on a coat and left the house.

Across the street, he knocked on his neighbor's door. The neighbor had no water pressure and his phone was dead. "That's odd don't you think?" Dunlap asked.

"I take it you missed Wheeler's address," the neighbor replied.

"When?"

"Forty-five minutes ago. It's an EMP weapon in space. Shut everything down."

Dunlap thought for a moment. "That means no police."

"It looks that way. You've got a gun, don't you?"

"Of course."

"The crazies will be crawling out of the woodwork tonight."

Dunlap nodded. "Take care."

"You too."

Back home, he pulled some food from the cupboard and water from the refrigerator, then took his wife and grandchildren to the basement, instructing them not to come upstairs unless he called for them. He lit two oil lamps and placed them on a cabinet, then started a fire in the small potbelly stove. Finally, he gave his wife an old Army-issue .45-caliber semiautomatic pistol.

"Is it that serious?" she asked.

"Just sit tight with the kids. I'm going to keep an eye out front." He leaned over and whispered in her ear, "If anyone comes down here unannounced, don't ask questions. Just shoot them."

Now, nearly an hour later, Dunlap sat in the dark, the kitchen window shade opened just enough that he could see the street out front. He stood and stretched his legs, then sat again. A moment later he heard a vehicle turn the corner at the top of the street. Peeking through the shades, he watched it stop three houses down. Five men climbed out of the back carrying rifles, then spread out, each one going to a different house. The last one walked up to the house across the street, stood at the front door for a moment, then kicked it open. A split-second later a flash, and the thunder of a shotgun blast echoed off the houses, rattling Dunlap's kitchen window.

"Wrong house," he said quietly. His neighbor stepped outside and looked down the street, then racked the pump shotgun and fired at the truck. Dunlap could hear the buckshot tearing through metal, then two more shots as the truck sped away. His neighbor turned and looked at the body lying on his front lawn, then walked back inside and closed the door.

Seconds later, Dunlap heard shots being fired at the truck farther down the street. He nodded. "Wrong neighborhood."

20

"I've never seen this city without lights." President Wheeler stood by the window looking out into the darkness, his mind running with thoughts of what might be happening out there. Over the last half-hour he heard sporadic gunfire and shouting in the distance, but mostly silence. He almost expected people to be marching in front of the White House, carrying signs reading, "Turn the Lights Back On!" But it was quiet outside. Quiet, and ominously dark.

He turned away from the window and faced the others in the room. With him were Vice President Jan Hutchens, Homeland Secretary Margaret Beck, and Chief of Staff Bob Larson, all dressed warmly. The White House was running on generator power, but Wheeler had instructed staff to use electricity only when and where absolutely necessary. He knew they would run out of fuel eventually and was trying to postpone that inevitability as long as possible.

He looked at Hutchens, Beck and Larson, thinking of what they faced. They were meeting with the idea of hammering out an early plan for responding to the blackout, but after thirty minutes of fits and starts, the discussion stalled. The problem was addressing an issue that completely overwhelmed them—like trying to stop arterial bleeding when all they had was a Band Aid.

"I think back to major disasters," Wheeler said, "and the solution—overall, at least, not in the details—was to mobilize agencies, send in recovery teams and supplies, throw money at it." He shook his head. "Apart from FEMA, nobody is out there."

"And FEMA is having problems," Secretary Beck said.

Wheeler nodded, then crossed the room to pour another cup of coffee. A moment later his secret service agent walked in. "Mr. President, Secretary Chambers is here."

Wheeler looked pleasantly surprised. Interior Secretary Douglas Chambers was one of the president's strongest allies and a close friend. He wasn't afraid to speak his mind, particularly when discussing serious issues. But the characteristic that stood out among all others, one that Wheeler appreciated most, was his ability to navigate serious problems and get right to the heart of the matter. Wheeler needed a large dose of that tonight.

"Show him in, John," he said.

"He's armed."

"I would be too if I didn't have you around. He's okay."

The Interior secretary entered the room, wearing a gray felt Stetson, a Carhartt parka and pac boots. Wheeler smiled. "You look like you stepped out of a Boot Barn catalog, Doug."

"It's snowing," Chambers replied. "Reminds me of Idaho." He looked around, nodding. "I like what you've done with the place. Oil lamps, a warm fire. Very 1870s." He greeted the vice president and Homeland secretary. "Ladies. Nice to see you." Then he turned to the chief of staff. "How are you, Bob?"

155

"I'm well, Mr. Chambers," Larson smiled. "How are you?"

"Okay, considering." Chambers hung his coat on a rack by the door, then sat. "I caught your video, Mr. President. The one dressing-down Burkov and Lee."

"I've been told it was a little over the top," Wheeler said.

"Wearing war paint would have been over the top. Personally, I thought it was just the right amount of crazy."

"Keep them guessing."

"From what I understand, sir, Russia has no electricity, North Korea and Iran are wall-to-wall craters. It doesn't sound like there's much guesswork involved."

"You drove across town to get here, didn't you?"

"Yes."

"What's happening out there?"

"People are burning cars in the streets. Some, because they're angry. Others . . ." He shrugged.

"Because they're cold."

"In Twin Falls they'll be burning timber."

"In the streets?"

"Safer than burning it in the forest." He paused. "There are mobs, some rioting, a lot of broken windows."

Wheeler shook his head. "We're two hours into this, Doug. I have a feeling we're about twenty-four hours from a complete breakdown in order if we can't get ahead of it and stay ahead of it. I'm scrambling to find people I can rely on for advice. Both chambers of Congress are in recess, and frankly, I'm not sure how many—if any—are going to make it back."

Chambers shrugged. "I don't see how that's a problem, considering the friction between the White House and Congress."

"I wasn't going to ask them to pass a bill. There's a possibility— perhaps a probability—that we may be going to war with Russia."

"Didn't we just shut off their lights?"

"We did. But that may not be the end of it."

"If it were me, Mr. President, I'd cross that bridge when I come to it. The Russians may call it a day, throw in the towel."

"Would you throw in the towel?"

Chambers shook his head. "No. But there's nothing you can do about it right now. Your first concern is out there." He pointed at the window. "What's FEMA doing?" he asked Secretary Beck.

"Moving food and water," Beck replied. "Blankets. But we can't communicate with field teams. We're losing satellites."

"That was bound to happen."

"No phones," Wheeler said. "No radio communication. We can't talk to anybody except NORAD. We've got soldiers from Marine Barracks bringing in Humvees for transportation. They might be able to coordinate with FEMA. The Army too—anybody that's got working communications equipment and transportation."

Chambers nodded. "Your focus, Mr. President, whether it's with FEMA or the military, should be on the big cities, urban centers. Small towns, rural areas, they'll get through this without a lot of help. But the cities . . . they're death traps. Large concentrations of people with no resources. People are scared, but they can't leave. And that element of society that feeds on disorder, lawlessness, they'll use this to their advantage. They'll try to turn this thing upside down."

Wheeler shook his head. "It's about as upside down as anything can be right now. I'm trying to imagine what things will be like in a week, and frankly, it's a little terrifying to think about."

"We take it a piece at a time, Mr. President. Otherwise, it's beyond any of us. Start with public safety in the cities."

"The National Guard will be helping with law enforcement."

"Just be sure we stand on the Constitution."

"You don't think we should use Guard troops?"

"You can't do this without them. The Guard is vital. And deploying them in cities doesn't violate the Posse Comitatus Act. Going beyond that, though—a declaration of martial law—will invite serious resistance. That's something we don't need or want."

"And if we lose control completely?"

"That's another bridge we cross if we come to it. But if I were in your shoes, I'd start by giving governors the freedom to do whatever they need to in their own states, starting with their Guard units. And I'm talking about complete autonomy. Do that and you eliminate a lot of problems you'll have if we try and control everybody. Be ready to give them what we're able to, but stay out of their hair."

"Relax our grip."

"No, Mr. President. Release our grip. Let states do whatever they want, however they want to do it. Wyoming, Montana, Idaho—states with largely rural populations aren't going to have the same kind of problems that California, New York or New Jersey will. Anywhere in the northeast, for that matter."

Wheeler nodded. "You think rural areas will be all right."

"You've got ranchers, farmers, people who are self-reliant to begin with. A lot of them have wells, so water isn't an insurmountable problem. And many small towns in agricultural areas have co-ops with food storage. Abundant hunting and fishing. These people were preppers before there was a prepper movement. And helping each other is second nature to them. That's one of the ironies in our society—ranchers in Montana, living miles apart from each other, are much closer than people living on top of each other in a Manhattan apartment building."

"People helping each other in order to survive."

"That's vital. At the same time, there are people in the prepper movement who are isolating themselves. The phrase 'helping others' is not in their lexicon. They don't factor into the neighborly mindset you find in most rural areas. But they don't concern us either."

"What should concern us," Secretary Beck said, "is the fringe element that has a history of making trouble for the government."

"You're talking about militias," Wheeler said.

"Yes. Not all of these are inherently bad. A lot of them—those that are more in tune with the prepper movement for the sake of self-preparedness—don't pose a problem. In our present situation, these people are out of sight, trying to keep what they have, protecting themselves. But there are groups out there who are clearly anti-government. They're could end up fighting us. If they see an opportunity—a lack of response on our part, or worse, a complete breakdown in the federal system—they could band together."

"With that in mind," Chambers said, "I come back to what I said earlier about adhering to the Constitution. And I mean sticking to it like glue. If we meet organized resistance, you'll bring in federal agents. But your greatest asset in a fight against rogue militias or any other anti-government group are county sheriffs. They're elected officials. They have greater authority than any federal cop. If you stand with the Constitution, they'll stand with you. The same goes for the military. These are men and women sworn to protect and defend the Constitution. No matter what happens in the days and weeks ahead, we need them backing us with zero reservations."

Wheeler nodded. "We're going to have another problem, depending on how long it takes to get electricity flowing again. Banking is shut down completely. Commerce of any kind."

"People will barter, Mr. President. Trade goods for services. A traditional economy that provides what people need to survive."

"I'm talking about the federal payroll. State, municipal—everybody's out of a paying job. At least for now. How long will our military, sheriff's departments and local police stay on the job?"

"Under the circumstances, I would hope they conduct themselves as patriots."

"Easy to say, Doug, until you can't feed your family." Wheeler shook his head. "We've gone from being the world's leading economy and global superpower, to a third world country."

"Actually, most third world countries have some form of economy," Vice President Hutchens said. "We have nothing."

"We can talk about rebuilding the economy down the road," Chambers said. "Right now, we need to focus on saving lives—first, from a public safety standpoint, then food, water and sanitation. With no fuel for food distribution, how do we prevent the starvation of millions of people?"

Wheeler crossed the room and stood in front of the fireplace, immediately feeling guilty as he thought of people burning cars to stay warm. His mind struggled to put it all in perspective—the seemingly impossible problem of food, water and heat. It all boiled down to electricity and moving goods.

"Are train locomotives computerized?" he asked.

"Not the older ones," Chambers replied.

"If we can get rail transport in motion, even on a limited basis, we can move supplies. From railheads we can move freight with military cargo trucks."

"But what freight? With no production underway, the goods we have on hand will be gone in days. A week or two at most."

"Israel and Saudi Arabia," Wheeler said. "If we can get shipments of food and refined diesel and gasoline—"

"Without electricity, you can't off-load freighters in port."

Wheeler shook his head, then turned and looked out the window. Snow was blowing past the pane of glass and piling up below. In the distance, the glow from a large fire was visible, most likely a building. Then he heard the intermittent pop-pop-pop of gunfire. He closed his eyes. "We're going to need a miracle," he said quietly.

21

6:00 p.m. Mountain Standard Time
Northwest Arizona

Neil Hayes sat on the tailgate of his pickup in the gas station parking lot, talking to his son Nathan, first officer of Delta flight 322, and the captain, Christopher McAvoy. After their successful landing on Highway 93, the pilots taxied to within a quarter-mile of the White Hills Chevron, then shut down the airliner in the middle of the road. Two more passenger jets landed safely and were parked behind the Delta jet.

Now, with more than six hundred passengers and crew milling about the gas station, and close to a hundred others who abandoned their cars stalled on the highway, the gas station was a hub of activity in the area. Generators were humming behind the station and in the small community across the highway.

Neil, Nathan and Christopher had been discussing the plight of the passengers—arranging some kind of transportation for them, and more immediately, what they would eat—when the drivers of the two semis that blocked the highway for the landings threaded their way through the crowd toward Neil's pickup. Neil stood as they approached. "I didn't get a chance to thank you guys for helping these planes land safely," he said, shaking their hands.

"Glad to help," one of the drivers said.

The other smiled and nodded at the pilots. "I felt like I could reach up and touch the belly of that jet when it came in overhead. That was really something."

Christopher stood and extended his hand. "Everyone on those planes—passengers and crew—owe you a debt of gratitude." He and Nathan shook hands with the drivers.

"I'm just glad you all got down in one piece," the driver replied. "Scares me to think what we'd be doing right now . . ." He left the thought hanging.

"You're not alone."

"So, here's the deal." The driver pointed over his shoulder. "We were talking to a few guys who live across the highway. They've got a couple of huge grills they use for outdoor events. They were talking about bringing them over and cooking up a meal for these folks."

"What have they got to cook?" Neil asked.

The driver smiled. "I'm hauling thirty-six thousand pounds of refrigerated beef—not that I'm giving up the whole load, but I'd donate enough to feed this crowd." He nodded at the other driver. "He's carrying produce and canned goods. Groceries."

"So how do you guys feel about a tailgate party?" Neil asked.

Nathan, Christopher, and the truck drivers nodded. "Sounds about right," Nathan smiled.

An hour later, residents of the White Hills area were manning six grills set up in the station parking lot. Others were setting banquet tables with chips, dips and salsas, salads, veggies, soft drinks and beer, and a mountain of grilled beef with barbecue sauce. A generator in back of the station supplied power to the canopy lights. A stereo played music.

There was a festival atmosphere among the people—airline passengers and crews, motorists, and residents of the area who turned out in force to help feed the people stranded by the EMP, now numbering close to a thousand.

"This is amazing, Dad," Nathan said.

Neil smiled. "This is the biggest party White Hills has ever seen. They're loving it."

Just then, the transceiver clipped to his belt broke squelch. "K7AZK, this is KG7DBD," a voice called.

Neil smiled. "Sounds like they got the repeater fired up." He keyed the mic, then spoke. "This is K7AZK. How's it going, Carl?"

"Equipment made it through okay, thanks to a phone call from your better half. We're hot and talking to a dozen radios in town."

"Pays to have an old transmitter, eh?"

"Vacuum tubes all the way."

"You've got full power?"

"Roger that. One hundred-mile radius."

"Any other repeaters running that you know of?"

"I've tried everybody in this end of the state. Nothing so far, but I'm still calling. I just wanted to touch base with you."

Neil nodded. "I appreciate the call. Any word from Nancy?"

"No, but she's probably busy unwrapping aluminum foil." Carl paused. "What's Nathan's status?"

"Safe. On the ground. Passengers and crew are fine, other than being stranded in the middle of the desert."

"I don't imagine they want to hang around very long."

"We're feeding them. A couple of truckers helped us block the highway for the landing. They're hauling beef and assorted groceries. We're having barbecue in the parking lot of the Chevron on 93."

"Save me some brisket. I'll be right down."

Neil chuckled. "Copy that, buddy."

"Stay in touch."

"Will do. K7AZK out."

"KG7DBD out."

"The radio guy on the mountain?" Nathan asked.

"Carl Ferguson."

Nathan nodded, then pointed at Neil's transceiver. "How did you manage to save that?"

Neil smiled. "I stuck it in the store's microwave."

"The oven?"

"Yeah. This, the ham radio under the dash and the CD player."

"You cooked them?"

Neil laughed. "No. The oven is shielded. It has to be to keep high frequency waves from affecting things outside the oven—pacemakers, stuff like that. The same shielding that keeps those frequencies from getting out, keeps frequencies like those in an EMP from getting in. But you have to unplug the oven from the electrical outlet. Otherwise it's acts like an antenna to the oven's chassis."

Nathan stared at him. "Some day when I get my degree in dad hacks, you can run this by me again."

Neil laughed. "Dad hacks. That's funny. Didn't you ever put a cell phone in a microwave and dial it with another phone?"

"Why would I?"

"To see if it would ring."

"Uh, no."

"Never mind. We're good. You guys got down in one piece, saved a lot of people. That's all that matters."

"Does it ring?"

"Nope. Signal can't get through the oven's shielding."

The two of them sat on the tailgate, eating barbecue beef and potato salad, watching people talking, laughing, sharing food and stories as the locals made perfect strangers feel right at home.

"Watching this," Nathan said, "all these people together, it makes me feel good."

"Me too, son," Neil smiled. "If other people can show strangers the same kind of compassion and generosity . . ." he looked around the parking lot, "we just might make it through this."

"Are you worried, Dad?"

Neil thought for a moment. "It's going to be a rough ride for sure. Not so much for people who live in rural areas like this. But the cities? No food or water—same as us, but most city people don't know how to grow anything. They don't hunt or fish. They'll starve. But their biggest problem is they can't get out. They're trapped. They can't pick up the phone and dial 911, and they're going to need help like they've never needed it before."

Nathan thought about that for a minute as he and his father sat in silence. He tried to imagine what things would be like, especially in big cities. His next thought was of his sister living near Baltimore. He turned to Neil. "I never asked if you heard anything from Naomi," he said. "With everything going on here—"

"It's understandable. Easy to get distracted. She texted me right after you guys touched down. Didn't say much other than she's coming home, and bringing a couple of friends."

"Do you know who they are?"

"I think they might be people she works with."

"Did she say anything else?"

"That she would monitor the ham radio frequencies." Neil looked at Nathan. "She'll be all right."

"I hope so." He paused. "I miss her, Dad."

"I do too, son."

22

8:45 p.m. Eastern Standard Time
National Security Agency
Fort Meade, Maryland

Naomi Hendricks, Scott Winter and Paul Lundgren stood in the NSA parking lot, looking up at the building. "I've never seen this place so dark," Hendricks said. Few windows were illuminated on the south side of the building. Those that were drew power from the facility's generators.

Lundgren pointed east to the suburbs, then north toward Baltimore. "It's spooky," he said. "More than a million people out there, and it's pitch black."

Hendricks nodded. "Time to get out of Dodge."

Lundgren and Winter tried starting their cars just to satisfy their curiosity. Winter's was completely dead. Lundgren got dashboard indicator lights, all of them flickering, but the car wouldn't start. Hendricks' F250 started and ran without any problem. She unwrapped the radios and replaced them in the dashboard, connecting power cables and antennas. Then she unwrapped her smartphone. It powered up, and while cell service was no longer up, the apps were operable. She closed up the back of the truck, then stood with Winter and Lundgren and took one last look at the building.

"It's been real," she said.

"As real as it gets," Winter added. Lundgren waved at the building, then the three of them climbed in and drove away.

From the NSA parking lot, they took Dennis Road to Canine, then caught Highway 32 and headed northwest, weaving through hundreds of cars stalled on the road. "This is worse than I thought it would be," Hendricks said.

"You weren't thinking we'd just breeze out of town, were you?" Winter asked.

"No. But I wasn't expecting to see every car registered in Maryland sitting in the middle of the road." They continued for another mile, then stopped short of the Highway 1 interchange, facing a massive pileup of cars. Hendricks flipped on the driving lights, bathing the scene in bright light.

"Wow," Lundgren said.

Winter shook his head. "This is like a scene out of a movie."

More than a hundred cars had crashed, most of them badly damaged, and the road was littered with broken glass, side mirrors and plastic bumpers. Hendricks picked her way through debris for a quarter-mile, then stopped. "I was afraid of this," she said. The road was blocked with wreckage—four cars tangled up on the right and a single car sitting across the left lane.

"Go back and take side streets?" Winter suggested.

"Hang on," Hendricks replied. She got out of the truck and grabbed a four-cell LED Maglite from behind the seat, then crossed the road to the car in the left lane and climbed on top of it. She shined the light down the road, trying to see if she could get through. A minute later she returned to the truck.

"The road doesn't look like it's blocked up ahead," she said. "We just need to move that car."

"How do you propose we do that?" Lundgren asked.

Hendricks smiled. "Drag it with the winch."

It took her just five minutes to pull the cable across the road, wrap it around the rear axle of the car, then engage the winch and drag the car out of the way. She climbed back into the cab and smiled at Winter and Lundgren. "Nothing to it."

Winter nodded. "This is going to be an interesting trip."

"I hope it stays at interesting," Hendricks replied.

"What else would it be?"

"Dangerous."

"Define dangerous."

"Dying at the hands of strangers."

Progress was slowed by two more pileups—at the I-95 interchange and the Highway 29 junction—neither of which blocked the road completely. After Highway 29 the number of stalled cars dwindled, and by Clarksville the left lane was unobstructed for the most part. At West Friendship they got on Interstate 70 westbound. Driving up the on-ramp, Hendricks checked her watch. The twenty-five miles from Fort Meade had taken an hour and fifteen minutes.

On I-70 they made good time, crossing into Pennsylvania at 10:45. Ten minutes later Hendricks pulled to the side of the road. "I need coffee," she said. She opened up the back, pulled out a parka and slipped it on, then pulled a blackened Coleman percolator and a propane burner from a box and set them on the tailgate. Two minutes later the coffee was perking, and the three of them stood together, bundled up against the cold.

"You know, Naomi, you're different than I expected," Winter said. "I mean, all I know about you is the way you are at work."

"I was thinking the same thing," she replied. "Not about expectations, but the fact that we've worked together as long as we have, and we really don't know each other."

Lundgren nodded. "All we ever talked about—other than what we were working on—was the news. Politics, global tension, war."

"It wears on you, doesn't it?" She set three travel mugs on the tailgate, then poured coffee. "I hope you guys don't need cream, because I don't have any. And the sugar is packed away pretty deep. I'm not going to dig for it."

"Wow," Winter said, sipping the black blend. "This is definitely not Starbucks."

"I know," Hendricks nodded. "This is good."

"No, this is crazy coffee."

They drank in silence for a few minutes, staring out into the darkness, looking for a single light anywhere. Lundgren set his cup on the tailgate. "Refill?" Hendricks asked.

Lundgren shook his head. "This should be a controlled substance, Naomi."

"Really? You guys think this is strong?"

"I feel like running through a wall."

"I drink this every morning."

Winter and Lundgren looked at each other, then laughed. "What."

Lundgren shrugged. "All this time we thought you were just hyperactive."

"Impulsive," Winter added. "Prone to delusional—"

Hendricks held up a hand. "Do you guys feel like walking?"

Lundgren laughed. "Actually, I feel like sprinting."

Three cups later, Hendricks was supercharged. It was all she could do to maintain a sane speed. But the truck was carrying a heavy load, and it was nighttime on a highway littered with stalled cars. She stayed in the left lane, then set the cruise control on seventy and forced herself to keep her foot away from the accelerator. Then the three of them talked.

"I never thanked you, Paul," Hendricks said, "for helping me back in the parking lot."

"When the power went out?" Lundgren asked.

"Yeah."

"What did I do?"

"You sat down next to me. You didn't try to comfort me. You didn't talk. You just sat with me." She paused. "You were just you."

Lundgren nodded. "Truthfully, that wasn't me. I'm a nerd. When it comes to interacting with people, I'm introverted, socially awkward . . . pretty much inept."

"You don't strike me that way."

"When I'm around you and Scott, I'm different. I'm comfortable. Working in Rampart is probably the best thing that ever happened to me as far as opening up. But when I'm somewhere else, around other people, I'm a nerd."

"Really."

"He's a nerd," Winter said.

What does that make you?"

"A geek."

"There's a difference?"

"Geeks are pretentious, long-winded on analytics—owing to the fact that we know everything. Addicted to gaming."

"How is that different from a nerd?"

"Nerds go to Space Camp," Lundgren replied.

Hendricks' first impulse was to laugh—it was funny. But she didn't want to hurt Lundgren's feelings. "He's serious," Winter said. "Nerds go to Space Camp." He paused. "After Space Camp, though, he was offered a professorship at Harvard."

"I was twenty-eight," Lundgren said. "I would have been the youngest person ever to fill the position."

"Wow," Hendricks said.

"Scott passed on a slot at MIT."

"Why would you guys take the NSA over that?"

Winter and Lundgren exchanged glances, then smiled. "NSA is the pinnacle of problem-solving," Winter said. "Threats to national security. It doesn't get any better than that."

Lundgren nodded. "And everybody hates us, which makes it totally cool."

"No dress code," Hendricks added. "At least in DEFSMAC."

Lundgren sighed. "I'm going to miss it."

"Me too."

"I'm trying to figure out what we'll do now," Winter said.

"Adapt."

"That's easy to say. But when I think about it, my mind draws a blank. Adapt to what?"

"Becoming a trapper," Lundgren said. "Or a blacksmith."

"Interesting you'd mention those, Paul. They were second and third on my list of majors in college."

"Hey, I'm just saying."

"Truth is," Hendricks said, "either one of those—trapping or blacksmithing—will end up being a lucrative trade before long." She paused. "Being good with hand tools, building things, growing vegetables, bathroom surgery—"

"Bathroom surgery?" Winter said. He laughed. "Where did that come from?"

"Well, not necessarily in the bathroom, but yes, the skills to cut someone open, remove what's bad and sew them shut."

"That's insane."

"Okay, what if." She paused. "What if tonight, tomorrow, maybe next week, you fall and break a leg? Or you cut yourself—a serious laceration. You're bleeding like crazy. Or you get shot."

"Naomi." Winter held up his hand.

"Do you know CPR? Could you set a fracture without an x-ray to look at?"

"No, and no."

"Ever cut down a tree with an ax? Field dress an elk?"

"I don't even know what that second one means."

"It's a whole new ball game, Scott. Everything we're used to—sitting behind a computer, analyzing data—it's not going to mean much now. About the only thing we did that we'll still be doing is threat assessment."

Lundgren turned and looked at her. "Threat assessment."

"Once people figure out the power isn't coming back on, and they realize that what they have in their cupboards is all there is, they'll get desperate. And desperate people have a nasty habit of doing desperate things."

"What does that mean out here? Out on the highway."

"People stopping you on the road and ripping you off. Taking everything you have. If you're lucky, they don't kill you."

On that note, conversation tapered off. Just outside of New Stanton, Hendricks stopped to stretch her legs, brew another batch of superman and pull some food out of the back. The three of them stood in the middle of the highway, looking around. The clouds had broken, and the sky was dark.

"Wow," Lundgren said. "Look at all the stars."

"We're in the middle of nowhere," Winter said. "Not that there would be any light from cities tonight."

"The sky where my parents live is jet black," Hendricks said. "The elevation is higher. The air's thinner. When your eyes adjust to the darkness, it's wall-to-wall stars." She walked to the back of the truck and opened it, then set up the burner and percolator.

"I'll take mine medium-rare if that's all right," Winter smiled, pulling on a coat.

"Lightweight," Hendricks replied.

"Hey, that last batch aged me twenty years."

Ten minutes later, they were sitting on the tailgate, sipping coffee and eating a sandwich. "What do you think it's like back home?" Lundgren asked.

Hendricks shrugged. "It's early. I think if you didn't see Wheeler's address to the nation before the EMP hit, you're probably thinking it's a power outage that'll be over soon."

"And if you saw the address?"

"You're busy trashing the city," Winter said. "The suburbs—Fort Meade, Laurel—they're probably quiet. But I'll bet they're setting cars on fire in Baltimore."

They ate in silence for another minute, then closed up the back. Hendricks had just poured the last of the coffee into her mug when the glow of lights appeared over a rise in the road behind them.

"Okay," she said, "we're not alone." She took her coffee cup to the cab, then returned, slipping a handgun into her coat pocket. Fifteen seconds later a pickup truck pulled up and stopped. The driver rolled down the window.

"You guys all right?" he asked.

"We're good," Hendricks replied. Her hands were in her pockets, her right hand holding the gun. "Thanks for asking."

The driver nodded, looking them over. He looked down the road ahead, then in his rearview mirror. Hendricks gripped the gun, her thumb on the safety. She was seconds away from pulling it out and telling the guy to beat it when he turned back to them. "Stay safe."

"Thanks." Hendricks waved as he pulled away. She watched the taillights disappear ahead of them. "I think we dodged a bullet. He was sizing us up, trying to decide who would win in a fight."

Winter looked down the road, then turned back to Hendricks. "You're set on this idea that someone's going to do us in."

"I think someone will try."

"And if they do, what's your plan?"

She pulled the gun from her pocket and held it up. Lundgren turned and walked to the cab of the truck. Winter followed. Thirty seconds later, Hendricks climbed in and closed her door. She stared through the windshield at the taillights in the distance, thinking. She wanted to ask Winter and Lundgren if either of them had ever fired a gun. But Lundgren's response when she showed him the pistol told her now was not the time. Still, she knew the chances of making it all the way to Arizona without being waylaid were nonexistent. It would happen, and when it did, she didn't want to be the only one armed. She would need help.

Hendricks stared ahead at the tail lights, now five miles down the road. A minute later, they disappeared altogether. She set the gun on the dashboard in front of her, then slipped the truck in gear and pulled away.

23

Tuesday, February 11
Interstate 70
Ohio

I t was just past midnight when Hendricks, Lundgren and Winter crossed into Ohio. The temperature was dropping and fog from the Ohio River shrouded the highway. Hendricks switched off the driving lights and slowed to fifty.

"With temperatures this low," she said, "and moisture in the air, we need to watch out for black ice."

"Murphy's Law," Winter replied. "I think we can plan on it tagging along the entire trip."

Five miles down the road the fog lifted. Hendricks switched on the auxiliary lights, then checked her side mirrors. A moment later she saw headlights about a half-mile behind. She watched for a few seconds, then saw a flashing red light. "No way," she said.

Winter leaned forward and checked his mirror. "Police?"

"Not tonight." The headlights behind her flashed.

"What's going on?" Winter asked.

"This isn't a cop," Hendricks replied, lifting her foot from the accelerator.

"You're stopping?" Lundgren said.

"I'm not going to get in a high-speed chase with whoever this is. We wreck the truck, it's over for us." She checked her mirror again as she slowed. "Scott, listen carefully. There's a pump shotgun behind the seat. It's loaded. When we stop, I'm going to get out and walk to the back of the truck. I want you to take the shotgun and get out your door as quietly as you can—don't shut it—then walk to the back. Stay next to the truck for cover, but in such a way that you can see what's happening. When I say now, rack the pump action. You know how to do that, right?"

"I think so."

"Keep your finger off the trigger unless I tell you to shoot."

"Please don't tell me to shoot, Naomi."

"Scott, if I say shoot, you point the shotgun at his chest and pull the trigger."

"Jesus," Winter whispered.

Hendricks stopped the truck in the middle of the lane, put it in neutral, then set the parking brake and left the engine running. She slipped her handgun inside her waistband in back, then pulled a small LED flashlight out of the glove box.

"Nobody talk," she said, opening her door. "Paul, lie down on the seat."

"Why?" Lundgren asked.

"If a stray bullet comes through the camper shell, I don't want it going through your head."

She climbed out of the truck and left the door open, then walked slowly to the rear. Halfway back she could see it was a pickup truck with a magnetic red light stuck to the roof. She held the flashlight in her left hand. With her right, she reached behind her for the gun.

"Hands where I can see them," a man's voice spoke. She heard a revolver being cocked.

She stopped, drew a slow breath, then started to raise her hands. "You're not going to like how this turns out," she said.

"We'll see about that," the man replied. He stood in front of his pickup, pointing the gun at her. "Open the back of the truck."

Hendricks took two slow steps backward, hands in front of her, keeping her eyes focused on his. Then she pointed the flashlight at his face and turned it on, blinding him momentarily. "Now, Scott," she said, pulling the gun from her waistband. The unmistakable sound of a shotgun chambering a round was followed by her quiet voice. "You're outnumbered. Drop the gun."

The man stood motionless. "Or what?"

Hendricks fired a shot past his left ear, through the windshield of his truck. "The next one's in your head."

He bent over slowly and set the gun on the pavement, then straightened up, hands in the air. Hendricks moved forward, training her gun on the man's head. "Scott, if he moves, shoot him." She picked up the revolver and opened the cylinder, then closed it and slipped the gun in her coat pocket. "Are you alone?"

"Yes," the man said.

She shined the light through the windshield, then moved to the driver's door. Raising her gun, she opened it and stepped back. The cab was empty. On the seat were two boxes of ammunition. She slipped them in her pocket, then looked in the bed of the truck. It was full of gas cans, a siphon hose and storage crates.

"You're stopping people and robbing them."

"Yes."

She walked back to the front of the truck and stood in front him, then pressed the barrel of the gun against the side of his head. "You remember when I said you're not going to like how this turns out?"

"Yes."

She stared at him for a moment, nodding slowly. Then in one fluid movement, she spun him around and shoved him face down over the front of the truck and fired three bullets past his head through the hood. "That's for pointing a gun at me," she said, stepping back. The man remained face down on the hood, trembling as Hendricks turned to Winter and reached for the shotgun. Pointing it at the grille, she fired a round of double-aught buckshot through the radiator. "That's for highway robbery."

Steam billowed from the front of the pickup as hot coolant poured onto the pavement. Winter stared, speechless, eyes wide, his heart pounding. Hendricks studied him for a moment, then offered him the shotgun. "Want to put one through the windshield?" He shook his head slowly. "Are you sure? It feels good." He stared at her in silence. "All right then," she said. "Let's get out of here."

Training the shotgun on the man, she backed up until she was next to the door of her truck, then looked in. Lundgren was lying in a fetal position on the floor. "You okay, Paul?" He didn't answer, but slowly moved back up onto the seat. Hendricks glanced back at the man. He was still lying across the hood of his truck. She and Winter climbed in and drove away.

It was five minutes before anyone spoke. Lundgren looked at Winter for a moment, then turned to Hendricks. "Nobody died back there, did they?" he said.

"No," Hendricks replied. "The guy's deaf, but not dead." She looked across at Winter. He was staring out his side window. "You okay, Scott?"

"I need a minute," Winter replied.

"You asked for a definition of dangerous. That was it."

"You? Or the other guy?"

"Did you even see what happened?"

"I did. It was like Bonnie and Clyde without Clyde."

"I mean before I started shooting."

Winter stared out the side window in silence, struggling to process what he had witnessed on the highway, his mind in turmoil. The difficulty wasn't in the shooting. Shocking as it was to him, he knew it was a matter of self-defense. It was that Hendricks—the woman he thought he knew, the woman he worked with closely for so long—could do that, and apparently with ease. It was a side to her he couldn't have imagined existed. He was boggled.

He finally turned to Hendricks and spoke. "When you're not working, what do you do?"

"What do you mean?" she replied.

"I've worked with you for six years, and I realized back there on the highway I don't really know you. What do you do in your free time, when you're not an intelligence analyst at NSA?"

She shrugged. "I rob convenience stores. I'll stick up a bank occasionally, but that's getting harder to do without getting shot." Lundgren and Winter stared at her for a moment, then Winter shook his head and turned back to the window. "I read, Scott," she continued. "I write. I watch movies. On weekends, I go hiking. Once in a while I'll go to Rita's and shoot pool, have a few shots of tequila."

"I shoot pool," Lundgren said.

"You're probably good at it. It's trigonometry."

"Rita's is a bar?" Winter asked.

"A neighborhood pub."

Winter nodded, then gazed out the window again. "I'm just trying to get a handle on this, Naomi. I feel like a six-year-old kid watching the nature channel. It's all about cute, furry animals until you see a leopard taking down a gazelle. Things are never the same after that. You're scarred."

"I'm sorry that happened back there—"

"It's all right," he said, holding up a hand. "I'm okay. I just need time to work this out. It's just . . ." He sighed. "This Jekyll and Hyde thing threw me. I'm trying to get my bearings."

Hendricks turned and stared at him. "Jekyll and Hyde." She paused. "You guys need to come to grips with a few things. First, if you hadn't backed me up with the shotgun, Scott, there's a good chance he would have shot me, then shot you and Paul, and left all three of us dead on the side of the road. Second, unless we're lucky—and I mean win-the-lottery-three-times-in-a-row lucky—something like that, or worse, is going to happen again."

"How can you be certain of that?" Winter asked.

Hendricks shook her head. "I don't know how to get you guys to understand how dangerous this is. Paul, back at the office you said people will kill you for a bottle of water. I don't know if you really believe that, or if it was just talk, but you were right. We're driving a truck. That by itself makes us a target—we have a vehicle that runs. And the back is full of food, water and fuel. Nobody knows that, but there are people out there who will stop us—tonight, tomorrow, whenever—to get the truck and whatever might be in the back. And they will not hesitate to kill us in the process.

"Third. Whether or not you get comfortable with any of this, know that I—the mild-mannered intelligence analyst who sits at a computer and tries to figure things out—will put a gun to someone's head and pull the trigger if it means keeping us alive." She paused. "Are we on the same page?"

"Yes," Winter said.

"Paul?"

Lundgren stared at her for five seconds before speaking. "Yes," he said quietly.

"Have either of you ever fired a gun before?" she asked.

"Does *Call of Duty* count?" Winter asked.

"Seriously, Scott? A video game? No." She paused. "The first chance we get, we're going to do some shooting. I want you guys to fire the shotgun. And the pistol. You need to get used to it."

"I'm okay with that," Winter replied.

Lundgren shook his head. "I'm not."

"Paul—"

"Why in the world would I?"

"Because it might save your life!" She paused, checking her emotion. "It might save mine."

There wasn't much talk after the incident on the highway. Winter fell asleep, crashing after the adrenalin rush he'd experienced. Then Lundgren dozed off. Hendricks focused on driving, listening to music on the CD player. It began snowing in Dayton, Ohio. By Indianapolis it was a foot deep on the highway. Hendricks pressed on, slower, in four-wheel drive. At 6 a.m. she turned off I-70 onto Highway 59, five miles outside Terre Haute. Dawn was breaking.

"I need to get some rest," she said. "We're going to find someplace out of the way and pitch the tents."

"There's snow on the ground," Lundgren said.

"Yeah. Crazy what happens in February."

Pulling into Clay City, twelve miles south of the interstate, she stopped in front of a gas station and convenience store. "You hear that?" she asked, rolling down her window. "That's a generator."

She pulled into the station, then went inside. A minute later, she returned. "They've got power, and they've got gas."

"How much is it?" Winter asked. "Fifty bucks a gallon?"

"Two seventy."

Hendricks considered this stop a bonus—the containers in back were untapped. She filled the truck tanks, then checked the oil and inspected the belts and hoses. Back inside, she paid for the gas, then quizzed the clerk about the motel across the street.

"Are they open for business?" she asked.

"They are," the clerk replied. "Henry and Arvella Gardner run the place. Good people."

"Thanks."

"Enjoy your stay."

Hendricks pulled across the street into the motel parking lot. "I was thinking we might end up camping somewhere," she said, "just to get some rest. It would be nice to stay here instead."

Winter nodded. "I'll take sleeping in a bed over sleeping on the ground any day."

"Same here," Lundgren said.

It was chilly in the motel, but there were lights in the office, and a woman standing behind the counter. She sized them up for a moment, then smiled. "You kids look like you could use a good rest."

"We've been driving all night," Hendricks replied. "Are you Arvella?"

"I am. You need rooms?"

"Yes. How much?"

"Well, here's the thing. Henry—that's my husband—he says money isn't going to mean much now. He says we're going to be bartering. At least the people who live around here."

"We've got a few things to trade."

"Whatever you have, you're going to need, traveling and all." She paused, smiling. "Besides, Henry and I would love the company. There's no one else here."

"I don't understand."

"There's no charge for the rooms."

"We couldn't do that, Arvella."

"Of course you can." She slid two room keys across the counter. "Now, the motel has solar, but it's a backup, so it doesn't run everything. The first three rooms have heat and hot water, but Henry shut off the breakers for the lights. You won't need them unless you stay the night. Then he can turn them back on for you."

"Thank you so much."

"Don't mention it. Now you kids go get some rest. When you get up, I'll cook breakfast for you."

Hendricks, Lundgren and Winter left the office and stood out front. There was traffic in the street—a dozen pickups and older cars. A truck was plowing snow. Down the street, a hardware store and a diner were lighted and open for business. Apart from the sound of generators, it could have been a normal morning in a small town.

"Maybe they didn't get the memo," Winter said.

Hendricks nodded. "Interesting."

They moved a few things out of the truck, locked it up, then retired to their rooms. As tired as she was, Hendricks was tempted to plop down on the bed and sleep in her clothes. But she undressed, then slipped under the covers. "Thank you, Arvella," she whispered. Then she was out.

24

1:10 p.m. Central Standard Time
Clay City, Indiana

Hendricks awoke at one in the afternoon, took a five-minute shower, then dressed and left her room. There was no response when she knocked on the door next to hers. She stood outside for a moment, looking down Clay City's main street. The snow storm had passed, and the sky was a brilliant blue. A foot of new snow lay on the ground.

"Nice day," she said. "I can use that." Entering the office, she heard conversation in a room to her right. She walked in to see Lundgren and Winter seated at a table with a man in his eighties.

"You must be Naomi," he smiled, standing.

"And you must be Henry," she nodded.

"Pleased to make your acquaintance. Your friends here tell me you had quite an adventure last night."

Hendricks smiled, glancing at Winter and Lundgren. "I was hoping we could keep that a secret."

"Oh, I wouldn't fuss over that if I were you," Henry said, taking his seat. "From the way these boys tell it, I'd say you're a good person to have around in a pinch."

"I don't know. I'd like to increase the odds in our favor. Is there somewhere we can do some shooting later on? A little practice?"

"Anywhere outside of town."

"No target range?"

"No. But there's a spot not far from here. It's wide open and flat. No wind today. Good time to shoot."

"Could you tell us how to get there?"

"If you don't mind me tagging along, I'll show you."

Arvella came in with two plates and set them in front of Lundgren and Winter. "You sleep all right?" she smiled at Hendricks.

"Best sleep I've had in a long time. Thank you again."

"You're welcome. I hope you're hungry."

"I am."

"I'll be right back."

Hendricks turned to Henry as Arvella left the room. "She's a sweetheart."

"One of a kind," he smiled. "Been together sixty-three years."

"Wow."

Winter glanced at Lundgren, eyebrows raised. "Sixty-three years," he mouthed silently.

Arvella returned with two more plates and coffee. She set them on the table, then sat. "So, you kids work for the NSA?"

"We did until last night," Winter said. "There wasn't much for us to do after the EMP hit."

Arvella and Henry were fascinated with talk of DEFSMAC and the discovery of the Iranian satellite, of the electromagnetic pulse and what it had done. When the topic turned to the bombing over Russia and the destruction of Iran and North Korea, Henry pointed a finger at Hendricks.

"That was bound to happen," he said. "Anyone who thinks it wasn't going to come to war with North Korea hasn't been paying attention. You can try and reason only so long." He nodded. "My guess is that politicians in Washington are a lot smarter today than they were yesterday."

"That assumes they've got the brainpower to process everything that happened," Lundgren said.

"I'll grant you that. But there are a few who can think. Their problem is going against the flow. It's lonely being the only one standing when everyone around you is sitting down."

Ninety minutes later, Hendricks, Winter and Lundgren stood with Henry at the edge of a two hundred-acre flat, three miles south of Clay City. With the blade on the front of his pickup, Henry cleared the snow from an area roughly fifty feet square, then set up three steel targets twenty-five feet away from the trucks.

"That's not very far," Winter said.

"We're starting with a pistol," Hendricks replied. "As firearms go, it's not a terribly accurate weapon." She pulled her 9-millimeter semiautomatic from her holster, then turned to face the targets and held the pistol in a grip for shooting, aiming toward the target. "Any movement in the wrist, no matter how small, moves the barrel of the gun, which moves the point at which the bullet will impact." She flexed her wrist to demonstrate the movement in the pistol. "If I move my wrist a quarter-inch—which isn't much—the end of the barrel twelve inches away will move one inch. Paul, how far off am I at twenty-five feet?"

"Twenty-five inches," Paul replied.

"Keep your wrist as rigid as you can when you shoot, and know that a handgun's range of accuracy—when adrenaline is pumping, and your heart is pounding—is no more than twenty-five feet. That's for the average shooter, not a marksman."

She walked back to the truck and picked up the shotgun. "There are a lot of fancy weapons out there, but when it comes to self-defense, nothing beats a pump shotgun. Loaded with double-aught buckshot, each pull of the trigger fires nine thirty-caliber pellets. Nothing short of a machine gun beats it, and against multiple attackers, it's a mowing machine.

"Finally, the rifle. If you have an attacker or attackers moving in on your position, and you can see them from a distance, it's your best bet. Take them out before they get close enough to kill you. Depending on how it's set up—the scope attached to it and the ammunition you're using—and the skill of the shooter, a bolt-action rifle is accurate to a thousand yards or more. That's over a half-mile."

Hendricks laid the shotgun on the tailgate and turned back to Winter and Lundgren. "Before we get started, a word about why we're doing this. Last night was a glimpse of what I think is ahead of us. I said it then and I'll say it again—we haven't seen the last of the bad guys, people who will kill us and take everything we have. I wish things were different, that this was just a road trip, three friends having fun. But here we are." She paused. "Get it through your heads that when someone points a gun at you, you'll die unless you kill them first. That's a horrible situation, but again, here we are.

"These are self-defense rules. Burn them into your brain. Number one—don't pull a gun unless you intend to fire it. Number two—don't fire it unless you intend to kill. There is no wounding to stop the bad guy. No warning shot. You shoot to kill, or you leave weapons alone. It's that simple. And on that note, understand that you don't have to do this. Paul, you've got reservations. I respect that. If you don't want to train with guns, don't. You too, Scott. But I meant what I said last night. Our lives will likely depend on knowing how to shoot these weapons, and shoot them effectively. That means fast and accurate. So, who's with me?"

"I am." Winter held up his hand.

Lundgren nodded slowly. "Me too."

Hendricks nodded. "I'll say thank you now, and again when you save my life." She put the 9-millimeter in her holster, then walked to the firing line and turned to face them. "Say when."

"When," Winter said.

Hendricks spun to her left, drawing the pistol and dropping to one knee as she turned, then fired six shots in three seconds, striking each target twice."

Henry nodded. "You've done this before."

"Many times," she replied. "And by the way guys, this—" she held up the pistol, "—is not just for killing bad guys. I love target shooting. It's fun. I do it a lot."

"Why did you kneel?" Lundgren asked.

"I'm moving my attacker's target. He has to change his point of aim while I'm getting ready to fire. Fractions of seconds count, and if I can slow him down a few tenths of a second, it gives me an advantage. But if dropping to a knee is going to slow you down on the trigger, don't do it. I can, because I practice."

She picked up an extra magazine, then returned to the firing line. "Nothing worse in a gunfight than an empty gun." She walked twenty-five feet to one side, then faced the targets and started shooting, moving across to the other side as she fired. The steel targets rang with each strike, a rapid ding-ding, ding-ding. When the magazine was empty, she ejected it and slid another one in, then released the slide and continued firing until the second one was empty, continually moving, left to right and back again, getting off twenty-eight shots in roughly eighteen seconds.

"Three things," she said, walking back to the truck. "First, moving and shooting. If you can move while you shoot, you're harder to hit. The other guy has to follow you while he's aiming. Second, rapid fire keeps the bad guy busy ducking behind cover. If you've got the ammo, put up a barrage. But know how to reload quickly—like, three seconds. Finally, not one of those shots was aimed. It's called point shooting. With practice, the handgun becomes an extension of your arm. You point it and shoot, just like lifting your arm and pointing your finger. It's much faster than aiming, and, like I said a minute ago, split-seconds count."

She paused, reloading the magazines from a box of ammo on the tailgate, then stood in front of Winter and Lundgren. "That's the basics of combat pistol shooting. I know it's a lot. We'll go through it again when you're behind the trigger. Paul, you want to go first?"

Lundgren glanced at Winter. "I guess."

"You're thrilled. Look at it this way, ten minutes from now, you'll wonder what the big deal was."

Winter chuckled. "That, or he'll never speak to you again."

"Thank you, Scott. Your turn is coming."

Lundgren sighed, then stepped to the firing line and stood next to Hendricks. "It's loud," she said. "The gun kicks a little. It can be a little unnerving until you get used to it."

Lundgren nodded. "Just tell me how it works."

"This is the safety. Up is on, down is off. Hold the gun firmly—like this—but not in a death grip. Place your other hand underneath, cupping the butt of the gun in your palm. Arms straight, elbows locked. Don't move your wrist. If you need to turn, pivot at your waist." She handed the gun to him. "Very important—keep the gun pointed down until you're ready to shoot, and keep your finger off the trigger until you're ready to pull it."

"How do I aim?"

She pointed at the front and rear sights. "Put the front dot between the two rear dots, then center them on your target."

Lundgren faced the targets and raised the gun, then closed his eyes and fired. The shot was deafening. He lowered the pistol, shaking his head. "My ears are ringing."

"Did you close your eyes?" Hendricks asked.

"Sort of," Lundgren replied.

"That doesn't help. Try it again."

Lundgren raised the gun and fired. Another miss.

"Move closer to the targets," Hendricks said. "And squeeze the trigger. Don't jerk it."

Lundgren moved five feet forward and fired again, missing again. Another five feet forward. Another shot and a miss. "Is this working right?" he asked, turning around.

Hendricks walked out and stood next to him, but slightly behind. "Shoot again." He did, and missed. "You're moving your wrist," she said. "Keep it rigid." She gripped his wrist and squeezed.

"I'm trying!"

"Paul. Listen. Close your eyes. Relax."

He looked at her. "Relax? Sure."

"Paul. Close your eyes." She paused, watching him. "Relax. Clear your mind." Another pause. "What do you hear?"

"You talking."

"What else?"

"Nothing."

"Picture the target in your mind—a big, square piece of steel, fifteen feet in front of you." He nodded. "When you're ready," she continued, "open your eyes and point at the target." Ten seconds later, he drew a slow breath and exhaled, then opened his eyes and raised the gun. "Pull the trigger," she said. He did, and the steel rang with the bullet strike. He turned and smiled at Hendricks. "Now shoot some steel," she said.

Lundgren faced the targets and paused, breathing. He raised the gun and started firing, first at the right-side target, then the left, and finally the middle, the steel ringing with each shot. "Piece of cake, once you get the hang of it," he nodded. He held up the gun with the slide locked open. "But I'm out." Hendricks stood next to him and showed him how to change magazines.

"Now you do it," she said.

Lundgren released the spent magazine and slid the fresh one in, then released the slide. He brought the pistol up and started firing with a sense of purpose, moving and shooting, hitting the steel with each shot. He pointed at a rock five feet beyond the targets and fired, hitting it. Then another rock. And another. "You're right," he said, walking back to the truck. "This is fun."

Hendricks smiled, reloading the magazines. She turned to Winter. "You ready?" He nodded, taking the gun and slipping the extra magazine into his coat pocket, then turned to face the targets. Raising the gun, he fired, hitting the middle target. Then he walked from left to right, firing until the magazine was empty, the steel ringing with each shot. When the slide locked open, he swapped magazines, then continued shooting, moving back and forth as he fired, hitting the steel every time.

Lundgren shook his head. "What the—"

"*Call of Duty*," Winter smiled, walking back to the truck.

"You were serious about that?" Hendricks said.

"Yeah."

"You've never fired a real gun."

"Nope."

"I wouldn't believe it if I hadn't seen it."

Over the next hour, they shot another five hundred rounds, and by the end of the pistol session, both Lundgren and Winter were showing remarkable proficiency in accuracy, point shooting, and lightning-fast magazine swaps.

They moved on to the shotgun, a weapon for which Lundgren quickly developed a liking. Henry had set up three empty paint buckets on top of the steel targets, and Lundgren managed to keep one flying through the air for three consecutive shots.

"Not bad for buckshot," Henry said.

Lundgren smiled. "This thing's a blast." Then he promptly burned his hand on the barrel.

"Friction," Hendricks said. "That much lead screaming down the barrel is going to warm things up."

"Note to self," Lundgren replied. "Let things cool off."

The sun was low in the sky when Hendricks pulled a black canvas bag from the back of the pickup and unzipped it, pulling out a high-powered rifle. "This is for long-distance calls," she said. "Composite stock, glass-bedded action, long-range scope."

"May I?" Henry asked. He turned toward the far end of the field and shouldered the rifle, sighting through the scope. "That is a thing of beauty," he smiled, handing it back to Hendricks.

"And you can hit a target a thousand yards away," Winter said.

"Yes. I don't mean everybody can, but I can."

Hendricks fired three shots at two hundred yards to check the scope's zero, then pulled a range finder from her bag and looked through it, scanning the far end of the field. "There's a rock about three feet in diameter just this side of that line of trees," she said. "It's nine hundred seventy yards away." She pulled binoculars from the bag and handed them to Henry.

"I see it," he said. "You won't hear steel from that distance, but I've got something better." He pulled three half-gallon plastic containers from the back of his truck and set them on the tailgate, then unscrewed the lids. "Ammonium nitrate and aluminum powder."

Winter looked at Lundgren. "That's what they use to blow up federal buildings," he said.

Henry smiled. "This is a much smaller, more manageable form. When Naomi said she wanted to do a little target shooting, I brought this along. Thought it might liven things up a bit."

Hendricks nodded. "If you like *Call of Duty*, Scott, you're going to love this."

"I can't hit anything at a thousand yards."

"I'll take the first shot, then we'll move it in to five hundred."

"Five hundred is still a long way off."

"Something tells me you'll be good at this."

Henry drove to the end of the field and placed the plastic bottle on top of the rock, then returned. Hendricks unfolded a tarp on the ground, then set up the rifle on a bipod. She handed Henry the binoculars. "Spot for me?"

"Sure." Henry held the binoculars as Hendricks pulled a smartphone from her coat pocket. She opened a ballistics app and tapped the screen a few times.

"It looks like we still have GPS satellites," she said. "Elevation is five hundred sixty-three feet. Temperature . . . I'm guessing around thirty." She entered the bullet weight, velocity and distance to target, then looked at Henry. "Three hundred fifty-three inches of drop."

"That's a fair bit of arc," he replied.

"A fair bit of arc?" Winter said. "That's thirty feet high."

"Up, over, and back down," Henry smiled.

Winter looked at Lundgren. "So, she does shoot hoops."

Hendricks settled on the tarp, her body turned at a slight angle to the target, legs spread. She dialed in thirty minutes of angle on the top turret of the scope, then rested her cheek on the stock. Holding the scope's crosshairs on the target, she exhaled slowly, then squeezed the trigger. A second later, a puff of white dust appeared in front of the rock.

"Eight inches low," Henry said.

Hendricks turned the turret three more clicks, then took aim, exhaled and squeezed the trigger. This time the jar exploded in an orange fireball twenty feet in diameter. A second later, the thunderclap of the explosion reached them.

"Holy cow!" Lundgren shouted. He and Winter stared at each other for a moment, then laughed.

"That was awesome," Winter said.

Henry turned to Hendricks, nodding. "Impressive shooting."

"Thank you," Hendricks said, kneeling on the tarp.

"I take it those are handloads."

"Dad's recipe."

"We used to say if you want accuracy, roll your own."

With the range finder they determined a five hundred-yard mark. Henry drove down and set up another jug, then returned. Hendricks had Winter lie down and settle in behind the rifle.

"Long-range precision is all about breathing," she said, "and squeezing the trigger. Find the jug in your scope, and center the crosshairs on it."

"Got it," Winter said.

"Now pull the rifle stock hard against your shoulder, and watch the jug in the scope."

"It's moving."

"With each beat of your heart."

"Yeah."

"So, relax, but hold the stock firmly in your hand."

"Got it."

Hendricks had him dry-fire the rifle to feel the trigger pull, then explained breathing—inhaling, then exhaling slowly, waiting for that moment when you're comfortable. You don't need air. "That's when you squeeze the trigger."

Winter nodded, then looked through the scope, gathering his mental focus, breathing, waiting. It took him three breaths to find his place. When he did, he squeezed the trigger. A split-second later the jug exploded in a fireball, this one close enough to feel its heat. He looked up at Hendricks. "Very cool."

"You want to try a thousand?" she asked.

"I do." He looked behind him. Lundgren nodded and gave him a thumbs up.

Five minutes later, the last jug was in place at the far end of the field, and Winter was lying prone behind the rifle. He looked through the scope for a few seconds. "That jug is really small," he said. "The crosshairs almost cover it."

"It's a target the size of a shoebox," Hendricks said, "more than a half-mile away. This is when breathing and trigger-squeeze matter."

Winter looked through the scope for another thirty seconds. He shifted his legs slightly, moved his head side to side, then rested on the stock again, breathing slowly. Ten seconds later he touched off the shot and the jug exploded in a fireball. A second later, the boom of the explosion.

Winter laughed, then got to his feet. "You were right, Naomi. I love it. And the explosion is cool, but just shooting at something that freaking far away and hitting it . . ." He nodded. "I love it."

"That rocked," Lundgren said.

"This is way better than gaming. I could do this all day."

Henry smiled. "It's fun blowing stuff up now and then."

They returned to the motel just as Arvella was pulling dinner from the oven. "You timed that just right," she said. "Everybody wash up and we'll eat."

They sat down to a meal of pot roast, mashed potatoes and gravy, and green beans. "This is delicious, Arvella," Hendricks said.

Arvella smiled. "I'm glad you like it, hon. It's nice having you kids around."

"It is," Henry agreed. "Making new friends is important."

"I noticed so many places are open for business," Hendricks said. "It's as if the blackout hasn't really affected that many people here."

"Folks around here are pretty independent. They don't like the idea of folding up because they lose electricity, or some other difficulty. Over the years we've had a few tornados blow through. People take cover. Afterward, everyone pulls together, rebuilding whatever was destroyed. This is going to last longer, but its effect on people here is pretty much the same. We buck up and stick together. We help each other."

"Generators are common in Clay City," Arvella said. "A lot of us put up solar just to help with the bills, but it comes in handy when the electricity is out altogether. You see the big water tank overhead down the street. That's the city supply. But there are a lot of wells around here too, with windmills for pumping. Every farm around here has a well, but the high school has one too, and a lot of the businesses. Water isn't a problem."

Henry nodded. "Clay City has a food cooperative. Growers put a certain amount of food in—and of course everybody around here cans and bottles food for storage—so having food isn't as big a problem as I imagine it might be in big cities."

"Think about people in big cities," Winter said. "Nobody grows their own food."

"I don't know anybody that hunts or fishes," Lundgren said. "Even a power outage that lasts a few days. Look at Hurricane Sandy. A day later, the stores are empty. People are high and dry."

"And they wait for the federal government to show up," Henry said, "with hot meals, even a bottle of water." He shook his head. "I don't know what's happening today, but my guess is the government is treading water right now along with everybody else."

"They can't do anything about this," Hendricks said. "A week from now, people will be starving. A month from now . . ."

"A month from now," Winter said, "they'll be trying to figure out where to bury the dead. And it won't be just from starvation. Disease from unsanitary conditions, bad drinking water."

Henry nodded. "The country's going to be tested. When this is over, months from now—maybe even years—it's going to be very different. The way people relate to each other, what really matters to them. It'll be interesting to see how we handle this."

The conversation moved from the dinner table to the living room where they sat in front of the fireplace with peach cobbler and coffee. After dessert, Henry left for several minutes, then returned with a half-dozen knives of different types, each one in a leather scabbard. He arranged them on the coffee table

"You made these," Hendricks said.

"It's a hobby of mine. Puts a little cash in my pocket now and then. The hardware store sells a few. Folks who want a good hunting knife will look me up."

Hendricks picked up a thirteen-inch knife with a drop-point blade made of Damascus steel, and a handle fashioned from a deer antler. "This is beautiful."

Henry nodded. "One of my favorites."

Lundgren glanced at Winter, then looked at Hendricks. "I've never heard anyone refer to a knife as being beautiful."

"Son," Henry chuckled, "you need to get out more." He picked up a wooden box. "I'm guessing you don't own a knife."

"Not outside the utensil drawer in my kitchen." He paused. "Which, of course, I left in Fort Meade."

Henry pulled out two four-inch pocket knives, both made by Case, one with a classic yellow handle. He handed it to Lundgren. "Every young man should have a good pocket knife." The other knife had an antique bone handle. He gave it to Winter. "You boys take good care of those, they'll last a long time."

Lundgren held the knife, then opened the blades. "This is the first pocket knife I've ever owned." He closed the blades, then held the knife up. "Thank you, Henry. This means a lot to me."

"Thanks, Henry," Winter smiled.

"You're welcome. Both of you." He turned to Hendricks. "That knife you're holding, I want you to have it."

"Oh, Henry," Hendricks said quietly. "This is very special."

"Something to remember us by."

Hendricks had planned on pushing on after dinner, but changed her mind. Now that they understood the dangers of the open road, Lundgren and Winter were nervous about traveling after dark. The day's target practice had instilled a fair amount of confidence in them. But if there was going to be trouble, they preferred dealing with it in daylight. "If I decide to head for the hills," Winter observed, "I want to know where they are."

"I'd like to be on the road by six," Hendricks told Arvella and Henry. "I hope we can see you in the morning to say goodbye."

"I'll have breakfast ready at five thirty," Arvella said. "Get a good night's rest. You have a long day ahead of you."

With that, Hendricks, Lundgren and Winter bid Henry and Arvella good night, then retired to their rooms for the longest rest they'd had in more than forty-eight hours.

25

4:00 p.m. Mountain Standard Time
Northwest Arizona

Neil Hayes and his son Nathan pulled away from the White Hills Chevron, driving south on Highway 93. Two hours earlier, a dozen school buses from the Clark County School District in Las Vegas arrived to ferry the airline passengers and crews to the Thomas and Mack Center where a shelter operation was underway for passengers stranded at McCarran International in Las Vegas. Nathan had stayed until the last passengers were on buses, at which time his captain, Christopher McAvoy, had released him from duty.

"If the day ever comes," McAvoy said, "I look forward to working with you again, Nathan. You're one of the best pilots I've ever flown with."

"Thanks, Mac," Nathan smiled, shaking hands.

"Neil," McAvoy said, "thanks for everything."

"Glad I could help, Captain," Neil replied. He handed McAvoy a slip of paper. "Here's how you can contact us if you need to. Or if you find yourself kicking around these parts and want to spend some time in the mountains, you're always welcome."

Now, as father and son headed home, Nathan stared out the side window, coming to grips with the way his life was in Thousand Oaks, California, and the way it would be in northern Arizona. He never cared for this area—a rocky desert cut by washes and spotted with creosote and mesquite brush. His mother and father loved what they called the 'stark beauty' of this landscape, particularly the rugged Black Mountains, and considered people who lived out here in the doublewides and otherwise code-resistant dwellings to be rough and tumble—the hardest of hard—clawing out an existence with their fingernails. As Nathan considered that, he realized they were the same kind of people who threw a banquet for the stranded passengers and crew of three airliners that dropped out of the sky into their desert. He turned and looked at his dad, realizing too that he was not much different. Neither was his mom, nor his sister.

"Does it bother you that I never got into the whole outdoors thing like Naomi did?" he asked.

"Does it bother me?" Neil replied. "No. We missed having you around for stuff like that, but I was never bothered."

"Disappointed?"

"No. Never."

Nathan turned back to the side window. "I hated sleeping on the ground."

Neil chuckled. "Fact is, I'm not crazy about sleeping on the ground. I liked it when I was a kid. Boy Scouts. Not so much these days."

"Did you like scouting?"

"I loved it. Most of what I know about being prepared, I learned in Boy Scouts. My dad filled in the gaps."

Nathan shook his head. "I always looked at Boy Scouts as a bunch of kids in archery tournaments, or paddling around in canoes."

"Helping little old ladies cross the street."

"Yeah."

"When I was twelve, our troop hiked into the Uinta mountains in northern Utah. Wilderness area. Twelve miles through seriously rugged country, carrying everything we needed for a week in the wilderness—clothes, cooking gear, fishing rod and tackle, first aid kit, tools—on our backs. We camped for a week. Cooked over a fire, bathed in an ice-cold lake, slept on the ground in tents. It rained, felt more like it ought to snow." He paused. "Never paddled a canoe. And I never shot in an archery tournament."

Nathan sighed. "I'm sorry, Dad."

"It's okay. Scouting's different these days. I'm not sure when it changed—mid '70s or early '80s. The emphasis shifted from outdoor skills to civics. I'm not sure they even teach kids how to start a fire anymore. I know they don't teach marksmanship."

"Preparing kids for a life as a military sniper."

Neil laughed. "That's funny. Anyway, yeah, the politically correct crowd, kicking and screaming until they get their way. And the kids pay the price, growing up barely knowing how to tie their shoes. The best part of scouting, at least in the '60s, was being prepared for anything that might happen, whether it was on a wilderness camping trip, or—and more to the point of scouting—anything that life might throw at you. It was cool knowing how to do that kind of stuff, reading maps and finding your way with a compass, first aid, building a shelter out of tree limbs and brush. It was survival.

"At the same time, scouting was about honor. It was about telling the truth, keeping your word and helping people. Doing your very best no matter what the circumstances." He paused. "Scouting turned young boys into men—men that young boys could look up to. Men that boys were proud to call Dad."

Nathan gazed out the side window in silence, then he turned to his father. "I feel like I let you guys down."

"How?" Neil asked.

"My lifestyle is so different from yours, even Naomi's."

"Nathan, you like jets and fast cars. I don't have a problem with that. And neither does your mother. And in case you're wondering, Naomi looks up to you. You're pretty special to her. So, do yourself a favor and don't hang on to this idea that because you're different than Naomi, or your mother and me, that somehow you're less than you ought to be. I don't care for opera, but I don't mind people who do. Life is about variety. Choices."

He paused. "I'm pretty sure I've told you this before, but in case you've forgotten, I'll repeat it. One of the proudest moments of my life—your mother's too—was when you started flying for Delta. Naomi thought that was about as neat as it gets. Being a commercial pilot. That demonstrates a discipline a lot of young people don't even dream of, let alone possess and practice. And to land that jet on the highway . . ." Neil shook his head. "Son, that puts you in a very special class with just a handful of people who can claim a 'miracle on the Hudson' moment."

"Mac was in control," Nathan replied.

"Your captain and I talked. Besides, I know a lot about flying. He couldn't have done it without you. Take that to heart and wear it with honor, Nathan. In my book, you're a hero."

Nathan looked at Neil for a moment, nodding slowly, then smiled. "Thanks, Dad."

"You're welcome. And, like it or not, you're smack dab in the middle of this family. Get used to it."

"I know. I appreciate you bringing it all home, Dad, but I didn't mean any of that to say I wasn't a part of the family. Just not plugged in all the way. But I always felt like if I got in a jam—I just couldn't figure something out—you were just a phone call away." He paused. "I can't tell you how I felt when Mac and I were dropping out of the sky with two hundred tons of airliner coming in at five hundred miles per hour, and trying to line up on a two-lane highway . . ." He looked out the side window, a lump rising in his throat, then turned back to his father, ". . . and I heard your voice on the radio."

"I know just how you felt," Neil replied. He squeezed Nathan's shoulder and smiled. "I know just how you felt."

Ten miles up the road, they were flagged down by a young man in his late teens standing next to a '76 Pontiac Bonneville—a vintage beater. Led Zeppelin's "Ramble On" was blasting from two home stereo speakers sitting on the rear window deck when Neil and Nathan pulled up and got out.

"You got any gas?" the young man asked.

"We do," Neil replied. "Where are you going?"

"Kingman."

"You live there?"

"Yeah."

Neil put five gallons in the car's tank, then twisted the cap on. "How much?" the young man asked.

"Nothing," Neil said.

"I've got some righteous weed. I'd part with a bud."

Neil smiled. "We're good."

"Right on, man. Thanks for the gas." The young man shook Neil's hand, then climbed in his car and started it.

"Some things never change," Neil said, watching the car pull away and head up the highway.

"How's that?" Nathan asked.

"That was me fifty years ago. Shoulder-length hair, two tons of Detroit steel, and a stereo that could wake the dead."

"Right on, man," Nathan smiled.

Neil laughed. "Righteous."

26

Wednesday, February 12
9:00 a.m. Eastern Standard Time
White House Situation Room
Washington, D.C.

President Wheeler sat down at the conference table in the Situation Room with Vice President Hutchens, Homeland Secretary Beck, Defense Secretary Wilkinson and Interior Secretary Chambers. The five of them had been working since six, then took a break to make a late breakfast of bacon, scrambled eggs and toast in the White House Mess, and brought it over to eat while they discussed ideas for dealing with the collapse.

The Situation Room had become Wheeler's command center, replacing the Oval Office as a meeting room. It was underground, and easier to warm. And it was next to the White House Mess, making it convenient to put together a quick meal while working. The four people who sat with him now had become his unofficial brain trust. "You're smart and you're available," Wheeler had told them when he asked them to stay on at the White House. Bob Larson, the chief of staff, had left to attend to his family, and the fact was, there wasn't much staff left. Moreover, anything Larson could do with regard to ideas, planning, or implementing strategy, could be handled by Hutchens or Chambers, leaving Beck to focus on FEMA and the crisis of food and water, and Wilkinson attending to matters concerning Russia, Iran and North Korea—three problems that Wheeler believed would rear their ugly heads.

There was still no word from the House Speaker, or any other members of Congress. Cabinet members other than Beck, Wilkinson and Chambers were also unaccounted for, a problem that didn't particularly bother Wheeler at this point other than being concerned for their safety. What he needed most was a small, lean, and trusted team of people who could call the White House home for an indefinite period of time, put up with colder-than-usual working temperatures, eat whatever they could find in the White House Mess, and, of course, do it without being paid.

"I'm fine as long as there's food, coffee, and a place to crash every once in a while," Chambers said. The others were in complete agreement, and over a period of seventy-two hours came to bond with each other in a way that was completely foreign to politicians, and even to problem-solving in general.

Wheeler poured coffee for everyone, then sat and sprinkled salt and pepper on his eggs. "Where are we with FEMA?" he asked Secretary Beck. "Last night you said they were having problems."

"There was a shooting at the Disaster Recovery Center in Detroit," Beck replied. "A man was demanding food. This was after our people announced there wasn't any more and asked everyone to go back to their homes. The man wouldn't take no for an answer. He pulled a gun. National Guard troops who were there in support of FEMA personnel told him to drop the weapon. He pointed the gun at the troops and they fired, killing him."

"Was anybody else injured?" Wheeler asked.

"No. But the remaining people, numbering more than a thousand, panicked briefly, then overran the facility, tearing it apart. Guard troops evacuated our people safely. I've instructed them not to return."

"This is not an isolated incident."

"No. There was a riot in Oakland. In Pittsburg a man drove a truck through a FEMA tent. People set fire to a facility in Seattle. And those are just the ones we've heard about. There's little communication between field operations and the top."

"And you think we should shut down the field operations."

"The food is gone, Mr. President. All we do by having FEMA personnel manning these DRCs—for no reason other than to maintain a presence—is put the lives of our people at risk."

Wheeler thought for a moment. "I guess it was fantasy to think people would maintain some sense of civility in this crisis."

"It was for inner cities," Secretary Chambers said. "I mentioned this the first night I was here. Urban areas are the most likely to fall apart, and the least likely to respond in a positive way to military and police presence. The fact that FEMA's DRCs have become a lightning rod isn't terribly surprising. People think it's the federal government's responsibility to take care of them. To feed them, give them whatever they need."

"Or want." Wheeler shook his head, then turned to Secretary Beck. "Shut it down for now, Margaret. We'll look at firing it up later on. Send your people home with our thanks for trying." He leaned forward, resting his elbows on the table and rubbing his temples with his fingertips, his eyes closed. The others watched him for a moment, then Chambers spoke.

"Implement martial law, Mr. President. I know it's the last thing you want to do. It's going to create a firestorm of resentment. Right now, we're in the early stages of urban rioting, which you would expect with a typical outage—widespread, but with pockets of service. The problem we face is this collapse is total. The power isn't coming back anytime soon, and most people out there know it. Seventy-two hours from now, anarchy will be breaking out. In two weeks, we'll be on the verge of civil war."

Wheeler stood and walked across the room, thinking about the likely response to martial law. At the same time, he knew he had no choice. He turned to his Defense secretary. "Patrick, mobilize the military. Get them on the streets. Establish a curfew."

"Yes, sir," Secretary Wilkinson replied. He consulted a list of military commands, then dialed a number on a satellite phone.

Wheeler turned to the others. "We've got to get word to the mayor. He'll need to be a part of this." He paused. "And we've got to figure out a way to communicate with people, to get the word out, whatever the word may be. Part of the problem right now is people are in the dark—and I don't mean lights. They're not hearing anything from us. For all practical purposes, there is no leadership."

"Ham radio is starting to come back up," Chambers said. "Not all operators have generator capability, but many of the repeater stations around the country do. And as they reestablish a network, we can pass the word along. It won't be a press briefing. But it'll do, as long as the people know it's coming from you, Mr. President."

Wheeler nodded. "Does anybody know if we're able to communicate on ham radio frequencies?"

"We can from the PEOC," Wilkinson said. "When we have someone to talk to, they'll hear us."

"Then let's start talking and see who's listening." He turned to Chambers. "I know this isn't your job, Doug, but you have experience with these systems."

Chambers smiled. "I suppose I didn't make this clear the other night when we were talking by the fire in the Oval Office. I'm at your disposal, Mr. President. I realize that little of what you'll be asking will have anything to do with Interior issues. But I'm here to do whatever I can."

"Thanks, Doug. I appreciate it. And I appreciate the rest of you hanging tough when you could be home with your families."

"I can only speak for myself," Vice President Hutchens said. "But I don't see that any of us have a choice. We make this work, regardless of the sacrifice. We pull this out of the fire, or else."

A moment later, Secretary Wilkinson's sat phone rang. He glanced at the display. "It's NORAD, Mr. President." He answered and listened, then put the phone on speaker. "I'm with the president, General Tuckett. The vice president is here as well, and Secretaries Beck and Chambers."

"Mr. President," Tuckett said, "Russian forces are attacking our military bases in Syria."

Wheeler set his fork on the plate. "Where exactly?"

"Al Tabaqah, in the northern part of the country, and Al Tanf, a crossing along the Jordan-Iraq-Syria borders.

"Are we responding?"

"Yes, sir. Air Force Raptors are engaging Russian aircraft. Apache helicopters, AC-130 gunships and Marine artillery are taking out ground forces." Tuckett paused. "Satellites show Russian warships moving in the Mediterranean. We think they may be preparing missile strikes against those bases. We're moving elements of the Sixth Fleet into striking range."

Wheeler turned to Wilkinson. "Your thoughts, Patrick."

"We've been at war with Russia since Monday evening—Friday, if you count the Persian Gulf. If we cat-and-mouse these people, it will go on and on. My advice would be take them out for good."

"Aircraft and ships?"

"Anything that moves and carries a Russian flag. Planes, ships, tanks and troops."

"You're saying we end it with the Russians."

"I don't see any point in prolonging the inevitable."

Wheeler thought for a moment. "General Tuckett?"

"Finish what we started last Friday, Mr. President. Take the Russians out of the picture. And, at the same time, do the Syrian rebels an enormous favor. The only reason we've been dancing around with al-Sharaa's forces is because the Russians were backing him, and we didn't want our forces in direct combat with them."

"This will change the face of the Middle East dramatically, Mr. President," Vice President Hutchens said.

"Are you saying don't do it?"

"On the contrary, I'm saying Syria will be a better place. This would cement our relationship with Jordan and Saudi Arabia. And if you pick up the phone and call Israel, they'll be falling over themselves to get jets up there and fight alongside us."

Wheeler nodded. "Doug?"

"We've got one foot in, one foot out, Mr. President," Chambers replied. "Drop the hammer. Be done with it."

"Does anybody think this complicates matters with Congress?"

"Authorization of war?" Hutchens said. "If you ask me, it's a continuation of what we brought against Russia on Friday after their unprovoked attack against our ships in the Gulf. And if we take what General Tuckett is saying at face value—that the Russian fleet in the Mediterranean is advancing for an attack—the War Powers Act would come into play."

"Patrick," Wheeler said, "will our fleet have problems neutralizing Russia's ships in the Mediterranean?"

"You mean could this turn into a protracted military operation?" Wilkinson said.

"Exactly."

"No, sir," Wilkinson replied. "We have the AGM-158, a long-range anti-ship missile. They're stealthy, they fly low and fast, and one will take out a destroyer." He paused. "A Navy missile cruiser carries between fifty and ninety. We give them the word, they take out Russia's navy. There won't be any ships left."

Wheeler considered that for a moment. "How long before our ships are within striking distance?"

"They're within striking distance now, sir. Five hundred miles."

"General Tuckett," Wheeler said, "commence a precision attack against the Russian fleet in the Mediterranean. Step up whatever the Air Force, Army and Marines are doing in and over Syria. And contact Israel's prime minister. Let them know what's happening and what we're doing about it."

"Right away, sir," Tuckett replied.

"Keep me posted, General."

"Of course, sir."

Wheeler stood and looked at the others seated at the table. They watched him for a moment, then Secretary Wilkinson spoke. "The balance of world power has shifted, Mr. President. Dramatically and irrevocably. The United States has been reduced to a third world country technologically. But we still have considerable military power overseas. A week from now Russia will be of no concern to us. We might consider bringing the bulk of our assets home."

Wheeler thought for a moment. "Leave enough in the Middle East to prevent a flare up."

"Yes, sir."

"And then?"

"We focus everything we have on rebuilding, getting our grid up and running, and our people fed."

Wheeler nodded, thinking. "You spend much time thinking about China, Patrick?"

"Yes, sir."

"So do I. I can't help but wonder what they're thinking right now. We talk about the balance of power . . . China's in the driver's seat. Globally, they run the show."

"I wonder if they can sit still, knowing that we'll rebuild and eventually resume our role as a superpower."

"You think they might move against us?"

"The door is wide open, Mr. President." Wilkinson paused. "We can fight small battles in the Middle East. But China . . . that's a war we wouldn't win under our present circumstances."

"They could walk in and make themselves at home."

"Eventually, sir. We have military strength, but very limited communications. We're hobbled. If China put their mind to it, they could take over the U.S." He looked at the others seated around the table. "And there's not much we could do about it."

27

7:20 a.m. Mountain Standard Time
Northwest Arizona

Nathan Hayes sat on the deck of his parents' home with a cup of coffee, watching the sunrise. The air was cold, crisp and still, the eastern sky a deep reddish-orange. He had seen Arizona sunsets before—salmon tones shot with burnt yellow and gold—but they were nothing like this. It was as if the sky were on fire.

He closed his eyes, drinking in the absolute stillness of the morning air, and realized he could tolerate this quite easily. It wasn't the dry and windy Arizona he was used to, but rather a beautiful mountain setting, picturesque and remarkably soothing. He gazed eastward into the sunrise, then drew a slow breath, momentarily overwhelmed by the beauty of it. "This is the most peaceful place I've ever been," he said aloud.

Nathan had never seen the mountain home. The last time he visited his parents, they lived in Kingman. And he didn't like Kingman much. So, when he visited, it was what his dad called a hit-

and-run—there for a few hours, then gone. He had a deep-rooted connection to Thousand Oaks that wasn't going to change any time soon. But he was clearly drawn to this morning on the mountain.

He watched the sunrise for a few more minutes, and was getting up to refill his cup when his mom and dad stepped out onto the deck. "There you are," Nancy smiled. She kissed his cheek, then moved to an empty chair on the other side of Nathan's. "Did you sleep all right?"

"I did," he replied. "Great, actually."

Neil held up a carafe filled with hot coffee. "Is this what you're looking for?"

"You saved me a trip," Nathan nodded.

Neil poured his cup full, then set the carafe on the table and sat next to Nancy, looking eastward. "What do you think?"

Nathan shook his head. "It's amazing. It's beautiful. Do you get this every morning?"

"No. Sometimes it's snowing. Rain in the summer. But when the weather is good, yeah, we get this."

"And it's so quiet."

"Not a lot of traffic up here," Nancy said.

Neil nodded. "Or neighbors yelling at each other."

"But you have to drive to town to shop," Nathan said.

"Small price," Neil replied. "You plan ahead and shop once a week. If you're down there for something else, pickup whatever you might need over the next few days."

"It's only twenty minutes from here," Nancy added. "Not terribly inconvenient."

"It grows on you," Neil said. "Of course, it's temporary. I mean, for you. I don't know how long it will take, but eventually they'll get things back up and running. When that happens, we'll get you back to California. Unless you find a way to get there earlier, and feel like you need to head out."

Nathan shook his head. "I'm fine here, Dad. I like it." He paused and sighed. "I just wish Naomi was here with us."

Nancy squeezed his shoulder. "She's on her way."

"I know. I can't help but worry about her, though."

"She'll be all right, son," Neil said. "She's got a couple of friends making the trip with her."

"I know. But if they're the guys she works with—the math geeks—I don't know that they'll be much help, other than calculating their odds of dying."

Neil shrugged. "Sometimes people like that will surprise you. Throw them in the thick of things."

"I'll just be glad when she's here."

"All of us will be glad when she's here," Nancy said. "Meanwhile, we keep her in prayer."

He nodded. "I know, Mom. I just hope God is listening."

28

The first two hours out of Clay City was an easy drive for Hendricks, Winter and Lundgren. There were fewer vehicles stalled on the road, all of them in the emergency lane on the right. Approaching St. Louis, they saw a few cars and trucks traveling on the side roads, two on the interstate. By ten miles the other side, traffic dropped to zero again.

Ninety miles southwest of St. Louis on Interstate 44, they stopped to brew coffee and grab snack food. Hendricks was at the back of the truck with Lundgren. Winter was standing in front with binoculars, scanning the landscape. He stopped and focused on the highway ahead of them.

"Naomi," he called out a moment later. "Check this out."

Hendricks walked to the front and took the binoculars. "What am I looking at?"

"Straight ahead, on the highway."

She climbed in the cab of the truck and rested the binoculars on the steering wheel for a steady view. Roughly a mile down the road, a pickup truck was parked next to a car. Standing between the vehicles, two men faced a woman and a child. Hendricks watched for several seconds, but couldn't tell what was going on.

"Pack it up, guys," she said, stepping out of the cab. She closed up the back of the truck, then walked to the front and pulled the shotgun from behind the seat.

"Looking for trouble, are we?" Lundgren asked.

"Intervention." She started the truck and pulled away, her heart beating faster as the truck accelerated, a dozen scenarios flashing through her mind, all of them ending with gunfire. Forty-five seconds later, she slowed, then rolled to a stop twenty feet behind the pickup, three feet left of its centerline.

"Can you see the car, Scott?" Hendricks asked.

Sitting on the right side, Winter leaned his head against the door glass. "Yes."

"Wait until I'm alongside their truck, then get out and cover me." She passed him the handgun. "There's one in the chamber. The safety's off. It's ready to fire." Winter took the gun and looked at it for a moment. "This is not like shooting at steel," Hendricks said.

"I know."

"Mind the adrenaline. Keep your finger off the trigger until you need to pull it."

"Right."

"You okay?"

He nodded. "I'm good. Be careful, Naomi."

"You too." She opened her door and slid off the seat, shotgun in hand, then walked to the other pickup. She paused at the rear, looking at two stickers on the tailgate, then she moved forward. At the driver's door she stopped and assessed the situation. The two men had their backs to her. Both wore cowboy hats and appeared to be

216

in their early seventies. The woman faced them, her back to the car. The child had moved to the front passenger seat. Then one of the men turned to see who pulled up behind them. Hendricks stood next to the left front fender of their pickup and racked the pump action. Both men turned and stepped back, eyes wide when they saw her pointing the shotgun at them. "Whoa!" one of them yelled, raising his hands in the air.

"Step away from the car," Hendricks said. Both men took several steps backward, hands raised. "Are these men bothering you?" she asked the woman.

The woman stared at Hendricks for a moment, then shook her head. "No. They stopped to help."

Hendricks stepped back, then held the shotgun with the muzzle pointed up, looking at the men. "Is this your truck?"

They glanced at each other. "Yes," one answered.

"You didn't steal it."

"No."

"You put those stickers on the tailgate?"

The man paused. "NRA?"

"De Oppresso Liber."

The man nodded. "To liberate the oppressed."

Hendricks shifted the shotgun, pointing the barrel at the ground, then walked around the front of the truck. "Army Special Forces," she said, standing in front of the men. "Green Beret."

"Yes, ma'am. Fifth Special Forces Group. Vietnam."

"Tip of the spear."

The man smiled and held out his hand. "Chris Tanner, at your service." They shook hands.

The other man leaned in and shook Hendricks' hand. "Miles Ackerman," he said, tipping his hat.

Hendricks exhaled, then smiled. "Naomi Hendricks. Sorry about the shotgun. We've had our share of drama on the road."

217

"No problem," Tanner said. "We're good?"

"Yes," she nodded. "We're good." She looked down the side of the pickup, then waved at Winter and Lundgren to join her.

Tanner nodded at the woman. "This young lady was stopped by some dirtbag in a pickup truck. He siphoned her gas and stole some tools from her trunk, then left her here."

"When?" Hendricks asked.

"Night before last," the woman replied. "About an hour after the power went out. My daughter and I were driving back to Springfield. This guy had a red light on the roof of his truck. I thought it was a policeman."

"Your car runs, other than being out of gas."

"Yes."

"We put gas in her car," Tanner said. "Enough to get her home. We were about to rustle up a little food when you pulled up."

Hendricks nodded, looking at the woman. "So, you've been out here for what . . . thirty-six hours?"

"I don't know how long it's been. We've got coats, of course. Gloves and hats. The cold wasn't too bad. We sat in the back seat cuddling, keeping each other warm."

"I'm Naomi," Hendricks said. "This is Scott and Paul."

"I'm Audrey," the woman smiled. "This is my daughter Evie."

Hendricks kneeled in front of the girl. "How old are you, Evie?"

"Eight," Evie replied.

"I'm sorry that you and your mom had to stay out here all alone."

"I wasn't scared."

"You're a big girl, aren't you?"

"Yes."

"Would you like a peanut butter and honey sandwich?"

Evie paused, glancing at Tanner and Ackerman, then back at Hendricks. "They have beef jerky."

Hendricks smiled. "I'm sure they do. They're cowboys."

Ten minutes later the two trucks were parked side by side on the highway, the seven travelers snacking on a variety of food—beef jerky, of course, as well as kipper snacks and crackers, peanut butter on apples, pineapple slices, and soup, warmed in a sauce pan on the propane burner.

Tanner walked to the cab of his truck and slipped a CD in the player. A few seconds later he was at the back of the truck singing along to Jerry Jeff Walker and smiling at Evie.

"My mom sings too," Evie said.

"Is that right?" Tanner said. He glanced at Audrey.

"I used to sing in bars," she said. "In a country band."

Tanner thought for a moment. "Go ahead," Ackerman said. "Get it out of your system." He walked to the cab and ejected the CD while Tanner rummaged through the back of his truck and produced a guitar case. Opening it, he pulled out a Martin acoustic, then sat on the tailgate and strummed it.

"I don't know much about guitars," Winter said, "but that looks like a nice one."

"Oh, it's nice all right," Hendricks replied. "How old is it?"

"Pushing fifty years," Tanner smiled, tuning it. "Bought it when I got back to the states." He paused. "I think this is one of the best things I did for my sanity—playing guitar, singing songs." He nodded, then started playing, his fingers plucking the strings, the guitar producing a deep, rich tone.

"*Take the ribbon from your hair,*" he sang, his voice a surprisingly smooth baritone. "*Shake it loose and let it fall. Layin' soft against my skin, like the shadows on the wall.*" He smiled at Audrey. "You know this one?"

She nodded. "Kristofferson." She began singing. "*Come and lay down by my side, 'til the early mornin' light. All I'm takin' is your time . . . help me make it through the night.*"

219

Hendricks had goose bumps. She turned and looked at Winter and Lundgren. They were mesmerized. She glanced at Ackerman. He smiled and nodded.

Tanner and Audrey launched into the chorus, their voices soaring in perfect harmony. "*I don't care who's right or wrong. I don't try to understand. Let the devil take tomorrow, 'cause tonight I need a friend.*" Tanner smiled at Audrey, his fingers dancing through the notes descending into the third verse. "*Yesterday is dead and gone. And tomorrow's out of sight. And it's sad to be alone . . . help me make it through the night.*"

Hendricks closed her eyes as the song drifted away on the morning breeze, the voices clean and clear, the steel strings ringing warmly. She drew a slow breath, then looked up at the sky and smiled, tears in her eyes.

"*Lord, it's sad to be alone . . . help me make it through the night.*"

The last notes faded into silence. Tanner looked at Evie. "You were right. Your mom can sing." He smiled at Audrey. "That was just about the prettiest thing I've ever heard."

"That was beautiful," Hendricks said. "It was . . ." she shook her head, "amazing."

"I'm just a sidekick," Ackerman said, "but I think you guys should take this on the road." He pointed at Tanner. "You outdid yourself on that one, pardner."

"That song made this whole trip worthwhile," Hendricks said. "If nothing else good happens, I've got that to hold on to."

Tanner and Audrey sang another song, "Louisiana Saturday Night," an up-tempo, honky-tonk tune, and Ackerman danced with Evie, swinging her around and lifting her up over his head. She held out her arms, laughing gleefully, and for that brief time there was no disaster, no stress or worry. They were seven people wrapped up in the moment—singing and dancing and laughing—and for those few minutes, all was right with the world.

But it couldn't last. They were packing things up when a flat-bed truck pulling a stock trailer rolled to a stop next to them. "You folks are about to have company," the driver said. "And they ain't friendly."

"Mr. Stokes?" Audrey said.

The driver climbed out of the truck and walked around the side. "Audrey?" he said. "Didn't expect to find you out here on the side of the road. Are you all right?"

"We are. It's a long story." She turned to the others. "Mr. Stokes is a rancher in Ash Grove."

"Are we looking at trouble?" Tanner asked.

"You are if you're still here five minutes from now," Stokes replied. "A bunch of militia knuckleheads are headed this way. They stopped me outside of Sullivan. Thought they'd help themselves to my horses. Didn't turn out like they thought it would."

Hendricks looked at Tanner and Ackerman. "Do we stay and fight?" she asked. "Or take off?"

Tanner looked at Ackerman. "What do you think?" he asked.

"I'm not wild about the idea of a running gun battle," Ackerman said. "We're a long way from any medical facility, and that's assuming we could find one that's up and running. If we take any hits— and I mean someone gets shot—we could have serious problems."

Stokes walked around the front of his truck. "If you folks don't mind, I'll be on my way. I can't afford to end up with dead horses."

Tanner nodded. "We appreciate the heads-up." He glanced at Audrey and Evie, then turned back to Stokes. "Would you mind if these two follow you in? They don't need to be here."

"Good idea," Stokes replied. "Whatever you decide to do, keep in mind these boys are armed to the teeth, and they won't think twice about killing every one of you if you've got something they want." He climbed in his truck and started it. Audrey and Evie said their goodbyes, then got in their car.

"Thanks for the song," Audrey said.

Tanner nodded. "It was my pleasure. You girls be safe."

"Goodbye, Evie," Hendricks waved.

They fell in behind the flatbed truck and drove away.

"Okay," Tanner said. "We can leave now and hope they don't catch up to us. Or we can deal with them. If we don't, we leave them to cause trouble for anybody else they run into." He turned to Hendricks. "What do you think?"

"We were stopped in Ohio," she said. "Middle of the night, a guy with a gun that wanted everything we have."

"What happened?"

"Short story, I took his gun away and shot his truck full of holes."

"So, what are you saying?"

"I've had it with thieves on the highway."

"The guy that stopped you, he's not dead."

"No."

"It might not be that easy with these guys."

"I know."

"You're prepared to use deadly force?"

"We do what we have to do."

Tanner looked up the highway behind them. There was a short rise in the road about a quarter-mile from them, another about a half-mile away, then a distant rise close to a mile. "It would be nice if we could stop them on that farthest hill. Disable the vehicles."

"With assault rifles?" Ackerman said. "A quarter of a mile is about all I'm good for."

"Yeah. Same here."

"Naomi's got a high-powered rifle," Winter said.

"How good are you with it?" Tanner asked.

"A minute of angle at a thousand yards," Hendricks replied.

"Under stress?"

Winter smiled. "I've seen her under stress. She's fearless."

Hendricks dug through her shooting bag and pulled out the range finder and binoculars. She handed the binoculars to Tanner.

"That rise on the horizon is out of our range," she said. "That's where we were when we spotted you guys down here. Driving distance was about a mile, which means when we see them coming over the top, they're about a minute away." She leaned against the side of the camper shell to steady the view in the range finder, focusing on a highway sign at the next closest rise. "The next one is a little over a thousand yards. From here, lying prone, I can hit radiators."

"How about tires?" Tanner asked.

"That's pushing it. I might get lucky."

"How far to the nearest rise?"

Hendricks refocused. "Four forty-five. Just over a quarter-mile."

"Miles and I can set up down there, off the side of the road, out of sight. Whatever you can't hit at a thousand yards, we stop them there." Tanner handed the binoculars back to Hendricks, then turned to Winter and Lundgren. "Can you back her up?"

"Yeah," Winter replied. Lundgren nodded.

"Okay, let's be clear—we're disabling vehicles. Nobody gets shot unless they shoot first. If they do, it's your life or theirs."

"Here they come," Hendricks said, looking through the binoculars. "At least I think it's them. Three trucks, camouflage paint."

"Let's go, Miles," Tanner said. They grabbed assault rifles, then took off running down the road.

Hendricks handed Winter the pistol and four extra magazines. "You remember how to reload," she said.

"Push the button on the side," Winter said. "Let the magazine drop to the ground, push the next one in until it locks, then release the slide."

"Fifty yards down there. Stand off the shoulder, just far enough down the slope that they can't see you. If they make it past Miles and Chris, let them go by, then come in from behind. If you have to shoot, be mindful of what's beyond your shot. Paul and I will be down here."

"Got it."

Hendricks pulled the rifle from her bag. "Paul, the shotgun's on the front seat. There's a box of shells in the glove compartment. Fill your pockets. Use the truck for cover. Stand in front. Stay low." She paused, looking down the road. "If any of those trucks make it this far, be ready to fire. Aim for center mass."

"What's center mass?" Lundgren asked.

"The widest part of the chest—the heart. Pull the trigger, then pump another round in and pull it again. Keep doing that until the threat is neutralized."

"You mean until everyone's dead."

"I'm sorry, Paul," Hendricks said, putting a hand on his arm. "I really am. But if these guys are truly bad, it's either them or us."

"I'm okay, Naomi." He paused. "Don't get shot."

"Stay brave, little brother."

Lundgren smiled at that. Hendricks kneeled on the asphalt, setting up the rifle. She opened a box of cartridges and loaded three magazines, then pulled out her phone and tapped the screen, moving through the ballistics setup. Lying prone behind the rifle, she twisted the turrets, setting the elevation and windage. Finally, she looked through the scope, holding the crosshairs just above the road a thousand yards away.

A quarter-mile down the road, Tanner and Ackerman sat behind a clump of brush twenty yards off the side of the road. "Ever think we'd be doing this again?" Ackerman asked.

"Hiding on a trail, waiting for the enemy?" Tanner said.

"Yeah."

"Can't say I did."

"You think she can hit anything from that distance?"

"We're about to find out."

Ten seconds later the trucks came up over the rise in single file, a half-mile away from Hendricks, a quarter-mile from Tanner and Ackerman. A moment later they heard a crack as Hendricks' first shot passed over them, twenty-eight feet above their heads. A second later the lead truck veered into the right-hand lane, exposing the front end of the second truck.

"She's good," Tanner said.

Another shot, and the second truck veered, exposing the third truck. A third shot, and a third hit. The first truck straightened out and kept coming. Three more shots were fired in rapid succession, followed by a ten-second pause. Then another shot, and the left front tire of the lead truck blew, sending the truck into the median. It rolled several times, coming to rest on its side.

"One down," Ackerman said.

Hendricks continued firing on the two trucks, both billowing steam from under the hood as they headed toward Tanner and Ackerman. When they were thirty feet away, Tanner and Ackerman stood and opened fire, aiming at the tires and engine compartments. The trailing truck drove into the median and rolled once. The lead truck passed them, rolling on flat tires. Tanner and Ackerman climbed the short slope, then crossed the highway to the wrecked vehicle, standing thirty feet away. Two men crawled out the windshield opening.

"On the ground!" Tanner yelled, pointing his rifle. The men swung their rifles up. Tanner and Ackerman fired. Both men fell.

"Cover me," Tanner said, moving in to check the bodies. Ackerman moved to the side, watching the bodies on the ground and the rear of the camper shell on the pickup. The shell was still attached. No one was getting out of the back.

"They're dead," Tanner said. He backed up, pointing his rifle at the back of the pickup. Ackerman moved closer, rifle shouldered, then looked inside. A single shot flew past his head. Ackerman leaned away for a moment, then stepped back and began firing. Ten shots later he stopped.

"Cover me," he said, stepping to the tailgate. He reached inside and checked the bodies. "They're toast."

"How many?"

"Three."

Down the highway, Hendricks stood and was moving to the rear of her truck just as the last pickup slid to a stop twenty feet away, engine knocking. The front doors opened, and two men bailed out, assault rifles blazing. Hendricks ducked alongside the rear of her truck and was sliding a full magazine into her rifle when three shots fired from behind the pickup tore through the fender next to her head. She dropped the rifle, flattened out on the pavement and was starting to roll underneath the truck when she looked up and saw both men standing over her, rifles pointed at her face. She heard the click of a trigger sear dropping. But there was no shot.

The next few seconds slowed to a crawl for Hendricks. Lying on her back, she saw blue sky above her, then the barrel of a shotgun. There was a flash and a deafening boom, then the harsh slap of muzzle blast hitting her in the face. She could feel the impact of the buckshot hitting one of the men squarely in the chest. There was a poof of dust and he was sailing backward, arms outstretched, his rifle flying end over end. A smoking shotgun shell fell to the ground next to her, followed by another boom, another blast from the muzzle of the shotgun, and the second man was sent flying.

The shooting stopped, and she rolled to a kneeling position, ears ringing. She heard Lundgren's muffled voice tell her to stay down, then felt his hand on her head as he stepped over her. Crouching next to the rear tire, she watched as he moved to the center of the highway, shotgun pointed at the camper shell of the camouflaged pickup. Thirty feet beyond him she saw Winter on the road, also moving to the center of the pavement, his pistol ready.

Hendricks reached for her rifle just as the tailgate on the camouflaged pickup dropped and five men scrambled out, brandishing weapons. They stared at Lundgren and Winter, and for a moment Hendricks hoped the men were smart enough to see the obvious—no matter how fast they were, at least two of them would die. Would they realize that and walk away? Then one of them fired a shot, just missing Lundgren, and gunfire erupted. Lundgren and Winter walked steadily toward the other men, firing as they moved, targeting and pulling the trigger as if they'd been doing it all their lives, miraculously untouched in the hail of bullets being fired at them.

As suddenly as it started, the gunfire stopped. Hendricks stood and looked around, then walked toward Lundgren and Winter. A man lying on the ground five feet in front of her turned over and pointed a pistol at Lundgren's back. Hendricks raised her rifle and fired a bullet through his head. Lundgren jumped and turned to see Hendricks kicking the pistol away from the man's hand, then kneeling next to him and checking his pulse. She stood and walked to the other men lying on the ground, checking them one by one.

"They're dead," she said. She turned to Lundgren and Winter. "Are you guys all right?"

Lundgren stared at her for a moment, then glanced at Winter. "We're okay," Winter said. "Are you all right?"

"Yes." She paused, looking at the dead men on the ground. "I can't believe what happened here." She looked at Winter and Lundgren. "We should all be dead right now."

Lundgren walked to the back of Hendricks' truck and sat on the tailgate, staring off into the trees south of the highway. Winter crossed the road and sat next to him. "You okay, buddy?" he asked. Lundgren nodded slowly, watching Hendricks. She was standing twenty feet away, looking across the fields to the north. She closed her eyes, savoring the warmth of the sun on her face, for a moment blocking the gun battle from her mind, thinking instead of Tanner and Audrey singing, laughing with Evie and joking with Winter and Lundgren. How happy they had been just thirty minutes ago. Now she felt empty, numb, emotionally detached. She opened her eyes and looked at Winter and Lundgren sitting silently on the tailgate staring at her, and her heart sank.

Ninety minutes later, the two pickup trucks pulled into a gas station on the outskirts of Ash Grove—Tanner and Ackerman in one; Hendricks, Winter and Lundgren in the other. Parked under the canopy was Mr. Stokes' flatbed truck and stock trailer. They walked inside, then stopped at the counter. A girl was stocking the cigarette rack.

"We're looking for the driver of the flatbed parked out front," Tanner said. "A rancher named Stokes."

The girl pointed behind them. They turned and saw two men sitting at a table, drinking coffee. One was Mr. Stokes. The other was a sheriff's deputy. Stokes waved to them.

"How did it go out there?" he asked.

They crossed the room. "Not good," Tanner said.

"I was afraid of that. This here is Hal Decker, Greene County deputy sheriff."

"How about we all pull up a chair and talk," Decker said.

The story was told exactly as it happened. The deputy asked questions. Tanner, Ackerman and Hendricks filled in the gaps. The bottom line was there were twelve men dead out on the interstate.

"We know these boys," Decker said. "They're from up in Phelps County. There's a group in Greene County too. They used to stick to themselves for the most part. But over the last year or so, they've taken to breaking and entering. Mostly cabins, but a few farm houses when no one was around. We knew who it was, but couldn't pin anything on them. Then two of them were shot and killed breaking into a home in Wheatland. Tough line of work to be in."

"I just wish this didn't have to happen," Hendricks said.

"Did you ask them to stand down?" Decker asked.

"We asked the first two men that got out of the truck," Tanner replied. "They raised their weapons to fire. We stopped them."

"And the second truck?"

"They came out firing," Hendricks said. "We didn't have a chance to say anything."

"You couldn't outrun them before it all started."

Tanner shook his head. "They would have been tailing us all the way. At some point, it was going to come down to a firefight."

Decker looked at Hendricks. "Sounds to me like it had to happen. I'm sorry to say that."

"I'm glad you folks are all right," Stokes said.

"Is Audrey okay?" Tanner asked.

"She's safe at home."

Decker sipped his coffee. "You folks mind telling me what you all do for a living?"

Hendricks shrugged. "Nothing now." She nodded at Winter and Lundgren. "We were intelligence analysts for the NSA."

Tanner and Ackerman leaned back. "No kidding," Decker said. "The ones that listen to our phone calls?"

"That would be the guys down the hall," Lundgren replied.

Decker nodded, then looked at Tanner and Ackerman. "How about you guys?"

"We're retired," Tanner said. "We were up in Iowa helping an old service buddy when the grid collapsed."

"Vietnam?" Stokes asked.

"Yes, sir."

"Thank you for your service."

"You're welcome."

Decker leaned back in his chair. "Where is everyone headed?"

"We're going back to Texas," Tanner replied.

"Arizona," Hendricks said. "My folks live there."

Decker nodded. "I don't know that there's anything else we need from you. I'll get with the Phelps County sheriff and explain the situation. He'll drive out and see what's what."

"Do you want to see IDs?" Hendricks asked. "Get a statement?"

"You just gave me a statement. And no, I don't need to see your IDs. Couldn't do anything with them anyway. NCIC is down." Decker stood. "You folks make yourselves at home, or be on your way. Whatever suits you." He paused. "I hope the rest of your trip—wherever you're headed—is less interesting." He nodded, then looked at Stokes. "Nice to see you, Avery."

"You too, Hal," Stokes replied.

With that, Decker left. "I guess I'll be on my way too," Stokes said. He stood and looked down at them for a moment. "Ash Grove's not a bad place to rest up if you need to. It's a friendly town."

"I think we'll be pushing on," Tanner said. "But thanks."

Stokes nodded, then tipped his hat. "You folks take care."

"Will do." Tanner stood and shook hands with Stokes, then watched him leave.

Nothing more was said at the table about the shooting on the highway. The five of them made small talk for another ten minutes, then walked outside to their trucks. "Is everybody all right?" Tanner asked, looking at Hendricks, Lundgren and Winter.

"Yeah," Winter replied. "Just trying to get used to this."

"You don't ever get used to it. You do what you have to do, and move on." He turned to Lundgren. "You okay, pardner?"

"Yeah," Lundgren nodded.

"Naomi?"

Hendricks was watching a truck with camouflage paint pull into the station. The driver got out and walked toward the front door, nodding at Hendricks and the others as he passed. She watched him for a few seconds, then turned back to Tanner. "I'm okay," she said.

He nodded, then looked at Ackerman. "What part of Arizona?" he asked, turning back to Hendricks.

"What?"

"You said you're going to Arizona."

"Northwest. A hundred miles east of Las Vegas."

"Mountains?"

"As a matter of fact, there are."

"Mind if we tag along?"

She smiled. "I was hoping you would."

29

Hendricks, Winter and Lundgren, now traveling with Tanner and Ackerman, were coming up on Stroud, Oklahoma, when they decided to drive through town and see what gas might be available. The plan to siphon fuel from abandoned cars had proved fruitless so far. After several attempts, they realized they weren't the only ones with that idea in mind, and since the collapse two days earlier, others had beaten them to it.

A number of small towns they stopped in along the way seemed to have weathered the collapse—at least the early stages of it—fairly well. A few businesses had generators running and were open for business, and there was traffic on the streets. This was not the case in Stroud. Exiting the interstate on North 8th Street, Hendricks, Winter, Lundgren, Tanner and Ackerman were confronted with what appeared to be a downsized version of the chaos that engulfed so many large, inner cities. Stores were gutted, in some cases torched, and the remains of vehicles, battered and burned, were everywhere. The strangest aspect to Hendricks and her traveling companions was the absence of people. They drove five blocks before they saw anybody, then, a man sitting in a lawn chair at the front entrance of a convenience store with a shotgun on his lap.

Hendricks and Tanner pulled their trucks into the parking lot, and Tanner got out. "Do you have gas?" he called out to the man.

The man remained silent for a moment, studying the travelers, then finally spoke. "Yes, and no. The underground tank has some in it, but there's no electricity and no generator."

Hendricks climbed out of her truck and walked around to Tanner. "I've got the fuel pump I was going to use for getting gas out of cars," she said. "But it's a long draw from an underground tank. I don't think it can pull from that depth."

Tanner turned back to the man. "If we can find a pump, will you let us get gas out of the underground tanks?"

"You got anything to trade?" the man asked.

"We've got cash," Hendricks said.

"Doesn't do me any good. What have you got to trade?"

"Guns and ammunition," Tanner replied.

"Talk to me."

"We fill both trucks and fifteen 5-gallon jugs. In trade, we give you an AR-15 and an ammo can of .223 hollow-points." The man shrugged. "That's a twelve hundred-dollar semiauto," Tanner said, "and six hundred rounds of robbery stoppers."

"Let me see the rifle."

Tanner opened the back of the truck and pulled out an AR-15 and a loaded magazine, then walked to the storefront and handed the rifle to the man. The man looked it over, then stood and walked around the side of the building. He inserted the magazine into the lower receiver, raised the rifle and pointed it at a fifty-five-gallon drum sitting on the ground behind the building, then pulled the trigger. A single shot punched through the drum. Then he emptied the magazine at it.

"Okay," the man nodded.

"How much hose do we need to reach the gas?" Tanner asked.

"Fifteen feet oughta do it. Twenty, to be sure. I can dip the tank when you're ready and give you an exact depth."

"Is there a hardware store open?"

"Left at the corner, five blocks down."

"We'll be right back."

Tanner walked to the back of his truck and opened it. Stacked on a blanket to one side were twelve AR-15s and seventeen semi-automatic handguns, all of them from the men killed in the shootout. On the opposite side of the pickup bed were a dozen metal ammo cans, each one holding six hundred rounds of .223 ammunition, and another six filled with rounds for the handguns.

"I'm guessing if we find a pump," Tanner said, "whoever has it will want to trade. I'm willing to give up an AR for a hundred and fifty gallons of gas, but I hate the idea of trading one for a pump."

"I've got the .357 mag I took off the guy in Ohio," Hendricks said. "Two cartons of ammo."

"You mind losing it?"

"No. It's a heavy hitter, but it's a revolver. Six rounds before you have to reload."

"All right. I'll check out the hardware store. You guys wait here just in case this guy decides to close early."

Tanner took the magnum and ammo from Hendricks, then drove to the hardware store. Thirty minutes later, he returned with the pump and hose. "It took three stops," he said, "but I found what we need. The guy was happy with the revolver. I talked him into parting with five 5-gallon gas jugs. I've got room for them. And I'd rather not have to worry about gas again before we reach the end of the line." He looked around. "There's a hitch. The pump is a hundred and ten volts, and this guy has no electricity."

"I've got an inverter on my truck," Hendricks said. "It'll put out one-ten."

Tanner nodded. "I picked up twenty-five feet of garden hose and extra couplings. We'll cut it in two—one for the inlet, the other for the outlet."

The owner of the gas station dipped the tank with a twenty-foot measuring stick. "Looks like you'll hit gas about nine feet down," he said. "Keep the hose off the bottom of the tank or it'll suck sand."

Tanner cut the hose in half, then crimped ends on the pieces that would screw into the pump. With the pump on the ground in front of Hendricks' truck and plugged into the inverter under the hood, Tanner and Ackerman filled the trucks first, then the jugs. It was slower than the station pumps, but it worked, and thirty minutes after they started, they had a full load of gas.

"I'm surprised none of the containers took a bullet during that gunfight," Hendricks said. "There are three holes in my fender, but everything inside looks okay."

"I still can't believe you guys came through a shootout like that without so much as a nick," Ackerman said. "We heard the shooting from up the road. It sounded like a war zone."

Hendricks nodded. In her mind it was nothing short of a miracle. She watched it, and she still couldn't believe it. "It wasn't our day to die," she said.

"Now you're talking like a warrior," Tanner replied.

"I'm just praying we get home without another gun battle. I'm not sure how much more of this I can handle."

"You want to try the side roads?" Ackerman asked. "Or stick to the interstate?"

Hendricks shrugged. "I think we're better off on the interstate. I feel like the further out in the sticks we get, the more likely it is we'll run into trouble. We can see farther on the interstate, spot trouble before we're on top of it."

"Longer drive on the side roads," Tanner said. "We'll use more gas." He looked at Winter and Lundgren. "Chime in, guys. You're in this too."

Lundgren glanced at Winter. "The odds are better on the interstate," he said. "Like Naomi said, we can see farther. That's a better advantage than not being seen on the side roads."

"I agree," Winter said. "Especially out here where it's mostly flat. We can see trouble a long way off."

"Ready to hit the road?" Tanner asked.

"Actually," Hendricks said, "I'm ready to call it a day. I'm frazzled. We should find a place to set up camp." She paused. "You guys have gear, right?"

"Yeah," Tanner replied. "We're set. As far as safety goes, I'm going to ask this guy if we can camp in the field behind his station. Assuming he's through shooting at that drum, I don't think we'll have any problems back there."

By sundown they had pitched tents and started a fire. The area was good. They could see a hundred yards in every direction, and the ground was covered with dry weeds—impossible to cross without making noise. Hendricks warmed a pot of stew over the fire. Tanner and Ackerman had a bag of hard rolls and butter. They ate, then relaxed around the fire.

"I've got a jug of tequila in the truck," Tanner said, "if anyone wants to take the edge off."

"Are you and Miles going to drink?" Hendricks asked.

"I'm not," Tanner replied.

"No," Ackerman said. "Do yourself a favor, Naomi. Have a couple of shots. You too," he nodded at Winter and Lundgren. "Relax. Chris and I will keep watch."

"Set 'em up," Hendricks nodded.

Tanner dug through the back of his truck, then returned to the fire with a half-gallon of Cuervo and three tumblers. He poured, then handed the glasses around. Hendricks turned to Winter and Lundgren and extended her glass. "I have no idea what we should drink to . . . living on the edge?"

"How about just living?" Lundgren said. Hendricks smiled. The three of them clinked glasses, then Hendricks tossed hers back. She shivered, then passed the glass back to Tanner.

"Another?" he asked.

She nodded. "Please."

He smiled and poured, then passed her the glass. "Three's the limit. Then we take away your pistol."

"Or unload it, anyway," Ackerman said.

Hendricks drank the second shot, then stood and walked to the back of her truck. Pulling out the range bag, she unclipped the holster from her belt and put the gun inside, then zipped the bag. Walking back to the fire, she handed the glass to Tanner.

"You sure about this?" he asked.

"I've drunk a lot of tequila, Chris. I know how—three shots, then stop." She smiled. "Or was it four? I forget."

"You're the boss."

Winter and Lundgren stared at her, still holding their first drink. "I've said this before, Naomi," Winter said. "I'll say it again. You are full of surprises."

Hendricks sat down with her drink and leaned back on one elbow. "The biggest surprise I've ever had," she said, "and I mean in my entire life, is you and Paul, standing on the highway behind my truck, firing at those guys with mind-boggling precision. And such fearlessness. You guys are heroes. You can think whatever you want about me, Scott. Call me amazing, whatever. You guys blew my mind." She looked at Lundgren. "When I was lying there on my back . . ." She put her thumb and index finger together, ". . . that far from being killed, and I looked up to see you standing over me with the shotgun . . ." She shook her head. "Boom," she said quietly. She leaned over and clinked her glass against Paul's, then Scott's, and tossed it back. She shivered, then turned to Tanner and Ackerman. "So, where do you guys live? What do you do?"

"I've got a small ranch outside of Big Spring, Texas," Tanner said. "I'm semi-retired. I work in a gun shop part time."

"You sell guns?"

"I'm a gunsmith."

"I live in Big Spring too," Ackerman said. "Retired, but I do odd jobs to stay busy. Carpentry, mostly."

"Do you guys prep?"

"Funny you'd ask that," Tanner replied. "A hard-core prepper wouldn't answer you, OPSEC being what it is."

"Operational security. The hard-core prepper's mantra. So where do you fit in?"

"I was an Eagle Scout. In my world, that's all the prep you need. You know how to find your way with a map. You can stop serious bleeding—you know how to save a life. And you have enough food to last a few weeks if there's a storm. That's about all there is to it."

Hendricks smiled. "My dad went through a phase. He had the camo, vests, boots—the whole show. He was thinking about getting a shipping container and turning it into a bunker. Bury it underground, load it up with food and water, guns and ammo."

"What happened?"

"Mom packed her bags."

"She left him?"

"No. She'd never leave him." She paused, thinking. "He woke up, figured out that survival means you want to blend. You wear T-shirts and jeans. And hiding in a bunker didn't make sense if the idea was to rebuild after some kind of collapse."

Tanner nodded. "Like the one we're in now."

"Yeah. Anyway, he and Mom have a place in the mountains east of Kingman. That's where we're headed."

"I've been to Kingman. Nice town. Hot in the summer."

"It is. Anyway, Dad was a Boy Scout too. Our family camped a lot. Fishing and hunting. I love the outdoors."

"It's good for the soul."

"Speaking of prepping," Ackerman said, "Chris and I have a friend up in Lewiston, Idaho. Serious outdoors guy—your basic Jeremiah Johnson. Knows the mountains in that area like the back of his hand. So, this businessman from Seattle hears about him somehow. He's got a ton of money and wants to build a prepper retreat up in Devil's Canyon. Real rugged area. You practically need a helicopter to get in and out. Anyway, they build this huge, underground house. He says it's almost five thousand square feet. Pantries and storage out the wazoo, generators, water purification systems. Everything. The guy spent almost a million on it. When it's finished, they build this dinky little cabin on top of it. It's weathered, made to look like no one's been in it for years. And that's all you see.

"Turns out this guy, the businessman—he's a CEO or something, smart when it comes to making money, but dumber than a bag of hammers when he's out in the woods—he insists on being the leader. And there's a dozen people involved in this besides this friend of ours and his wife. And they spend half their lives in those mountains. But this Bill Gates knockoff wants to be the boss. Crazy."

"Last we heard," Tanner said, "it was falling apart. The guy had everyone wearing Army fatigues, marching around, drilling for incursions. He'd come down on weekends and get everybody up there to rehearse for the apocalypse, the end of the world as we know it. It was a joke. Kyle and his wife—they're the friends of ours—are two of the nicest people you could meet. They'd give you the shirt off the back. But they don't put up with stupid."

Ackerman nodded. "In fairness, I've got to say this about preppers who think like that. It's fine to go full-bore, battle-ready, wrap your place in razor wire. Batten down the hatches and pity the poor soul who stumbles onto your place in need of help." Ackerman shook his head. "But it's not for me. If you're the type that won't help people, you're not going to get along with anybody living with you in a box underground."

"Roger that," Tanner said. "If that's how they want to play it, more power to them. But personally, I think they lose in the end."

The five of them sat in silence for a minute, then Hendricks spoke. "I keep thinking I'll wake up from this, and it'll just be a bad dream. But it's happening. It's in your face." She shook her head. "That first night when we were stopped by that guy on the highway, I had it in my head what I needed to do, and I did it. It was almost automatic. Scott was totally freaked out. We did some target shooting the next day. I wanted him and Paul to get used to firing guns. Then we're in a full-blown shootout." She sighed. "We left a dozen people dead back there."

Tanner and Ackerman glanced at each other. Hendricks was struggling to come to grips with a situation they'd been in many times, decades earlier in Vietnam. Like a lot of combat veterans, they didn't talk about it. But Hendricks didn't have their training, the ability to deal with combat and still sleep at night. She was approaching a tipping point emotionally. "How do you live with that?" she asked. "When you think about what happened, what do you do?" She nodded. "I need to know."

"You tell yourself it was necessary," Tanner said quietly. "You plug that into the part of your brain that deals with right and wrong, and every time it comes back to you—the memory of what you did—you remind yourself it was necessary. That's it. It had to be done. You move on. You don't dwell on it."

"You know what a sheep dog is?" Ackerman asked.

Hendricks nodded. "Someone who protects people who can't protect themselves."

"When a person—a sheep dog—carries a concealed weapon, they accept the fact that they may end up killing someone to protect the innocent. Or they don't carry. It's that simple. One of the first questions a person is asked when they apply for a job as a policeman, is can you take someone's life if the situation requires it? People need to think long and hard about that if they're going to be a cop, or a private citizen who carries. In the end, there are a lot of bad people out there who will take innocent lives without a second thought. Those of us who carry—whether we're everyday Joes or the cop on the street—accept the responsibility that comes with being a sheep dog. That means training, discipline, and knowing the law. It also means accepting the fact that it's necessary."

Hendricks nodded, thinking. She knew there was nothing easy about this. And it wasn't going to go away anytime soon—the experience would stay with her long after tonight. But she knew too, that with their help she'd get past it. She looked at Tanner and Ackerman. "Thank you," she said quietly.

They nodded. "You're welcome," Tanner said. "Anything we can do to help."

"Feel like singing another song?"

He smiled. "I'd love to."

30

Thursday, February 13
6:00 a.m. Central Standard Time
Stroud, Oklahoma

Hendricks awoke to the smell of coffee and breakfast. Tanner and Ackerman had a fire going, with bacon, eggs, and hash browns on a griddle. She dressed, then crawled out of her tent and pulled on her parka.

"It's cold this morning," she said.

Tanner smiled. "But it's not snowing." He poured a cup of coffee and held it out to her.

"Thanks."

"Sleep all right?" Ackerman asked.

"I did." She sipped the coffee. "I'm good. Thanks—both of you—for last night."

"Anytime," Tanner replied.

Hendricks smiled, then stepped over to the tent where Winter and Lundgren were sleeping. "You guys awake?"

Lundgren's muffled voice came from inside. "Yeah."

"Breakfast is on." She returned to the fire and stood, turning slowly, looking across the field. The sun wasn't over the horizon yet, but it was light, and she could see in all directions. Looking south, she saw people digging through a dumpster behind a store at the far end of the field. She watched them for a minute, sipping her coffee, then noticed the smoke from the fire drifting that direction. The smell of bacon and eggs wouldn't be far behind.

"We're going to have company," she said.

Tanner looked up from the griddle. "Friendly, I hope."

"Hungry, I'd say."

Tanner and Ackerman turned and looked south, watching the people for a moment. A few seconds later the people stepped back from the dumpster and looked toward the gas station. They spotted the camp and started walking toward it.

"I hope you don't mind feeding the neighbors," Hendricks said, watching them approach.

"I hope they don't mind scrambled eggs," Tanner replied. Ackerman stepped to the back of their pickup and threw a blanket over the rifles, then pulled eggs and bacon and a bag of hash browns from the cooler. Tanner lifted the percolator from the coals and poured the coffee into a thermos, then started another batch brewing. A minute later, a man and woman in their late thirties and a boy in his early teens walked up and stopped by the fire.

"Good morning," Hendricks said.

"Morning," the man replied. "That food sure smells good."

Tanner set a helping of eggs, hash browns and four strips of bacon on a plate. "Join us for breakfast?" he said, handing the plate to the man. Tanner served up two more plates, handing them to the woman and the boy. Ackerman poured coffee.

The man looked at Tanner and Ackerman, then Hendricks. "Thank you," he said. "We're grateful." The three of them sat on the ground and began eating. After a few bites, the man nodded. "This is the best breakfast I've ever had."

"When you're hungry," Tanner said, "anything tastes good. Even my cooking."

"No," the woman said. "This is delicious."

"You live here?" Ackerman asked.

"Yeah," the man answered.

"I guess you're out of food."

The man nodded silently. The woman glanced at him, then turned to Tanner. "We were in Chandler visiting friends when the power went out," she said. "Our car wouldn't run. We got a ride back the next day, but when we got home—"

"Verlene," the man said.

The woman looked down at her plate, then glanced at the others standing around the fire. "Someone had broken in. They took everything we had."

"Verlene!"

"Easy, friend," Ackerman said.

The woman looked at her husband defiantly. "It doesn't matter anymore, Chet. It's gone. We make the best of it."

"The best of it would have been that boy of yours not shooting his mouth off." He turned to Tanner and Ackerman. "We had six months of food and water, everything we'd need if things fell apart. We had guns, ammo, gasoline, propane, heaters. Bastards took it all." He nodded at the boy. "The kid there told his friends about everything we had."

"They wouldn't have done this, Dad," the boy said.

"It's who they told!"

The boy stepped away from the fire, then walked to the front of Tanner's pickup and looked across the field. Hendricks watched for a minute, then walked over and stood next to him. She ate a piece of bacon in silence, then nodded. "It's better when it's hot."

"I'm not hungry," the boy replied.

"When did you eat last?"

"Night before last."

They stood together for a minute, then the boy started crying. "I can't do anything right," he said. He set his plate on the hood of the pickup, then turned and started off across the field.

"Just leave him be," the man called out. "He'll be back. This is where the food is."

Tanner stood up from the fire. "This is where our food is," he said. "Now, you're welcome to share it with us as long as you relax a little. You can't fight around our campfire." He stepped over to the man and refilled his coffee cup. "Any idea who took your stuff?"

"Yeah. Can't do anything about. Cops don't care. I'm unarmed. I can't go in alone."

Tanner nodded slowly. "Okay. Well, let's eat. Maybe we can figure something out. Meanwhile, I don't want the kid wandering around angry. He's your boy, but you're eating my breakfast. That gives me a say in the matter."

"Yes, sir," the man said quietly.

"You don't have to call me sir. My name's Chris." Tanner held out his hand. The man shook it.

"Chet. This is my wife, Verlene. The boy's name is Nick."

"Is it okay if my friend Naomi brings him back?"

"Yes, sir."

"Chris."

Forty-five minutes later, the group was finished with breakfast. Lundgren and Winter got up just in time to grab a quick bite, then help break camp. With the gear stowed in the trucks, the group stood around the campfire, finishing the last of the coffee.

"So, Chet," Tanner said, "where do you think your stuff is?"

"A guy who lives off Highway 99," Chet replied. "He's got it."

"You're sure."

"One of our neighbors saw his truck backed into our driveway. They said he made three trips."

"You know him."

"His kid is friends with one of the boys Nick was talking to."

"What kind of guy is he?"

"The kind who'll steal everything you have."

Tanner nodded. "Does he do drugs?"

"No. He runs a business in town. A tire shop."

"So, he's not likely to do anything crazy."

"Crazy?"

"Like shoot all of us if we show up at his place."

"Before the power went out," Chet replied, "I'd say no. Today? I don't know."

"There's only two ways this goes down," Ackerman said. "We get lucky and nobody's home. We break in and steal it back. Or he's home and we confront him. Either way, we're going to need more than the trucks we have to haul everything out of there."

"You know anybody who can help?" Tanner asked Chet.

"I've got a couple of friends. They have trucks that run. They're both flatbeds."

Tanner nodded. "You say you lost guns."

"Yeah."

"Are you any good with them?"

"I can hit what I'm aiming at."

"That's all that matters."

31

8:30 a.m. Central Standard Time
Stroud, Oklahoma

Four trucks pulled onto the long gravel drive of a farmhouse six miles outside of town and stopped a hundred yards from the front door. "That's his truck," Chet said, pointing at a pickup parked alongside the house.

"So, he's home," Tanner replied.

The plan called for Hendricks and Lundgren to hang back at the end of the driveway with the two flatbed trucks and their drivers. Hendricks would scope things with her rifle. Tanner, Ackerman, Winter and Chet would drive to the house, then Tanner and Chet would walk to the front door while Ackerman and Winter covered them. If the owner came out with a weapon, Hendricks was their element of surprise.

Tanner and Chet were thirty feet from the front door when the owner stepped outside with a shotgun. "Hold it right there, boys," he said. "What's going on?"

Tanner glanced at Chet, then looked at the man standing on the porch. "This man says you've got something that belongs to him."

"Is that right?"

"We're here to take it back."

The man nodded slowly, then raised the shotgun. A split-second later a rifle shot sounded from the end of the driveway and a bullet punched through the wooden face of the step he stood on, three inches below his feet. He jumped back and stood next to the screen door, looking at the pickup truck a hundred yards away.

"Lay the shotgun down," Tanner said, "or she puts a bullet through your heart." The man stood motionless, staring at Tanner. Five seconds later, Tanner shouted, "You want to do this the hard way?" A moment later he saw movement inside the house. Then a gunshot, and a bullet tore through the screen and passed over his head. He ducked down next to the truck. Ackerman and Chet took cover on the opposite side. Leaning over the hood of the pickup, Hendricks watched the front door through the riflescope, ready to squeeze off another round. She saw a woman inside, wearing an apron and holding a pistol with both hands.

"Tanner!" she yelled. "It's his wife!"

"She dies too, mister," Tanner said. "Put the weapon down and tell her to do the same. I'm not going to ask you again."

Hendricks waited five seconds then fired again, putting a bullet through the front of the house four inches to the right of the man's head. The man dropped the shotgun and yelled. "Eleanor! Put the gun down and come out with your hands up! Do it now!"

Hendricks watched through the scope as the woman set the gun on a coffee table and crossed the room to the front door. Putting both hands on the screen in front of her, she pushed it open and stepped outside, then raised her hands over her head.

"I told you this was bound to happen," she told the man.

"Not now, Eleanor," the man replied.

"We've got enough food to feed a dozen people, and you have to take more."

"Eleanor!"

"You're lucky I don't set you on fire while you sleep."

"Calm down," Tanner said. "Anybody else inside?"

"No," the woman replied.

"Where's the food you took?" he asked the man.

"A shipping container in back," the man said.

"It's locked," the woman said. "The key's in the house."

"Get it," Tanner said. He turned to Ackerman. "Go with her." Ackerman stepped up on the porch, then followed her inside.

Chet's friends pulled their trucks around the back of the house and backed them in next to the container. The man unlocked the doors and swung them open, then Tanner and Chet stepped inside. Dozens of boxes were stacked along one wall. Sealed food-storage buckets were stacked against the opposite side. Farther back were propane tanks and heaters, as well as jugs filled with gasoline.

"Where are the guns?" Chet asked the man."

"I don't have your guns," the man replied.

"They're in the house," the woman said. "In a closet." The man glared at his wife. "I told you you'd regret this," she said.

Thirty minutes later the trucks were loaded. Before leaving, Tanner and Hendricks walked into the kitchen and opened the cupboards. They were full, as was the pantry. He turned to the owner. "You've got all this, and you steal another man's food?" He pushed the man against the wall. "You're lucky I don't beat the living—"

"Chris," Hendricks interrupted. "Let's leave well enough alone."

Tanner nodded, then turned back to the owner. "We're sticking around for a while. You bother Chet and his family—you steal his food, any of his stuff—we'll kill you. Got it?"

The man stared at Tanner defiantly. "The sheriff happens to be a friend of mine."

"Good," Tanner replied. "You can give him a message next time you see him. If he's involved in this with you, we've got a bullet for him too." He paused. "Any other time, a thief is a stinking lowlife. This week, he's a dead, stinking lowlife."

Back at Chet's house, they unloaded everything and packed it into the basement. "Better than the garage," Tanner said. "People usually think twice before they break into a home. Not so much with a garage."

The friends with flatbeds told Chet they'd hang out with him for a few days until things cooled down. "You guys have weapons?" Ackerman asked.

"AR-15s. But not a lot of ammunition."

"Two twenty-three?"

"Yeah."

Ackerman gave Chet and his friends two cans—twelve hundred rounds—of ammo. Then Tanner stepped outside with Chet. "Your son wasn't trying to cause trouble when he told his friends about your preps," Tanner said. "He was proud of what you were doing. He thought it was important." Chet looked down, nodding slowly. "Chet," Tanner continued, "these are tough times. And they're going to get tougher. Show the boy what kind of man you really are. Give him a reason to look up to you." Tanner put his hand on Chet's shoulder. "Teach him how to be that kind of man."

"Thanks, Chris," Chet said. "For everything."

"You're welcome," Tanner smiled. "You'll be fine. Stay safe. Take care of your family."

32

2:30 p.m. Mountain Standard Time
West Central Idaho

The prepper compound in the Seven Devils Mountains was about as isolated as a place can be and still be reached when it's needed. Located just east of the Oregon border, the seventy-acre plot of private land was accessible only by four-wheel-drive, making it ideal for what preppers refer to as a bugout retreat.

The main building on the property was underground—forty-six hundred square feet of bedrooms, bathrooms, an expansive kitchen and dining facility, a recreation room, and three separate storage areas. Complimenting this were a sophisticated water filtration and purification system working in tandem with the water well, an air recirculation system, and a diesel generator.

Above ground was a simple cabin, approximately twenty feet square, built from timber cut on the property. Although the cabin had a living room, kitchen, bedroom and bath, it served only as an entry point to the underground quarters.

As with many prepper retreats, considerable work had been done to maximize the defense of those living here against attempts to infiltrate the premises and overthrow the occupants. The twelve acres immediately surrounding the cabin were fenced and topped with razor wire, and fougasse booby traps, trip wires and anti-vehicular ditches were hidden across the terrain. The entire area was observable from a number of rock outcroppings on the slope behind the cabin, and when the compound was in use by the preppers, operational security—or OPSEC, in the jargon of hard-core preppers—called for snipers manning these outposts day and night, communicating with other members by two-way radio.

The last deterrence against invasion was the cabin itself. Doors and window shutters were steel reinforced. Built into the foyer was a 'mantrap'—essentially a pit beneath a trapdoor. Inside the living area, cupboards and closets were booby-trapped.

Entrance to the property was by way of a single, severely rutted road that appeared to be more of a river bed, strewn with large rocks, making passage difficult. There was no gate. There were no locks. There was only a sign at the fence line declaring that trespassers would be shot on sight.

Apart from occasional visits by the owners, during which food, ammunition and other provisions were stockpiled, the property had been vacant until the grid collapse. Twelve hours later, fourteen men and women arrived and set up camp, preparing to hunker down for the long haul.

These were preppers with a militaristic view of preparing for disasters. They believed survival depended on a highly structured lifestyle of unbendable rules and strict discipline. They wore camouflage and carried assault weapons. They used military jargon and communicated with hand signals when running drills aimed at putting down attempts to overtake them. In short, they were rooted in a pseudomilitary lifestyle.

Despite the discipline, the emotional makeup of the group was unpredictable, and by day three of the collapse there was considerable friction. What began as small, seemingly insignificant differences of opinion grew into arguments. Some members began isolating themselves from others. Tension grew. Shouting was common.

Then their leader, a man named Mitchell, turned away three elk hunters who were left stranded after the EMP shut down their truck. With backpacks, hunting rifles and personal gear, the three men hiked twelve miles through two feet of snow from their camp, eventually stumbling onto the preppers' retreat. Crossing the perimeter in dense trees, they were met by three armed men.

"You're trespassing," a prepper named Thompson said.

One of the hunters, a man named King, shifted his backpack. "We need help," he said. He pulled the rifle from his shoulder and was immediately faced with three AR-15s pointed at him.

"You're trespassing," Thompson repeated. The preppers spread out, training their weapons on the hunters.

King held up his hands. "We just need a ride to the highway."

"That's not going to happen," Thompson said.

The hunters looked at each other, then back at the preppers. "What's the problem?" King asked.

"I've said it twice," Thompson replied. "You're trespassing. That makes three. I'm not going to tell you again."

"Look, we're in trouble," King said. He took a step toward Thompson. Thompson fired a shot into the ground in front of King, then pointed the rifle at his face.

"Are you serious?" King said. He stared at Thompson, then at the other preppers. "We've run out of food. Our truck won't run. We don't have phones. We've been hiking all day and we're exhausted. All we need is a ride."

Thompson stared at King for a few seconds, then he pulled out a handheld transceiver. "Ballroom, this is Doorman," he spoke.

"Go ahead, Doorman," a voice replied.

"We need reinforcements at point Tango."

"Is there a problem?"

"Intruders."

For the next five minutes the two groups stood in silence, staring at each other. King's initial impulse was to leave, but he thought he might be able to reason with whoever showed up. A light snow began falling as six more men arrived, all of them armed.

Mitchell stopped in front of the hunters. "Who are you?"

"We've been hunting elk on the other side of the ridge," King replied. "We were breaking camp two days ago when we discovered our truck wouldn't run. We stayed another night, but didn't have provisions to make it any longer, so we decided to hike out. We left this morning at daybreak. The idea was to move east, hoping to find a cabin, somebody who might be able to help us."

Mitchell shook his head. "We can't help you."

"If we could get some food," King said, "and rest for the night, we'll finish hiking out on our own."

"No food," Mitchell replied.

"You're saying you guys don't have any food?"

"I'm saying we're not going to feed you."

"Can you give us a ride to the highway?"

"No."

King exhaled loudly. He looked at his hunting partners, then back at Mitchell. Mitchell stared in silence. Then one of the men who came down from the cabin with him spoke.

"We could give them a ride down to that logging camp."

"Shut up, Ward," Mitchell snapped.

Ward looked at the ground for a moment, then at the hunters. He shrugged.

Mitchell pointed behind the hunters. "Go back to the fence line. Cross over. Then walk south until you hit the corner. From there you can go wherever you want, as long as you don't come back here on my land."

King stared at Mitchell for a few seconds. Then Mitchell fired a burst from his rifle in the air. King fell backward in the snow. He lay there for a moment, then slipped out of the pack's shoulder straps and stood. Lifting the pack from the ground, his friends helped him get it back on his shoulders.

He stared at Mitchell again. "Mighty neighborly of you, friend," he said quietly. "Mighty neighborly."

Mitchell smiled. "Get the hell off my property."

The three hunters turned and walked away.

Back at the cabin, the men who confronted the hunters stood with the others in the recreation room. "This is exactly what I said would happen," Mitchell said. "Someone shows up needing something—food, shelter, whatever. And we deviate from the plan. From protocol. We feed them or give them a ride. A few days later, everybody shows up looking for a handout."

Ward nodded. "I understand, but—"

"No," Mitchell interrupted. "I don't think you do. When I tell someone to leave, and you tell me we should give them a ride, you're ignoring my orders."

Ward held up his hand. "I get it. You're the boss. I'm not sure why, because you're not any smarter than the rest of us. And you sure as hell don't know anything about living in the mountains. But apart from that, this isn't the Army. A military operation. There are no orders. There's only—"

"If we don't have a chain of command," Mitchell said, "we're—"

"I wasn't through," Ward said.

"Kyle." Ward's wife Julie stepped forward.

Ward stared at Mitchell. "When we started this group, it was with the idea that we would take care of each other as brothers, sisters, husbands and wives. Friends. I understand the need for security.

But to turn away men who could die of exposure before they reach someone who will help them, goes against everything I believe."

"You believe in survival?" Mitchell asked.

"Not at the expense of other people."

"That's where we differ."

"Mitchell, the differences between you and me are far too numerous to get into right now." Ward turned to his wife. Julie was not wild about the idea of taking refuge in an underground shelter in the wilderness with a group of people led by Mitchell. His manner irritated her, and for the most part, when he was in the room, she wasn't. Ward knew her feelings, but was torn. Until now.

He turned back to Mitchell. "Let me ask you something. Would you rather be alone with a year's supply of food, or share your last meal with someone you don't even know?" Mitchell stared at Ward in silence. "That's what I thought," Ward said. He turned to Julie. "Get your things together."

"What are you doing?" Mitchell asked.

"My wife and I are leaving."

"No, you're not."

"You can't stop us. We're taking what we brought and we're driving out of here."

"You won't get half a mile in this snow."

Ward smiled. "I grew up in Idaho. I forget more about driving in this kind of weather than you'll know if you live to be a hundred." Ward started to leave the room, then turned back. "Another thing someone like you will never understand, when you're in the wilderness, and it's winter, and someone shows up at your door needing help, you damn well take them in."

"In a grid collapse?" Mitchell replied. "When your survival depends on OPSEC?"

Ward clenched his jaw, then spoke quietly. "Mitchell, I don't care if the earth is falling into the sun. You help people when they need it." He paused. "And if I hear the word OPSEC come out of your mouth again before I leave . . ." Mitchell squared off with Ward and the two men stared at each other in silence. Then Ward nodded and left the room.

It was dark when Kyle and Julie Ward pulled away from the cabin in a heavy snow storm, their truck chained on all four tires and loaded with provisions—food, clothing, and medical supplies, as well as weapons and ammunition. It wasn't all they brought to the property over the last eighteen months. But it was all the truck could carry and still have room for the elk hunters.

"I'm thinking they'd head south along the fence line," Kyle said. "From there, they'd pick up the road."

"If they can find it," Julie replied. "This storm is getting bad." She looked out the side window. "If it were me out there, I'd probably shelter."

"They might do that," Kyle said.

The truck pushed through the snow—bouncing, sliding, at times bogging down as it spun the tires, but pulling through. Julie switched on the roof-mounted spotlight and swept the beam side to side, looking for any sign of the elk hunters. Several minutes later, the snow was so heavy the spotlight was useless due to the light reflecting off the flakes. Five minutes after that, Kyle shut off the headlights in order to see the ground ahead of him, leaving the amber parking lights on.

He shook his head. "This is bad. If we find the hunters—and that's a big if—we may not get off the mountain tonight."

Julie held up her hand. "Did you hear that? It sounded like a gunshot." Kyle stopped the truck. Both of them rolled down their windows and listened. Kyle shook his head. Julie stared out the window, straining to hear, then reached over and honked the horn three times. A moment later they heard another gunshot.

"That's a rifle," Kyle said. "It came from your side." He switched on the spotlight and shined the beam to the right of the truck, then climbed out and walked around the front.

Then he heard someone yell, "We're east of you! Fifty yards south of the road!"

Kyle climbed in the truck and pulled forward slowly, listening. When he heard the man yell again, he turned off the road, heading due south, picking his way through thick patches of scrub oak. Two minutes later he saw three men standing in front of a yellow tent, waving their arms. He pulled up to them and stopped.

"We came to take you guys into town," he said, "but I don't think we can make it out now. If we can get this truck in close, we'll raise a tarp over the back of it and extend it over your tent. That'll give us some shelter. We'll wait out the storm."

"Sounds like a workable plan." The man glanced at his hunting partners, then looked at Kyle. "I hesitate to ask because of the reception we got earlier—"

"That was them, not us. We've got food."

Julie opened the back of the truck and dug through boxes, pulling out two bunches of bananas, a bag of oranges, a bag of apples, and a bottle of fruit juice. "Start with this," she said. "It'll be easier on your stomach if you haven't eaten for more than a day."

"Thank you, ma'am," the man said, taking the items from her. He held out his other hand. "Everett King." He pointed to his friends. "This is Burke Abbott and Jordan Stanley."

"I'm Julie Ward," she smiled, shaking hands. "That's my husband, Kyle."

"We met earlier," Everett said.

With that, Everett, Burke and Jordan retreated to their tent to eat while Kyle and Julie backed the truck in and strung up a tarp, running from the midpoint of the camper shell to the back side of the tent, draped to the ground on both sides. The hunters climbed out of the tent and opened up the front, then stood with Kyle and Julie underneath the tarp.

"Cozy," Everett said.

"Let's hope the wind doesn't pick up," Kyle replied, "or we can kiss cozy goodbye."

Julie pulled out a bag of hard rolls. "Here's some carbs." She tossed a jar of peanut butter to Everett. "And protein. Spread that on apple slices. Does a body good."

Everett held up the jar of peanut butter. "Been a big fan of this since I was a kid."

Julie nodded. "That makes three of us."

"Five of us," Burke and Jordan added.

Kyle pulled out tins of sardines, a bag of raw cashews and a mason jar filled with homemade beef jerky. They ate and talked.

"You're a lifesaver, Kyle," Everett said. "Julie. We appreciate this more than we can say."

"You're welcome," Kyle replied. "And I'm really sorry about those guys back up the road."

"They do what they think they have to," Everett said. "Problem is, when someone's stranded . . ."

"Starving," Burke added.

"Oh, I brought that up," Kyle said, "just before Julie and I packed our bags."

"What are they doing up there?" Jordan asked. "What's with the commando act?"

"You guys know what happened? Why your truck won't run?"

"No," Everett replied. "And it's not just the truck. Our flashlights, watches . . . nothing works."

"There was a high-altitude nuclear detonation. It caused an electromagnetic pulse that fried anything electronic. Your truck has a computer. LED flashlights have an integrated circuit on the back of the diode. Your watches are electronic."

"You're saying everything electronic is dead?"

"Yes. Computers, cell phones, everything. And there's no electricity. No running water. Nothing's being delivered because fuel can't be pumped." Kyle paused. "It's all of North America."

"For how long?"

"It'll be months before they get electrical power back, and even then, it'll be spotty. It could be a year or more for some parts of the country. And the economy, banking . . ." Kyle shrugged.

"What about banking?" Burke asked.

"We're partners in a financial investment firm," Jordan said. "San Francisco."

"Everything stored on servers," Kyle said. "It's gone."

Everett, Burke and Jordan stared at each other, absorbing this information. They looked back at Kyle, then glanced at Julie. "So, you guys are preppers," Everett said. "That place is your hideout—your end-of-the-world, get-lost compound."

"Was," Kyle replied.

"But that's the idea. Come up here and escape the crazies."

"I'm not sure who the crazies are anymore."

33

Friday, February 14
5:00 a.m. Mountain Standard Time
West Central Idaho

It was still dark when Kyle woke up. He lay on his back, sleeping bag pulled snugly around his face, and stared at the ceiling of the camper shell. He and Julie had unloaded a portion of what was packed in the back of their truck to make room for sleeping, but it was still cramped. He checked his watch, slipped out of his bag and pulled on his boots, then twisted the handle of the camper shell door and pushed it open. A foot and a half of new snow had fallen overnight, bringing the total depth to more than thirty inches. The sky was clear, the temperature a bone-chilling twenty-five below zero.

He stepped over to the elk hunters' tent. "You guys alive and kicking?" he said.

"Yeah," a voice replied. "Time to get up?"

"As much as I hate to say it. And it's seriously cold, so bundle up." Kyle cleared an area of snow between the two trucks, then lowered the tailgate on his. He reached in and shook Julie. "It's morning, sweetheart. Rise and shine."

"What time is it?" she asked.

"Five."

"Seriously?"

"Yeah. I want to get out of here—off the mountain and down into town. I'll make coffee, but we'll wait to eat until we get there."

It took twenty minutes to clear snow so the truck could move. With Kyle, Everett and Julie in the front seat, and Burke and Jordan in the back with their gear, the truck spun its way back up to the road, then down the mountain to Riggins.

An hour and a half after they left the campsite, they were standing behind their pickup truck in the parking lot of Rosie's Bar and Steakhouse, eating breakfast off the tailgate—bacon and eggs, and pancakes with syrup. They sat on three-legged camp stools and ate as the sun came up and the town of Riggins, population 440, started moving. Most vehicles were pickups, and most of those had a blade on the front for moving snow. A pickup pulled into the parking lot and started plowing. Five minutes later another truck pulled in and a man and a woman got out and unlocked the front door.

"You open for business?" Kyle called out.

"We will be in a few minutes," the man answered.

After they finished eating, Kyle and Julie packed everything in the back of the truck. Then they went inside.

"Bar's open," the woman said. "But we're not cooking, and we're out of coffee."

"Hold that thought," Kyle said. He went back outside to the pickup and returned a minute later with a three-pound can of Folgers. "It's yours," he said, handing it to the woman.

"Drinks are on the house," she smiled. "Let me get a drip going and I'll be right with you. Sit wherever you'd like."

They sat at the bar and turned their stools to face the front windows, watching activity along Riggins' main street. "So, Kyle," Everett said, "Where do you and Julie call home when you're not playing army in the mountains?"

"Lewiston," Kyle said. "About a hundred miles north of here."

"I know Lewiston," Everett replied. "We fished for steelhead on the Snake River a couple of years ago."

"I don't know what your plan is," Julie said, "but you could do a lot worse than northern Idaho."

"Is that an invitation?" Everett asked.

"You guys are welcome at our place," Kyle said. "We've got plenty of room. An extra vehicle. And we've got food."

"We don't want to impose."

Kyle chuckled. "This is just me, but these days there is no imposing. There's only helping, and being helped."

"Amen to that," the waitress said, walking up behind the bar. "What can I get you folks?"

"I'll have a cup of that coffee when it's ready," Julie said. "With a splash of Irish cream."

Kyle looked at Everett, Burke and Jordan. "You guys don't have to work today, do you?" he asked. Everett smiled. Kyle turned to the waitress. "Wild Turkey. Neat."

"Jack Daniels," Everett said. "Neat also." Jordan and Burke ordered the same.

"Drinking at eight in the morning," Julie said. "Not exactly what I had in mind for Valentine's Day."

Kyle stared at her. "You're right. It's Valentine's Day."

"Don't worry, sweetheart. You can get me flowers later. Right now, there's nowhere I'd rather be than in this bar." She turned to the others and lifted her coffee cup. "Here's to not being buried in snow on the mountain."

34

11:00 a.m. Mountain Standard Time
Interstate 40
New Mexico

The road trip was winding down. Stopped outside Gallup, New Mexico for a meal break, Hendricks, Lundgren, Winter, Tanner and Ackerman were seven hours from their destination in Arizona. They were upbeat after the strain of the last few days, and were looking forward to putting this trip behind them.

"I'm tired of framing things with crosshairs," Hendricks said, eating an apple. "Especially people."

"Well, you're good at it," Tanner said. "You've saved lives."

"I've taken lives too. That's a balancing act I don't like."

"Remember what we talked about the other night around the campfire?"

"I know, Chris. It's necessary. And don't take this wrong, because I have the utmost respect for men and women who fight for our country, but I couldn't kill people for a living."

"You make it sound like assassination," Ackerman said.

"I'm sorry, Miles. That didn't come out right. That's not what I meant." Hendricks paused and drew a deep breath. "I'm just tired of the trigger." She paused again, then sat upright and laughed. "That was weird."

"What," Tanner said.

"Have you ever heard that phrase before? Tired of the trigger?"

"No. Why?"

"My husband said it to me."

"You're married?"

"I was. He was killed in Iraq." Tanner and Ackerman glanced at each other. "He was a Marine scout sniper," Hendricks continued. "I was wondering if that was a phrase soldiers use."

"It might be for snipers," Ackerman said. "But I never heard anyone say it."

"Naomi," Lundgren said, "we worked together six years and you never said a word about being married." Hendricks nodded slowly. "Why?" Lundgren asked.

She shrugged. "I don't know."

"That explains a lot," Winter said.

"A lot about what?" Hendricks asked.

"The way you can shoot."

"My dad taught me how to shoot." She paused. "Ryan—my husband—taught me how to face fear."

"Okay," Winter nodded. "That explains a lot too."

Hendricks stood and brushed off the seat of her pants, then began stowing the meal gear in the back of the truck. The others watched her for a moment.

"You okay, Naomi?" Lundgren asked.

"I'm just tired," she replied. "Actually, I'm not tired. I'm weary. I am so weary I can't stand it. I just . . . I don't know whether I want to laugh or cry."

Tanner put his trash in the bag, then faced Hendricks. He placed his hands on her shoulders and looked her squarely in the eyes. "I'm not breaking out the tequila," he said, winking.

She smiled, but her lower lip was quivering, and the look in her eyes told him she was running on empty. He put his arms around her. "You're almost home," he said. She nodded and drew a deep breath, then turned away.

"I feel like such a baby," she said, wiping a tear from her cheek. "I've cried more in the last few days than . . ." She sighed. "This trip's been an emotional roller coaster for me."

""You're not alone with those feelings."

She turned back and hugged him. "Thanks, Chris. I don't know what we would have done without you and Miles."

"You wouldn't have lasted two minutes."

"Actually, we were on day three."

"I'm kidding, Naomi."

"I'm sorry, Chris. I feel like I'm asleep at the wheel. I'm running on autopilot."

"You want Miles to drive your truck?"

"I'll be okay. I'm in familiar territory now. Close to home."

They packed up the trucks, then climbed in and drove away, Tanner and Ackerman in the lead. Traffic picked up after they crossed into Arizona, and by the time they reached Holbrook, it seemed as if life—at least on the highway—had returned to normal.

"I don't get it," Winter said, watching a car pass them on the left. "It's like there's an anti-EMP dome over the state."

Hendricks smiled. "Arizona doesn't have a vehicle inspection. So, there are a lot of older cars on the road—what some might call less-than-reliable."

"So less reliable means working transportation," Lundgren said.

"Yeah." She paused. "Arizona has a mind of its own. They don't change their clocks twice a year. They don't register firearms. And you can carry weapons, concealed or open, anywhere you want without a license. Unless, of course, there's a sign on the door prohibiting it."

"That's crazy," Winter said.

"Maybe. On the other hand, the crime rate is low. People don't stick up convenience stores because they don't know who's packing. There aren't a lot of home invasions."

"And with the collapse? What do they do now?"

"They pick sides. Kind of like we did in Missouri and Oklahoma." She paused. "My dad used to say that in any given group of people—ten, or ten thousand—the majority will be straight-thinking people. Common sense will prevail. There will be a few who rock the boat. But when everybody else gets tired of it, they take the troublemakers out back and throw them around a little. Things have a way of working out."

"Equilibrium," Winter said.

"Exactly. So, while you've got idiots who are going to try and take what other people have, around here the other people are armed. Not a lot of soft targets."

It was just past 1 p.m. when they reached Winslow. They stopped to fill the tanks with gas from the containers and grab snack food.

"How far to Kingman?" Tanner asked.

"Two hundred miles," Hendricks said. "Four hours, if we don't run into trouble."

"Trouble?" Tanner smiled. "What could possibly go wrong?"

"Don't get me started."

Twenty minutes later they were on the road again with Hendricks in the lead. She was on a high, thinking about home, singing Bachman-Turner Overdrive's "Roll On Down the Highway" and rocking in her seat. She smiled at Winter and Lundgren, drumming on the steering wheel with both hands. Then she paused, looking through the windshield. Her eyes narrowed for a moment, then she jumped on the brakes.

"What's going on?" Lundgren asked.

"That's a choke point," she said. A half-mile away, two pickups were angle-parked, one on each side of the road. Four men stepped onto the highway carrying rifles, then walked to the centerline. Hendricks shifted into reverse and stomped the accelerator, looking in her side mirror as the truck took off backward. A moment later, a bullet punched through the windshield, passing between her and Lundgren, shattering the cab's rear window.

"Get down!" she shouted. Before Lundgren and Winter could react, three more rounds hit the windshield in rapid succession. The first took out the rearview mirror. The second hit Hendricks in the neck. The third hit Lundgren in the chest.

For a split-second, Hendricks froze, staring at four neat, clean bullet holes in the windshield, each one the size of a pencil. Out of the corner of her eye she saw Lundgren fall forward. She heard Winter shout. She realized her foot was still on the accelerator, the truck racing down the highway in reverse, engine screaming. She hit the brakes and turned the steering wheel hard. The truck spun around, coming to a stop with the rear end facing the shooters. Then she fell against the side window.

"We need to catch up," Ackerman said.

"I know," Tanner replied. "I should have used the bathroom when we stopped for coffee."

"If a man's gotta go, a man's gotta go."

"That sounds like something John Wayne would say."

Ackerman laughed. "A man's gotta do what a man's gotta do."

"Same thing."

They came up over a rise and saw Hendricks' pickup off the side of the road in a cloud of dust. Two trucks were parked beyond it, and men with rifles were running toward them. "We've got trouble," Tanner said. He slid to a stop next to Hendricks' truck.

"Naomi and Paul were shot," Winter called out, running to Tanner's truck.

Tanner opened his door and started to get out, but Ackerman grabbed his arm. "Are they alive?" he asked.

"Yes."

"Can they make it back to Winslow?"

"I doubt it. Paul's been hit in the chest. Naomi's hit in the neck. They're bleeding badly."

"Chris," Ackerman said, "Those guys are thirty seconds away. We need to hold them off while Scott works on Naomi and Paul."

Tanner turned back to Winter. "Can you get a safe distance down the highway and take care of them?"

"I think so," Winter replied.

"Get out of range, but keep us in sight."

"Got it." Winter ran back to Hendricks' truck and opened the driver's door slowly, pushing Hendricks to the middle of the seat, then climbed in and drove away.

Tanner backed his truck around until it was sideways in the road, then both men climbed out and pulled rifles and ammo cans from the back. At three hundred yards, they began firing at the men approaching, using the truck for cover.

Winter drove a quarter mile down the road and pulled off into the dirt, then retrieved Hendricks' trauma bag from the rear of the truck. Back inside the cab, he pressed a half-dozen gauze pads against Naomi's wound. The bullet had passed between her trachea and neck muscle, just missing the carotid artery and jugular vein. Still, the bleeding was profuse, and his priority was to get it under control. He couldn't work on Lundgren without her help.

Hendricks opened her eyes and straightened up, grabbing Winter's hand. "What are you doing?"

"You've been shot, Naomi," he replied. "Can you hold these pads against your neck? I need to check Paul."

She held the pads, then tried to turn and look at Lundgren, but was stopped by searing pain, a sensation of being stabbed in the neck. "What happened?" She pulled her hand away from her neck and looked at the blood-soaked gauze, then glanced up at the bullet holes in the windshield. A moment later she heard gunfire in the distance, and suddenly everything came back to her.

"Oh, my God!" she shouted. "Paul!" She tried turning again but was stabbed with neck pain. Stepping out of the truck, she twisted the side mirror to look at the wound. When she lifted the gauze, she saw the bullet hole and blood running down her neck. She dropped the pads on the ground and pulled two rolls of gauze from the trauma bag, then tore the paper from one and pressed it in between her throat and neck muscle. Holding it in place, she kneeled on the seat next to Lundgren.

"He's hit in the chest," Winter said.

Hendricks checked his pulse. It was rapid, thready. "He's going into shock. We've got to lay him on the seat and get his legs up. Grab one of those poly bins out of the back." Winter climbed out of the truck as Hendricks pulled Lundgren down on the seat and tore open the front of his shirt. There was a single bullet hole four inches below his collarbone, three inches to the left of his sternum. "Dear God," she whispered, knowing that if the bullet had hit a half-inch to the right, he would have been dead before he fell over.

Winter returned to the passenger door with the bin. He lifted Lundgren's legs, then placed the bin underneath. "How is he?" he asked quietly.

"Alive," Hendricks replied. "But the bullet went through his lung." She pulled the collar of his coat to the side, examining his neck. The blood vessels were distended. "It's collapsing."

"His lung?"

"I know what to do, Scott. But I need your help. You can't get distracted by bullet holes and blood." She stared at him for a moment. "Can you do this?"

Blood had soaked the roll of gauze Hendricks was pressing against her neck, and was dripping on Lundgren's chest and running down his side. Winter watched it pool on the seat, then looked up at her. "Whatever you say, Naomi."

She tossed the blood-soaked gauze and opened the second roll, pressing it against her neck. "We need a jug of water up here. And some clean cloth. In my duffel bag are T-shirts. Grab three. And bring a lid from the other poly bin."

She dug through the trauma bag and pulled out a bottle of alcohol, a stack of gauze pads, a Bic pen, a Ziploc bag, and a roll of surgical tape. When Winter returned with the items from the back, she placed the lid on the floor and laid the shirts on it.

"Scott, I have to hold this roll of gauze against my neck, and I can't work on Paul with just one hand."

"Tell me what to do."

They were interrupted by the sound of gunfire coming from down the highway. "Is that Chris and Miles?" she asked

"Yeah. They're fighting bad guys."

"You've got to work fast, Scott. First, wash your hands. Hold them out while I pour water over them." Winter cleaned his hands as best he could with plain water, then dried them on a T-shirt. "Now clean his chest around the wound with alcohol." When he finished, she handed him the pen. "Pull the ink cartridge out."

"This goes in the bullet hole."

"Yes."

Winter gripped the tip of the pen in his teeth and pulled it out, then he poured alcohol over the plastic tube. "Anything special?" he asked, holding the tapered end over the hole.

"Point the end of it away from your face."

He started the tube into the wound. At a half-inch in, a red mist sprayed out the end. Lundgren's chest fell and the veins in his neck relaxed. "Amazing," he said.

"Pull it out, but keep it handy. You may need it again. Soak two gauze pads in alcohol and place them over the wound." While he was doing that, Hendricks replaced the soaked gauze on her neck with a fresh roll. "Now put the Ziploc over the gauze and tape it on three sides."

"It lets air out, but keeps it from coming in."

"A valve. You seem to know what you're doing. I should just pass out and get it over with."

Winter smiled. "How are you doing?"

"I'm losing my peripheral vision."

"You're white as a sheet."

"You're going to have to drive us back into Winslow and find a doctor."

"Chris and Miles can help."

Hendricks winced as she turned to look up the highway. "Criminy, that hurts." She pivoted at her waist, then held up a hand to shade her eyes. In the distance, a dozen men were running across the desert toward Tanner's truck. It was a coordinated ambush, and Hendricks knew that Tanner and Ackerman were about a minute away from being completely outgunned. She turned back to Winter and nearly fell over from dizziness.

"Scott," she said, hanging on to the driver's door, "get the rifle out of my bag and set it up on the highway." She pulled her smartphone from a pocket and opened the ballistics app, then handed it to him. "There are three magazines loaded, five rounds in each."

Winter grabbed a roll of gauze. "Naomi, you're bleeding out." He unwrapped the gauze and pressed it against her neck, soaking up the blood. She held it in place.

"Range your shots, adjust the scope turrets—"

"I know what to do."

She paused, hanging on to the door. Then she fell over.

"Where the hell are all these guys coming from!" Tanner yelled. "It's like someone rolled over a freakin' rock!" He fired a half-dozen more shots, then dropped the magazine onto the pavement and slipped in another. "Miles, take cover behind the tire. We've got to figure this out."

Tanner sat on the pavement with his back to the front wheel. Ackerman leaned up against the rear wheel. They looked at each other for a moment, then Tanner shook his head. "We're in deep shit, buddy."

"I know," Miles replied.

"How many have we taken out?"

"Eight or nine."

"There are at least fifteen left. And we don't know how many more are out there hiding in those gullies."

"The numbers aren't the problem, Chris."

"I know. It's their rifles. They're full auto." Tanner leaned over and glanced underneath the pickup. A dozen men were advancing on their position, and others were still coming up onto the highway from both sides of the road. "We've got about a minute before we're overrun."

Ackerman grabbed a handful of cartridges from an ammo can and loaded empty magazines, looking back down the highway toward Hendricks' pickup a half-mile away. "I wish we had the lady on that long gun right now. If these guys started dropping from shots they couldn't even hear, they'd bug out."

"Ain't gonna happen."

"I know." There was a lull in the shooting and the air was silent. Ackerman leaned back and closed his eyes for a moment, breathing in the smell of mesquite and dirt. "I miss Texas."

Just then a shot came in over their heads from the direction of Hendricks' pickup. Tanner leaned over and looked underneath his truck. Fifty yards away, a man standing at the side of the road fell. Five seconds later another shot rang out and another man fell. Then another, and another. Suddenly Ackerman stood and started around the back of the truck.

"Miles!" Tanner shouted. "Get back here!" Gunfire erupted as soon as Ackerman stepped into the open. He fired three shots, then fell backward. "Miles!" Tanner yelled. He crawled to Ackerman and pulled him back to cover. Blood was soaking through his shirt.

"That was stupid," Ackerman said, looking up at Tanner.

"A little," Tanner nodded. "Fatigue, adrenaline." He tore Ackerman's shirt open, exposing a hole in his chest, pouring blood. "A death wish." He pulled a bandana from his pocket and pressed it against the wound. "It happens."

"Not to us," Ackerman smiled. "It was stupid." His head rolled to the side, then he snapped it back. "My blood pressure's falling, Chris. I'm blacking out."

Tanner lifted the bandana. The bullet hole was still bleeding, but not profusely. Then he saw blood pooling on the pavement under Ackerman's leg. He tore the pants leg open and saw blood spurting from a bullet hole. "Jesus," he whispered. He knew from his Army training that it was an artery, and that Ackerman would be dead in ninety seconds if he couldn't stop the flow of blood.

He pulled off his belt and cinched it around Ackerman's thigh three inches above the bullet hole, then tightened it. The bleeding slowed, but it wasn't going to be enough. Ackerman's hand slid off his chest. He was losing consciousness. Tanner grabbed the bandana and squeezed the blood from it, then wadded it into a ball and pushed it in between the belt and Ackerman's groin as a compress directly over the femoral artery, then cinched the belt again. This time the flow of blood stopped.

"Still with me, Miles?" Tanner said. Ackerman was unresponsive, eyes closed. Tanner slapped his face. "Talk to me, Miles."

Ackerman raised his hand a few inches. "How we doin', pardner?" he said. His eyes remained closed, his voice thin, distant.

"We're good. We're almost there."

Tanner knew he had to get Ackerman out of there. Gunfire was still coming from the direction of Hendricks' pickup. He leaned over and looked underneath the truck at the highway on the other side, counting five bodies lying on the ground, and at least that many more on the sides of the road. The rest were running back toward their trucks. He opened the driver's door, then lifted Ackerman to his feet and pushed him across the seat.

"Stay with me, buddy," he said, getting in behind the wheel. He looked at the chest wound. The flow of blood had almost stopped, barely oozing. But the leg wound was bleeding again. He refastened the belt, cinching it tight, slowing the blood flow, but he couldn't stop it completely. He slipped the truck into gear and punched it, spinning the tires as the truck slid around, heading east.

Lying on the highway, Winter watched through the riflescope as Tanner's truck approached. He saw a man opening the driver's door of one of the pickups behind Tanner. Placing the crosshairs of the scope between his shoulder blades, he squeezed the trigger and the man fell. Across the road, another man was heading toward the other pickup. Winter waited until he stopped at the door, then pulled the trigger again, dropping him. Finally, he put a bullet through each of the back tires of both trucks, then stood and carried the rifle to the back of Hendricks' pickup. He was closing the tailgate when Tanner's truck slid to a stop fifty feet away.

"Miles is hit," Tanner shouted at him. "He's in bad shape."

"Head into town," Winter said. "I'll be right behind you."

Tanner pulled away, stomping the gas pedal. As the truck picked up speed, his mind drifted back to an ambush fifty years earlier in the jungles of Vietnam. Tanner and Ackerman were in a Medevac chopper along with eight other soldiers who were wounded. That day, though, it was Tanner who was lying in a pool of blood, and Ackerman working on him. He couldn't see, but he remembered being on the edge of consciousness when Ackerman grabbed his hand and gripped it, telling him to hang tight. That was the last thing he remembered before passing out.

Now, racing down the highway, Tanner reached over and grabbed Ackerman's wrist, checking for a pulse. He couldn't feel one. "Miles!" he shouted, but there was no response. He swore, flooring the gas pedal. The speedometer was pegged. In his mirror, he saw Hendricks' truck behind him, keeping pace. Then he passed a road sign—Winslow 8 miles. He'd be there in four minutes.

"Hang tight, buddy," he whispered, gripping Ackerman's hand. "Hang tight."

35

Miles Ackerman lay unconscious on an examination table as the doctor, an elderly general practitioner named Silas Davenport, leaned over the leg wound. "Suture," he spoke quietly, adjusting the magnifiers clipped to his glasses. Chris Tanner—gowned, gloved and masked—picked up a clamp holding a curved needle with black nylon thread attached and handed it to the doctor. "More light, please," Davenport said. Scott Winter, also gowned, gloved and masked, moved closer with a high intensity flashlight.

The family clinic was running on a small generator, but the bulk of the electricity was going to the X-ray machine and the autoclave. On top of that, there were no nurses or assistants. When Tanner and Winter arrived with their wounded friends, Davenport informed them that the only way he could help them was if they assisted.

He started by stabilizing Ackerman, the most critically wounded, replacing the belt around his thigh with a pneumatic tourniquet, and administering an intravenous blood-volume expander consisting of two liters of Gelofusine. He turned his attention to Lundgren, cleaning the wound, inserting a chest tube to relieve the pneumothorax, and starting an IV of dextrose and water. The bullet, which had come to rest beneath the skin on Lundgren's back, would be removed after he finished treating Ackerman.

Next, Davenport treated Hendricks' neck wound. The bullet had passed completely through, exiting next to her third cervical vertebra, leaving no fragments and no damage to the veins, arteries and tendons in her neck. He sterilized the wounds, applied a dressing, a bandage, and a cervical collar to hold everything in place and limit motion in her neck, and started an IV drip.

"Mr. Ackerman will need an infusion of whole blood," Davenport said. "The problem is cross-matching. I can't do that here."

"He's O-negative," Tanner replied. "So am I."

"You're certain of this."

"We served together in Vietnam. He gave me blood."

Davenport nodded. "We'll repair the artery, then do blood."

The three of them scrubbed, then donned surgical gowns, gloves and masks. Davenport gave Tanner a crash course in surgical instruments—how to clamp gauze sponges or a curved suture needle, how to pass a scalpel to the surgeon, and most importantly, how to keep a sterile environment sterile. Davenport turned to Ackerman and swabbed the wound with Betadine.

"Ready?" he asked Tanner and Winter. They nodded. He stepped in close and flipped the magnifiers down. "Sponge."

Two hours later, Tanner and Winter stepped outside. Tanner walked around his pickup, surveying the damage. The passenger side was riddled with bullet holes, and the door glass was shattered. But the truck wasn't leaking anything, and it ran. He turned to Hendricks' truck. It was in similar shape, with bullet holes in the windshield, down one side and across the tailgate. He looked underneath, then stood, nodding.

"The trucks look okay," he said. He lowered the tailgate on his pickup, and the two of them sat. "Ever done anything like that?" Tanner asked. "Surgery?"

"No," Winter replied. "It was interesting, though."

"You can learn a lot just by watching."

"Were you a medic in Vietnam?"

"No. I was an A-Team weapons NCO. But you don't get to be a Green Beret without a big chunk of medical training. Soldiers in the field have a way of getting shot to pieces, and there's not always a medic around to patch you up."

"What did Miles do?"

"He was a commo NCO. A-Team communications." Tanner paused, then put a hand on Winter's shoulder. "Miles and I would be dead right now if you hadn't stepped up with Naomi's rifle."

"You can thank Naomi for that. She told me what to do."

"When?"

"Right before she passed out."

"She taught you how to shoot long-range precision while she was doctoring her neck?"

Winter smiled. "No. She taught me how to shoot yesterday. Today she told me how to range my shots."

Tanner nodded. "Well, that was damned good shooting."

"For a mathematician?"

"For anybody."

A minute later, Davenport joined them in the parking lot. "Barring an infection," he said, "Mr. Ackerman will be fine. He lost a lot of blood, and it will take time for his body to replenish vital elements. And he'll be on crutches for a week or so. Ms. Hendricks lost quite a bit of blood as well, though not as much as Mr. Ackerman. But she'll be fine in a few days. Same with Mr. Lundgren."

"Thanks, Doc," Tanner said.

Davenport nodded, looking at the side of Tanner's truck. "You people did this town a favor out there on the highway. I hate to say that—I delivered most of those boys as babies. Watched them grow up. Then, over the years, I watched them throw their lives away. When the power went out, they hit every clinic and pharmacy in town. Stole all the drugs they could find. Then they stormed the police department." He shook his head. "A lot of good people are dead because of them."

"These guys killed police officers?"

"Police officers, private citizens. They're taking over this town by force, and they'll stop at nothing to achieve that."

"What about the police that are left?"

"They're outnumbered and outgunned." Davenport paused. "I could be wrong, but it strikes me that you and your friend in there have a particular skill set we could use around here."

Tanner's mind drifted back over the last three weeks. He and Ackerman had gone out on a limb to help their friend in Iowa. He was struggling with alcohol and drug addiction, and after years of bouncing in and out of rehab, it was apparent he had lost interest in leading a normal, productive life. Tanner and Ackerman spent two agonizing weeks working with him—with family, friends, doctors and therapists at the VA. When it became obvious the man no longer cared about anything—himself included—Tanner and Ackerman cut their losses and headed back home.

Then the EMP hit. As they were making their way through traffic outside Des Moines, an airliner nosedived into a field four hundred yards away, exploding in a fireball. There was nothing they could do but watch. From that point on, the trip had become a struggle of life and death, a surreal mix of making friends and killing strangers. Right now, standing outside this clinic, Tanner wanted nothing more than to be back home in Big Spring, Texas.

He looked at Davenport, then stood and closed the tailgate. "De oppresso liber," Davenport said, looking at the sticker on the back of the truck. "To liberate the oppressed." He looked at Tanner. "You didn't say you were Special Forces."

Tanner looked down, shaking his head. He knew he had no choice. He glanced at Davenport. "Still am."

An hour later, Tanner and Winter were standing in Silas Davenport's kitchen. Hendricks, Lundgren and Ackerman were in bedrooms down the hall. "Up until Monday night, we had a thriving bed and breakfast," Silas said, nodding at his wife, Muriel. "Now we've got a big, empty house. You folks are welcome to stay as long as you want—at least until your friends get back on their feet."

"We appreciate the hospitality," Tanner said. "And again, thanks for patching up our wounded."

"Glad I could help."

"The police that are still around, do you know how we can get a hold of them, see if we can come up with some kind of a plan?"

"They're lying low for now," Silas said, "like everyone else around town. But we can find them. As far as a plan goes, I know someone that could be a big help. Name's Harlan Hicks. He's a little eccentric, but he's got more armament than anybody around here, law enforcement included. He's a man you want on your side."

"Eccentric?"

"He's a conspiracy theorist," Muriel said.

Silas nodded. "Got himself a website and a radio station."

"A conspiracy theorist," Tanner said. "Like, who killed JFK?"

"JFK, CIA, black helicopters. You name it."

"He thinks the federal government is involved in the grid collapse," Muriel said.

"The federal government is involved in the grid collapse?" Tanner smiled at Winter. "Naomi's going to love this."

36

Saturday, February 15
7:00 a.m. Mountain Standard Time
Winslow, Arizona

"You have got to be kidding me." Hendricks looked out the living room window as a military M-35 cargo truck pulled in the Davenports' driveway. "A deuce and a half?"

Muriel Davenport looked across the room from the kitchen and smiled. "That's Harlan."

"I hate to be the one to say this," Winter said, crossing the living room. He stood next to Hendricks and gently elbowed her. "I think you just got out-trucked."

"He's got a fifty-caliber machine gun in the back," Silas said.

"You're joking," Tanner replied.

"No, sir."

"A fifty-caliber machine gun?" Winter asked.

"Right out of your video game," Hendricks replied.

Tanner nodded. "That would have come in handy yesterday."

Silas crossed the room to the front door. "It still might. Like I said, Harlan's a man you want on your side." He opened the door and Hicks stepped inside.

"Doc," Hicks said, shaking hands with Silas. "How's it going?"

"Shaping up to be a nice day. You hungry?"

"I ate breakfast a couple of hours ago. But I'd take a cup of coffee." He glanced at the others. "Bed and breakfast up and running?"

"Something like that." Silas made introductions, then ushered everyone into the kitchen where Muriel was putting breakfast on the table. Winter poured coffee. Tanner pulled homemade biscuits from the oven, popped them into a basket, then set them on the table next to a serving dish filled with cream gravy.

"Compliments of Texas," he said.

"You know what?" Hicks nodded. "I changed my mind."

"I thought you might," Muriel smiled, setting another plate on the table. "This is the lightest gravy I've ever tasted."

"Mom's recipe," Tanner said.

"Looks like solar power finally paid off," Hicks said. "This is probably one of the few working kitchens around."

"Nothing like a hot breakfast," Silas nodded.

They passed around plates of pancakes, bacon, sausage and eggs, and started eating and making small talk. Hicks nodded at Hendricks' cervical collar. "I take it that's not for whiplash."

"I was shot through the neck," she replied.

"Seriously?"

"These folks got caught in an ambush outside of town," Silas said. "The local thugs."

Hendricks and Tanner described the shooting to Hicks, and the mad dash to the clinic for medical help. "We've got two others down the hall, recuperating from gunshot wounds," Tanner said.

Hicks turned to Silas. "Are these the same guys who shot up everything the night of the collapse? I thought they disappeared."

"Doesn't look like it," Silas replied.

"Why are they stopping traffic on the highway?"

"Targets of opportunity," Tanner said.

Hicks looked at him. "Can any of you shoot?"

"All of us can shoot."

"What do you say we take these SOBs down a notch or two?"

"Define 'take them down a notch or two.'"

"Track 'em down. Kill 'em. Bury the bodies in the desert. Or don't bury them. Let the buzzards pick their bones clean."

Tanner turned to Hendricks. "Your thoughts?" he said.

Hendricks shook her head. "I'm not sure how to respond to that." She looked at Hicks. "You paint a vivid picture."

"I have a vivid imagination," Hicks replied. He turned to Tanner. "What kind of weapons have you got?"

"Assault rifles. Handguns. A pump shotgun."

"That's okay for mopping up."

"What have you got?"

Hicks smiled. "RPGs."

"RPGs."

"Rocket-propelled grenade launchers."

"I know what they are. I'm surprised you have them."

"I know a guy who knows a guy, who's friends with someone's brother. He knows a guy."

"Who knows a guy."

"Exactly."

"Don't you need a federal firearms license to own RPGs?"

Hicks shrugged. "I don't know. I didn't ask." He paused. "Anyway, yeah, RPGS. I've got Claymore mines, grenades—frag, smoke and thermite. I've got a truckload of M-16s."

"I know you have to have a federal license to own M-16s."

"You've got a thing about licenses, don't you? You realize they add to a bloated bureaucracy, right?"

Tanner laughed. "A bloated bureaucracy. I'm curious, how well do you get along with the police?"

"And we were just starting to make headway." Hicks looked around the table, then back at Tanner. "Why would you bring up the police? What possible good can come from that?"

"I take it you don't see eye to eye."

"That would be one way to put it."

Tanner held up his hands. "Hey, I'm just saying. If we're going after these guys, with lethal force, it might not hurt to have the law on our side. Crazy as that might sound."

Hicks stared at Tanner for a moment, then picked up his fork. He took a bite of biscuit with gravy, then looked at Tanner again as he chewed slowly. "So, what do you think?" Tanner asked.

"Good gravy," Hicks nodded. "You make this in a skillet?"

"Crock pot. Back to the cops, it's not like you have to wear a uniform and a badge."

"Look, this is all well and good. I mean, I like blowing stuff up as much as the next guy. But working with the police . . ." He paused, shaking his head. "That isn't a good fit for me."

"From what Doc tells me, people in your town are being killed. I don't see how a good fit has anything to do with that."

Hicks took another bite of biscuit and gravy, nodding while he chewed. "This is really good gravy."

"People in your town are being killed, Harlan."

"I know. I heard you. I'm thinking."

"Take your time. Kick it around while you enjoy the gravy. You want some more bacon? Pancakes, maybe?"

Hicks chewed another bite of biscuit, then pointed a fork at Tanner. "Tell you what. You give me this recipe, I'll help you."

Tanner laughed. "You're a piece of work, Harlan."

"Deal?"

"Deal."

Muriel smiled. "The way to a man's heart."

"Now that I think about it," Hicks said, "there is one bright spot to working with the cops, or at least having access to their building. They have an antenna tower I could use. Maybe some radios that didn't get fried. I want to see if I can get out on ham frequencies, find out who's out there and what's happening."

"You have a ham radio license?" Hendricks asked.

Hicks stared at her for a moment. "What is it with you guys and licenses? When I said a bloated bureaucracy, what I really meant was the federal government keeping tabs on civilians. And when the time is right, the New World Order swoops in with their black helicopters and riot squads. They round everybody up and stick them in detention centers, then reeducate them."

"I haven't heard that one in a while—the New World Order."

"You haven't been paying attention."

"Black helicopters."

"Like locusts descending in swarms across America, stripping the citizenry of their constitutional rights. Liberty. Freedom."

Hendricks nodded. "I see." She looked at Tanner and Winter, then back at Hicks. "How do you feel about intelligence agencies?"

Silas smiled at Muriel. "Here we go."

"The CIA?" Hicks said. "A wretched hive of scum and villainy."

"I didn't take you for a Star Wars fan," Hendricks replied.

"Did you know the CIA played around with mind control, dosing human subjects—unwitting human subjects—with LSD?"

"That's old news. Really old news."

"They did that?" Tanner asked. "Mind control with LSD?"

Hendricks nodded. "MK Ultra."

"It was psychological torture," Hicks said. "And it messed up a bunch of people. Permanently. Some died."

"How about the NSA?"

"Right up there with the CIA. A cesspool of spies."

"Before we get into a deep and meaningful relationship, you should know that some of us work for the NSA."

Hicks stared at Hendricks for a moment, then looked at Silas. "News to me," Silas said.

Hicks stood. "Doc, Muriel. Thanks for breakfast. I'd love to stick around, but I'm not going to." He headed for the front door.

Hendricks got up from the table. "Harlan. Wait a minute."

Hicks turned. "Do you really work for the NSA? Or are you just pushing my buttons?" She walked down the hall to her bedroom, then returned thirty seconds later and handed him a photo ID card on a lanyard. He examined the watermark on the front of the card, then flipped it over and saw the embedded chip, the barcode and the magnetic strip on the back.

"National Security Agency," she said. "Senior intelligence analyst, DEFSMAC." She took the card from him and smiled, patting his shoulder. "I really couldn't care less about your thoughts on the federal government, intelligence agencies, and especially the New World Order and black helicopters. All I care about right now is getting some law and order back in this town. Helping the people of Winslow." She paused. "So please, sit back down and enjoy your breakfast. Quit being so paranoid. It's annoying."

Both of them returned to the table and sat. Hendricks glanced at Winter and Tanner. Tanner was grinning. He passed the basket of biscuits to Hicks. "Have another."

Hicks took a biscuit and set it on his plate, eyeing Tanner with suspicion. "I'm afraid to ask what you do."

Tanner leaned in and whispered. "Chopper pilot. New World Order." He smiled.

"You're joking."

"I guess I'd have to be. There is no New World Order. There's no Illuminati. FEMA isn't building concentration camps, and—"

"Cut me some slack, okay?"

"Sorry."

"So, you don't work for the government."

"My friend Miles—he's down the hall recuperating—and I fought in Vietnam." Tanner reached in his pocket and pulled out a silver coin, then handed it to Hicks. "Not sure if that fits your definition of working for the government."

Hicks examined the coin. It was worn, its once-sharp and clean edges now smooth, rounded. On one side was a beret, a sword and a scroll, with the words 'De Oppresso Liber.' On the other, a shield with a diagonal flash—the flag of the Republic of Vietnam. "You guys were Green Beret," he said.

"Yes, sir," Tanner nodded.

"That's up there." He paused. "Ever make napalm out of Ivory soap flakes and gasoline?"

"All the time. In fifty-five-gallon drums. Tie a loop of det cord around the bottom and set it off . . . you've got a sky full of fire."

"Then it works? Soap flakes and gasoline?"

"Like a charm."

Hicks nodded, looking around the table at the others. "Well, this morning hasn't been a complete loss."

"Hey, you know how to make napalm. And when I give you the recipe, you'll know how to make cream gravy."

"Napalm and gravy."

Tanner smiled. "You scored, buddy."

37

President Wheeler sat down at the conference table, then turned on the wall screen and waited for General Tuckett at NORAD to connect. The timing of this meeting—5:30 a.m. in Washington, 3:30 in Colorado Springs—was the most reliable for transmission from a ground station to a satellite, and back to another ground station. Five days into the grid collapse, communication through satellites was degraded, and getting worse.

The problems began at the moment of detonation of the nuclear weapon in orbit. Low-Earth orbiting satellites in the weapon's line of sight lost operations capability almost immediately, suffering the same effects as ground-based electronics. And while LEO satellites that were not in line of sight of the weapon at the moment of detonation suffered no immediate effects, they too would fail over time as their orbits took them through a belt of intense radiation that would destroy solar panels powering the satellites.

Compounding the problem of space radiation were the subsequent detonations of eight nuclear weapons over Russia. This portion of the radiation formed an elongated belt reaching thousands of miles into space, extending into the orbits of geosynchronous-Earth orbiting satellites—twenty-two thousand miles above the earth's surface. Most of these satellites were tasked with communications.

And finally, communication through GEO satellites that were unaffected by space-borne radiation, suffered from a distortion of radio waves near the earth's surface created by scattered electrons trapped within the earth's magnetic field.

In short, communications between NORAD and the White House, and NORAD and most other military installations, were becoming increasingly unreliable. This morning's meeting between President Wheeler and General Tuckett would use two satellites in a single GEO network, one of which was optimum for voice transmission through a satellite phone, the other for video. It was hoped the combination would allow a fifteen-minute conversation.

Wheeler checked his watch, then glanced back at the wall screen. A moment later it flickered to life. "NORAD here," General Tuckett spoke. "How's the reception?" The video feed was broken by intermittent white noise.

"I'd adjust the rabbit ears," Wheeler replied, "but there aren't any. Try the phone."

Five seconds later the sat phone rang. "Test," Tuckett said. "One, two, three."

"You're breaking up. But what I lose on the phone is coming through the video, and vice versa." Wheeler shrugged. "We'll get by. What's new? What are you hearing out there?"

"I spoke with Offut Air Force Base in Nebraska at midnight. Their people are communicating with HF radio."

"What's HF?"

"High frequency. Ham radio operators use it to talk without repeaters. A waveform in that frequency can skip between the ionosphere and the ground halfway around the globe. It's how they talk to people on the other side of the planet."

"Interesting. Who are they talking to?"

"Operators on the west coast, east coast, Canada. Cities are the worst in terms of food, water, breakdown in social order. Not so bad out in the sticks."

Wheeler nodded. "We knew that would happen. We've got military out in force here in DC. They're working with what law enforcement is still available to maintain the peace, pressing civilians into service—neighborhood watch groups."

"Untrained?"

"They're doing what they can—arming them, showing them which end of the gun to point. The problem is Jane and John Doe trying to figure out who the bad guys are."

"They're locking down neighborhoods here in the Springs," Tuckett said. "Nobody gets in without proof of identity. Offut tells me they're doing the same in suburban areas around Omaha. We're trying to get the word out to other bases, but communication . . . well, you get the idea."

"I'd like to think they can figure it out on their own."

"Military? Or civilians?"

"Both." Wheeler stared at the screen for a moment, then shifted in his chair. "What's happening with our overseas forces?"

"Communication gaps there as well. Our instructions to field commanders—when we could still reach them—was to defend themselves, but no further offensive operations."

"In Syria?"

"Russian forces were defeated. Easily. With Moscow out of the picture, they've lost interest in fighting."

"That's a bright spot." Wheeler paused. "Back to this high-frequency form of communication, is this something we can use to communicate with the public?"

"Provided they have the means to receive it. Some frequencies work better during the day. Others at night."

Wheeler nodded. "It sounds promising."

"I'll get some COMMs people from Joint Base Andrews to look over the equipment in the White House Ops Center. I'm not sure what's there, but they can get things set up."

"I appreciate it, General."

"We'll talk again tonight?"

"Yes."

"Twenty-two hundred."

"I'll be here."

Tuckett paused, then signed off. "NORAD out."

Wheeler shut off the phone and video screen, then leaned back in his chair and surveyed the notepads, binders, loose papers and pens scattered across the table top. For nearly a week this room had served as headquarters for the dozen or so people involved in the most intense problem-solving process any of them had ever experienced, and this conference table reflected that effort. The phrase 'controlled clutter' came to mind, and although he was organized by nature, he wouldn't touch a single item lest he upset the process.

He glanced at three whiteboards that had been hung on the opposite wall, a recent addition to the situation room. On the left board were the most pressing problems and various details concerning them—electricity, of course, and the word was printed across the top of the board and underlined. Food and water were next, followed by the words 'civil unrest,' also underlined. Below these were sanitation, medical, law enforcement and communications. Toward the bottom, seemingly unrelated to anything else on the board, were the words 'burial of the dead.'

On the center board were the names of people and the tasks they were handling. At the bottom were incidental comments and ideas. The board on the right was home to items such as shipping ports, truck and rail transport, and nuclear power plant generators.

Wheeler crossed the room to the boards and picked up a pen, then wrote 'HF radio' with a question mark next to communications, followed by 'JBA.' He returned to his chair and sat, scanning the boards and thinking, chasing ideas he couldn't quite lay his hands on. He shook his head, then glanced at the clock on the wall. He was riding on three hours of sleep for the fourth night in a row. He carefully moved the papers in front of him, then put his feet up on the table, leaned back in the chair, and closed his eyes.

Forty-five minutes later, he awoke to find Spencer Cochran, the Speaker of the House, standing over him. Wheeler stared up at him. "You get separated from the tour group?" he asked. Cochran frowned. Wheeler's relationship with the Speaker wasn't the warmest. Prior to the midterm elections, Cochran had been the minority leader, frequently skewering the president when grandstanding before the cameras. When the Republicans lost the majority and Cochran was elected Speaker, he made it his mission to thwart everything the president attempted to push through Congress.

"Seriously," Wheeler said, "why are you here?"

"I heard the U.S. is in an undeclared war," Cochran replied.

"Is that a problem?"

"The House should have been consulted."

"The House shouldn't go on vacation before a grid collapse." Wheeler stood and left the room to get a cup of coffee.

"You're familiar with the Constitution," Cochran said, following the president down the hallway.

Wheeler laughed. "Are you?" He walked into the White House Mess kitchen. "I'm not in the mood for a fight, Spence," he said. "I'm up to my eyeballs in the worst disaster that's ever hit this country. Federal agencies are overwhelmed. FEMA is treading water. Frankly, if you can't see your way to pitch in and help us, I'd just as soon you leave." He rinsed out the coffee pot, then brewed a fresh batch. During the five minutes it took for the drip to finish, neither man spoke. Wheeler pulled two cups from the cupboard, filled them, and handed one to Cochran.

"Thank you," Cochran said.

"You're welcome." Wheeler left the kitchen and returned to the Situation Room. He pulled a chair away from the table and motioned for Cochran to sit, then stood in front of the whiteboards, sipping coffee. A minute later he turned and set the cup on the table, then folded his arms. "How was the ice fishing?"

"Cold."

"Hence the name." Wheeler paused. "Spence, you're smart. And I need all the smart I can get."

"I'm here."

"No Democrats. No Republicans."

"Agreed."

"If I sense so much as a hint of partisanship, I won't ask you to leave. I'll have the Secret Service remove you and detain you."

Cochran paused. "Agreed."

Wheeler continued staring, then nodded. "Do you know what happened?"

"Bits and pieces. My brother and I were fishing. No phones, no laptops, no news—nothing that would interrupt our outing. Driving back, we saw cars all over the place but had no idea what happened until I talked to my wife. She watched your address." He paused. "I take it you know who did this."

"North Korea and Iran. They launched a nuclear warhead into orbit. The Russians provided a launch vehicle that would lift it."

"And you retaliated."

"Our strike groups in the Sea of Japan and Persian Gulf hit North Korea and Iran. Subs in the North Atlantic launched eight Tridents. They detonated over Russia at altitude, taking down their grid."

"So, we've got two world superpowers reduced to what—third world countries?"

"Third world countries are better off than we are."

Cochran nodded slowly. "Any counterretaliation?"

"Nothing from Iran and North Korea. They're toast. Russian troops and aircraft made moves in the Middle East, going after U.S. air bases in Syria. We stopped them."

"What's the big picture here? The U.S."

"No power. Anywhere. No running water in the cities. No food. No fuel. No medical facilities."

"What's FEMA doing?"

"Nothing. Rioting shut down the facilities that were up and running. There was no more food or water to hand out, no reason to put their lives at risk. I told Margaret Beck to close shop and sit tight."

"And there is no food whatsoever?"

"What was in warehouses has been appropriated and distributed. It was gone in under an hour. It's December, so there's not a crop coming in. There are some areas that are still growing this time of year. But you have the problem of moving that food anywhere. Trucking is limited by the lack of fuel. Like food, there are local supplies of gasoline and diesel—Texas, Louisiana, California. But we can't move anything in quantities that will make a difference. A few trucks, sure. They pick up a load of tomatoes in Texas or lettuce in Arizona, and drive it somewhere. Best case, they feed a few hundred people." Wheeler paused. "We need trainloads of food, trainloads of fuel. And trains to move it all."

"What about civil unrest?"

"Rioting began within hours, but was short lived. Inner city gangs started going door to door, stealing whatever they could lay their hands on and killing anyone who got in their way. That tapered off when apartment dwellers demonstrated a willingness to take a baseball bat to someone's head."

"What are the police doing?"

"The ones that are still around are working with National Guard troops to establish order. But moving Guard troops has been difficult, so law enforcement, as it were, is spread thin."

"What's the status of nuclear power plants? Can they maintain cooling operations?"

"As of right now, yes. They have emergency generators running on diesel, but there will come a time—and it's not far off—when they run out of fuel. I don't need to tell you what that will be like."

Cochran nodded, thinking. "Don't refineries have reserves?"

"It's going to run out, Spence. There's no way around it."

"And the nation is in the dark—I don't mean lights. I mean hearing anything from anyone in power. From you."

"Communications are practically nonexistent right now. That may change as ham radio operations return to service."

Cochran pointed at the bottom of the whiteboard on the left. "Burial of the dead?"

Wheeler stood and crossed the room. "The number of dead is rising," he said quietly. "Planes that were in the air when the EMP hit dropped out of the sky. FAA tried to get the word out, but they only had forty-five minutes. We have no way of knowing how many died in air crashes, but reports of wreckage in rural areas—hundreds of planes." Wheeler sat and sipped his coffee. "Violence, hypothermia, fires, disease. Another week and we're looking at starvation. I've asked the Army Corps of Engineers to come up with a plan for burial of the dead. That means bulldozers. No funerals."

Cochran looked at the whiteboards again, trying to wrap his head around the big picture. "This is . . ." He paused, then looked from the boards to the president. "This is disastrous."

"Hurricane Katrina, Rita, Harvey—those were disasters. This is apocalyptic. Three hundred million people in the U.S. are without electricity and running water. No sanitation. No medical services." Wheeler paused. "They're living on borrowed time, Spence."

Cochran stared at the president in silence, face to face with the enormity of the situation and the utter lack of resources Wheeler had to work with. He was scraping things together with his fingernails. Cochran's mind went back to the bitter rivalry he had waged since becoming Speaker, and a burning sense of shame washed over him. He looked at the floor and shook his head.

As if reading his thoughts, Wheeler stood and walked around the table, then sat on the edge in front of Cochran. "What do you say we move ahead?" he asked quietly.

Cochran nodded. "Thank you, Mr. President."

"I can't emphasize this strongly enough. Partisan politics is a thing of the past. This country is burning down, and people are dying. We're not politicians anymore. We're firefighters." He paused. "The question is, are you with us? Are you ready to roll up your sleeves and truly help your country?"

"I am."

"Lock, stock and barrel."

"Yes."

"Welcome aboard, Spence." Wheeler shook Cochran's hand. "It's good to have you back."

38

Monday, February 17
6:15 a.m. Mountain Standard Time
Winslow, Arizona

Hendricks, Winter and Tanner arrived at the Winslow Police Department to find a partially burned building with the glass broken out of the front window frames. Inside, offices had been trashed. Hendricks surveyed the damage in the lobby. "Let's hope the transmitter room is in better shape."

The plan was to turn the station's radio system into a VHF repeater, beginning with the replacement of most of the radio gear which had fried in the EMP. Before the repeater, though, they would set up a high-power base station for calling and listening. They found the room down the hall, and were in the process of sorting through equipment when Harlan Hicks walked in with a cardboard box.

"Radio parts," he said. "Spare gear I had lying around." He lifted a transceiver and an amplifier out of the box and set them on the desk. "Two hundred fifty watts and that monster antenna tower out back should get us some distance." He crossed the room to the equipment rack and studied the gear, then slipped between the wall and rack and began disconnecting various components.

"Remind me again why we're doing this," Tanner said.

"Communications is a priority right now," Hicks said. "The only thing worse than a nationwide blackout is not being able to talk to anybody, find out what's happening in different areas. People are scared right now. They're starting to realize that nobody is coming to save them—not the police or the sheriff, and not the federal government. The world they knew with electricity, running water, TV and radio, the internet . . . all the activities that made life real—movies, restaurants, ball games—it doesn't exist anymore." He paused. "Anyway, the longer things go on with no communication—no word from anybody about what's happening—the more likely it is that some group, like those idiots on the highway that you guys ran into, tries to take over. And as much as I hate the government, I don't like the idea of tribalism—a bunch of freaking warlords going at it, trying to take over a country that's falling apart."

"I wouldn't mind being able to contact my family," Hendricks said. "I haven't talked to anybody since the collapse."

"Where are they?"

"Kingman."

"I'm not sure what other repeaters are running between here and there—we won't be able to hit Kingman directly—but we can find out as soon as we get this gear set up."

Hendricks sat at the desk and studied the radio and amplifier. "Do we know what the local repeater frequencies are?"

"I printed out a directory, a list of everybody that uses VHF and UHF statewide. Police, sheriff, search and rescue, utility companies. It's all there. As far as talking to each other on these radios, though, and I mean using handhelds to communicate with each other, I don't really give a hoot what local protocol is."

"Let me guess," Tanner said. "We'll use whatever frequency we damn well please."

"Now you're in tune. There's no FCC anymore. So yeah, whatever frequency we damn well please. When we fire this up, we'll scan frequencies for traffic. If we find any, we'll decide what to use for calling, and what to use for chitchat."

Hendricks poured a cup of coffee from a thermos, then sat in a swivel chair and turned to face Hicks. "Harlan," she said, "the other day at breakfast when I told you I don't care what you think about intelligence agencies, the New World Order, stuff like that, I didn't mean it the way it probably sounded."

"It sounded pretty much the way you said it," Hicks replied.

"I mean—"

"I know what you mean. Apology accepted."

"I want you to know I'm not crazy about a lot of what goes on at the NSA. Reading everyone's emails, listening to phone calls, spying on civilians. And I think the CIA has a lot to answer for."

Hicks stepped out from behind the equipment rack and looked at Hendricks. "I'm not sure what you're looking for. Absolution?"

"No. I find myself thinking about what this country is going to be like without sixteen intelligence agencies digging into who knows what, for the benefit of who knows who, and I wonder if we might be better off without them."

"Uh, Naomi," Winter said, "this is just me—your conscience—but when it comes to national security, there is some agency stuff that's nice to have. Like DEFSMAC."

"I don't have a problem with DEFSMAC," Hicks said. "And the people you guys work with—NORAD, NORTHCOM—without them, nobody knows what's up there. We've got missiles coming in over the Pole and nobody has a clue." He paused. "I haven't been completely honest with you guys."

"What about?" Hendricks said.

"I used to work for NSA."

"No way."

"And I'm a little embarrassed about my response to you when you told me you guys worked for them. I'm sorry."

"I'm surprised that someone like you—"

"A conspiracy theorist?"

"Yeah."

"You wouldn't be if you knew what I did."

"Try me."

"I worked in Access Operations. S321."

"Infiltrating networks," Winter said.

"Brute-force attacks. We worked with the CIA."

"Harlan!" Hendricks threw up her hands.

"What better reason for not liking them than knowing them."

"Well, you've already said you're sorry. I just . . . wow."

"Anyway, we—hackers in 321 and the CIA—conducted cyberwarfare against foreign governments, breaking into networks, sabotaging servers, routers, firewalls. When we weren't crashing systems, we were leaving implants that would give us control. We could see everything they were doing, and affect the outcome. We had access to banking, finance." He paused. "The CIA was dispensing with antiquated methods—staging coups. With the new software, a lot of which I helped write, they could collapse economies."

Tanner laughed. "Toppling governments from a laptop."

"Pretty much," Hicks nodded.

"It wasn't just foreign governments you hacked," Winter said.

"Nope. Domestic too. We were tapped into everyone. Anyway, when Snowden went rogue, a bunch of us slipped out the back door quietly. We didn't want to be the ones left holding the bag when some Congressional committee came down on the program."

"And guys like you are always the ones left holding the bag," Hendricks said. "Not the people at the top who told you to do it."

Tanner chuckled. "And I thought this was going to be boring—flipping switches and turning knobs."

Hicks slipped from behind the rack and pulled the end of a coaxial cable across the floor. He screwed the connector to the back of the amplifier, connected the transceiver, then turned to Tanner. "Flip that switch." Tanner reached over and powered up the radio. Indicator lights flickered, then illuminated. Needles swept across the face of meters. A faint hum emanated from the amplifier.

Hicks nodded. "Now let's see if anybody's listening." He sat behind the desk and tuned the transceiver to 144.000 MHz, then keyed the microphone. "This is station WKG70 in Winslow, Arizona. Anybody out there?" He listened for a few seconds, then called again. "WKG70 calling on one forty-four megahertz. Anybody copy?" Still no reply. He continued calling, increasing the frequency in 25-kHz steps with each attempt. Finally, at 147.350 MHz, he heard a man's voice fading in and out.

"—continuity from the station switchyard, southwest through substation thirty-four." Five seconds of silence was followed by more talk. "No. We're at substation thirty-four, not fifty-four. Repeat, thirty-four . . . three four."

Hicks keyed the microphone. "This is station WKG70 in Winslow, Arizona. Who's talking, please?"

There was a pause, then, "APS line crew here."

"Yes, thank you. What's your location?"

"Ninety miles southwest of Phoenix."

"You're getting electric up?"

"Trying to. We're repairing transmission lines."

Tanner glanced at Hendricks. "Who's APS?"

"Arizona Public Service," she said. "They're the electrical utility for the Palo Verde Nuclear Generating Station."

Hicks keyed the mic. "You guys working with Palo Verde?"

"Most of us. We've got some field crews from other utilities."

"Is Palo Verde running?"

"Not quite, but they're getting there."

"Any idea how long?"

"A few days."

"That's good news."

"Who did you say you are?"

"WKG70 in Winslow. We just finished setting up a radio here. We're trying to find out what our area of coverage is, get a line of communication going."

"Roger that. Lines of communication. Lines of electrical service. Both good things right now. And FYI, the signal you're receiving is going through a repeater in Payson. Our crews are using that to talk to engineers at Palo Verde."

"That helps. We appreciate it." Hicks paused. "I'll let you get back to it. Good luck. Be safe."

"Always safe. We try not to rely on luck."

"Got it. We'll talk later."

"We'll be on this frequency. Give us a day or two. We'll should have some lights on."

"Thank you, sir."

"APS line crew out."

"WKG70 out."

"Palo Verde supplies L.A. with electricity," Hicks said. "Ports at Long Beach and Los Angeles. If they get power that far, they can offload ships."

"They'll need trains to move anything," Tanner said.

"One thing at a time. Electricity first. Then railroads."

Hendricks crossed the room to the window and looked out at the street beyond, thinking, then turned to Hicks. "Harlan, do you have a satellite phone?"

"Yes," he replied.

"I need it."

39

The control room of Palo Verde Nuclear Generating Station's Unit 1 was crowded with engineers pouring over electrical schematics when the plant's director of operations walked in. "Talk to me," he said. "Where are we?"

The plant's senior engineer, Jack Davis, looked up from the schematics. "Containment building checks out—steam generator, coolant pump, pressurizer, injection tank. Turbine building's good—condenser, feedwater pumps and heaters." He waved his arm around the perimeter of the control room. "Every system in here has been triple checked, down to the meters, switches and dials. We're ready to take the Unit one generator online tomorrow at noon."

The control rooms of the plant were untouched by the EMP, owing to their location three stories underground, and the fact that their concrete floors, walls and ceilings were reinforced by crisscrossed steel rebar and wire mesh—in effect, a Faraday cage. Elsewhere in the plant, systems had been protected in time to prevent damage, and at this point, the engineers were in the initial stages of an extensive point-by-point startup procedure.

Of all the preventive measures taken, the most drastic in terms of methods employed was the isolation of large power transformers, a critical step in protecting the electrical infrastructure. LPTs were expensive and difficult to replace, in some cases requiring a lead time of years before delivery. Under normal circumstances, these transformers would be isolated from all incoming and outgoing transmission lines by climbing the towers nearest the LPT, insulating the lines, then performing a clean disconnect. Due to the location of some transformers—an hour or more from any field crews with boom trucks—and the fact that time was running out, a last resort tactic was devised by crews with field radios or phones. Calls were made to brothers, cousins, uncles—anyone with a high-powered rifle and a truck—requesting they race to the towers and shoot line insulators, thus cutting the connections.

With just minutes to spare before the EMP hit, all LPTs in Palo Verde's southwest region, from Arizona to California, had been successfully isolated. Apart from the protection of LPTs, calls were made to Palo Verde's major customers—Southern California Edison, the Southern California Public Power Authority, and the Los Angeles Department of Power and Water—with instructions to protect at all costs local utility infrastructure, particularly areas involving the ports at Long Beach and Los Angeles. The ability to offload ships and move freight from ports would be essential.

Now, a week and a half after the collapse, line crews were restringing transmission lines, establishing continuity from switchyards, through transformers, to relay stations and beyond. In the control room of Unit 1, Jack Davis consulted a list of field crews and the radio frequencies they were using, and was calling for updates.

"How are we looking downstream?" the director asked.

"Good," Davis replied. "Better than I expected, actually. We'll have transmission capability across Arizona by the time this unit goes online tomorrow. I can't get through to California crews, but I've got some of our guys in the field driving southwest for better radio access. We should know something within an hour or so."

"Can we contact the ports?"

"By radio only, and they've got the same problem. There are only a handful of repeaters between us and them, and down by the state line, the gap is too big. Someone's got to drive seventy-five miles to make radio contact."

The director nodded, looking around the control room. "You know, Jack, if someone had told me ten days ago that we would take this plant offline and run on emergency diesel generators for a week and a half, lose transmission lines at twenty-two junctions, and be ready to deliver juice by tomorrow at noon . . ."

Davis smiled. "I know. Impossible. But here we are."

"Due in no small part to cutting corners."

"Nothing critical."

The director nodded. "You know that, and I know that. But the INPO would have a cow over this."

Davis chuckled. "Do they even exist today?"

"If they do, they'll find a car that runs, drive here with an inspection list as long as you are tall, and get in our face."

"When they get here, they can start by thanking us for the ability to flip a switch on the wall and have lights. After that, they can pound sand for all I care."

The director laughed. "I won't tell anyone you said that." He took one last look around before leaving the room. "Thanks for all your hard work, Jack. Your people pulled it off."

Davis smiled. "Someone up there likes us."

40

7:30 a.m. Mountain Standard Time
Hualapai Mountains
Northwest Arizona

Neil and Nathan Hayes sat in a draw on the southwest side of Dean Peak, watching a bull elk and six cows slowly moving up the rocky slope north of them. Neil was sitting in front, watching through binoculars. Nathan sat right behind him, straddling him and resting the forearm of the rifle on his right shoulder, watching the elk through the scope.

"You see them?" Neil said quietly.

"Yeah," Nathan replied. "A bull in front. The cows are coming up behind him."

"About a hundred yards above them—"

"I can't judge a hundred yards from this distance."

"Okay." Neil paused. "Sweep up with your scope, straight above the elk, until you come to a clearing. There are some white rocks on the left, right before the trees start again."

"I see it."

"The elk are making their way up through the trees. When they come out into the clearing, I'll use the elk call. The bull should stop. It'll be broadside to you." He paused, shifting his position.

"I can't shoot if you're going to be moving, Dad."

"I know. I'm sitting on a rock, and it's not very soft. Slide back for a sec." Nathan moved backward, then Neil adjusted his position. "Okay," he said. "That's better." Nathan moved back in behind Neil, then rested the rifle on his shoulder again. "You remember your aim point?" Neil asked.

Nathan nodded. "Right behind the shoulder."

"When the bull turns—and it will when I call it—give me a second to plug my ears. I'll hold still, and you squeeze off the shot."

"Got it."

They sat in silence as the elk climbed another forty yards up the slope, zigzagging their way to the top, then stopped. "Now?" Nathan asked.

"They're still in the trees," Neil replied. "They'll move. Give them a few more seconds."

"So, Dad, is this legal?"

"No. We don't have a tag. But, under the circumstances, I'd be surprised if Game and Fish had a problem with it. That's one of the benefits of living in the mountains—they're crawling with food." He held up his hand. "Here they come. Find the bull in your scope and position your crosshairs."

Nathan moved the rifle slowly. "I see him."

"Remember your breathing."

"Yep."

"And squeeze the trigger."

"Call the elk, Dad."

Neil put the elk call to his lips and blew. A bugling sound echoed across the draw and the bull stopped, then turned broadside. Neil plugged his ears with his fingers, closed his eyes to shield them from the muzzle blast, then held as still as he could. "Anytime," he said. A second later, Nathan squeezed the trigger. The rifle recoiled off Neil's shoulder, then dropped back down. Neil opened his eyes in time to see the bull drop in its tracks. "Beautiful shot, son. Dead on." He stood and hung the binoculars around his neck, then reached down and gave Nathan a hand up.

Nathan drew a deep breath and exhaled. "That was easier than I thought it would be."

"Shooting a high-powered rifle?" Neil asked. "Or taking the life of an animal?"

Nathan thought for a moment. "Shopping for meat."

Neil nodded. "Good point of view. And in case you're wondering, there's nothing like an elk burger grilled over charcoal."

Ten minutes later they were gutting the elk. "This is the first time I've seen an animal this big, inside out," Nathan said.

"You okay?" Neil asked.

"Yeah. I just . . . you don't see this every day."

"No, you don't."

"I guess Naomi's done this before."

"She has."

"Did it bother her?"

"At first. She got used to it."

"I wish we'd hear something from her."

Neil straightened up, wiping the blade of his knife on his pants. "I do too, Nathan."

"You've tried her on the radio."

"Five times a day. I don't know if she's in range of a working repeater."

"I guess we just wait."

"Smartest thing we can do is to follow your mom's lead."

"Pray."

"That's it."

They finished field-dressing the elk, then quartered it and bagged the meat. Nathan looked at the carcass as Neil was tying the bags to their backpacks. "That's a lot of leftovers," he said.

"Not much in the way of meat, though," Neil replied. "Bits and pieces in the ribs and along the spine. It's more work than it's worth. As far as leaving it behind, the mountain has a cleanup crew—mountain lions and vultures. They'll take care of this."

"So that's it?"

"That's it." Neil helped Nathan with his pack, then shouldered the second one. They stood side by side for a minute as Neil got his bearings. "Down this slope to the draw," he pointed. "The truck's about a half-mile further down."

"Good," Nathan said. "I'd hate to hike up this mountain loaded like we are."

"Yeah. A rule of thumb—though sometimes it can't be helped—shoot your game uphill from your truck."

It was 10:00 a.m. when they reached the pickup. They had just loaded the packs in the back when Neil's transceiver broke squelch. It was Carl Ferguson calling. "K7AZK, this is KG7DBD."

Neil pulled the handset from his belt. "Hey, Carl."

"Where are you?"

"About a mile north of your tower. Nathan and I are hunting."

"I just heard from Naomi."

Neil paused, staring at Nathan, then broke into a grin. "You just made my day, old friend. How is she?"

"Alive and kickin'. She's in Winslow. Apparently, they just got a repeater up. She was able to hit a tower in Flagstaff, who passed word through Williams, then Seligman. The Seligman relay couldn't reach me, but he was able to hit a mobile on I-40. They called me."

"What did she say?"

"Not much, going through that many people. Kinda like the telephone game. Words change."

"But she's okay."

"She is."

"Did she say what her plan is?"

"She's staying put for a few days. Doing something there with people she's traveling with."

Neil sighed. "I hope she's all right."

"Didn't I just say she is?"

"You did. And I thank you for that, Carl." He paused, his eyes closed. "Like I said, you made my day."

"You bag an elk?"

"We did."

"Burgers tonight?"

Neil laughed. "Tomorrow or the next day. I'll let you know."

"Don't forget me, buddy."

"Never. Thanks again."

"Anytime. KG7DBD clear."

"K7AZK clear."

Neil clipped the radio to his belt, then looked at Nathan with tears in his eyes. The two of them hugged. "Thank you, Lord." Neil whispered.

"Amen," Nathan added. He paused, then looked at his father. "You okay, Dad?"

"Never better, son."

"Me too."

With that, the two of them climbed in the truck and drove away, headed for home.

41

Wednesday, February 19
12:00 p.m. Eastern Standard Time
White House Situation Room
Washington, D.C.

President Wheeler sat at the conference table in the Situation Room, flanked by Vice President Hutchens and Chairman of the Joint Chiefs Thomas Macfarland. They had been reviewing plans drawn up by the Army Corps of Engineers for burying the dead. Wheeler shook his head, deeply anguished, dispirited, his mood bordering on despair.

"There's no way around it, Mr. President," Macfarland said. "We have to resort to mass graves."

"I know, General," Wheeler replied quietly. "I know. Too many bodies." He paused and closed his eyes, rubbing his temples with the fingers of both hands, then leaned back and sighed. "Too many bodies," he whispered. He appeared to be on the verge of tears. Macfarland shifted in his seat, exchanging glances with Hutchens.

Hutchens nodded toward the door and they stood, getting ready to leave. Just then, Interior secretary Doug Chambers burst into the room, out of breath from running.

"Arizona has power," he said.

Wheeler turned and stared at Chambers, eyes wide, then stood. "Where did you hear this?"

"In the operations center. General Tuckett at NORAD received a phone call. It came through satellite, someone in Winslow, Arizona. They've been monitoring ham radio bands, trying to establish lines of communication. They talked to repair crews working with the Palo Verde nuclear power plant. The plant has one unit up and running, generating nine hundred megawatts. Phoenix and Tucson have power." He paused and grasped the president by the shoulders. "So do the shipping ports at Long Beach and Los Angeles."

Wheeler stared at Chambers in silence. Then he looked at Hutchens. Finally, he lowered himself into his chair and leaned forward, then buried his face in his hands and wept quietly. The vice president stood behind him and leaned over. "There's your miracle, Mr. President," she whispered.

PART III

THE RECOVERY

42

Saturday, February 22

Twelve days into the collapse saw little change. Fewer than one hundred hospitals across the nation were operating—and those only on emergency power with minimal services. Police and fire departments were practically nonexistent, as were all other municipal services. There was no business, no banking, no jobs or payroll. The nation had simply shut down.

The rioting and chaos that overwhelmed metropolitan areas in the first forty-eight hours was losing momentum. There were still random acts of violence and vandalism, but for the most part, people had chosen either to sit it out with a wait-and-see position, hoping the power would return and with it, a semblance of normal life, or leave the cities with whatever they could carry on their back, setting up camps in outlying areas and using whatever they could find for shelter from the cold.

Meanwhile, trading posts were popping up in most rural areas as well as metropolitan areas. In streets and parking lots, people gathered to trade goods—a dozen eggs for a half-pound of coffee, sugar for bar soap, a horse-drawn wagon for a hunting rifle and ammunition. In most places, trading was protected by armed agents appointed by a town council or a neighborhood group. There were disagreements over the asking price of a certain service or product, but for the most part, people recognized that the only way they could acquire necessities was through peaceful commerce.

As time went on, word spread of goods and services available in neighboring towns or areas of a city. People moved from one trading post to another, traveling in groups for safety, shopping for goods by day and settling down in camps for the night. It was a throw-back not just to the nineteenth century when hunters, trappers and explorers traded animal skins and furs for provisions, but to the dawn of civilization when prehistoric cultures practiced the earliest form of commerce—trade transactions.

As people moved backward from a cash-based economy and toward a preelectric society, Palo Verde Nuclear Generating Station in Arizona threw the final switch in its startup procedure on the plant's Unit 1 on February 18th, delivering electricity across four transmission corridors to areas in Arizona and southern California. Coupled with service being restored to the ports at Long Beach and Los Angeles, and the return to operating status of those ports, this marked the turning point in the collapse. It was by no means an end to the problems, but limited electrical service and functioning ports meant that food, water and fuel could begin moving. The next step in that process would be the ability to move freight by rail. And efforts by BNSF Railway and the Union Pacific Railroad to reestablish freight delivery were beginning to produce results.

Both railway companies had in their equipment inventories a combined total of fifteen thousand locomotives. Of these, roughly three thousand were more than twenty years old, and still operable following the EMP. They would run, and could pull the same freight that newer locomotives could. The problem was in regulating train traffic across rail lines, a process normally controlled by computerized traffic control centers scattered across the U.S.

BNSF and Union Pacific were working together to devise methods of moving freight over shared routes safely. Traffic control would be handled manually—by running trains on a single rail no closer than thirty minutes apart with strict limits on track switches, and with radio links in trains using a common frequency. Visibility of the rail line ahead and behind was crucial—there would be no rail traffic at night or in weather limiting visibility to less than a mile.

Meanwhile, operations were underway at rail yards and corridors in and out of the Long Beach and Los Angeles ports, preparing for the return of intermodal freight moving from the west coast in all directions, and trucking companies were assembling fleets of older tractors that were operable, combining them with tankers, flatbeds and box trailers for delivering goods.

Electricity, ports, trains and trucks, though limited in terms of reach, signaled the beginning of the nation's recovery.

43

President Wheeler and Vice President Hutchens were rearranging papers on the conference table, sliding stacks to the center, as National Security Advisor William Denton looked on. It was his first time back in the White House since the collapse, and he was surprised to see the state of the Situation Room.

"I take it this is where things get done," he said.

"It is," Wheeler replied. "It's warmer than the Emergency Operations Center, and it's a short walk to the White House Mess kitchen. That's where we take out meals when we're working down here."

"I'd lend a hand, but I have a feeling I'd upset what appears to be a delicate balance between order and chaos."

"And you'd be right, Bill. I just want to clear a place, so you can sit and have room to take notes, a spot to lean your elbows if nothing else. Give us thirty seconds and you can pull up a chair."

A moment later, General Tuckett appeared on the video screen. "You folks awake?" he asked.

"Ready to roll," Wheeler replied. "I'm just clearing a spot for the National Security Advisor."

"Welcome back, Bill," Tuckett smiled. "How are you?"

"I'm well, General Tuckett. How are things in the Springs?"

"Quieting down."

"Glad to hear it."

"Mr. President, you got my message about power coming back up in parts of Arizona."

"I did," Wheeler replied. "It was an answer to prayer."

"It was the best news we've had since this began." Tuckett paused. "You remember Naomi Hendricks?"

Wheeler glanced at Hutchens and Denton, then back at the video screen. "She's the analyst with Rampart who called during our briefing on the tenth."

"Yes. And she's the one who called me about the power in Arizona. She's with some people in Winslow, monitoring radio traffic. They talked to Palo Verde's repair crews."

"What is she doing in Winslow?"

"She's trying to get home." Tuckett paused. "It's a long story. Anyway, she called again late last night with more good news. Union Pacific and BNSF railway are getting a number of locomotives running—roughly a thousand older models that don't have the extensive computerization that newer models do—and are working to reestablish freight service out of Long Beach and Los Angeles."

"What can they move with those older locomotives?"

"Anything that newer ones can—tankers for diesel, gasoline and oil, water too, I suppose. Boxcars, flatcars. They can move anything that's sitting in port right now."

"Excellent news, General. This is exciting. Are there limitations on routes? Or can they go anywhere?"

"The limitations have to do with multiple trains traveling the same route. Traffic is normally handled by computerized control points. They're down, of course, but what we're hearing is that both rail lines—UP and BNSF—are working on a manual control system using radios. They're working out the details, but the bottom line is they're close to running.

"Now then, refineries in California and Texas are getting ready to fill rail tankers with gasoline and diesel—"

"Texas has power?"

"Limited power, but yes, Texas is restoring electrical service. Like Arizona, it's a slow process, but the lights are coming back on in a number of cities."

"And this comes from Hendricks and her people on radios?"

"Most of it. They're monitoring VHF and UHF during the day, and calling on HF during the night when skip conditions let them cover long distances."

"That's amazing," Wheeler nodded. "Truly amazing. General, next time you talk to Hendricks and her people, give them our deepest thanks for their efforts."

"I will, Mr. President."

"Anything else?"

"That's it for now."

"Electricity, ports, trains and communications . . ." Wheeler paused, smiling. "We're almost out of the woods."

"We can see the edge of the trees, Mr. President." Tuckett paused. "Twenty-two hundred tonight?"

"I'll be here, General."

"Good day, Mr. President."

Wheeler disconnected, then turned to Hutchens and Denton. "Your thoughts?

"You already said it, Mr. President," Hutchens said. "It's truly amazing. We should be able to get diesel fuel to nuclear power plants to run generators, so the possibility of cores melting down won't be as pressing a concern now. With the ability to move freight—and I assume that would include food and water—will you bring FEMA back into the picture?"

"Yes. Now that we're able to move goods, I'll have Secretary Beck get her people set up."

"Mr. President," Denton said, "now that we can say we're on the road to recovery, we need to look at the details of repairing our technological infrastructure—the ability to access data, but more importantly, recover what was lost in the collapse. Records of all kinds—banking and finance, insurance, medical, anything like that. Recovery of them, as opposed to rebuilding them, moves us ahead significantly."

"Is it possible to recover that kind of information?" Wheeler asked. "I thought it was lost for good. And rebuilding the infrastructure—the technological infrastructure—I thought we'd be back at square one, starting from scratch."

"Certain aspects, yes. We start over. But not everything. I spent some time with Matthew Donovan's IT people at NSA, getting an accurate assessment of what's involved in repair and recovery. From a strictly technological standpoint—computer systems, servers, internet connectivity—we're sitting in the 1950s, maybe early '60s. None of this existed. But what we have now that we didn't have then is the knowledge. We know how computers work as well as the software that runs them, how to connect those computers with twisted-pair cables through switches, and so on."

"We don't have to reinvent the wheel, just repair it."

"Exactly. I'm told that a lot of equipment may be undamaged, but only that equipment that was not running when the EMP hit. Nothing that was plugged in survived. But equipment that was not powered up and had no physical connection to line voltage through a power cord could have survived.

"Now then, equipment that was plugged in and running might be repairable. We talk about computers being fried, but when the EMP hit, only certain components burned out. New, undamaged components are sitting in a box on a shelf at an electronics store. It's a matter of someone with diagnostic skills opening the computer, testing circuit boards, then replacing the damaged parts.

"Moving on from that, the Ethernet—which is the technology that makes up networks—still exists in large part. There are servers and switch devices that link networks, and, like the computers, they'll need repair. But the lines—the wiring and fiber optics—are still in place and undamaged."

Wheeler nodded. "So, you're saying that while it took decades to get to where we were right before the collapse, it may take just weeks or months to get back there."

"In general terms, yes. We just have to get people with the skills. The tools and the necessary parts are out there."

"Mr. President," Hutchens said, "with radio communications available in some areas—Ms. Hendricks and her people come to mind—we can coordinate a workforce of sorts."

"Absolutely," Denton said. "We start with the people at NSA and other intelligence agencies. These are people that have the knowledge and the access to other people with the same capabilities. Then we put the word out via radio that we need people with the skills to diagnose and repair electronic equipment. And we find someone who can manage an operation like that, coordinate people in different areas." He paused. "With electricity, we could have a functioning internet in several weeks—in some areas, at least."

"The thing that comes to my mind concerning electricity," Wheeler said, "is that what we've got right now is part of Arizona, part of Texas, and part of California. Service will spread from there, but my understanding is that at some point—a number of points in geographic terms—electrical service will hit a roadblock. And that roadblock is the absence of functioning large power transformers. Those areas will be in the dark until the transformers are replaced, and from what I understand, that could take years." He paused. "We don't yet know where the dead transformers are—what areas will not have electricity until they're replaced. But it could well be that rural areas—farms and ranches—have power tomorrow, but New York City, D.C. or Chicago, remain in the dark for years."

Denton nodded slowly, thinking. "Radio communication is a priority. We need someone who can focus on that and that alone. Until we have the ability to talk to people, the rest of this is just us sitting in a room, spitballing."

"Doug Chambers is already putting things together," Wheeler said. "With this information from General Tuckett coming out of Winslow, I think Chambers can make strides. I'll have a sit-down with him today." He paused, looking from Denton to Hutchens. "I think Tuckett's call and this conversation have moved us ahead more than anything else that's happened since the collapse. We've been inching ahead, wringing our hands. Now we're rolling."

"Something else to keep in mind, Mr. President," Denton said. "At the moment of the collapse, America's wealth—roughly one hundred trillion dollars—stopped moving. It's not lost, but it's dormant. It's critical that financial records stored on computers and servers—information on hard drives—be preserved. Everything from neighborhood banks to Wall Street investment firms. Our economy depends on it. If we lose that, we're toast."

Wheeler nodded. "So, what you're saying is right now we're visiting the nineteenth century. If we're not careful, we'll be stuck there, trading buffalo hides for coffee and flour."

"If not that, Mr. President, something very close to it."

44

10:00 a.m. Mountain Standard Time
Lewiston, Idaho

Kyle and Julie Ward, along with Everett King, Burke Abbott and Jordan Stanley, walked among the tables set up in a parking lot that faced Lewiston's main street. In another time this would have been a swap meet. Today it was called a trading post, and it was crowded with people bartering goods and services. Tables were set up with staples—coffee, sugar, flour and cereal grains. Others were piled with soap, detergents and cleaning supplies. And still others held hand tools, knives, axes, various weapons and ammunition. There were no price tags. Offers to trade were made and countered, odds and ends were added to sweeten deals, and transactions were completed with a handshake.

"This is your basic general store," Kyle said. "Literally, everything from soup to nuts." They stopped at a table with medicinal supplies—isopropyl alcohol, hydrogen peroxide, ointments, essential oils, pain relievers and antihistamines, as well as dozens of other items. "Is everything here on a barter basis?" Kyle asked the elderly couple sitting behind the table.

"Oh, yes," the woman smiled. "No one takes cash."

"Anybody take precious metals?" Burke asked.

"There was a guy here earlier, asking the same thing," the man replied. "He had a bag of silver dimes and quarters. I told him there was nothing I could do with it. I wasn't interested."

"Despite the value of silver? Before the collapse it was trading at fifteen dollars an ounce."

"And now it's worthless." The man waved at the other tables. "Look around you, son. Everyone here is trading things they can use—coffee, sugar, coats and blankets, guns and goats. Whatever the item is, it will be put to use. A bag of coins . . . you can't eat it, you can't milk it, you can't build a shed with it. You trade it to someone, and they trade it to someone else, and then someone after that. But in the end, someone is stuck with a bag of coins that's just that—a bag of coins. They can't be used for anything meaningful."

"I see your point," Burke replied. He looked at Everett and Jordan, his partners in a prominent investment firm. "Ever think you'd see the day when gold and silver is worthless?"

"Now if you boys have real estate," the man said, "land that can be farmed, that's a different story."

"You can't argue with real estate," Everett nodded. "We'll keep that in mind. Thanks for your time."

With that, they moved on, past the pens holding chickens, rabbits and ducks, the ice buckets filled with fresh salmon and steelhead, and horses in a makeshift corral with saddles, bridles and other tack placed nearby. There was a table piled high with how-to books. Another with bolts of fabric, spools of thread, yarn and knitting needles, and another table with a sign that read 'Medical Advice.'

Toward the end of the parking lot was a table with stacks of metal boxes, some the size of a cereal box, others no bigger than a paperback book. "What are these?" Everett asked the man seated behind the table.

"Electronic control modules," he replied. "Computers for cars and trucks."

Everett picked one up and examined it. "These are what died in the collapse?"

"Yes, sir. Fried by the EMP. Your car won't run without it." The man paused. "What do you drive?"

"Twenty fifteen Dodge Ram, three-quarter ton."

The man pulled a catalog from the stack and thumbed through it. "Six point four Hemi?"

"Yes."

The man smiled at Everett, closed the book, then pulled an ECM from the bottom of a stack. "Gotcha covered," he said, setting the module on the table.

"Is this guaranteed to work?"

"Yep. Any ECM that wasn't plugged into a power source when the EMP went off is good. These are units from my salvage yard."

"What do you want for it?"

The man smiled. "The question is, what's it worth to get your truck running?" Everett nodded, looking the ECM over. "I'd take that parka you're wearing," the man said.

"It's the only one I've got."

Kyle stepped in and unzipped his coat. "How about this one?" he asked, handing it to the man.

"I can't let you do that," Everett said.

"Sure, you can. I've got three more at home." Kyle looked at the man. "Try it on. See what you think."

The man put the coat on and zipped it up. He held his arms out and twisted at the hips, then leaned over, stretching. "Feels good," he said, straightening up. "What's the insulation? Thinsulate?"

"PrimaLoft."

The man nodded. "Can you get the truck down here?"

"It's up in the mountains. Seven Devils, west of Riggins."

"I know the area," the man nodded. "Rough going." He looked around the parking lot for a few seconds, then back at Kyle. "You know anybody with ammo for a three hundred Win Mag?"

Kyle nodded. "I've got handloads."

"I know a guy who's looking for match-grade stuff. Something with better accuracy than over-the-counter loads."

"He'll like these."

"You busy tomorrow?"

Kyle looked at Everett. "Are we busy tomorrow?"

"Nope," Everett replied.

"Be here at nine in the morning with five boxes of ammo—one hundred rounds. He'll drive you up to your truck and install the ECM, make sure it runs."

"He'll drive two hundred miles round trip and repair the truck for a hundred rounds of ammo?"

The man nodded. "He needs good ammo. Your buddy needs his truck. Everybody's happy."

"Can't argue with that," Kyle smiled. "We appreciate it."

"See you tomorrow morning."

Everett smiled at Kyle as they walked away from the table. "Interesting place of business."

"It is," Kyle said. He looked across the parking lot to see his wife Julie standing by a chicken pen. She waved him over. "And I have a feeling I'm going to be spending a lot of time here."

45

2:30 p.m. Mountain Standard Time
Northwest Arizona

Neil and Nathan Hayes stood with Carl Ferguson on the Hayes' deck, tending a charcoal grill laden with tenderloin steaks from the elk Neil and Nathan shot the previous Monday. After butchering the elk, Neil split it up with several other homeowners on the mountain. Despite the cold winter temperatures, there wasn't a reliable method of refrigerating the meat for more than a few days. Sharing it with others while it was fresh eliminated the possibility of spoilage.

"You know," Carl said, "there's something about the smell of meat grilling, mixed with the scent of ponderosa pine . . ." He paused, smiling. "Good for the soul."

"Roger that," Neil said, turning the steaks. "And when it comes to grilling meat, nothing beats elk."

"I don't know if I've ever eaten elk," Nathan said.

"You've eaten elk," Neil replied. "You just don't remember it."

"Did I like it?"

"You did. You didn't realize it at the time, but you did."

"Everybody likes elk," Carl added.

"So, Carl," Neil said, "the solar panels we put up on the repeater. They're working all right?"

"Seem to be."

"I guess you haven't heard anything from Naomi."

"Not since her call last week."

Neil sighed. "Sure would be nice to see her."

Carl watched Neil for a moment, then put a hand on his shoulder. "She'll get here. Maybe not soon, but she'll get here. She'll be all right, you guys will hug, smile, all that fun stuff. And then she'll tell you a horrifying story of driving cross-country with bad guys around every turn, bandits trying to hijack her—"

"Carl. Do you think this is helping?"

"Sure. I give you a frightening alternative to what's actually going on with her, then you can tell me I'm crazy and relax."

"Whatever."

Carl smiled and clapped Neil on the back. "See there? You're relaxing already."

A minute later, Nancy stepped out onto the deck. "How are we doing? Getting close?"

"Two minutes," Neil said.

Nancy set a platter next to the grill. "Everything else is ready."

"What have we got beside this meat?"

"Beans. Potato salad.

"Sounds just right."

Five minutes later they were sitting down at the dining room table. Neil said grace, asking for a blessing over Naomi and her friends. "I can't wait to have her back home," Nancy said as they started to eat.

"When was the last time we were all together here?" Neil asked.

"Before Naomi started at NSA. Five years at least. Ryan was on leave and was here with her."

With the mention of Naomi's husband, a momentary silence fell on the dinner table. Then Carl cleared his throat and spoke. "From what I gather, Naomi and her friends over in Winslow have established a communications hub. Jumping through repeaters with a conversation makes for spotty information, but it sounds like they're talking to APS crews who are getting electricity back up. Not sure when, but I think we may get power back before long."

Neil nodded. "I've been thinking about driving over there."

"Winslow?" Nancy asked.

"Yeah. See if I could help with anything. Meet her friends. See what's happening."

"You want to talk to her face to face."

"I do."

"Give her a hug."

"Yes."

"Tell her you love her."

Neil set his fork down and gazed at his wife for a moment, then reached over and squeezed her hand. "Yes."

"Have you got gas to make the trip?"

"Nope."

She smiled. "Sounds like you might be staying put."

46

Naomi Hendricks and Harlan Hicks pulled into the vacant Flying J Truck Stop on the east side of Winslow and crossed to the tire shop located in the northeast corner of the parking lot. They were there to pick up Hicks' cargo truck. The tire shop had been closed since the collapse, but the manager, a friend of Hicks, had agreed to replace the front tires in exchange for an M-16 and a thousand rounds of ammo.

Hendricks and Hicks pulled up in front of the building, then walked into the service bay. The manager was just finishing, and lowered the floor jack. "You want these old skins?" he asked. He stood by two tires leaning up against a workbench, both completely bald. "They might be worth something . . . stick 'em in a museum, the oldest tires ever to roll on pavement."

Hendricks laughed. "The thinnest tires ever to hold air."

"Are you two having fun?" Hicks asked.

"Sorry," the manager replied. "It's just . . ." He chuckled. "Never mind. Show me the rifle." Hicks walked back to Hendricks' pickup, then returned with the M-16 and two ammo cans. The manager whistled, taking the rifle from Hicks. "She's a beauty."

"Worth four of those tires."

"I know. I owe you."

Hicks turned to Hendricks. "You heard him."

Hendricks shook her head. "I doubt I'll be around when you square with him on this. But yeah, I heard him." She pointed a finger at the manager. "I heard you." She smiled and turned to leave. "You all right if I head back to the station, Harlan?"

"Sure," Hicks replied. "I'll be along in a few minutes."

"See you in a bit."

Hendricks backed away from the garage, then drove across the parking lot and pulled out on Transcon Lane. At East 3rd Street, she turned right, heading back to the police station, looking around as she drove. Winslow was a lot like Stroud, Oklahoma—nobody on the street. A lot of stalled cars, but nothing moving.

Passing the U-Haul dealership, she saw four pickup trucks with shells in a vacant lot across the street, and eight men dressed in camouflage standing next to them. She stared for a moment, then stomped the accelerator to the floor, her mind suddenly racing. She knew who these people were, and she was fifteen blocks from the police station, her truck unable to outrun the pickups that were now pulling out on the street behind her and accelerating rapidly.

They caught up with her at Cottonwood Avenue, following her in single file. Then she heard gunfire and felt the bullets impacting the back of the truck. She pressed the gas pedal as hard as she could, but the truck was topped out at 105 miles per hour, flying down the street with four pickups right behind. She shook her head, praying that no one else was on the street.

Then a shot came through the back of the camper shell and punched out through the windshield. She slid down in the seat as low as she could while still being able to see over the dashboard. A moment later, the lead pickup pulled out to pass her on the left. She swerved at it, and the pickup slowed. Then it moved ahead again, this time pulling alongside.

Hendricks drew her 9-millimeter from its holster and tucked it under her right leg, then rolled down her window. She thought about swerving hard, trying to run the pickup off the left side of the street, but at this speed, there was a good chance she would end up rolling her truck. Another burst of gunfire came from behind, all of the shots exiting through her windshield. She knew that one more volley and the windshield would drop out.

Looking to her left, she saw the passenger window on the pickup rolling down, and a man shifting in the seat with an assault rifle in his hands. She glanced in the mirror and saw the three trucks following her, the lead truck less than ten feet from her bumper. A shot came through the driver's side window, passing right in front of her face and shattering the passenger side glass. Then two more shots. She drew a deep breath and exhaled slowly, then fired three blind shots at the truck. It dropped back for a moment, then pulled up again. This time, Hendricks sat up and faced the truck, firing three more shots, hitting the passenger in the head. When he slumped forward, she fired four more, killing the driver.

Then she braced herself and jumped on the brakes with both feet. The truck following slammed into the back of her, smashing the front end, then both trucks slid to a stop, tires smoking. Hendricks jumped out and walked to the rear, quickly assessing the situation. The truck behind hers was billowing steam from the radiator. It wasn't going anywhere. The windshield was shattered in two places. "Seatbelts, idiots," she said. She fired four shots through the windshield—two at the driver, two at the passenger, killing both.

Now the men in the second and third trucks were out and moving forward. Knowing she couldn't take all of them, she glanced behind her and saw the truck that had pulled alongside her piled up against a tree two blocks down the street. It was no longer a threat. With only three bullets left in her pistol and needing to throw up a barrage, she ejected the magazine and slipped in a fresh one. She walked to the middle of the street, pulling the trigger as fast as she could, emptying the magazine at the four men. They scrambled for cover behind the rear pickup, and Hendricks ran back to the cab of her truck, climbed in and took off down the street.

Back at the tire shop, Hicks and the manager were standing next to the cargo truck talking when they heard gunfire. "Gotta go," Hicks said. He climbed in his truck and drove out of the parking lot, then sped down the street, the truck belching black smoke. Turning on to 3rd Street, he saw the pickups stopped in the middle of the road six blocks ahead, and a gunfight raging. Then he saw Hendricks run back to her truck and leave.

Hicks was pushing the M-35 as fast as it would go, but it wasn't built for speed. Before he could reach the other pickups, two of them pulled out, chasing Hendricks. Ten seconds later he drove past the wrecked pickup. Ahead, he saw Hendricks' truck with the two in pursuit, and catching up to her.

"Step on it, Naomi," he said.

Hendricks was now three blocks from the station. She switched on the ham radio hanging under the dashboard and keyed the mic. "Mayday, mayday!" she yelled. "You guys there?"

"We're here," Tanner answered. "What's going on?"

"Shots fired. I've got bad guys right behind me. Get outside and be ready. I'm fifteen seconds away, and I'm coming in hot." She hit a bump in the road and the corner of the windshield dropped in. She reached into the glove box for a pair of sunglasses and put them on just as the windshield flew back into the cab, hitting her in the face.

She raised her arm underneath it and pushed it aside, then got ready for a sliding turn into the parking lot.

Chris Tanner, Miles Ackerman, Scott Winter and Paul Lundgren ran outside with assault rifles just as Hendricks drifted her truck through the intersection of 3rd Street and Prairie Avenue, then bounced into the parking lot and slid to a stop, the two pickups right behind her. "Naomi!" Tanner yelled. "Stay in the truck and get down!" Then Tanner, Ackerman, Winter and Lundgren fanned out, guns blazing at the pickups as their drivers and passengers returned fire, standing behind the open doors for cover.

Five seconds later, Hicks' cargo truck came around the corner, headed for the parking lot. Glancing at the position of the two pick-ups, he turned slightly to the left to get a better angle on the closest one, then swerved into the rear, knocking it into the second truck and flipping it on its side. Rolling to a stop in front of the build-ing, he jumped out and climbed into the back, pulling up the can-vas cover on the rear. Then the .50-caliber machine gun roared to life, filling the air with thunder as eight hundred rounds per minute shredded the two pickups, reducing them to scrap metal.

The firing stopped a minute later, and Hendricks moved up onto the seat to see what was happening. Hicks was bending over in the back of his truck. A moment later, he stood and turned to the rear, holding a rocket-propelled grenade launcher on his shoulder. "Oh, my God," Hendricks said, and she ducked as the grenade flew over her truck with a loud whoosh. A split-second later, a deafening ex-plosion, and a shock wave rocked her truck. She heard Hicks laugh, then another whoosh, and another explosion.

She waited for a third, but heard nothing. Opening the door of her truck slowly, she climbed out and looked behind her. Where the two pickups had been, only twisted metal and burned asphalt remained. She stared for a moment, then turned and looked across the parking lot where Ackerman, Winter and Lundgren held rifles on two survivors sitting on the ground. She brushed glass from her face, then crossed the parking lot toward the cargo truck. Tanner and Hicks were standing behind it, talking.

"You're crazy, Harlan," Tanner said.

"I know," Hicks laughed. "But it was great, wasn't it?"

"Yeah," Tanner smiled, "it was. A fifty-cal blazing away, and an RPG to light things up. Leaves no doubt." Tanner clapped Hicks on the back, then turned and walked over to Hendricks. Her face was smeared with blood from dozens of small cuts. He pulled a bandana from his pocket and brushed away particles of glass that were still stuck to her. "You okay?"

"Yes," she replied. "Thanks." She squeezed his arm, then walked away and sat alone against the side of the building, trembling. She leaned her head back and closed her eyes. "I'm through with this," she said quietly. "I'm going home."

An hour later, four Navajo County sheriff's deputies were loading the men, handcuffed and shackled, into pickup trucks parked in front. The sheriff had taken statements from Hendricks and the others. Now he stood by the front door of the station, looking at the blackened asphalt and pieces of twisted metal by the parking lot entrance, shaking his head. "You definitely left an impression."

"What happens to these guys now?" Tanner asked.

"They'll sit in a jail cell in Holbrook until we can put together a trial," the sheriff replied. "We'll need you folks to testify."

"Some of us are headed to Kingman," Hendricks said.

"How can we contact you?"

"VHF radio. One forty-six, four forty."

The sheriff jotted the number in a notebook, then closed it. He looked around the parking lot again, then turned to the five of them. "I want to thank you all for stepping up. Our people have been spread pretty thin. And Winslow . . . well, they've got almost nothing left in the way of law enforcement. Two of my deputies will be staying, but if any of you can stick around, it would be a big help." Tanner and Ackerman nodded. The sheriff paused, then shook hands with everyone. "You folks be safe. I'll be in touch."

Walking back to his truck, he stopped at the rear of the cargo truck and looked inside at the .50-caliber machine gun, and a pile of brass that would fill a wheelbarrow. "Is that an M-2?"

"Yep," Hicks replied. "That's ol' Ma Duce."

"Light the tires and kick the fires, eh?" The sheriff chuckled, then walked away shaking his head.

47

Wednesday, February 26
7:30 a.m. Pacific Standard Time
Long Beach, California

B NSF 557 was the first train to leave the port at Long Beach since the collapse—a mile of tankers and freight cars pulled by five locomotives. It would take the Alameda Corridor out of port and head north through Los Angeles. At 26th Street it would jog back to the southeast, then make a long, slow turn back north to San Bernardino. From there, the train would head northwest through Barstow, Bakersfield, Fresno and Stockton, dropping freight cars along the way. The six tankers filled with diesel would be taken all the way to the Columbia nuclear generating station, located ten miles outside of Richland, Washington. Then the locomotives would return to California for another load.

Other trains would carry loads north through Nevada and Idaho, Oregon, Utah, Wyoming and Montana. And still others would carry freight to Colorado and New Mexico. Meanwhile, rail yards in the Dallas-Fort Worth area were readying locomotives to pull freight cars to states in the Midwest and further east.

It was precisely 7:30 a.m. when 557 left the rail yard and began the slow pull up the Corridor, the engines roaring under the load of nearly sixty thousand tons. Two miles later, the train reached forty miles per hour—the speed limit for this stretch—and the engineer eased back on the throttle control. The conductor leaned toward the windshield, looking ahead at the Pacific Coast Highway overpass. He grinned and turned to the engineer.

"Check it out," he said. At least a hundred people stood on the overpass, cheering and waving American flags as the train approached. The conductor leaned out the side window and waved back. The engineer pulled the air horn lanyard. At the next overpass, Sepulveda Boulevard, more people were gathered to cheer them on. And at every street-level crossing, people stood behind the barricade, waving flags and cheering.

Finally, at the 405 overpass, people standing on top unfurled a thirty-foot flag, hanging it from the chain link fence. The engineer looked up as the locomotive passed under the Stars and Stripes. "You know," he said, "I've been railroading for more than thirty years." He paused, nodding. "This is the first time I feel like I'm doing something that really matters."

48

It was the largest group of people assembled in the Situation Room since February tenth, the day of the collapse. Sitting at the conference table with the president were Vice President Jan Hutchens, Secretary of State Elaine Richardson, Secretary of Homeland Security Margaret Beck, Secretary of Defense Patrick Wilkinson, National Security Advisor William Denton, and Speaker of the House Spencer Cochran. The topic of discussion was the continuing blackout in the largest metropolitan areas of the country.

"Trains are moving," President Wheeler said. "And we're grateful for that. But electricity is a different story. Spotty doesn't begin to describe the coverage."

"Phoenix," William Denton said. "Tucson, Dallas, Fort Worth, El Paso. That's a lot of people with lights, Mr. President."

"I know," Wheeler replied. "It just seems ironic that . . ." he paused referring to a list, "Waco, Texas has electricity. Barstow, California. St. George, Utah. Gila Bend, Arizona." He paused and looked around the table. "Gila Bend, Arizona?"

"Seventy miles southwest of Phoenix," Doug Chambers replied.

Wheeler looked at Chambers and cocked his head. "I take it you've been there."

"Yes, Mr. President."

"Any idea how many people live in Gila Bend?"

"A couple thousand."

"Meanwhile, New York City, home to eight million, minus a hundred thousand or so who have died since the collapse, is in the dark. New Jersey, Pennsylvania, Ohio—in fact, the entire eastern seaboard—are still in the dark. The Pacific Northwest. Kansas, Nebraska, the Dakotas, Illinois, Wisconsin, Michigan. People are starving. They're freezing." He paused. "They're dying." He leaned back in his chair and stared at the ceiling for a moment, then looked around the table. "I guess there's no way to get electricity from Arizona and Texas all the way to the east coast."

"Not without large power transformers," Secretary Beck replied.

"She's right," Denton said. "Utility companies can string power lines wherever they want. But without LPTs," he shrugged, "there's only so far electricity can run before it needs to be boosted."

Wheeler shook his head. "How in the world did we not protect the transformers? Texas and Arizona did."

"They weren't doing that based on information passed down from the top," Denton said. "Utility companies in Texas and Arizona took the initiative to—"

"I know, Bill. It was a rhetorical question. I'm trying to come to grips with how stupid some people can be, beginning with administrations over the last twenty years—ours included—who ignored the threat of EMP. We knew this was a possibility. A threat."

Secretary of Defense Patrick Wilkinson leaned forward in his chair. "Mr. President, at the time of the initial report to Congress—two thousand four, I believe—there were a number of experts who felt the risk to the nation as outlined was exaggerated. A number of people in the military—those who had experience in field tests of tactical nuclear weapons—questioned whether EMP posed any threat at all."

Wheeler looked at Wilkinson. "Ever wonder what a conversation with those people might sound like today?"

"Mr. President," Beck said, "There were serious budget considerations. The proposals by appropriations committees for hardening the electrical infrastructure were far beyond what the administration at the time was willing to accept."

Wheeler glanced at Beck, then stood and looked at the others. "Is there anyone sitting at this table who can say a hundred billion dollars is too much to spend to prevent the loss of what—a million lives? Ten million lives? Do we even know how many people have died? That's on us, people. That's on this administration and Congress, and every administration and Congress for the last eighteen years." The room was silent as he walked slowly around the table, shaking his head, grumbling. "We spend nearly eight billion for TSA to pat down passengers boarding commercial flights for the sake of national security. Thirty billion on cyber security. Eighty billion on intelligence agencies. And when we talk about infrastructure spending, it's roads and bridges. Not a cent on the electrical grid, which, according to everyone in the industry, is falling apart." Returning to his chair, he sat. "Eighteen years we've known about the possibility of an EMP attack and the consequences. Eighteen years!"

No one spoke. There was nothing to say. For a full minute the silence continued, then Wheeler stood and walked toward the door. "I have nothing else," he said quietly. "If anybody comes up with anything," he paused, "I don't know where I'll be. Somewhere screaming." He reached for the doorknob just as Bob Larson, the chief of staff, pushed the door open from outside the room, nearly knocking the president over.

"I'm sorry, Mr. President," Larson said.

"If this isn't good news," Wheeler replied, "you can turn around and head back down the hallway."

Larson paused, staring at the president, then the others in the room. "Sir, I don't know if it's good news or bad."

"Let's have it, then we'll decide."

"General Tuckett called the Emergency Operations Center. The base commander at Fort Dix reports that freighters are docking at the Newark-Elizabeth Marine Terminal at Newark Bay. That information comes from the Port Authority. They're trying to figure out what to do with them."

"With the freighters?"

"Yes, Mr. President."

"Whose freighters are they?"

"China's."

Wheeler leaned back, staring at Larson for a moment as if not comprehending what he was saying. He looked at the others around the table, then back at Larson. "Are you saying Chinese freighters are docked in the Port of New Jersey?"

"Yes, sir."

"Do we know what they're carrying?"

"Not all of them, sir. Most of them are container ships. But several are deck-loaded with heavy equipment and dozens of trucks—semis with tankers and large flatbed trailers. The bills of lading presented to the Port Authority declare the equipment as power transformers and transformer repair parts. The trucks and flatbeds are for moving the transformers. The tankers are carrying fuel for the trucks."

Wheeler turned to the others and held up his hands. "Anybody care to venture a guess as to why China, after nearly destroying our economy and teaming up with Russia—a collaborator in the attack against us—is giving us power transformers, trucks and other equipment to repair our electric grid?"

"Do we care why?" Secretary Beck asked.

Spencer Cochran smiled. "I think I know why, Mr. President. In simple terms, China wants the game to continue."

"I don't follow you."

"I played football in high school. Three years—sophomore JV, then junior and senior on varsity. My junior year we were nine and one. We took State. Senior year we were undefeated."

"Jump to the chase, Spence."

"There were games that were so lopsided, we felt like it was a waste of time even playing. I remember the coach in the locker room after one game. He talked about humility—playing to win, but winning with grace. He reminded us that without an opposing team, there is no game. There's no challenge. No point. It's an adversarial view, Mr. President. We can ask why, or we can accept that win, lose or draw, China wants a game."

49

Saturday, March 21
7:00 a.m. Mountain Standard Time
Winslow, Arizona

Naomi Hendricks stood at the back of her pickup in the Davenports' driveway, packing the last few items for the trip. With help from Harlan Hicks, she had found a windshield for her truck, as well as a door glass and tail lights, from a salvage yard. The rest of the damage—bullet holes and a bent tailgate and bumper—wouldn't affect the truck's roadworthiness in getting her, Scott Winter and Paul Lundgren, home.

Miles Ackerman was under the hood, checking the belts and hoses, and fluid levels. Chris Tanner was on his hands and knees looking underneath, making sure there were no leaks. "Everything's good," he said, getting to his feet. Hendricks closed the back of the truck and walked to the front.

"No damage?" she asked.

"Nothing that matters."

"This truck's been through a lot."

"Like it's owner," Ackerman smiled, closing the hood. He wiped his hands on a rag. "You're good for this trip?"

"Yeah," Hendricks nodded. "We'll be fine."

Winter and Lundgren joined them by the front of the truck. "I seem to remember you saying that when we were leaving Fort Meade two weeks ago," Winter said.

She smiled, thinking back. "I find myself wondering how I'll tell my mom and dad about this trip without freaking them out."

"Keep it simple," Ackerman said. "Say nothing. Let them wonder." He smiled, then put his arms around Hendricks and hugged her. "Take care, kiddo."

"You too, Miles," she said. She turned and hugged Tanner. "Thank you, Chris, for everything. You guys were awesome."

"You're welcome," he said. "And thank you."

"So, you guys will be all right without us?" she asked.

Tanner glanced at Ackerman. "We'll figure it out."

"You know how to find us?"

"Got it mapped." He nodded. "Give us a week or so and we'll head that direction." He turned to Winter and Lundgren. Lundgren extended his hand. Tanner smiled and pulled him in for a hug. "We're family." Then he hugged Winter. "You guys take care."

Winter nodded. "We'll try."

"And keep her out of trouble."

"Okay, that's asking a lot."

Silas and Muriel stepped outside with a plate of brownies and a thermos of coffee. "You kids all set?" Silas asked.

"Ready to roll," Hendricks replied.

Muriel handed Hendricks the plate. "Something for the trip."

"Thank you, Muriel," Hendricks said.

"You're welcome, sweetheart." They hugged, then Muriel took Hendricks' hand. "You take good care, Naomi. And come back to see us when things settle down." She turned to Winter and Lundgren. "All of you. We want to see you again soon."

Hendricks nodded. "We'll be back."

Silas handed Hendricks the thermos. "Here's a little Joe to go with those brownies."

"Thanks, Doc." She opened the driver's door and set the thermos on the seat and the plate on the dashboard, then turned back and hugged him. "I was hoping Harlan would be here."

As if on cue, a horn sounded down the street, and Harlan Hicks pulled up to the curb in his cargo truck. "Sorry I'm late," he said, walking up the driveway. "Got stuck in traffic."

Hendricks smiled. "Thanks for coming, Harlan." She held out her arms, and for a moment he just looked at her. "Come here," she said. "Give me a hug."

He sighed and put his arms around her. "This doesn't change anything. You're still a spy."

"I know," she replied, hugging him. "And you're still a crazy conspiracy theorist." She paused, stepping back. "You'll contact General Tuckett on the sat phone with updates?"

"You never said anything—"

"Harlan, we talked about this. I gave you the number."

"You know the CIA has people at Cheyenne Mountain, right? They're embedded with NORAD."

"The CIA has people everywhere. Besides, what would you do if they weren't out there getting on your nerves?" She hugged him again. "Thank you for everything," she said.

He smiled. "You're welcome. Stay safe. And come back for a visit when you can."

"Absolutely."

"Doc knows how to reach me."

Hendricks nodded. "See you around, Harlan."

"Vaya con Dios, Naomi."

Hendricks turned to Winter and Lundgren. "Let's hit the road." They climbed in the truck and waved at the others, then backed out of the driveway and drove away.

Fifteen minutes later, they reached the place on the highway where the shootout took place. The trucks were still there, now dragged off the side of the road. Everything else had been removed from the scene. Lundgren shifted in his seat.

"You okay?" Winter asked.

"I don't like this place," Lundgren replied.

They drove past the trucks in silence. A mile down the road Lundgren relaxed. "Okay," Hendricks said, "picking up where we left off two weeks ago. Are you guys nervous about making this trip?"

"A little," Winter replied.

"I'm nervous about everything now," Lundgren said.

"I guess getting shot will do that to you."

"Even before that. Driving away from the NSA parking lot that first night, I had no idea what to expect. Cars stalled everywhere, some wrecked. And the darkness. I hated that feeling—the anxiety. Like standing in front of your bedroom closet with your hand on the doorknob, wondering if there's a boogeyman in there."

Winter turned and looked at Lundgren. "You mean when you were a kid, right?"

"No. That morning when I was getting ready for work." He pulled a brownie from the plate on the dashboard and took a bite. "These are good," he nodded.

Winter watched him for a moment, then glanced at Hendricks She shrugged. "Anyway," Winter said, "I'll never forget this trip." He paused. "The gunfights . . ."

Lundgren looked at him for a moment, then glanced at Hendricks. "You know," he said quietly, "I was thinking, since no one is shooting at us and we're not bleeding to death, could we maybe talk about something happy? It's a really nice day. And the sky is so blue in Arizona! I can't get over that."

Hendricks nodded, then noticed something down the road. "Check it out." She pointed at a sign.

"Meteor Crater, next right," Paul read. "Is that—"

"Meteor Crater."

"That's right. It's in Arizona."

"It's five miles down that road."

Lundgren smiled. There was a look of excitement in his eyes that she hadn't seen in a long time. He leaned forward in anticipation, and for a moment she thought he might start bouncing on the seat. "This is very cool," he said quietly.

The narrow strip of asphalt ran south through the desert, past brush and rock outcroppings, eventually climbing up to a parking lot. The visitors center appeared untouched, the window and door glass unbroken. Winter tried the front door. "It's locked," he said.

Hendricks nodded. "No problem." She walked to the end of the building and climbed the chain link fence.

"Should we be doing that?" Lundgren asked.

"Yeah," Winter replied. "We should."

Behind the building was a field of boulders. They hiked through it, finally reaching the edge of the crater, then stared down into the bottom. It was immense—a nearly symmetrical hole in the desert.

"Thirty-nine hundred feet across," Lundgren said. "More than five hundred feet deep." He paused, looking across to the other rim, then turned to Hendricks and Winter. "Did you know it's actually called Barringer Crater?"

"No," Winter replied. "I didn't."

"Daniel Barringer. He was the first to suggest it might have been formed by a meteorite impact. The meteor was one hundred sixty feet across, traveling twelve miles per second. It broke up when it hit

the atmosphere. The pieces vaporized when they hit the ground."
He paused. "I'm rattling."

Winter laughed. "Go for it."

Lundgren started down the path to the bottom, continuing his
recitation of everything he ever read about Meteor Crater. Hendricks
smiled at Winter. "That is one happy guy."

"This is right up there with Space Camp," Winter replied. Reaching the bottom, they walked across to the center of the basin where
a rock peak jutted up from the crater floor. Lundgren climbed to the
top and raised his arms over his head, beaming, then shouted. Hendricks smiled and snapped a picture of him with her phone. Winter
climbed up next to him and she took another.

A minute later they climbed down and walked over to Hendricks.
Lundgren grinned and put his arms around her. "Thanks, Mom."

She laughed. "You're welcome, Paul."

It was twelve noon when Hendricks pulled off the side of the
interstate and pointed to a range of mountains thirty miles away.
"See that tallest peak in the middle?" she said.

"That's home?" Winter asked.

"That's home." She reached for the ham radio under the dash and
tuned to the frequency of Carl Ferguson's repeater located on top of
the peak. "K7AZK, this is K7AZQ." She waited ten seconds, then
called again. "K7AZK, this is K7AZQ. Anybody home?"

A moment later she heard her father's voice. "Naomi!" he said.
"Where are you?"

"We're about a half-hour away. We just dropped out of the
mountains west of Willow Creek."

Neil paused. When he spoke again, his voice cracked. "It's good
to hear your voice, sweetheart. So, so good."

Hendricks nodded, holding the mic. "Dad . . ." She paused. A
tear rolled down her cheek, then she broke down.

"Are you okay?" he asked.

She nodded again, wiping away the tears. "Yes," she whispered, struggling to get the words out. "I'm just really happy right now." Lundgren put his arm around her shoulders and squeezed, then he and Scott climbed out of the truck and stood by the side of the road, looking at the mountains in the distance.

Nathan Hayes had been standing outside on the deck for the last fifteen minutes, listening. Then he heard a vehicle coming down the road past the ranger station. Five minutes later he saw Naomi's truck winding its way up the dirt road to the house.

"She's here!" he called out. He ran inside and followed Neil and Nancy downstairs and out the front door. They waved as the truck pulled up out front, then walked down the steps. Neil opened the driver's door, and Naomi stepped out, smiling. For a moment they just looked at each other, then Neil hugged her.

"It's good to have you home," he said. She nodded, tears in her eyes. Then Nancy stepped in.

"My turn," she said. She hugged Naomi, then pulled back looking at her. "What happened to your neck?"

"What happened to her truck?" Nathan asked.

"It's a long story," Naomi replied. "A very long story." She paused. "Paul, Scott, meet my mom and dad, and my brother Nathan." They went to shake hands with Neil. He smiled and hugged them. Then Nancy hugged them. They looked at Nathan for a moment.

"It's a thing around here," he said. "All I can say is you'd better get used to it." And they hugged.

Upstairs, Naomi moved through the house, looking in bedrooms, at pictures on the wall in the hallway, at her mother's collection of antique bottling jars and porcelain roosters on a shelf in the kitchen, as if rediscovering her life with a family. She smiled at her father's pictures of cowboys on horseback, riding through aspens, across streams, towering mountains and blazing sunsets in the background. Over the fireplace was a framed picture of his father sitting on a palomino in a meadow against a backdrop of the mountains of Idaho. Then she noticed a string of Christmas lights along the ceiling over the fireplace, hanging down both sides to the hearth.

"That brings back memories," she said, turning to her dad. "Christmas lights in March. I always thought it was fun having them up long after Christmas, turning them on every night."

He plugged them in and smiled. "Welcome home, Naomi."

That night she lay in bed, thinking. For a few minutes, thoughts of the road trip filled her head—Chris and Miles, Paul and Scott, Harlan, the gun battles. She thought of Audrey Lane singing, her daughter Evie eating beef jerky and apples, of sharing breakfast with Chet and Verlene and their son Nick. Henry and Arvella, Silas and Muriel. Good and bad, it was an experience she would never forget. Now in the comfort and safety of home, she set it aside, letting in thoughts of the mountain, of the deer and elk, of hiking and camping and relaxing in the outdoors. She smiled, thinking of just being with her family again. And in that moment she felt happiness she had never experienced before. She felt peace and contentment. But most of all, she felt truly at home.

50

Monday, June 1

President Wheeler had taken on faith the idea that China's gift of power transformers and repair equipment was a sign of trust, a signal that there could be common ground between the two nations in the wake of such economic devastation. Spencer Cochran's observation that China wanted to 'keep the game going' was a stretch in Wheeler's mind. But he didn't see an alternative that made sense. In the end, regardless of why China reached out to help the United States, the fact they did enabled the U.S. to turn the corner in the recovery effort.

In the weeks following the arrival of the first vessels from China, additional shipments of food arrived from Israel, along with solar energy equipment—panels, inverters, batteries and cabling. Saudi Arabia sent tankers carrying diesel fuel and gasoline, and freighters carrying tanker trucks. More freighters from China docked with electronics—servers, routers, switches and hard drives. The ports at Los Angeles and Long Beach were in full swing, and ports in Galveston, Brownsville and Corpus Christi, Texas, were preparing to re-sume operations. With the installation of large power transformers in New Jersey and Charleston, South Carolina, east coast shipping was not far behind.

By mid-March, railroads were expanding their reach, and with the availability of fuel, trucking companies were resurgent. FEMA Disaster Recovery Centers were up and running across the nation, with daily shipments of food and water arriving by truck in 165 cities. By early April, segments of the internet were restored, and on Monday, May 4th, President Wheeler gave his first address to the nation since the day of the collapse, this one on YouTube. It was viewed by 800,000 people.

These gains were significant in Wheeler's mind, and to a gov-ernment that was slowly putting itself back together. Portions of the Southwest and Northeast were returning to some semblance of normalcy with business and small-scale banking underway. But the reality facing the rest of the country was that as of June 1st—four months after the initial loss of power—one hundred sixty million people in thirty states were still without electricity and running water. And even as most in his administration touted the recovery, President Wheeler knew that in the final analysis, the bulk of the country over which he presided lived in the nineteenth century. And it would remain that way through the end of the year.

In any sense that mattered, America was starting over.

51

There isn't a happy ending. As I write this—one year to the day since the grid collapse—more than thirty million people living in the United States are still without power and running water. There has been a massive migration of people from areas still crippled by the collapse to areas that have recovered, putting a tremendous burden on those places. Cities with power are overcrowded. Crime is rampant. Homelessness has become epidemic. People are still bartering because money is scarce. Jobs are too.

No one knows how many died. Estimates put the number at close to fifteen million, most of those from starvation, but also from dysentery, cholera and other diseases caused by bad water and unsanitary conditions. An estimated five million froze to death. And of course, there were the jets falling out of the sky.

When I think of the number of people who died, my mind goes back to the night of the collapse. At seven minutes past six, I saw the distant flash in the sky, and I knew in that moment that the death toll would be staggering. There was simply no other possible outcome. I knew before it happened that the collapse of the electrical grid caused by an EMP would result in so much damage, it would be impossible to repair in months, let alone weeks. And people just couldn't make it that long.

As it turned out, repairing the grid in a year has proved impossible. And today, no one can say when—or if— things will ever be the way they were.

While the migration to cities continues, millions of people have chosen to live off the land. Knowledge of farming has become one of the most sought-after skills, second to medical expertise. People have claimed land—much as they did when settlers were moving west in the 1800s—dug wells, tilled the land and planted crops, then traded at large farmers markets. In some cases, a hundred people or more will be working a single farm, with dozens of families, homes built with hand tools, even schools. Although a throwback to more than a century earlier, the way of life that today has come to be known as 'Prairie Pride' is actually more productive—certainly less violent— than life in any major urban area. Some are saying that until power has been fully restored, the migration into cities with electricity will most likely reverse, with people opting for a rural, farming lifestyle despite the hardships.

Chris and Miles are back in Big Spring, Texas. They stopped here on their way through. Scott and Paul were still here, and we spent time hiking and doing a little fishing. It was during their visit that Mom and Dad and Nathan learned the details of our trip from Fort Meade. It was a conversation fraught with anxiety, especially for Mom, but with Chris and Miles, it went much easier than it ever would have without them. They stayed a week, then headed out. A month later, Scott and Paul went to California. They're working at the Port of Long Beach managing logistics.

I've been working with a group in Kingman who teach people life-sustaining skills. These include gardening, animal husbandry, carpentry, automotive repair, stuff like that. I'm teaching advanced first aid and lifesaving. I also work with our church in an outreach helping people get back on their feet. It's funny, but when I look back on my life at NSA, as rewarding as that was in a highly technical and analytical way, it's nothing compared to what I do now.

People helping people is, I believe, what got this country through the early stages of the collapse. As I search the internet, I am moved by the countless stories of those who gave selflessly to others. And I know the same compassion demonstrated by so many in those first weeks and months will continue as America rebuilds, bringing communities together, forming bonds that can never be broken.

As I consider that aspect of humanity and the impact it had, I know too that being prepared for disaster mitigated the death toll. At the same time, I can't help but wonder how different things would have been if more people took the time to look ahead and consider what their lives might be like if a catastrophe struck. I think back to disasters like Hurricane Sandy, Ike and Rita—even relatively minor events like the snowstorms that buried areas in the Northeast, leaving people without food and other basic necessities—and I ask myself, how could people not think it would ever happen to them?

From an early age, my parents instilled in me the idea that it is impossible to know when disaster will strike. From minor events like a snow storm or a power outage, to serious calamities like a stock market crash, we don't realize how bad it can be until we're left sitting there empty-handed. Dad was a Boy Scout, and I think I was eight or nine when he first talked about their motto—be prepared. As I grew older, I enjoyed being involved in activities that built on that phrase, whether it was learning outdoor skills, life-saving techniques, or just buying food and other necessities and putting it away, or bottling and preserving food from our own garden.

There was so much we did as a family when I was growing up that I now realize was simply building security, safety, self-sufficiency. As a kid, it was fun. Today, I see it was critical—I wouldn't be writing this had I not known how to prepare.

The hurricanes I mentioned—Sandy, Ike and Rita—seemed for such a long time to be the benchmark for what could go wrong, and a perfect illustration of the need to be ready. Now it's the grid collapse. Never has there been an event so disastrous, so far-reaching or long-lasting, or one that has taken so many lives. And never has there been a better example that I can point to and say, "No one knows what tomorrow brings."

Epilogue

WASHINGTON, March 1, 4:15 p.m. EDT (AP) - In an address before a joint session of Congress today, President Edmund Wheeler announced he would sit down for one-on-one talks with Zhu Xiannian, president of China, with a goal of establishing a trade agreement that, in his words, "would usher in a new era of trust and cooperation between our two countries." He went on to say, "China extended an olive branch in America's hour of need. We are grateful to President Zhu, and for his help we are indebted. Now we turn the page and begin a new chapter, building a bond that will demonstrate to the world that like swords of the finest steel, alliances forged in the fires of conflict may be strong and enduring."

According to sources close to the president, Zhu indicated in early discussions a willingness to open up internet access in China to social media platforms and search engines, a sign that he may soften his stance on the free exchange of information in his country. Even more striking was the revelation that he would strive to end the theft of intellectual property originating within his borders, the first open admission to the existence of cyber theft in China, and an indication of an entirely new approach to conducting business on a global scale, with respect for all countries.

Later in his address, President Wheeler announced changes to domestic policy, including his desire for sweeping infrastructure legislation that would address the nation's aging electrical grid, and the need for hardening areas of the infrastructure to prevent losses, such as those occurring in last year's grid collapse.

Stocks rallied on today's news, with the Dow Jones Industrials climbing 27 points to a high of 850.

CPSIA information can be obtained
at www.ICGtesting.com
Printed in the USA
LVHW031547140619
621259LV00001B/55

9 780997 985719

JUL 1 5 2019